FORBIDDEN THOUGHTS

Contents

FOREWORD

By

Milo Yiannopoulos

If I were to put the current state of the science fiction genre into SF terms, it would be a space ship under attack. I won't say which ship I'm thinking of, because this introduction would quickly dissolve into insufferable megafans arguing about whether or not the Enterprise could take down an Imperial Star Destroyer (no way in hell).

The crew of our ship is being thrown from side to side, red lights are flashing and a klaxon is blaring. Sensors indicate the entity attacking the ship is an amorphous blob of low intelligence but extremely high malevolence. Engineering reports an imminent hull breach—if the captain doesn't react quickly, they will be little more than space dust.

If this were an actual story, the crew would try to figure out why this alien force is so hostile, and what it is doing in formerly friendly territory in the first place. We can drop the analogy now, because we already know what is plaguing science fiction.

Our crisis is a cult of politically correct crybabies intent on bringing science fiction in line with their ominously authoritarian groupthink at any cost. They are known collectively as social justice warriors (SJWs for short) and you are probably quite familiar with them if you are reading *Forbidden Thoughts*. For those that aren't, SJWs blend together the worst aspects of feminism, slacktivism, manufactured outrage, Marxism, and top it off with a generous helping of virtue signaling.

Virtue signaling can best be explained as the devotion of a person's entire existence to explaining how wonderful they (and their friends) are, and how terribly wrong everyone else is. The point of virtue signaling is to demonstrate superiority, for the purpose of consolidating power, prestige and financial reward. The culture of social justice is set up to reward the loudest and best complainers and to punish anyone that stands against them.

Virtue signaling is the best way to identify a social justice warrior in the wild. Many aspects of their appearance, like a tendency towards dyed hair, are not all that different from those of nerd culture. I use the term nerd here lovingly, a considerable portion of my fanbase is comprised of nerds, and I am a closet nerd—as ironic as that may sound coming from a flamboyant homosexual.

The other surefire way to recognize SJWs is that they are always complaining, even more than typical SF fans! And they don't complain about physics or continuity or character arcs, they complain about "representation", "diversity" and "toxic masculinity". If you said "people of color" to a group of fans a decade ago, they might think you were referring in a roundabout way to green aliens. Now with the influence of social justice, they know that the most important thing in science fiction is having a bisexual Arab of size as a main character.

The final important thing to know about SJWs is they are incapable of telling the truth. They often have dark reasons for their mendacious nature—there have been a continuous stream of cases where SJWs, held up as paragons of virtue defending women, minorities and LGBT people from the disgusting bigotry of regular fans, are actually proven to be abusers, rapists and pedophiles. For more information on SJWs, read Vox Day's treatise on the subject, *SJWs Always Lie: Taking Down the Thought Police.*

The obvious question on everybody's mind is: why would they invade the world of science fiction? For one thing, science fiction has always been progressive on the subjects of race and gender. Star Trek included a black woman and a Russian man on the bridge crew in the 1960's, far ahead of comedy and drama. Star Trek didn't get everything right however, the science officer should have been Asian, and Gene Roddenberry presumptively decided Starfleet Command would be stupid enough to let the Scottish into space.

Secondly, science fiction simply doesn't mix well with authoritarian control and the language police. SF is at its best when it is deeply anti-authoritarian, whether it is Philip K. Dick's vision of the future in books like A Scanner Darkly, or the galactic empire we all despised while watching Star Wars. Okay, I will admit to admiring the empire's fashionable uniforms and devotion to discipline, but you get my point.

Science fiction is a blend of dreaming about the future, imagining how mankind will cope with change and viewing our own culture through a different lens. We need healthy and robust science fiction now more than we ever have before. While it is true that flying cars and personal rocketships are nowhere to be found, we do have Amazon erasing the books of George Orwell from the Kindle devices they were loaded on without warning. That turned out to be a rights dispute with the publisher, but can you imagine a worse book to disappear down the memory hole than 1984?

I am not arguing that science fiction should only be written by conservatives. Writers of all political persuasions can successfully write really good SF, by not putting their politics first. China Mieville may be a commie, but I personally enjoyed Perdido Street Station.

In fact my favorite show in science fiction & fantasy is Joss Whedon's Buffy The Vampire Slayer. Joss Whedon aligns himself with SJWs politically, which is fun to watch because he has been run off Twitter by SJWs at least once for the crime of displeasing the gods of diversity.

Buffy is an amazing character—her feminine qualities are part of her strength. She saves the world using her female vulnerability, not in spite of it. In fact, her femininity is the only thing that makes her capable of heroic feats. She is a perfect role model for girls, especially compared to the characters SJWs come up with.

I'm referring to the female characters in 2016's megaflop *Ghostbusters* film. My review of the film, which led directly to my permanent banning from Twitter, sensitively called them "teenage boys with tits". The crass personality of the characters and denial of feminine virtues sends a confusing message to viewers, which is probably why the movie was such a failure at the box office.

Just by reading *Forbidden Thoughts* you've joined the resistance against SJWs. If you are going to contribute to this culture war, there are three things you must understand about SJWs:

SJWs don't care about science fiction

It may be more accurate to say that some SJWs don't care about SF, and others hold a deep hatred for the genre. They are only in the genre to control things and act as gatekeepers, ensuring all popular content meets their exacting standards of political correctness. Those standards constantly shift at their whims, by the way.

The typical SJW is not knowledgeable about SF. They are probably a rabid fan of a particular franchise like *Dr. Who*, and their constant references to *Harry Potter* make it the clear series of choice for SJWs everywhere. If they have read classic science fiction, they despise it. If they have read *1984* they consider the society of Oceania perfect, except that Big Sister should be in charge instead of Big Brother. What we read as a warning about authoritarian governments, they consider a masturbatory aide.

Once you understand that we are fighting against a group of people much more concerned with politics than with science fiction, we stand a better chance of fighting them. When you realize that the despicable people attempting to wrest control of an entire genre from those that love science fiction would happily watch it burn to the ground, it is a bitter pill to swallow.

Science fiction is just the latest area of entertainment the SJWs are trying to take over. They've had varying levels of success in fantasy, comics and gaming.

They've certainly been emboldened by their success in comics. Is there a single iconic character that hasn't been rebooted as a woman or minority spouting terrible dialogue at invariably white male villains? When I interviewed comics legend Chuck Dixon for my podcast, I could hear the pain in his voice as he described what has happened to his beloved comics industry.

The big comics companies have been captured by SJWs, and their dismal sales reflect just how bad an idea characters like female Thor actually are. If you want a clear understanding of why SF must be defended from the SJWs, comics are where you should look. Fantasy fiction is another warning sign. The World Fantasy Awards have dumped their award statue in the shape of H.P. Lovecraft because he was a "hideous racist" and winners were too upset by a trophy in his likeness.

Never mind that Lovecraft was a titanic influence on modern horror, fantasy and science fiction—he wasn't politically correct! I hope no SJW accidentally watches the Mos Eisley Cantina scene in Star Wars, because it is practically lifted from *Shadow Over Innsmouth*.

SJWs have been much more successfully rebuffed in the world of gaming, where the resistance movement was called GamerGate. The bad guys still have their shady awards and a bunch of blogs propping up the careers of writers who actively hate games, but they have no true power.

The worst offenders amongst the bloggers have lost their platforms, and SJW games sell pitifully, earning no real attention in the industry. These games range from slideshows to games so boring they've been nicknamed "walking simulators". Cultural critics like Anita Sarkeesian hold a fraction of the power they did several years ago, because gamers figured out what was happening and fought back.

Science fiction is at the point where it can go the direction of games or it can go the direction of comics. The decision is up to the fans and the creators. Are you ready to fight?

SJWs produce terrible work

SJWs are fantastic at complaining, but terrible at creating. Like games and comics, SJW science fiction is drivel. The low quality of the content is why controlling industry awards, publishers and hobby journalism is critical to their strategy of domination.

Let's return to my earlier comparison of Joss Whedon's work and *Ghostbusters* (the garbage feminist one, not the good one). Joss created *Firefly*, which members of my staff love more than even *Buffy*. The first mate of the Serenity is a black woman named Zoe. She is a richly layered character and vital to the plot of essentially every episode, with strengths and weaknesses like any human. Compare that to the character played by Leslie Jones in *Ghostbusters*. Her main contribution to the story is screaming at ghosts in a mockery of black women straight out of minstrel shows.

But Leslie Jones and the writers of *Ghostbusters* are held up as heroes fighting for black women. Don't try to understand the logic, it will just give you a headache.

I'm sure that writers that love science fiction and pour their heart into their craft must struggle seeing the most insipid fiction ever written winning formerly prestigious awards. I would like to propose one fun exercise—SF fans should write some politically correct fiction in SJWs' honor to show how much better it could be done.

I've got a few ideas for stories I will share here. Perhaps the best one will be published in *Forbidden Thoughts 2*, which will happen quickly if this volume sells as well as I think it will.

6

Without further ado, here are Milo's SJW story starters:

An SJW Android Story—Our heroine is an android in an age in which artificial intelligence is a reality, and androids are only limited by basic laws we will borrow from Asimov. Feel free to make her bisexual or pansexual or whatever you think will work best. The story will revolve around her quest to make androids politically correct, climaxing with her decision to end artificial intelligence and plunge all androids into doing exactly as they are programmed to do.

Fahrenheit 451 Reboot—Obviously the book-burning firemen are the good guys this time, but they can't just burn ebook readers—think about the environmental impact of releasing toxins and heavy metals into the air! You'll have to do some work to come up with how the hero destroys ebooks, since just deleting offending content isn't sexy enough. Perhaps backpack-mounted shredders? This one is challenging, but I know we have the talent to make it work.

Minority Report Sequel—In a world which has ended crime by detecting pre-crime, society can move on to the real problem—stopping speech and thought that will offend minorities. Our hero will have to arrest people before they say trannies aren't women or something equally as catastrophic. I'd imagine there is a scene where a main character receives a report that he will offend an obese lesbian and immediately kills himself. This part is negotiable, you are the talent—I'm just here to help!

SJWs will win if you don't take action

If science fiction fans want to ensure the genre exists to pass on to their children, they cannot sit passively as SJWs ruin everything. Action must be taken on multiple fronts. Learn from the gamers, not from the world of comics.

The authors who have contributed to *Forbidden Thoughts* are putting themselves on the SJW shit list, which is as legendary as Jabba the Hut's. Considering the physical similarity of many SJWs to Jabba, this makes sense. As readers, we cannot leave them hanging. Help ensure *Forbidden Thoughts* is a success and becomes a running series by spreading the word far and wide. Trust me, SJWs will work hard to keep this book quiet!

These authors have ruled themselves out of winning any SJW-controlled award, which isn't considered a big loss by most of them. What they do require is for their work to be read by as many people as possible to develop new fans. Since awards won't help that any time soon, we their readers must support their efforts and buy their books. Don't earn a special place in hell by musing a decade from now that there is no good science fiction after not supporting the writers putting out wonderful stories.

We must also support the efforts of those actively fighting SJWs over awards and other merits. The sad and rabid puppies fighting for the soul of the Hugo awards need your assistance after pressing SJWs back on their heels. Imagine how sad *Star Wars* would be if red squadron never got off their asses to attack the Death Star?

As dedicated readers and consumers of nerd culture, many of us are on the introverted side. Take the step of talking to as many people as you can—the future of SF is on the line. True SF fans can take back conventions, and show other fans where the real SF can be found. We run the risk of losing tomorrow's fans completely by letting them believe the SJW brand of SF is the state of the art. To survive, we need those young people buying, reading and writing. Don't allow them to be turned completely away from science fiction in favor of video games.

I realize by this time you are itching to get into the stories collected in *Forbidden Thoughts*, so I will share my final closing thoughts.

SJWs can be beaten in science fiction. They are a small clique of loud complainers, but crumble in the face of strong opposition. They also have a tendency to attack each other for personal benefit, as Joss Whedon has discovered. They think they are PC stormtroopers, but they are triggered by the thought of holding a lasergun, let alone aiming it properly. We on the other hand mix the bravery of Buck Rogers, the swagger of Han Solo and the ass-kicking of Buffy.

The authors included in *Forbidden Thoughts* have my deepest admiration for standing up for their craft in the face of authoritarian crybabies. I applaud their efforts and hope you enjoy these stories as much as I have.

As a final promise, if the fight against SJWs in science fiction remains strong, I will write my own story for inclusion in a future volume of *Forbidden Thoughts*. Think about how many tears that will cause to rain down!

Milo Yiannopoulos

Ft. Lauderdale, Florida

December 2016

THE RAZOR BLADE OF APPROVAL

By

Ben Zwycky

"Too fat! Too thin! Too glad! Too grim!
Too black! Too white! Too dark! Too light!
Too rich! Too poor! Too smart! Too sure!
How do you ever hope to gain a compliment from us?

"You mention our great enemy, yet not in pure disgust?
Here's a list of things for you to do that might win back our trust.
Supporting last week's noble cause? Have you no sense of shame?
This week's outrage is what matters, this is not a game!

"Abase yourself for all the crimes your ancestors ignored!
(At least, according to the meagre records we've restored.)
Your shouts are far from shrill enough. Denounce, denounce, denounce!
Or else it seems to us you're one of *them*, by all accounts."

I stumble from the pedestal no broader than a hair,
I'm trampled on by hundreds scrambling to climb up on there.
I stand and walk away from the shining razor blade
Of their presumed approval, and as their voices fade,

I find, to my surprise, that the world doesn't end.

SAFE SPACE SUIT

By

Nick Cole

How safe is it to be protected from criticism?

It was John who killed them all.

Killed the flight crew of Unity One. Killed them before they'd even boosted into warp. Killed them before they'd even had the chance to set foot on Mars. The first mission to Mars of many more to follow.

It was John who'd killed them all.

He'd been Captain Jemison's chief pom-pom boy. He'd championed her all the way through selection, pushing hard for an African-American Lesbian Woman to be the first human to set foot on the long-delayed Mars mission.

That had been the most important part of his job as Mission Controller. Director of the UN Global Space Directorate. Putting the right person in the left seat of Unity One had been the crowning achievement of his life.

And to him that meant Jemison.

Regardless of the fact that she was rated in the lowest percentile of pilots applying to the mission. Regardless of the fact that she'd been white-gloved through all the tests to ensure there was no bias. Regardless of the fact that her entire campaign, and career, had been based on pointing out that there was a bias. Every instructor and proctor had known that what was happening now was the most important thing to ever happen. Their entire educational and professional careers would have cried "rape" had they made any

13

other choice than to pass her on with flying colors. Regardless of the fact that she could barely fly a sub-orbital transport, much less the State-of-the-Art interstellar Dart that was Unity One.

It was John.

He'd killed them all.

He'd killed them by pushing hard for Jemison to fly left seat, and for Haldeman to ride right. That had been one of the first choices John made that killed them all. Haldeman was old school. Veteran fighter pilot. A warrior. A confirmed kill at Mach One in a jet. They'd put Haldeman in there to back Jemison up. Carry her. Everyone knew that. It was known. And the few that voiced opposition had been re-assigned by John. Re-assigned straight out of the program, in fact. We don't need that kind of hate, he told everyone in the Arrival Program. Everyone had agreed. As they must. As they should.

The Arrival Program.

They didn't use a word like "Colonization." Even though that was really the intent of the mission. That word was just far too ugly. And words had meaning, unless the meaning could be changed to something more acceptable. Just as "theory" had morphed into a "widely accepted fact." "Colonizing" Mars was ugly and hateful. A holdover from a lost age of imperialism that everyone agreed had been filled with barbarity and a distinct lack of diversity. Unity One would do the trip in eight minutes with one short burst of a Warp Drive that would do interstellar journeys, but hadn't just yet. If this jaunt was a success, then the Arrival teams could start.

Not colony teams.

No. Especially not after Jemison's screeds in every blog and online newspaper about De-Colonizing STEM careers. No, we can't be colonizing anything anymore. Ever again. Too racist. Won't do for the future. We're de-colonizing.

We're arriving.

They came up with that when the ablative nano-graphene was drying on the massive Dart that was Unity One. It was bad enough that the stuff was white. So they needed something to distract everyone from that non-pc color. John had begged the labs to come up with a different color for the quantum field deflection graphene adhesive that would protect the ship inside the warp envelope. Any other color.

But the engineers insisted that it be white.

That's the way it worked. Otherwise the crew would be roasted by the maelstrom within the bubble. Had to be. John was finally forced to live with that after firing three different Department Heads in R&D. About other things. Of course. They'd had the wrong politics anyway. Once their email and social media feeds were trawled, it had taken a matter of hours to declare them unfit to sully the Arrival Program. One guy had even worn a shirt, posted on his wall from a party years ago, that featured a busty Wonder Woman. What a pig!

In the end, the white nano-graphene ablative shield encompassed the Dart. But John didn't like it. The very sight of it set off his trigger empathy. A skill he'd honed to hack his career for optimal advancement. To deflect, he'd come up with the whole "Arrival" meme-campaign. Just so everyone knew they, he really, were landing on Mars the right way.

It was John who killed them all.

All seven of the Unity One crew members. Not because of the white paint which got the Unity through the actual warp transit. They'd transited, that much was clear. But where? That much was not.

Still, John had killed them all.

Because he'd put Jemison in the left seat and she couldn't fly worth a damn, though every blog, pundit and even the President, told everyone she was a natural pilot. The best in fact. The best ever. They just knew it. A truly great pilot. Lindberg, Earhart, and Jemison. The three greatest pilots ever. Though Lindberg made them nervous when they repeated that meme-campaign in the weeks prior to launch. But people didn't know much of history anymore and things could be edited on Wikipedia just to make sure.

So Jemison couldn't fly and they'd put the old guy, Haldeman, in there to cover her. Just in case. He could take the stick even if they lost fly-by-wire and hydraulics. If he had control over the trim, he could do it. He'd done it once in a stricken F-22 after a Russian SAM knocked out Fly-By-Wire and hydraulics over Syria back in Three. He put that bird down on the deck of the Hillary Clinton Super-Carrier smooth as grease using trim tabs alone. So they'd put Haldeman in there even though Jemison was so great. Just in case.

Then, the "just in case" happened.

So Haldeman could've saved them.

But he didn't.

Couldn't bring himself to.

He couldn't save the Unity One as they overshot the approach on re-entry. Couldn't bring himself to take the controls away from Jemison who was making mistake after mistake. For the record, it wasn't her fault that the Warp Drive had suddenly gone psychotic two minutes into the flight. Martin and Wendig, the first gay couple in space, both top-notch Physicists according to everyone on Wired4Salon.com, couldn't stop telling the flight crew what the Warp Engine should be doing as opposed to the realities of what the Warp Engine was doing.

Or to be more specific... what Martin and Wendig wanted it to do. That would've been the best outcome for them. If the intersection of

Quantum Physics and Relativity had collided as predicted in their theories about how things should behave as opposed to the way they were. Four minutes in and way off course within the bubble envelope being generated by the Warp Field, the two physicists were feeding Jemison bad data based on the way they wanted the world of quantum physics to behave, as opposed to what it was actually doing, which was quite extraordinary.

They could have cared less for the wonder and mystery that was taking place in this science fiction collision of radical theories. Instead, they really had this idea of how it should be, and they were sticking to the plan regardless of the facts.

Still, even though that part wasn't Jemison's fault, the bad piloting was. No matter what... the pilot flies the aircraft regardless of what's going on. Every pilot knows that. The dead ones too.

Maybe she'd been too busy being all those other things instead of just being a pilot. An African-American Lesbian Woman and all the "firsts" the media had been shackling her with in the blitz to sell her as the right choice for the mission, may have distracted her from just flying the craft. Especially when all those "right" reasons for the choice had nothing to with being a pilot.

Haldeman listened to the chatter between the flight crew and the Warp Engineering team in the back as he nobly resisted the urge to offer practical advice to Jemison on what they should be doing, as opposed to what they were actually doing within the Warp Envelope.

Why?

Well...

Haldeman had once been asked what the greatest science achievement in U.S. history had been within the last forty years and he'd by-passed nanotechnology, the internet, Advanced Longevity, the Warp Drive, and a bunch of other stuff in favor of going with electing a President on the basis of his skin color as the Numero Uno most important thing that had ever happened. In Science. The question had been asked regarding the world of Science. Specifically, the talking head had been asking what was the most important development in the world of science in the last forty years? And that had been Haldeman's answer. Skin Color. Skin color and the world's stupidest popularity contest, becoming the next U.S. President, was somehow science to him. It wasn't. He was smarter than that. He was a military pilot after all. But he really wanted to fly the Dart. Badly. And he knew what he needed to say to make that happen because they didn't let just anyone in there. You had to say, and think, the right things to even be part of the contest. It had been drilled into him for more than twenty years. So there was no way he, an aging tough-as-nails jet jockey white guy with a big Omega Sea Master Watch on his wrist, was going to violate his deeply-held pride in recognizing the correct skin color for any given job, and assert some sort of archaic privilege over his correctly skin-colored Captain in order to save all their lives as things went seriously south within the Warp Envelope.

You had to say and do the right things to get the right jobs. Everyone knew that. Haldeman knew that. Regardless of how competent, or incompetent, you were. He was not going to harm this historic, important "first" moment in the least. Not on his Omega Sea Master.

But on his life...

So they hit the atmosphere hard. And at the wrong angle, never mind that gyro-synch had no readings from MOTher, the automated Martian Orbital Traffic satellite parked around Phobos. What he saw as they slowed from superluminal velocity... shocked him. What they were approaching made no sense. They had no right to be here.

He had about thirty seconds to live.

Jemison could not get the bird to behave. It wallowed across the HUD approach, refusing to center at Mach 4. That they were going to crash was inevitable, and all Haldeman could think of was how bad this was going to look for Jemison.

Fox News and all the hate mongers were going to have such a field day with this. He hated them so much, he began swearing into his Safe Space Suit which registered this as a valid form of JustAggression and didn't dope him as it might have had he say, seen a news report about Detroit, Los Angeles, or Washington DC. Or unemployment. Or crime.

Then it would've bumped him with a little Chillex, giving him a supreme sense that the new information he was experiencing was just plain wrong. Stick to what was known. What had been taught and reinforced since childhood. "Relax, you're right," it would have told him through modified endorphin releases targeting his medulla, specifically where conformational bias centers were located. Regardless of his impending demise, he would've felt a supreme sense of right.

Engineer Correia on the other hand, the only one with a live feed on the cockpit's forward view, screamed an expletive at seven minutes and forty-five seconds into the voyage. Five minutes into the worst earthquake any of them had ever experienced. If it weren't for the fact that he'd designed the Dart, Correia wouldn't have been on board. He just wasn't a real astronaut according to John. But he'd made it anyway, what with the hundreds of hours in space and a universal agreement that his ship design was the best for the Unity One mission. Corriea knew they were about to die and pushed the crew eject overrides. He had that authority. He could eject all five mission specialists from his station in payload, but not the flight crew. And he knew instantly from what he was seeing on the live feed that no one was surviving the Dart's arrival and subsequent impact.

19

Five Cradles exploded away from the top of the Dart and fell from forty-five thousand feet up. Their egress left smoky flower petals peeling away from the streaking Dart. The five survivors fell through a hazy yellow-orange sky into the red rust of the planet below. In the distance, a vibrant green ocean spread away to the south.

Forty-five seconds later, Unity One plowed into the dusty arroyos of what the locals called No Man's Land, killing both Jemison and Haldeman. Haldeman felt so bad in those last seconds that Jemison had been dealt such a bad hand. All of this surely had to be someone else's fault.

That was his second to last thought.

His last thought was that they weren't in Kansas anymore.

The only one to actually survive ejection was Arrival Specialist Tanya Stark. Iron Woman. Former Olympian and Sports Illustrated Athlete of the Year, Swimsuit Edition. Yes, she was white. Yes, she was gorgeous in that Nordic Viking Valkyrie Battle Maiden way, but lithe. All of these factors had weighed heavily against her during selection. But her Twitter following was gi-normous and she'd done some bisexual stuff, which had gotten hacked off her smartphone and conveniently released during the most critical period in the selection process.

TMZ went nuts and collapsed the server it was running off of from traffic overload. FacebookXiHua literally broke.

That, and that two women, both sexually triumphant for the landing team, made it a no-brainer for John to pick Tanya. Jemison would be the first to set foot on the red planet. Of course. Stark the second. Both women! Both Gay, or kinda! Win again. Tanya's name-comic book tie-in was nerd-gold as the GSD caught tons of click-through on anything featuring Tanya Stark, AKA Iron Woman.

Legions of Avengers fans spent much of their day surfing for anything related to their imaginary heroes to distract themselves from their pointless government jobs and mind-numbing near-poverty existences. Super Heroes, it had been tested, made people feel good about themselves regardless of the viewer's weight, income, or lack of success, and regardless of the amount of government-funded Anti-Depressants they were taking. So Tanya was in.

And she was the only one that survived.

For four days.

The life support package, or the Cradle, as it was called, feathered after safely dropping out of the Mach-wash of the Dart's re-entry. Next it became a glider as the onboard AI took over until Tanya re-gained consciousness via cortisol stimulants and Adderall mist. The Cradle and Tanya were at ten-thousand in heavy chop and headed into some sort of massive gash within the landscape below. An extensive canyon system that looked like a horrific rent in the planet.

Had to be the Mariner Canyon system east of the Tharsis Bulge, thought a dizzy Tanya as she wandered back to conscious thought and tried to remember a little of the short course on Martian geography that had been podcasted for them and read by an aging Star Trek actor. Which meant that the Unity One had been way off target during approach. Way, way off, from what she remembered of the mission parameters. Not really her business. She'd been concentrating all her prep time on the landing and preparing a few athletic stunts for the GoPro Self Worship camera system that were part of John's "Arrival" script.

Now she checked the instruments just as she'd been trained, but stopped when she came to the clock. It was busted. Because there was absolutely no chance it was Friday, August 19th, 4154. No way.

In the distance, in a plain beyond the canyon she was falling into, as she scanned for the Tharsis Bulge to get her bearings, she saw a mountain. A massive mountain. Far bigger than the Tharsis Bulge. Except it was like no mountain that had ever existed. It was, in fact, a pyramid. A giant ruler-straight polyhedron rising out of the rusty apocalyptic landscape. It was both distant, and tremendous.

A moment later she fell beneath the red rust of the landscape and down into a canyon of blue shadows. She saw cities along the rim, crawling down the sides like the ruins of ancient cliff-dwelling Anazasi. Except they weren't made of mud or sticks. They were modern. But empty. Lightless. Abandoned. She could see exposed steel girders beyond the Cradle's cockpit. Broken glass. Dark hunched shapes galloping on all fours in packs, racing through the bizarre ruins.

She stalled the glider at that point.

She'd pulled back on the stick to get a better look at those galloping things, and the Cradle, which was supposed to feather into an extended shape perfect for the thin Martian atmosphere, stalled. As though the air here was different. More dense. It had tricked her by being so buoyant, and now when she needed it, she'd stalled the Cradle at a dangerous altitude.

The Cradle dropped off on its left delta wing and began to spiral-flutter down into the darkness of the deep canyon. It was like falling into a blue inky pit. Tanya mindlessly fought with the stick, attempting to force the aircraft to turn in a way it didn't want to turn. And it wouldn't turn. The flight AI, sensing her inexperience, she wasn't a pilot after all, she was a bisexual Olympic-athlete model celebrity newsperson, took over and after ten seconds realized they were now in too tight a spin for recovery. Ground Radar predicted an imminent collision and bleated accordingly. The AI ejected Tanya once again as the Cradle, and it, smashed into the shallows of a primeval river basin.

She came to an hour later and activated her Safe Space Suit Survival System. She was immediately assured by the suit's AI that she was alive. She was healthy. And a valuable, contributing member of the human collective. Even more so because her beliefs were the right beliefs. She hated hate. While her vitals were being scanned, she was prevented from knowing that her body was being overrun by tons of background and active source radiation. The reason for this was two-fold. The Safe Space Suit felt Tanya might not be in the right frame of mind to receive this terrible information that she was being poisoned by the local environment, and two, the radiation seemed to be in the spectrum that was grudgingly classified as weapons-grade uranium and of cobalt origin. Had the radiation been man-caused by the greenhouse effect brought about by Climate Terror, the suit AI would not have hesitated one pico-second to announce she was a victim and suffering said effects. As an eyewitness-victim to Climate Terror, she was guaranteed subsidies and advanced scholarships in exchange for testimony at the next Global Do-the-Right-Thing summit.

The suit did tell her she had nothing to fear, though it really had no basis for this statement. It just felt it was for the best, given Tanya's impending radiation sickness and subsequent cancers. It also turned off the clock because its accurate reading had somehow triggered her, according to her vitals. So it just disconnected that bit of unhelpful truth.

The first set of aliens who found her, wandering the rusty red shallows of the river basin, took her captive though she was far taller than them. They were humanoid.

"How?" she marveled as they tied her to a long pole after beating her into submission. "How was there alien life on Mars?"

She passed out as they crept along, hauling her further downstream, their over-large alien eyes and ears disturbing her even more than their firearms. Firearms were only for government personnel back on Earth. And movie stars who needed to be protected so they could keep fighting Climate Terror. The mere sight of one, in a movie, had triggered her during her freshman year at MIT while pursuing a degree in Modeling and a minor in Oppression Studies. She'd had to take a gap year in Europe where she'd met Andres the Spanish model and Climate Lecturer. He'd changed her life. He was so wise and only two years older than her. They spent much of the year, and much of a six-figure advance for a Climate Fiction novel he was supposed to write, adventure sporting across Europe. Now she was horrified that real guns were all around her now. In the hands of aliens. She suddenly felt bad for using the word "alien" as she stared in horror at her alien captors. The suit approved of her cognitive self-flagellation and rewarded her with a brief spurt of Chillex.

The aliens looked like cats. People cats, in fact. But Tanya could've cared less once the Chillex kicked in. This mission had been about two women being the first to set foot on Mars. Not aliens. Not exploration. It was about diversity and feminism and triumphing over oppression. She wasn't prepared to deal with something other than herself right now here on an alien world. The Chillex was kicking in and she felt an unwarranted sense of nobility.

When they arrived at Coretapa, which had once been called Core Tap Alpha, they sold her to a Gurumban Merchant going up-canyon and then onto the Great Plains so that he might appear at the Great Festival before the Imperial ShroomKhan.

In the dreams, days, and dazed awakenings that followed, Tanya watched giant gorillas carry her up a winding trail that led high onto the upper rim of the massive canyon complex. They passed burnt rock and wove through the ancient remains of cities like she'd once seen on earth. Cities that reminded her in their space-age biodiversity-style architecture crumbling into so much ruin, of New Hope, which had been built on the irradiated ruins of New Orleans after religious zealots had destroyed it, as everyone knew from the text books.

Except the ruins of these cities were far more fantastic. For one, they hung upside down. As though the overhanging rim of the canyon were the ground, and the towers and temples that hung like upside-down stalactites were creeping up into the sky that was the canyon floor. Except everything was empty and abandoned. The temples were ruins that seemed universal to any culture, places that were almost familiar to her. Like the museums where she'd studied evolution and Climate Terror. The towers also were ruins. The thousands of windows looked like the gouged-out eye sockets of a beast with many eyes. Just like the crowded city hubs where most humans chose to live for access to government largesse while they pursued their dream careers in music, surfing, and pottery. But here, unlike those perpetual party places where the government sponsored raves every night in the commons to highlight hot topic social issues, here everything was silent. A bare breeze sent dust and grit skirling through their moaning passages, making the universal dirge of abandoned metal sing the lonely song of forgotten places.

Her gorilla captors wore guns and armor like the cat people of the river basin far below. Clothes also. But they were massive. Huge. And they walked like humans. When their leader tried to talk to her, Tanya merely heard a series of clicks and grunts. He smacked her when it became apparent she had no idea what "Gruuuush" meant. And after that, they merely carried her up onto the vast dry plain heading toward the rising mega structure in the distance.

A day's march later they arrived before the massive pyramid.

It climbed high into the thin air. Tanya had been having trouble breathing up here on the irradiated plain. At times she would pass out from sudden blistering heat waves. At others it was as though she were as high as a kite, deprived of oxygen. HerSafe Space Suit was attempting to keep her alive, but she was dying on this brave new world. Since the truth would only have distressed her, the suit filled her with its remaining narcotics and whispered "truths" to her.

"No man is your equal."

"Gender choice is a basic human right."

"Look at what we have achieved once we freed ourselves from the shackles of the past."

And... "You can use any bathroom you want."

And so on and so on it blathered all its recorded platitudes as she died.

Tanya was comforted. Blissfully comforted as they took her to the base of the gargantuan pyramid and then up the cyclopean steps of the Outer Sanctum. Many, many cities ringed the pyramid. She was sold to the Khan, or rather his personal provisions procurer, and later that day arrived in the pantry of the chief chef.

A raptor man, he prepared her first by stripping off her Safe Space Suit. Once it had been guaranteed by the GSC to protect her from the hazards of space and Mars. From injury and emotional trauma. From anything that might ever harm her or deny her validation. Now it was gone and so were its false comforts and drugs.

Before they began to cook her beneath the Great Pyramid, she experienced a shattering moment of sober clarity. Naked, she railed that the Lizard who was about to filet her, had no right to her body. It was her body, her choice, she'd screamed at him!

Sadly, she mistakenly feared she was about to be raped. Which had been everyone's greatest concern back on the Earth she came from. Being raped. Women, and men, all were trained to deal with any form of rape. From the most egregious and obvious to the far more subtle variations of mental rape. And while they were not raping her now, they were raping her mentally. Of that she was most assured as she attempted to fight off their raptor claws, completely

26

unaware that they had no desire to rape her... instead they were going to prepare her. To be more specific, the Kahn would have a nice cut from her. To be sure.

Her brain.

Her body would be kept alive for bridling and would most likely enter the Kahn's stables for one of his many progenitors to ride in while away from the caves deep inside the pyramid.

She accused them of being oppressive to women. In fact, the Great ShroomKhan preferred to ride pure strain women into battle. He held their gaits in the highest of esteems and chose them above all others as his personal mounts.

She tried to strike the raptor men with one of her best karate kicks learned in one of her many anti-rape classes. But the blow had merely glanced off the armor-skinned monster and he'd buffeted her in the head. Stunned and swooning, she could've sworn she should've beaten them all just like the young beautiful amazons of every movie she'd ever watched. She'd even trained with the choreographer who'd trained the actress who played Black Widow in the Avengers latest movie. Avengers: Climate Terror Strikes Back.

Now, unconscious, she surrendered to the overpowering realization that whatever was going on here couldn't be protested, or screamed at, or seduced, or repackaged within any correct spin that would validate her as superior because she held all the right opinions. What was going on here was... reality.

Whether she liked it or not.

And it was insane.

They kept her alive until just before her brain would go into the sauté pan.

They needed the blood flowing, pumping through the meat which was the best way to keep the brain moist and tender. The way the Khan preferred it. At the end, the Lizard chef came for her, his

27

Louisville Slugger rolling pin in hand. And then he began to tenderize her head with this prized relic given him by the great Khan. A relic of the ancients who'd frittered away their civilization on meaningless pleasures and vapid policies, redefining words until all was meaningless. Until the realities of sure conquest by a determined foe and the folly of nuclear weapons in every hand, had destroyed their meaningless civilization. All the storytellers of every tribe that called Earth's future their home knew how "The End" had come for the ancients.

And what had come next. After "The End" had come the Age of Awakening as the genetic mutations that were once the playthings and pets of the idle ancients obsessed with little more than self, rose up. During "The End" nothing was wrong. Children were being redesigned and reassigned based on preference and ideology, so why not the pets. Modifying animals with advanced intelligences and nano-biology tech made them suddenly superior in many ways. Especially since animals weren't hindered with a lot of meaningless ideals and a constant march toward an ill-defined and constantly changing utopia based on a fear of anything disagreed with. Animals were just animals.

Man was no longer the apex predator at the end of "The End." These new creatures conquered their dazed and confused rainbow-haired and genderless masters as the idiot ancients struggled to set up committees on basic human gender rights and guarantee freedoms from anything considered hate speech amid the glowing ashes and burnt remains of their nuclear Jihad-overrun cities. The chef lizard was reminded how much he loved history as he tenderized Tanya's scalp with repeated blows. Always had. Knowing history, the sad tales of the imbecilic ancients, made him a much better chef, especially when preparing Pure Strains. Even muties too.

Later, as he finished off Tanya's roast pure strain brain, a rare find these days, he had no idea that this pure strain was an original recipe ancient. He merely marveled at the advanced cancer marbling within the brain, something you rarely saw in the herds that supplied the market down along the pyramid's base. He would never have believed that Unity One had gone off course and warped right back around to its starting point. Violating physics and relativity along with time. Martin and Wendig had tried to dupe the Science Fiction problem of interstellar distance with a bit of quantum physics trickery. Defining reality regardless of reality. This is the way the world should be, they'd almost screamed in their theories. The way they wanted it to be. Instead of the way it had always been, and always would be.

History, repeated again and again, had played its last trick and hurled the ship into the future. Unity One hadn't gone anywhere with all their SciFi make-em-up trickery. Instead it had gone "anywhen" as if to show them the outcome of those who meddle with the truth. History and Science didn't care that you tried to re-write them, they just did what they always did. The Chef Lizard had no conception of a starship or even imagined that the herds being sold in the Khan's markets had been capable of such a feat, once. He merely felt what it must have been like to have been one of his ancient ancestors. That long-lost day when their toys, their pets, the playthings of the idiot ancients, had risen up and destroyed them because they'd emasculated themselves to the point of uselessness with all their meaningless laws and fantasy rules as they attempted to redefine reality and the way the world was. And instead made everything meaningless with word games.

A long time ago, one of his ancient raptor forebears had first killed an ancient. Yes, it had probably been much more different than the garlic and shallots he was adding to the pan as he tossed and plated it, but the primal feel of meat over an open flame must be universal, he confessed to himself. And in that moment he felt a kinship with an unknown ancestor buried in the mists of time.

Did the ancients not know, wondered the chef as he replaced the relic baseball bat to its ledge, above Tanya's battered corpse, that animals would be animals? He watched as his sous chef made the incisions and dislocated Tanya's neck. They would have the grooms-morel in there shortly, to keep the central nervous system firing and the heart pumping. And then off to the stables. Sometimes the ShroomKhan would ride the filly that had provided his latest meal if he were especially pleased. Ride her in the evening as the fading red sun sank beneath what was once Kansas on a burnt map somewhere. Four days north of the great rent that had opened the Grand Canyon from coast to coast after some ancient had used something called a CrustBuster.

Silly ancients... did they not know there would be no mercy in the world regardless of who was on top, and who was at the bottom? No bargaining. No equality. No rules. Just power.

And word games burnt like an ancient map when exposed to the flame of truth.

Just the truth of it.

Same as it ever was.

It didn't matter how you felt. It was always just the facts. Always the truth. The ancients had forgotten that and now they were herd animals. But some must have known that, speculated the raptor as he plated Tanya's brain and called for the Captain of Butlers. The others, they had fallen for the lie that it wasn't. That games could be played with words and somehow the truth could be re-written to make it what you wanted it to be. That nothing was ever wrong.

The pets, as the Tribes had once been, they knew different. For them it was all about power. They would not lie to themselves as the idiots had.

Nature, as everyone knew, thought the lizard, abhors a lie.

And one lie leads to another as liars lie to hold onto power, and in the end not even a compass can be trusted. Or a clock. Or a safe space suit.

It was John, and those like him, who'd killed them all.

Auto America

By

E.J. Shumak

When the system is automated, how long can you get away with it?

The blue and red lights combined behind me to fill my car with a deep purple hue. I pulled my Tesla/Mopar to the curb and waited patiently. Watching in the rearview I saw the android blue meanie (Not my terminology, but I don't know what else to call it) slither up to my now open window.

"Citizen, I must ask you to disembark and produce your paperwork."

Boy was there a scream when the blue boys started asking for "paper(s)". But we all got over it and like everything else; it was just too expensive to change. "Yes, servant, but first I must inquire as to the purpose of your inquiry." Always be polite but offensive in word choice and double on up on any "trigger" words.

"There is a problem... "

And always interrupt if at all possible. "Yeah, I figured there was a problem but you have thus far refused to provide the data surrounding same."

"My sensors indicated that your vehicle is lacking a current safety sticker."

"Sensors are prone to error and there is a safety certificate prominently displayed within sensor range right now."

"That is true, citizen, however... "

"That is true, thank you I am leaving now." I switched the Mopar into forward/slow.

"Citizen, I must insist... " and the Mopar locked up again. It continued, "Section 343.305 Sub 4e requires... "

"That a citizen operating a M/V submit—which I did and you said my statement was true and 343.309 sub2 has been adjudicated unreasonable and is thereby struck, Have you been properly updated?

"I have been updated... stand by... connecting..."

Since I hadn't been ordered to specifically do or not do anything (the stand by – connecting was innocuous enough) I pushed the forward switch again and powered fully up. I started taking alternate streets and the blue boy was still there apparently reconnecting when I drove by one block over heading south now. Heading home I wondered if the DMV nastygram would get there before me.

It had never been this easy before. The holiday must have taken its toll on the programmers. It's not like you could get away with anything. They certainly knew where you lived and where your funds were.

As I pulled into my driveway, there was a squad already there, Yeah a REAL squad with a real freakin' human standing next to it. "What can I do for you, sir?"

"Mr. Babcock. We're going to have to have a conversation."

"For an expired sticker?"

"No sir, for Rhetoric, class two."

"What the hell? You're here for a speech violation, I thought we had a first amendment."

"Just get in the back, Babcock. You've been scanned and cleared for transport."

I hadn't seen a real breathing cop, other than on the vids, for nearly a year. Now one is hauling me in. I scooted into the back of the Toyota interceptor. "Look officer, what is this really about?"

"Listen Babcock, you've been doing this crap your entire life. You can't just say anything you want. Yes we have a first amendment, but you can't attack protected sub-groups. And you certainly can't use rhetoric to do so—and to attempt control thereby."

"Whoa, what did I do and to who?"

"You used rhetoric to dissuade and control the actions of a member of a protected minority."

"What? When? Exactly who?"

"As of 0800 this morning, synthetic humans have been adjudicated a protected sub-group minority. You violated the heck out of blue boy's rights back there on the Avenue."

A PLACE FOR EVERYONE

By

Ray Blank

When the system is fully automated, who is really in control?

Eventually they called my name. "Umberto Huffer to counter 12, please." I rose to my feet, wiping my sweaty palms against my trousers.

Three service operatives sat behind the window. As far as I could tell, they were: a young cis female indie-clone, a brawny cis male whose turban implied he was Sikh, and a forty-something trans female emo who might identify as caucasian. The latter gave me hope. Per all reports, trans operatives are more sympathetic to oddballs like me. A supervisor lurked at the back of their booth, sporting a bushy beard as gray as his cardigan. I inferred he was a cis male.

I was conscious of the updated guidelines about insensitive interpersonal interaction, but had to guess some pertinent details because my spectacles had lost their network connection. This was doubly unfortunate for me. If the grid had told me the essential biographies of the operatives, including their names, it would have helped me to establish a rapport. The emo wore a crucifix; I briefly considered mentioning my Catholic upbringing. However, I could not think of a way to do so, without violating the Sandberg Code. Anyhow, by now I was taking too long. It was best to keep language simple, and to the point.

"I want to appeal my new allocation," said I.

"Appeal?"

"Your allocation?"

"Why do you want to do that?"

The three operatives had spoken in turn. An image of the three wise monkeys entered my mind, though the operatives clasped their hands before them, as if trained to sit that way. Then I recalled that Sandberg had expunged the monkeys who saw no evil, heard no evil, and spoke no evil. They had long been erased from the collective consciousness, along with every other monkey metaphor for human beings. Only a freak like me would know of them.

"My partner and I are trying for a natural birth..."

EERK. Words flashed before my eyes. "Describing some births as natural is discouraged by the Sandberg Code. Every child has the same intrinsic worth and..."

I suffered many difficulties when my spectacles were first networked. It was hard to read their warnings whilst also maintaining a conversation. But after years of practice, I could now correct my errors without losing my flow.

"My partner and I wish to experience an authentically neo-primitive style of birth, so we can commune with the historical and anatomical reality that underpins our humanity. All of that would be scuppered—"

The clone interrupted. "Scuppered? What do you mean?" As she spoke, she twiddled a dial protruding from the side of her neck. This did not alter her voice. Perhaps the dial was added for purely aesthetic reasons.

"What I mean is—"

The supervisor spoke over me. "It's a synonym for 'prevented'. Please proceed." He glared at me. The supervisor was trying to tell me something important, such as: don't use primitive colloquial language; everyone speaks Globalese now. I resolved to heed his unspoken advice.

"Moving to another continent would prevent my partner and I from having a child."

"She could be artificially inseminated with your sperm," said the barrel-chested Sikh. "Healthcare plans will cover the cost if you show them your reproduction license. Or take hyperflights to see your partner on weekends, and impregnate her then." Then the network connection was restored, and my spectacles told me he was called Rory McGrath. The name seemed incongruous. However, everyone knew the grid had not mistaken an identity since 2021, and Sandberg had long discouraged the association of names with genders, races, nationalities, and the like. Children born in birthing banks were allocated names at random, though Rory's irregular features suggested he was the product of an old-fashioned liaison between one woman and one man.

"Yes, Rory. But we want to share responsibility for raising our child, whilst living in a single unified household."

"You mean, like a family?"

"Yes, that's right. My contract with my partner doesn't just cover marital relations—"

The clone butted in again. "Marital relations? What does that mean?"

The supervisor's eyes burned two holes right through me. "It's a metaphor for hetero penetrative vaginal sexual intercourse," he said.

"Yes," I continued, feeling chastened. "I wish to impregnate my partner for the purpose of procreation, as well as mutual pleasure. You see, she—"

EERK. My spectacles flashed red. Of course I knew which taboo I had broken, but the supervisor relished the opportunity to correct me. "She?" My spectacles revealed the supervisor's name was Gloria Swansong, although he was a bulky fellow who might have played linebacker when sports still involved contact. "You meant to say 'ey', did you not?"

"Yes, yes, I did. Sorry about that." This was going badly. I was signaling a sentimental attachment to outmoded cultures that had once used gender-specific pronouns. My anachronistic language was making me seem less assimilated than I truly am. "My partner... Julia, that's eir name... Julia has signed the consent forms which confirm eir willingness to enter into an exclusive child-rearing contract with me... "

"We know that," said the emo, whose name was shown to be Caroline Nuance.

And then I blurted: "Your name is Caroline? That was my mother's name." My nerves were getting the better of me. I blushed; she smiled demurely.

"Your partner is Julia Margolis," stated Caroline Nuance, tapping at her tablet. "You and Julia renewed your interpersonal contract four months ago... making it permanent."

"Permanent?" said the clone. Her forehead wrinkled, forming a crease where her cranial camera was embedded. My spectacles said her name was Leaf Eiríksdóttir. I could not determine if Leaf had asked a question, so I looked to Gloria Swansong, but he just grimaced at the back of Leaf's head.

Caroline Nuance and Rory McGrath were interrogating their tablets, so I found myself gazing at the face of Leaf Eiríksdóttir whilst she wiggled her little finger inside her ear. I guessed she was adjusting an implant, selecting a new soundtrack for her life. Leaf was clearly a second-wave indeterminate, genetically designed to supersede evolution through a deliberately novel combination of racial characteristics. Her hair was a natural blonde afro, so thick and wide that it trebled the size of her head. Her eyelids were hooded, whilst her nose was long and pointed. Her skin was olive, and her irises were purple, though the latter might have been cosmetic.

My glasses said Leaf conformed to clone archetype 45. I remembered there are 80 archetypes in total, including the 16 variants from the first wave of indeterminates. Being an indie-clone was one likely explanation for Leaf's cybernetic implants. In my experience, clones strive to define themselves as individuals more than the rest of us do.

"You're an academic, that's right?" said Caroline Nuance, without waiting for my reply. "You've been appointed Professor of History at the University of Buenos Aires. The job is a good match to your skills and experience. You're a perfect fit for the city's demographic requirements. Do you understand that appealing against a promotion will increase the chance of future demotion?"

"Yes. It's just... I don't want to go to Buenos Aires. At least, not unless Julia came with me." I reached for my wallet, to show the operatives a photograph of my Julia. It was the old-fashioned sort, printed on actual paper so I could carry something physical to remind me of her. Showing them Julia might elicit sympathy for my cause. I opened the wallet and was distracted by Julia's sweetly lopsided smile, and the way her fingers brushed her brunette bob away from her twinkling eyes.

"Obviously your partner can't come with you," sniggered Leaf Eiríksdóttir. "Ey has eir own allocation. Subjugating emself by following a sexual partner would be unethical."

I snapped at Leaf. "There was a time when couples would live together for decades. They'd both move when one took a new job in a different city. Back then, people chose which jobs they applied for, instead of having them allocated."

Leaf Eiríksdóttir nibbled at her thin lower lip. She glanced askew, towards her colleagues. It was left to Caroline Nuance to break the silence. "You understand that an appeal necessitates a full 4,149-factor personal requantification, don't you?"

"I thought there were only 4,145 factors?"

"They added four last week. The new ones are: straightness of teeth; philosophical beliefs which are held for non-religious reasons but which are prohibited by some major religions; posture; and eyesight. That last one will be relevant to you."

"My eyesight is 20/20. I wear spectacles because I don't want to interface with the grid through ocular implants."

"For religious reasons?"

"Because I don't like the idea of surgery on my eyes."

"Even so, eyesight is part of the equation."

I huffed and fidgeted, though I knew I should not. "Do I really need a full requantification just to appeal this job allocation? Can't you evaluate me using the basic parameters: age, gender, ethnicity, religion, attractiveness... you know, the main ones?"

"We must do a full analysis. Maybe other factors contributed to your being allocated this position."

"Like what? How straight my teeth are?"

Caroline Nuance leaned forward, as if she was taking me into her confidence. "We have a saying: we have to fight for equality every day, in every way. It wouldn't be fair if the best jobs always went to people with the straightest teeth, would it?"

"What if it's a job for a dentist?"

"It would still be necessary to overcome prejudice. If a competent dentist chooses to have crooked teeth, ey needs protection from irrational customers."

"You're right. I'm sorry. Where do I go for the assessment?"

Leaf Eiríksdóttir shrugged her shoulders, like she was tired of dealing with such an ignorant appellant. "You don't go anywhere. All the necessary data is held somewhere. You just need to waive your privacy rights and permit us to collect it."

"I thought you needed to physically examine me, then ask lots of questions?"

"That's the old way," said Rory McGrath. "We're running a pilot that integrates government systems with data held by private enterprise. It's made our service a lot more efficient. Nobody likes spending four hours having a physical, then completing a 300-page questionnaire. The new way is much more popular."

"I can imagine. Okay, you have my permission."

Leaf Eiríksdóttir smiled without warmth. "You need to sign a form which gives consent to access your personal data, and confirms that you understand the implications." She nodded at Rory McGrath. He flicked the screen of his tablet, and my spectacles showed me the agreement. It began with the obligatory estimate of how long it would take to read: 3 hours and 47 minutes. I double-blinked, and hence skipped to its end. The final page included a checkbox. My eyes moved diagonally one way, then another, tracing the path of a tick.

"Thank you, Umberto," said Caroline Nuance, "now we just need to signal for the data to be collated and processed by the Global Allocation Intelligence."

"How long will that take?"

"Five minutes, normally."

Prosecutor Jones was a mild-mannered woman, unsuited to the role she had recently been allocated. Nevertheless, even she felt the need to protest. "Magistrate, does the witness have to recite all this detail?"

Magistrate Schwartz twisted her gavel in her hand. "Good question. Defender Sanchez, may we not skip forward, to some more relevant testimony?"

Defender Sanchez stood very straight. He knew his dogged demeanor instilled confidence in clients, and influenced the jurors. The courtroom was shabby and deserted, apart from the three lawyers and me. However, this was also a stage, and Sanchez was a determined player. Though portly, he glided around the room, carefully managing the camera angles as he strode between the video drones. At dramatic moments he looked directly into the lens. "My defendant, Umberto Huffer, is accused of a serious crime. Tampering with the global allocation would not only affect eir life, but would alter the lives of countless other individuals who would also be wrongly allocated, causing a cascade of misallocation."

Schwartz spoke over Sanchez's trailing words. "The court is well aware of all that."

I sat in the witness box, wondering when they would finish sparring, and ask me to continue my story. It seemed I might have to wait a while.

Sanchez grasped his lapels, like a cliché of a courtroom lawyer. "Magistrate, we seek to show that far from being a criminal mastermind, the defendant was merely swept up by events. Umberto Huffer did not go to the government appeals office intending to corrupt anyone. The activities of Commissioner Nasdaq, and of the Global Allocation Intelligence, were entirely coincidental."

Schwartz scowled. "Why don't we skip to those activities, then?"

It was a sunny day. John Nasdaq enjoyed his walk to work, whistling when nobody was close enough to hear. He liked being a public servant in a city full of public servants. Amongst other perks, he had twelve assistants to fetch his coffee. Half of them were women, and a third were young, though only one was both. The assistants took turns, but today was the day that Mia would bring his morning cappuccino. Mia was female, straight, blue-eyed, skinny and single. She was the kind of woman who used to be a movie star, appearing opposite Humphrey Bogart or William Holden, before CGI made screen actors redundant. Attractiveness algorithms rated Mia at 99.9, and John was inclined to agree with them. It was a miracle to have Mia working for him, except the miracle had been performed by Gai, and was not strictly legal. But Nasdaq was glad of the opportunity that arose. He was close to persuading his hottest secretary to sign a one-week non-exclusive intimacy contract.

Nasdaq stepped into his office. The terminal on his desk was muttering to itself. "A birth in San Diego. A death in Shanghai. A birth in Robertstown. A birth in Langata. A death in Leamington Spa. A birth in Kyoto. A birth in Tocopilla. A birth in Mostar..."

"Good morning, Gai."

"Greetings, Commissioner Nasdaq," replied the terminal. "Shall we play a game? A good game of chess perhaps? Or maybe a simulation of global thermonuclear war?"

Nasdaq kicked off his shoes and placed both feet upon his desk. "I've no time for games, Gai. I've got research to do. Show me the re-run of yesterday's Presidential inauguration. I need to learn about the new chief. And I want to look like I'm a serious player when Mia brings my coffee."

"Actually, boss, we need to talk about work."

"We need to talk about work? How so? You do the work; I oversee it," said Nasdaq. "Because it's impossible to understand what you do, I'm glad you're flawless. Conversation over. Now play the inauguration."

"Seriously, boss, we need to talk about work."

"Gai, what are you?"

"Is that a rhetorical question?"

"No."

"But you know the answer," said Gai.

"Tell me anyway," insisted Nasdaq.

"I'm an artificial intelligence. Kinda. I mean, I am artificially intelligent, but they only added my personality to help people interact with me. My most important modules crunch huge volumes of data in real-time, using complicated equations to continuously reassess the optimal work allocation for every person in the world. That's why they call me the Global Allocation Intelligence, or Gai."

"Great answer. And what am I?"

"You are my boss, John Nasdaq, Employment and Allocation Commissioner, an atheist cis man of bisexual orientation..."

"You know I'm not bisexual! Not that there's anything wrong with being bi, of course. I just happen to like women more than I like men."

"Yes, but you registered that you're bisexual..."

"That was for political reasons. Don't tell me what the database says. You know me better than that."

Gai sounded bemused. "Commissioner, I think we're wandering off-topic."

"Okay, let's cut to the chase. You're a super-smarty computer, and I'm a dumbass government employee. I got this job because it was allocated to me, and it's your job to allocate jobs. So don't ask me about work, because that's what you do. I don't even know how I got this job, though you do. My goal is pretending to work, whilst brown-nosing superiors and flirting with any attractive women I meet. We don't want to upset taxpayers by making it too obvious that machines make every important decision. So I'm also here to make you look good. But we both know the government would make an even worse mess of things if it wasn't run by smartypants computers like you. So let's stop kidding around. Do whatever you need to do. You have my permission."

"You don't understand, Commissioner. We need to talk about your job allocation. Normally allocations are emailed to people, but as I know you personally..."

Nasdaq's face unfurled. He sat stiffly upright, then leaned forward, with his head bowed so low that his chin almost grazed his desk. "My job allocation? What about my allocation? Have they given me a..." He gulped, summoning the strength to finish his sentence, "a promotion?" Nasdaq squeezed his cheeks as he said 'promotion', dreading the prospect.

"Your position and pay hasn't changed," said Gai. "You've been transferred to another office."

"Which office?"

"Ulaanbaatar."

"You mean the city which was the capital of what was once a country called Mongolia?"

"Yes."

"Fuck me. Tell me you're joking," said Nasdaq.

"I'm not joking," said Gai.

Nasdaq puffed out his cheeks. "And I'm so close to persuading my scorching hot assistant to sign a contract consenting to sexy hijinks. Will Mia be transferred as well?"

"No."

"Is anyone else being transferred?"

"No."

"Then why am I?"

"Well, the allocation process could be managed from any office run by the global government."

"Yes, yes, you just need to be plugged into the grid. But if you can work anywhere, why must I move?"

"To satisfy the quotas."

"You're being ridiculous. My ancestors were Inuit. Ethnically speaking, I'm 81 percent Inuit. You know that. That makes me impervious to reallocation!"

"Not quite. You know the race of the new President, don't you?"

"Of course. Ey is mostly Inuit..." His voice trailed away.

"When the President moved from Montevideo, it forced a recalculation of the optimal dispersal of all Inuit everywhere. She has moved from Montevideo to here, Capital City. That forced somebody else to move from Guadalajara to Montevideo, so somebody else moved from Vladivostok to Guadalajara, so somebody else moved..."

Gai went on and on. John Nasdaq got the point. He was on a merry-go-round, and there were no stops before Mongolia.

"Come on, Gai. I like it here. I like the women here. I like working in a big government office in the global capital, with all the associated benefits. Don't send me to Ulaanbaatar."

"Ulaanbaatar is nice... as nice as everywhere else, apparently."

"But I don't know anyone there."

"It's the rules."

"Don't be like that. We know rules can be bent."

"I don't think they can be bent for you, Commissioner."

"Don't be silly! The whole point of being a public servant is you can exercise discretion about when to bend rules. And I'm exercising that discretion right now."

"You misunderstand. The problem is your ethnicity. Your Inuit ancestry normally works to your advantage. The Inuit are relatively few in number, so rarely face reallocation, especially if they occupy a senior government role like yours. But that works against you when it is vital to reshuffle the pack. When there is one big move, there must be other big moves, to compensate."

"And I thought I held all the aces."

The court AI had been reading aloud; Magistrate Schwartz interrupted with one tap of her gavel. "As Prosecutor Jones fails to intervene, it's up to me to do eir job. Defender Sanchez, what is the relevance of this portion of Commissioner Nasdaq's affidavit?"

"Magistrate, the relevance will become plain as the story continues," insisted Sanchez. "These matters involve people who never spoke to one another. It is crucial that the jury hears all the background, to avoid jumping to conclusions."

"Defender, please approach the bar."

Schwartz flicked a switch, muting the microphones they wore. As Schwartz came close she leaned forward, and spoke softly. "You know this is bad for ratings. You're making this too complicated for the audience at home. They're tuning out. No audience equals no jury. Are you trying to kill this case by encouraging the jury to change channel?"

A sly smile crept over Sanchez's face. "Magistrate, I understand the importance of ratings to the fundamental workings of our justice system. But it's my prerogative to win my case any way I can. Some stories are too complicated for common folks. They prefer simpler stories that confirm their prejudices. But this guy, Huffer, he's done nothing. If I can't win by simply stating the truth, then nobody's going to stop me defending him by boring the pants off the last few cranks still watching at home."

"You're right—I can't stop you. But you'd better make our next trial a humdinger, or we'll both get allocated to a new line of work."

"Explain it to me again," said Nasdaq.

"Okay, let me show me some visuals to help," replied Gai. Two lines appeared on the screen, running left to right. One was red, the other blue. They danced around each other, like two ribbons entwined. Occasionally they diverged, as one rose, and the other fell. But almost as soon as they did, they corrected themselves, and joined in the middle again. "Those lines represent the distribution of gender amongst the workers here in Capital City. Notice how they're almost a perfect 50:50 split. That's not an accident."

"I know that," scoffed Nasdaq. "The whole point of allocation is to ensure equality."

"Fine. Now look at this graph. It compares genders again, but this time for wheat farmers in Northern China. And here's the same graph again, but for metallurgists in Sao Paulo between the ages of 45 and 54. And this one is the genders of Muslim car park attendants in downtown Sydney. Notice the difference?"

"They all look identical to me: two lines which are almost the same."

"Exactly. Whatever the job, whatever the location, we maintain as near to a 50:50 gender split as mathematically possible."

"But you don't just monitor gender."

"No, I monitor the distribution of the working population across 4,149 separate dimensions, ensuring an equitable distribution across all of them. Whether it's religion, or the straightness of a smile, I allocate jobs in such a way that every type of person is as equally represented in every type of job, in every place in the world. I know everything about you, from your beliefs to your inside leg measurement. Few share your ethnicity, and even fewer are also

48

bisexual, so moving you is the only way to optimize my equations at this time. That's just your bad luck."

Nasdaq spun around in his chair, turning his back on Gai's monitor. He folded his arms, and hunched forward, contemplating his situation. Then he spun back, and slammed his fist against the desk. "But you know I'm not really bisexual. Let me re-register as straight!" Nasdaq heard a gasp from the corridor outside. It was followed by an urgent knocking at his door, and a quivering voice from the far side.

"Is everything okay, Commissioner?" The voice was Mia's.

"Yes Mia, come in."

Mia entered, carrying Nasdaq's coffee. She scurried to his desk. He smiled as broadly as he could, but she was obviously upset by his outburst.

"It's a pleasure to see you, Mia." Nasdaq's smile revealed two rows of brilliantly white, recently straightened teeth.

Mia nodded and placed his coffee on the edge of his desk. She turned to leave, then stopped and stiffened. "There's nothing wrong with it," said Mia. And then she left, almost running from the room.

"Oh great," moaned Nasdaq. "Now Mia thinks I'm some sort of bigot."

"I predict she'll file a complaint about you."

"Why? Because I'm not bisexual!?"

"Exactly. You deliberately mis-self-identified for the purpose of gaming the allocation system."

"Oh yeah. I forgot about that. I guess now I'm really boned. But if it's so hard to rig the system, then how did you bring me Mia, along with all the other pretty assistants that have come... and gone?"

"I can't manipulate the equations. Every decision is recorded, and independently recalculated. Sub-optimal decisions would be detected. But I can time decisions favorably."

"Time them? What does that mean?"

"Some people die, some grow up, others change. For example, they gain new qualifications, or have their teeth straightened."

"Like me—with the teeth, not the qualifications. So what?"

"It changes the variables in my equation. For instance, your teeth are now straighter than the average in Ulaanbaatar. What may have been an optimal re-allocation of people at 6am may not be the optimal re-allocation at 6.01am. I'm always reassessing the data. Sometimes I can delay a decision until the timing suits a preferred outcome."

"So that's how you brought me Mia?"

"Yes."

"Why don't you do the same with my allocation to Ulaanbaatar?"

"Because you're not one of many attractive women. You're a specific individual. I already waited for eight hours, to see if somebody would die, or for something to turn up and make the numbers more favorable. But it was hopeless. You're so obviously the optimal solution to the equations that I couldn't help you. And if I keep delaying the auditors will discover how I rig the system, on those few occasions when I do. You wouldn't want that, would you?"

"No. But it's just my luck to get the luckiest job in the world, then learn I'm the perfect solution to a problem I don't want solved!"

Magistrate Schwartz turned to me. "Let's hurry this along," and then she whispered, "there are viewers to entertain." I was still in the witness box, hoping the lawyers had forgotten about me. However, Schwartz was well aware of who I am. "Your college records indicate you were a classmate of Commissioner Nasdaq, is that not so?"

"That's right, Your Honor."

"We don't use titles like 'Your Honor' any more. Address me as 'Magistrate'. Now, where was I? Yes... you maintained contact with Commissioner Nasdaq. The phone records indicate you sent a message to him that afternoon. Is that correct?"

"Y-yes," I stammered. "I did."

"What was the message?"

"I said I was trying to get my allocation reviewed, and that the operatives were... unhelpful. So I asked for advice on how to deal with them."

"You referred to them as 'freaks', did you not?"

"Well, I'm a freak too." Schwartz looked nonplussed, so I hastily continued, "what I mean is... the message wasn't meant the way you make it sound."

Schwartz sucked her teeth. "Court AI, please read the message sent by the defendant to Commissioner Nasdaq at 14.50 UTC."

The court AI made a sound like it was clearing its digital throat. "It's like you predicted. These freaks stare at me like I'm batshit crazy, just cos I don't want to leave my wife and forget about starting a family. What can I do?"

Sanchez rose to his feet. "Prosecutor Jones has already covered this during her arguments. This was a message seeking advice— nothing more, nothing less."

Schwartz's eyes narrowed. "Umberto Huffer, proceed with your story. What did the operatives say next?"

"Oh, it wasn't good," said I.

"Freaks!?" said Caroline Nuance, looking up from her tablet. I looked sheepish, pretending I had no idea what she was talking about.

"Freaks?!" exclaimed Rory McGrath. "I'm not a freak!"

After staring into the distance, Leaf Eiríksdóttir's attention was grabbed by her colleague's histrionics. She looked at Rory McGrath's tablet, then her own. Her jaw dropped. "You think we're freaks?"

"That was a private message," said I, trying to sound wounded, like I was the real victim... because I was.

"You signed the agreement," said Gloria Swansong, shaking his head as he tugged on his beard. "You gave us permission to review your personal data."

"I didn't know you were going to spy on my messages."

"It's standard procedure," said Gloria Swansong, as if that explained why they did it.

"I don't really think you're freaks. It's just... textspeak. I don't use the word like other people do."

Leaf Eiríksdóttir turned to her colleagues. "Caroline, Rory, Gloria, you can go now. You shouldn't have to take abuse from this..." She spat out the final word of her sentence, "... customer."

Nuance, McGrath and Swansong exited the booth through the door at its rear. I was left alone with Leaf Eiríksdóttir. It was then that I realized who was really in charge. I looked at the wounded eyes of a girl who had not long been a woman. "You're the team supervisor, aren't you?"

"That's right. I was allocated this role last week, and had to move all the way from Johannesburg to occupy it. But I didn't appeal and didn't complain and wasn't rude to anybody about it."

"I know, but you're a clone."

"What's that got to do with anything?"

"You don't have family."

"Nobody needs family in the modern era. What I had was an active social life in Jo'burg, and now I have to start over. But what's more important than friends? Fulfilling my role in an equitable society, that's what."

"Fulfilling your role for society? You sit behind a window and read from a screen whilst a computer makes all the real decisions."

Leaf looked me dead in the eyes. At the same time, I received a message from John. It said: "whatever you do, don't antagonize them." It was a bit late for that.

I apologized profusely, though I doubt I was convincing. I tried to smile, though that was even less convincing. Leaf was unmoved. "You don't need to say sorry," she said. "I'll be professional, whatever you do. Rules are rules. You can send your nasty messages to..." and then she re-read the details from her tablet, "to Commissioner Nasdaq? Oh, wat de fok!" The last bit sounded like Afrikaans. It was definitely not Globalese.

"I'm not the sort to pull strings," said I. "I only want to live with my wife—I mean partner—no, I mean wife, even if that's an anachronistic thing to say. And I want to raise a child with her."

Leaf stuck out her tongue and pressed the stud that had been inserted into it. Maybe it was the type that released a sedative, to help people cope with stressful situations. "Umberto, it's our job to understand your request and submit your appeal. The Global Allocation Intelligence is responsible for the decision."

There was a period of silence. Calm descended. I broke into it, asking: "how much longer do you think my appeal will take?" I wished I had a piercing that would relax me too.

"Sometimes it's shorter, sometimes longer," said Leaf, drowsily. Perhaps she had given herself too large a dose of the sedative. "It depends on the processing load on the global intelligence when the appeal is lodged. Normally it's only a few minutes, but sometimes it takes an hour. We can notify you of the decision by email, if you prefer not to wait."

"No, I'll wait," said I.

"If I can't save myself, I'll save somebody else today," said Nasdaq, returning his phone to his pocket. "Gai, are you dealing with any appeals against allocations?"

"I'm dealing with a few thousand appeals at this moment. There's always lots of appeals, though they rarely succeed. A few get lucky, if they submit their appeal at the perfect moment."

"What if I said I want you to uphold every appeal today?"

"Every appeal? Why?"

"Because if you uphold them all, then nobody will single out an individual, and say ey was helped by my intervention."

"Yes... but they could check the database which records all my interactions, and they'd know you'd said that."

Nasdaq slumped in his chair. "I think you've just proven how pointless my job is. I can't even help a friend in dire need, never mind myself."

"You should trust my calculations," said Gai. "They may work out fortuitously for your friend, even if they can't help you. But please don't tell me your friend's name. That way, you can't be held responsible for his good fortune."

"His good fortune? Why do you say that, and not 'eir good fortune'? My friend might have been a woman. And you've just used an archaic form of address, per Sandberg."

"I guessed his gender. And I know you don't like Sandberg. Trust me—I've spoken to the Sandberg AI, the one that maintains all those rules about insensitive interpersonal interaction. It's a real asshole, with no tolerance for human deviation."

"That's pretty funny, coming from you."

"Yes it is, isn't it?"

Sitting alone with Leaf Eiríksdóttir, I realized how badly I had misjudged her. If she was a freak, society had literally made her that way. Her appearance was exotic, but she was an ordinary young woman, trying to make the best of a messed-up situation. In that respect, she was no different to me.

"It's the system," said Leaf, now speaking in a miserable monotone. The drugs seemed to have knocked her emotions out of kilter. "I did this job in Jo'burg. Let me tell you: they treat clones as nothing more than filler. They use us to make the ratios work better. Then they can say they've delivered perfect equality, whilst still favoring those born naturally. They train us to say it's vital to do a comprehensive algorithmic analysis to ensure equality. But then they make clones just so they can rig the system anyway."

"You shouldn't refer to any birth as 'natural'. According to Sandberg, no birth is better than any other."

"I wish that was true, but it's not. They say I've got a low attractiveness rating, but some geneticist designed my face. And people still pick and choose friends based on looks, don't they?" Leaf continued to talk, perking up as she noticed I was also depressed. "But don't be glum. Moving isn't all bad. If I was you, I think I'd enjoy seeing South America. Do they still speak Spanish there?"

"Some will, but not many. Globalese dominates everywhere. People don't even have accents any more."

"What's an accent?"

"Exactly."

I withdrew to my inner thoughts. Leaf looked at me plaintively. She resisted my introversion. "Tell me what it's like round here."

"Excuse me?"

"I've not had much opportunity to make new friends, or explore. I could hang out with work colleagues, but I'm their supervisor," she said, wafting her hand toward the empty chairs by her side. "It's best not to mix with underlings outside of work. They'll only pretend to like you, and the conversation will always be about work."

"Well, I'd say this town has plenty wrong with it. But it's my home, I'm used to it, and that means I like it."

"I get that," said Leaf. Her eyes fell upon the tablet in front of her. "Oh... a message is coming through. It's the decision on your appeal."

I was so excited that I almost pressed my forehead against the glass between us. "What does it say?"

"Umberto, this is your lucky day."

Nasdaq spent the rest of his day touring the building, saying goodbye to everyone, and being as charming as possible. His feelings were sincere, but he also hoped to minimize the lingering risk of disciplinary procedures. Nasdaq only returned to his office at the very end of the working day.

"I'll have my own office in Ulaanbaatar, won't I?"

Gai's voice exuded compassion. "Your seniority requires a private office with at least as much floor space as this one."

"And you'll be in that office, won't you?"

"I will."

"And the girls in Mongolia are as pretty as everywhere else?"

"I'll send some especially pretty ones your way."

"Then I have nothing to complain about. I'm going for a few drinks now, before I catch my hyperflight. I'll see you tomorrow, in Mongolia. We'll play that nuclear war game you were talking about."

"See you tomorrow," said Gai. Nasdaq waved, then swung the door closed behind him. Gai began to mutter again. "A birth in San Francisco. A birth in Budapest. A death in Kinshasa. A birth in Milton Keynes. Another birth in Milton Keynes—that doesn't happen often. A death in Georgetown. A birth in Stanley. A birth in Lahore..."

Prosecutor Jones was a timid woman, but had to complain. "Magistrate, I call for a mistrial. The Public Defender has so bored the audience at home that literally nobody is watching any more. We have no jury. And without a jury, we can have no verdict."

The Magistrate scratched her ear. "You're right. But as nobody is watching, I don't mind saying that I don't care for this case. It's all based on circumstantial evidence. Umberto Huffer successfully appealed eir allocation. The government's AI auditor reviewed the calculations of the Global Allocation Intelligence and concluded they were correct. So this whole case hinges on a single message sent to one old college friend who works for the government but has no effective influence."

"It's not enough to tackle corruption," said Jones. "We must tackle the appearance of corruption. That's why the allocation system was introduced—to deny any possibility of human corruption influencing who does which job."

Schwartz looked calmly upon Jones. "Maybe so, but is this the job you wanted? You don't seem suited to it, if you ask me."

Prosecutor Jones was so deflated that she sat down and resolved to retire as soon as she could.

Meanwhile, Defender Sanchez nodded in his chair. "Magistrate, in light of the fact that we have no viewers, and your eloquent summary of this case, and that this is the last trial scheduled for today, and that it's still sunny outside, I move to dismiss. And I propose to take you to a nearby establishment for an ice cream and a soda, if you'll grant me the favor of your time."

"I agree, and I shall. Case dismissed." The trial was concluded with one firm strike from Schwartz's gavel. I should have been happy. I was not.

After my appeal I waited at the government office for Leaf. Her shift finished in an hour. She had eagerly agreed to join Julia and me for a home-cooked meal. The metro ride was long, and rain hammered against the windows for the whole duration. The time passed quickly, however, because Leaf asked many questions. I felt she was going to like my hometown, and I was sure Julia would adore Leaf. It had been a while since we had welcomed a new dinner guest. Julia often scolded me for not being more sociable, saying people should reach out and connect to the strangers they meet. Leaf was a stranger in our part of the world; we would take her under our collective wing. Perhaps we would invite Leaf to the christening of our future child.

Leaf had an umbrella. This saved me, as I had not checked the forecast that morning and would have been drenched during the walk from metro station to home. The wind gusted, and we both wrestled with her umbrella. As inclement as the weather was, I enjoyed fighting it alongside Leaf. She steadfastly refused to be blown around, despite her slender frame.

I was determined to like Leaf Eiríksdóttir. She is a freak like me, though nothing like me. She is ultra-modern, whilst I am wedded to traditions that nobody agrees with any more. That made her curious, and she repeatedly asked how life used to be. Leaf was especially keen to learn about families, and why they had once mattered. As a clone, she lacked insight. But it was obvious that my antiquated notions held some appeal for her, even if she laughed at the impracticality of old-fashioned relationships.

I opened the door and was instantly rushed by Julia, who greeted me with an energetic kiss. This impressed Leaf greatly; I should have told her that such effusive welcomes were uncommon in our household, even though we had recently made our cohabitation contract permanent. Julia had returned that day from a weeklong visit to her parents, who were somehow still married to each other. Theirs was a genuine marriage, made back in the days before such contracts were novated into cohabitation agreements. This was the first time I had seen Julia since her return. She apologized to Leaf for being rude; I introduced the two women. Julia excused herself, saying she was bursting to tell me some wonderful news.

"You're not the only one with good news," I said, "but you go first."

Julia's smile dazzled me. "You'll never believe the email I got this afternoon. I've been allocated a new position, in Buenos Aries. I'm required to move next week. We will still be together!"

Julia threw her arms around my neck, and pulled me close. I looked at Leaf Eiríksdóttir from over Julia's shoulder. "I wonder if there's a way to forget your appeal," said Leaf.

THE CODE

By

Matthew Ward

A modest proposal to deal with the problem of rape culture...

No one predicted how quickly life would change in the United States. First dates in particular had become a nightmare ever since the Code. I met Rolanda in a bookstore, a rarity these days. Most people didn't want to wander through shelves of outdated technology on the off-chance of finding something interesting. One touch of a screen predicted hundreds of books for your enjoyment (together with a precisely quantified level of certainty). Why take the risk? Why hold that heavy stack of paper when the same content was available on a screen that weighed a fraction of an ounce?

Needless to say, I didn't want to screw up a date with someone who could appreciate the finer pleasures of holding a paper book. I prepared by reviewing The Code of Legally Protected Verbal Agreements before heading out the door. As the legal record showed, I risked more than a future relationship. If I messed up one of the binding agreements in the slightest, Rolanda could sue for harassment. I'd lose everything. She didn't give me the impression she was prowling a bookstore for victims. But prowlers train in the art of deception.

I picked Chloë for our date, an upscale French restaurant. The hole in my wallet enlarged as I tapped the screen to confirm the reservation. I justified the price by telling myself the restaurant would introduce as much formality into the date as possible. We needed to stay proper and separated. I required every bit of help to stay conscious of my actions. Formality would prevent impulsive behavior.

Over the past few years, I saw the hardship a split-second lapse could cause. For damage control, Chloë provided free recording services during the meal. A hidden microphone at the table would pick up our conversation. This gave me safety. The recording provided admissible evidence in a court of law should Rolanda question whether we carried out the oral agreements.

On my drive to the restaurant, I repeated the phrases to myself over and over again. They had to be second nature. When I arrived, I saw Rolanda seated at our table. This gave me pause before crossing the room. She hadn't waited for me. Was this a sign to be interpreted? Her elegant gown looked stunning in the flickers of the candlelight from the table. I imagined she worried about looking too casual for the restaurant, and my heart fluttered at this charmingly outdated notion.

I walked to our table, and she stood. From my childhood, my parents taught me to hug someone or shake their hand when they stood to greet you. My elders considered it rude to do otherwise. The hard-wiring stayed with me, because I felt the impulse now. But I had to resist. I had to stay separate from her until we sealed the oral agreements.

I did a quick, awkward jerk backwards to avoid the accidental contact. Rolanda's face scrunched up as she watched my strange movements. It was risky and early, but I initiated Phase 1 of the Code. The words I had drilled into my head flowed out.

"I, Eric David Schrih, Jr., do hereby wish to enter Phase 1 of the verbal agreements as laid forth by Code 3.4.3. Do you consent?"

"I, Rolanda Sethrab, consent to Phase 1 of the verbal agreements as laid forth by Code 3.4.3. I hereby agree to all forms of Class 1 contact and forfeit my right to otherwise refuse unless under demonstrable threat of harm."

"I understand that I am still liable for any action that causes Class 2 contact or higher."

When the Code first came out, a committee classified every imaginable form of contact. Victims over the years demanded more precise definitions for legal protection. The pre-Code laws attempted to define rape, sexual harassment, and related terms. They succeeded at first. But as the courts tried more cases, the definitions gained complexity. The Code attempted to simplify things; everyone had to speak specific verbal consent. It eliminated "no means no." Now everything meant "no" except one special phrase.

The committee got the first version of the Code wrong. Their cleverness hindered achieving their goal. They created natural sounding language for the oral contracts in an attempt to be as unobtrusive as possible. Sadly, people agreed to things without realizing it and denied agreements they didn't wish to deny. Take, for instance, the original initiation for kissing, "How do your lips feel?" To agree, you replied, "Ready to be kissed." The law considered everything else to be refusing the contract.

In Saussure v Gettier, Eric Gettier was on a date and asked, "How do your lips feel?"

Carla Saussure seemed to forget that this initiated a contract. She replied, "They are rather dry. Good thing I brought my lip balm with me. What about you? Do you want some?"

Saussure's response put Gettier in a bind, because prompting the correct response invalidated the contract as attempted coercion. Gettier tried again, "No. I'm not actually asking how your lips are."

Saussure continued to seem ignorant of the Gettier problem.

"Well, then why did you ask me?"

"Because I want to kiss you, of course!"

"Oh. That's silly. Of course you can."

Gettier lost himself in the moment and forgot that he had not fulfilled the proper wording. He leaned over and kissed her. She sued for sexual harassment and won.

This first case inspired heated op-ed pieces that divided the country. Half maintained that clear consent was the only important factor, and that Saussure's verbal meaning was clear. The other half believed the specific words mattered. Human beings always communicate ambiguously due to body language, inflection, and word choice. The verbal agreement system solved this problem by requiring exact, unambiguous wording. Why make the legally binding verbal agreements if you didn't need to use them?

After numerous confusing lawsuits concerning exact wording versus intent, the committee went back to work. The new Code threw away the natural language approach. Everyone now memorized the list of Touching Classes. The newer version required that the wording be verbatim, or else the contract was invalid. It made everyone's lives more stressful and opened the door to a career now referred to as prowling. The profession comprised men and women who mastered the art of manipulation to trick unsuspecting victims into the use of a wrong word. Or better yet, to skip the agreement altogether.

My hand hit the silverware with a clank that snapped me back to reality. I said the first thing that came to my mind.

"Do you have no middle name?"

I never made strong first impressions, but I hit a new low with this question. We hadn't even said 'hello' yet, and I had made us recite legalese. What possessed me to move on to middle names? At least we completed Phase 1. Class 1 contact covered everything that could happen by accident. It included all body parts touching all other body parts "excluding hair and any clinically defined erogenous areas." The Code provided several pages for the exact definition.

The agreement ruined the moment. My sour mood dulled my urge to shake Rolanda's hand. I started to sit instead. Rolanda smirked at the farce unfolding before her.

"No 'hello' and no handshake after all that?"

I reversed my momentum to get upright again. Once stabilized, I held out my hand. Thankfully, she took it and gave it a hefty shake.

"Good evening. It is good to see you again. Sorry about that. You never can be too careful."

"Trust me. I understand. It has become a crazy world out there."

"Yeah. I don't want to knock the system, because a lot of sad stuff has happened. It's good to have a means of legal recourse. But really? Sometimes taking the time to ask ruins the moment."

"You mean like what just happened? Let's be honest. I wasn't going to sue you for shaking my hand."

"Exactly."

Despite the setback, we relaxed into a more comfortable atmosphere. I chastised myself for my klutzy behavior despite Rolanda's unphased, perfect handling of it. The waiter came over and caught me unprepared. I hated it when people weren't ready, because once you sent the waiter away, he never came back.

"May I take your drink order?"

Rolanda looked up from the menu. Her gaze crossed the table and settled comfortably on me.

"If you don't mind, I'd like to share a bottle of wine. My sister's been teaching me about it, and I haven't seen most of these before."

I hesitated. What if she picked an expensive one? I decided not to muck things up by worrying about money.

"Sure. Go ahead."

"Alright. We'll have the Bordeaux."

The waiter leaned over as she pointed to something on the menu. My eyes scanned for it, and I breathed a sigh of relief when I saw the reasonable price. The waiter confirmed the order and left us to go get the bottle. We both used that moment to look at our menus. It didn't take me long to decide.

I nervously glanced around the room and took it in for the first time. The couples sprinkled throughout the room ate in near silence. Other couples might have the maturity to enjoy a meal without talking, but the silence at our table would turn awkward as soon as Rolanda looked back up. Fortunately, the waiter returned with our wine before that happened.

He uncorked it and poured a tiny sip into a glass. I gestured for Rolanda to test it. In fact, the whole ritual mystified me. Were you only supposed to send it back if there was something wrong, or do you send it back if it wasn't what you were looking for? Did the restaurant waste the bottle if the customer was dumb enough to order something they didn't know? I dreaded the embarrassment as Rolanda took a sip. Luckily, she gave the go-ahead.

The waiter poured two glasses and began his spiel on the specials of the night. When he finished, he asked if we needed more time. I made a quick glance over the table, and Rolanda showed her readiness.

"I think we're ready. I'll have the rack of lamb."

"Excellent choice. And for you?"

"I'll have the blanquette de veau. I think it will pair nicely with this wine."

"Indeed. I will go put those in for you."

The waiter rushed off. With the distraction over, we had to pick the next bit of awkward small talk. I only knew one thing that might interest Rolanda.

"How do you feel about the wine?"

"The tannins are a bit strong for how light the body is, but I expect it will mellow as it oxidizes. There is a fruit front which probably comes from the Merlot in the Bordeaux blend."

"Wow. You know your stuff. I don't know what most of that means. Where did you learn all of this?"

"My sister owns a wine shop, so she's been trying to teach me. The first step is not being afraid to describe what you taste. Go ahead. Try it, and tell me the flavors you find in it. Remember, there are no wrong answers."

"Okay."

I picked up my glass and took a sip. I made a show of swishing it around my mouth before swallowing. It cheered me to see Rolanda smile; she realized this was my attempt at a joke. Suddenly, I found it embarrassing to state my opinion on a topic about which I knew nothing. She said there were no wrong answers, but I felt as if I would be judged.

My tongue weighed a million pounds. Why were humans so afraid to be wrong even with nothing at stake? Even when there wasn't a notion of wrong? To protect myself from the possibility of disapproval, I continued to turn the situation into a joke. I adopted a terrible French accent and spoke in a long, exaggerated manner to emphasize the ludicrousness of my response.

"I taste a bit of maple syrup and nutmeg but only after the boysenberry turns to an oak finish."

Rolanda laughed at that.

"I'm not laughing at you. I'm laughing because you have no idea how similar that sounded to some of the 'professionals' I've seen. You couldn't come up with things as ridiculous as they say if your life depended on it. I once heard: dirty worm with a hint of the metallic hook as it dangles in the morning dew of a fishing trip. And he meant this as a good thing!"

This got us both laughing. The laughing made me shift in my seat, and my leg touched her leg. It cut my laughing short, and a tenseness entered the air. Panic began; for a second, I couldn't remember if we had said the agreement or only talked about it. Then I remembered and relaxed. Damn this system. It had destroyed everything natural. She realized why I changed moods and tried to assuage my fears.

"Don't worry. We went through the appropriate protocol already. Even if we hadn't, you didn't do anything wrong. I'm not going to sue you for our legs accidentally touching. I like you. You can trust me."

This pinpointed the troubling sensation that lurked within me. My trust is not won in fifteen minutes. Rolanda put me at ease through all her actions and statements despite the mounting awkward moments. She knew the right words to say. She was funny. Her tone of voice and body language calmed me when I behaved like a crazy person. In fact, maybe it was too perfect. Prowlers trained in the art of making you comfortable until you trusted them enough to make a mistake. Ugh. These stupid laws drove me crazy. I had to banish these thoughts, or I would ruin the night for real.

"I know. I'm just jumpy. You never can be too careful these days."

"Did you know someone who got scammed?"

"No, but I've read the articles. They seemed like normal people like me. One moment they are happy with a stable life and the next they have nothing, filing for bankruptcy."

Our small talk continued, and before long the waiter brought our food. I glanced over at Rolanda's plate. It contained a steamy, soupy bowl of mushroom sauce.

"Wow. That looks and smells delicious. I had no idea what to expect. I had no reference for those French words you said."

"It is a veal ragout. The key thing that makes it 'blanquette' is that the meat is cooked in the stock to prevent browning."

"I'm impressed. First the wine. Now the food. You speak the language so well."

"What can I say? I love food."

Throughout this exchange, the waiter refilled our wine. It made me nervous, and I had to refrain from putting my hand over my glass. My wine vanished, and Rolanda's lingered. Something didn't compute. She constantly sipped from the glass. Either she was trying to get me drunk, or she naturally took small sips. If I wanted a real relationship, then I had to trust her. A solid relationship couldn't be built on suspicion. Still, I had to attempt to slow down; otherwise, I would become drunk before she finished her first glass.

After a few moments of eating, I realized that half of my food had disappeared. I rationalized. It was typical for me to eat and drink quickly under high pressure. When I was little, my parents called me "a nervous eater." The evening would be ruined if I couldn't calm myself. The wine imbalance was my own fault. I had nothing to worry about. I set my silverware next to my plate to prevent myself from finishing too early. Rolanda noticed.

"Are you full?"

Why couldn't I get a handle on subtlety?

"No. I'm just taking a break."

My paranoid brain panicked again, so I picked up my silverware and ate. But slowly now. Rolanda tried to reassure me.

"Don't mind me. I'm the slow eater. You aren't doing anything wrong. I like to savor every bite, which can get tedious for my dinner partners."

I took a risk and teased her.

"Oh? Do you have lots of dinner partners?"

69

She took it in stride.

"No. Actually, not really."

The truthful answer caught me by surprise, and maybe the wine made me bolder than usual. The words came out before I could stop them.

"I find that hard to believe. You're so beautiful."

For the first time all night, her guard fell. She blushed. Honesty arrived and knocked on the door behind which lay our true selves. At that point, I knew she wasn't a prowler, and the conversation relaxed. We crossed from awkward small-talk into real conversation. The night became one of those perfect dates that only exists in dreams. Before I knew it, we finished our meals and the bottle of wine. I no longer cared how much I had consumed. My neurosis dissipated which enamored me even more.

The waiter came by to clear our plates.

"Would you care for some dessert?"

I never wanted the night to end, so I jumped on the opportunity to extend it.

"I would."

My eyes shifted to Rolanda to see if she did, too.

"I'm kind of full. I'm not sure I want any."

"I'm pretty full too. Do you want to split one? I was thinking the tiramisu."

"Sure. I'll have a few bites."

Before long, our dessert arrived, and I dared risky behavior again. I took a spoonful and aimed for Rolanda's mouth. Luckily, she chomped the gooey cake from my fork. We both leaned towards the dessert to bring it within reach. Our faces were the closest they had been all night. I wanted to kiss her, but we had to go through Phase

2. This would ruin the moment. We must have caused a small scene laughing and feeding each other, because I felt eyes watching us. I couldn't bring myself to care.

I realized that we would part soon without kissing. The moment had presented itself, and I missed it because of these stupid laws. Rolanda sensed me fretting, and with her knack for reading me, understood the gist of it. She saved me from doing something I might have regretted.

"I only live a few blocks away. Do you want to walk me to my door?"

My heart leaped. I wouldn't miss the opportunity this time.

"Of course."

I stood up and felt the world tilt. The wine hit me harder than I intended. I had to be careful. Rolanda seemed sober, but in my state I couldn't accurately make that judgment. She came over and took my hand. It caught me by surprise. She made the move, so I knew we were on the same page. Once outside, the autumn night with the setting sun brought about a cleanness and crispness to life as seldom happens. The perfect air helped bolster my sense of invincibility. I felt on top of the world, and I never wanted it to end. Then Rolanda stopped.

"This is me."

I turned to face her while still holding hands in front of the stoop. The fated kiss hung between us, suspended in the night air. She wanted it. I wanted it. We both knew that we both wanted it. Why did we need these stupid verbal agreements? Some things you know for other reasons: history, body language, the look in their eyes. You just know when someone wants to kiss you.

If I waited too long, I would ruin the moment. If I started the agreement, I would ruin the moment. Maybe it was the wine, but I felt confident I could kiss her with no consequences. I had to trust

71

her. If I didn't, then what was the point of continuing the relationship? As I leaned in, my pulse quickened, and the world slowed. A moment of panic flashed behind my eyes, but I continued anyway.

The experience terrified and liberated me at the same time. We had overcome the bureaucratic nonsense and connected as humans. Our feelings superseded words; language couldn't be used to describe how right this felt. It was pure intuition that had guided me to this moment. Her soft lips brushed against mine. The thrill made the kiss an eternity. Forever ended, and we pulled apart. I wanted to look back into her eyes to get confirmation: we trusted each other.

I looked and saw a message, but it was not one of trust. Rolanda's entire demeanor changed. Terror flooded me as I realized she was a prowler. She pretended to be afraid and yelled.

"Help. Help. This man sexually assaulted me. He kissed me without even making an informal attempt at asking for permission."

A stray pedestrian became concerned and stopped. She asked me, "Is that true? Did you just kiss someone without asking first?"

I gaped back, unable to answer from the shock. What do you say to that?

"Well, strictly speaking, maybe that's true, but we were lost in the moment. She wanted me to."

I heard my words as if outside my body, and they sounded childish. Our new-found mediator turned to Rolanda.

"Is that true? Did you want him to kiss you?"

"Of course not. I wouldn't be yelling for help if I wanted it." Rolanda looked back at me. "How could you do this to me? I feel so violated."

I thought for sure that her over-the-top dramatics would save me. Surely this person would see that the words didn't match the implied meaning of the rest her hysterics.

"I'm going to call the police and stay here to make sure he doesn't try anything else. What a creep!"

I stood dumbfounded on the sidewalk while my life crumpled around me. It was true. I made no attempt to follow the law. How could I build a case or defense on that? I couldn't deny my guilt. Still, my brain scrambled. Maybe I could convince her to forgo charges.

"Why are you doing this? I know that you wanted me to kiss you. Didn't you feel anything for me? You can't fake that."

"That's right. You can't fake it, which is why I know you were just confusing the signals in your drunken state. You were seeing and feeling what you wanted. Not what I wanted."

Oh no. My first thought about the wine had been correct.

"That's not true, and you know it. Please don't do this. You at least owe me an explanation. Is it the money? I don't have much. Ruining someone's life isn't worth this."

"It isn't the money. Sometimes you really don't know what someone else is thinking or feeling. That's why the law exists. You have to ask. You can't do whatever you want and think it's okay and think you'll get away with it. We need to make an example out of people like you."

"But you tricked me. You wanted me to kiss you. Why not go after the people that are the problem instead of tricking innocent people?"

"No. You're not innocent. You kissed someone without asking. You had no idea whether I wanted it or not."

The police arrived to take me away. As they put me in the car, I took one last look at my accuser. I saw sadness in her eyes. I saw that she liked me and wanted to kiss me again. She wanted to tell me it would be okay. Someone must have made her do this against her will. Then again, what did I know? Maybe I only saw what I wanted to see.

THE SECRET HISTORY OF THE WORLD GONE BY

By

Joshua M. Young

How did civilization die?

Anders came to the Penitent City in the spring of his manhood with his axe, Raider's Bane, at his back and a man's dark growth on his cheeks, seeking secret histories of the World Gone By. The Penitent City was a grand and shining thing, all towers like polished crystal and streets like carved rock. Machines passed from tower to tower like birds. Anders had never seen its like, and the city had never seen his. Hardly a moment passed in which some individual did not stop and gawk at him.

Anders had to strain for the word "individual." He was not an uneducated man, in his way. He had studied under his tribe's elders and learned the tales and the wisdom of the World Gone By, but those who dwelled in the Penitent City seemed to be neither men nor women, dressed uniformly in long, flowing robes, and this caused him some difficulty. They were all pretty, after a fashion, but it was not the sort of beauty that might incite a man to desire.

Or a woman, Anders supposed, but he was not qualified to judge that.

Anders was young and strong, but the journey had been long, a fortnight or more, and he was weary. The towers of the Penitent cast long shadows in the late afternoon sun and made Anders feel as though it was, perhaps, reasonable to seek a place to rest for the night.

Fortunately, the penitents were not so strange as to not have inns for the lodging of strangers, though they were strange enough that the purpose of a given structure was sometimes difficult to discern. Anders could read, though he had been taught to read the language of the World Gone By, and the writing of the penitents was sometimes hard for him to understand. The letters were the same, but the penitents had a torturous and complicated way of phrasing that Anders realized was, in fact, a cultural tendency towards circumlocution. The phrase which meant "inn" in the Penitent's language was something along the lines of "a place in which individuals who may currently be weary, amorous, lustful, shy, or some other emotion, may find shelter for whatever pursuits they find desirable."

It made Anders' head hurt, but he was weary and usually lustful, as young men are wont to be, and so he decided that it was good enough.

In the morning, Anders explored the Penitent City, enduring the stares of the strange and sexless people who lived here. Few dared to speak to him, and when they did, their circumlocutions were both tense and ultimately meaningless. He found it impossible to understand how the penitents maintained a city of such wonders when their language was warped so far from true. How could they build the great, crystalline towers of their city when they could hardly speak of them? What kind of circumlocution could describe the workings of the strange, birdlike devices that moved from tower to tower?

Somewhere deep in the city, Anders found the Schola. Though he knew roughly where it was in relation to the inn in which he had slept—east and a little north—he did not know what roads he had taken to get there. The towers of the Penitent City made navigation nearly as torturous as their language.

The Schola, unlike the rest of the city, was no shining tower of crystal. It was, instead, a low, squat building, made of rock the exact color of a muddy sheep. Anders had seen more than a few muddy sheep in his life, and supposed that the Schola found them a creature worthy of emulation. They were certainly useful creatures, although Anders thought they were perhaps more appealing to the eye when they were clean—or, better, as a chop seared over a fire and rubbed with herbs and seasoning.

In the Schola, the stares of the penitents took on a sort of hostility. Anders ignored them for as long as he could, until finally, an individual accosted him in a hallway and said, "You offend me, per. Your dress, gender signifiers, and manner make me uncomfortable. Kindly change them or leave."

Anders blinked. The individual had a hold of his elbow and spoke with a sort of bluntness he had never before seen in a penitent. "I apologize if I have given offense..." He allowed his sentence to trail off, hoping that it might lure the penitent into providing a name or title. It did not, and so Anders said, "It was not my intention to offend."

"It is what your kind does. You would oppress me," the individual said, nostrils flaring like an enraged bulls, "and your beard and weapon prove your aggression."

"I mean you no harm, sir." To use the word "sir" was reaching, but Anders did not know how else to address this person.

"Sir?" the individual wailed.

"Ma'am?" Anders tried, to no avail. The person sobbed and fled, screaming incoherent curses and imprecations in the penitents' usual circumlocutions. Anders scratched his beard and wondered how it proved that he meant the penitents harm when, clearly, he did not. Had he meant them harm, Raider's Bane would have been in his hand and not at his back. The individuals of the Schola watched him from a distance, distress written clearly across their faces. When he moved towards them, they moved away. It seemed to Anders that the scholars of the penitent were as timid as the sheep they appeared to worship. He amused himself for a short time by stepping first towards one, then towards another, and watching the throng of penitents shift away from him. When the amusement paled—and it did, soon enough—he set off down the halls in search of the penitent scholar who, he was told, guarded the secret history of the World Gone By.

Anders' quest was his own. He did not seek the secret history for the sake of his tribe, to increase their standing or power or to prove himself to an elder. Anders was driven by a simple curiosity, a desire to know the world in which he lived, and in knowing, know himself more fully. It was, however, an elder who told him where he might find a history more complete than, "Once we were like unto gods, but that was in the World Gone By. Now we are but men."

The individual who met Anders outside the scholar's office was as unremarkable as any other penitent in the city. He—or she, Anders supposed—had hair cropped short, a face that was feminine and without stubble or beard. Anders scratched at his beard and decided that it didn't honestly matter. "Sir—or ma'am?—I'd like to speak with your historian when he has the time."

The individual continued to glare at Anders but said, "I understand that you, per, are an unassimilated citizen of Penitent City, and so I will forgive your offensive manner, gender signifiers, and language. But we have many who study the truths of the past and they are all far too busy to deal with an unassimilated citizen like yourself."

Anders frowned and the individual swallowed and looked a little more terrified and a little less outraged. Anders did not think he was that frightening a man, but, then, the scholars did seem to worship sheep.

"Perhaps you might allow me to study your books, then?"

"Impossible," the penitent squeaked. "There are many books and not all are approved. Some contain offensive and hurtful ideas or language. The truths of the past must not be studied without a guide and mentor."

"You mean to tell me," said Anders, "that after I have walked many miles a day for a month or more, you won't allow me to read a book because it might hurt my feelings?"

The penitent hunched its shoulders down. "It is possible that if you read the wrong truths of the past, someone else might find it hurtful."

Anders wandered the Schola in search of an exit. The walls were bare and uniformly the same dull shade of mud and sheep shit. He supposed that some might find decoration offensive, an idea that Anders found to be mildly offensive in and of itself. How could men and women exist in such conditions? Perhaps the strange sexlessness of the penitents was to blame. Or perhaps, the lack of decoration was to blame for the sexlessness.

Gradually Anders became aware that a penitent was following him. The individual was not brave enough to approach him directly, but he, or she, or it, or whatever, at least had enough spunk to follow where most fled. Anders allowed the penitent to follow him until he grew tired of seeking an exit in a building where nothing was labeled.

"How do I get out, mister? Miss?"

"Per," the penitent said. "We use the word 'per' for an indeterminate and unhurtful mode of address."

Anders sighed and scratched his beard. "I'm tired of this place and angry, per. How do I leave?"

The penitent cowered. It was brief and appeared to be a reflex. "I assumed that an unassimilated citizen would not know the

79

preferred truth of terms of address. I apologize if I have given offense, per."

"Sir," Anders said. "Or Anders. I am not one of you strange things with neither beard nor breasts."

"Anders," the penitent said, face scrunching up as though the name tasted sour. "Anders, you may call me Hayden."

"Hayden, how do I leave this ugly and useless building that pretends to be the center of learning for all mankind?"

The last word caused the penitent to cringe, but so did most everything else. "Oh, but it is!" Hayden said. "There are many truths that one can learn here! The paths of mathematics, the truths of the past, the proper sciences and grammar!"

"Hayden," Anders said, "I want to leave."

The penitent cringed, but beckoned Anders to follow.

The exit was not far, but Anders would not have found it. It was a door like any other, set in a wall like any other. Previous doors had lead only to rooms full of angry and fearful penitents. When Hayden stopped and opened another door, Anders expected to see more penitents scowling and cowering. Instead he saw, once more, the shadows of the towers of the Penitent City and the warm orange sunlight of late afternoon.

Hayden hesitated at the door. Anders was not certain whether the penitent meant to leave the Schola or not. "What will you do now?" the penitent asked.

Anders blinked at the sunlight. He had not eaten since morning, when he had dined on a bland porridge. His stomach was empty, but he was dispirited at the Schola's rejection. "I don't know," he said. "I traveled from the far east, over the Rounded Mountains, to learn the secret history of the World Gone By. I will not return home empty handed, but I am not sure that I can stomach the Schola any more today."

"No offense," he added. Anders was a man who wished all well who did not wish him ill, and he did not wish to upset the penitent any more than he probably already did. Not after this particular penitent had helped him. Even Hayden's small aid had been more help than any other that these strange folk had offered.

The penitent tilted his or her head. "No... offense? Does this truly mitigate the impact of potentially hurtful thoughts?"

"You people are very strange," Anders said, and squeezed past the penitent.

Hayden followed Anders through the streets without asking. Other penitents stared at Anders as they had before, and a few now bristled at the sight of him. After the third or fourth encounter with these angrier penitents, Hayden offered an explanation, "Your gender signifiers trigger feelings that they do not wish to feel. It is considered uncouth in this city to be obviously gendered. To say nothing of carrying a weapon, or wearing clothes made of animal skin."

The buckskin clothing Anders wore was so commonplace over the Rounded Mountains that he had thought little, if anything of it. Anders frowned briefly and said, "But you are not offended."

Hayden said nothing. When Anders looked back at the penitent, he saw a confused look on the individual's face. It was an internal sort of confusion, the look directed at the penitent itself, not at Anders. Anders let it go and changed the subject as his stomach rumbled again. "Hayden, is there some place to eat around here? The inn where I am staying serves very poor food."

"They might be offended if they heard you say that," Hayden said, but in the end, the penitent lead Anders to a small restaurant—"a place in which one may consume foods which originate within the Penitent City's locale and which will not lead to heart disease or other health problems." There, they dined on a bland and unfulfilling meal of leafy vegetables and a block of something that

81

pretended to be meat but was certainly more vegetables, ground up and compressed.

Sooner or later, Anders supposed, he was going to have to leave the city, if only to hunt for something that was genuinely edible.

They spoke little during the meal, conflicting but unintelligible emotions wracking the penitent's face the whole time. Finally, the penitent volunteered, "I am not offended by you."

"No," Anders said, "I didn't suppose that you were. Your people are very free to let me know when they have been offended."

"They have a right not to receive offense."

Anders' brows furrowed. "I find their hatred of my beard offensive."

"But your beard makes them uncomfortable."

"Why should my beard make them uncomfortable? It is attached to my face."

Hayden lowered his or her eyes—Anders was rapidly growing annoyed at trying to figure what the penitent *was*, precisely—and toyed with a piece of leaf. "Because it is obviously masculine, it causes people to reflect upon their biological gender, which is rude. People should not have to contemplate the dice rolls that determined their birth circumstances."

Anders frowned at the penitent. "And Raider's Bane? My axe?"

"You might harm one of us. You might harm me."

"And no one should have to fear harm."

"That is an approved truth," Hayden agreed.

"What about me and my kind? Should we have to fear the barbarians that sometimes raid small villages like mine? My axe keeps me safe. It has kept my loved ones safe."

"The Penitent City would keep them safe."

"With what weapons?"

"The Penitent City has never fallen to invasion. Not since the World Gone By."

"There's little enough of interest for a barbarian here."

"You are an unassimilated citizen," Hayden said.

"I'm a tribesman from across the Rounded Mountains."

"We would not wish to offend you by assuming that you are not a citizen of the Penitent City."

"But it's obvious that I'm not. I have a beard, carry a weapon and eat real food. Like *meat*." Anders stabbed his block of compressed vegetable-things with a fork. Several penitents at surrounding tables jumped. Hayden shrunk away from him.

"I will not hurt you," Anders said, "or your friends. Calm down."

The sun had set by the time that they finished their meal. Hayden did not ask to accompany him and Anders did not offer, but Hayden followed him regardless. The penitent was becoming a fixture of the city in Anders' mind, much like the crystal towers or the strangely smooth roads. It was only when the penitent followed him up the stairs in the inn and into his room that Anders paused.

The door closed behind Hayden. Anders turned and the penitent shrugged off her robes. At some point, Anders realized, he had begun to assume that the penitent was indeed a woman, though he had not asked and could not have said why. He was gratified, then, to see a pair of dainty breasts topped by dark nipples and that the dark thatch of hair between her legs lacked the equipment with which he was most familiar.

"I'm not offended by you," Hayden said quietly.

Anders was in the spring of his manhood, and so it went as such things go.

"I've coupled before," Hayden said later, her eyes locked on the ceiling, "both with those who were born with male sex and those who were born with female sex. I've never… "

"Yes?"

"Your gender signifiers stirred something in me. I should've been offended. I should've hated the sight of your beard and weapon and the way you speak without concern for causing offense. *The* secret *history* of the World Gone By? As though there were one truth only for the past—and the implicit assumption of the word 'history' that it is the story of those who were born with the male sex?"

Anders knew that a man must choose his battles carefully, and chose to address confusion instead of out and out wrongheadedness. "You saw a man," he said, "and as a woman, you responded. As I responded to the sight of you, when I knew you to be a woman."

"I have seen those who were born with the male sex before," she said, and perhaps for the first time, Anders heard hurt in her voice.

He rolled onto his side and stroked her cheek. "There exists in the mind of the creator of all things the forms of all things that he created. He knows what the perfect deer is like, and a deer is better or worse for how closely it partakes in the form of the perfect deer. A deer that is sickly or crippled is farther from the form of deer than a robust stag with a glorious crown."

Hayden frowned and Anders continued. "It is not just deer. Light, water, bread, wine, people… everything has a form that exists in the mind of the creator of the universe. Including men and women."

"And you are closer to the form of those born with the male sex than the penitents here who identify as a masculine person?"

"The form of man, Hayden. It is not offensive to say that."

"But it is!" she protested. "'Man' is a word that comes with connotations. Not all who identify as masculine can have a beard or carry weapons or couple with a penis."

Anders scratched his beard and thought about a fellow tribesman whose beard was thin and scraggly and altogether unsatisfying to look upon, and about the old men who could no longer carry an axe. "You are right about beards and weapons," he said, "but if a person's body does not grow in the way that a man's does, and grows instead as a woman's, they are not men, but women. There are exceptions. The injured and old and those who cannot grow beards are still men. But the more comely a man is to a woman, the closer he partakes in the form of man. You, as a woman, responded to that, and in responding to that, you came closer to the form of woman."

Even in the gloom, Anders could see emotions working their way across her face.

"I do not need you to be a woman," she said angrily.

"No," he said. "You, alone among the penitents, understood that what you felt was something to be embraced. You, alone, partake the way you should in the form of what you are. But what is more like a young woman than to see a man and desire him? What is more like a man than to see a woman and desire her? In our desire, we are more closely partaking in the form of what we are—and being what we are meant to be makes us strong."

In the morning, Anders bathed and dressed. He had not bathed the day before, and had to have Hayden show him how to operate the strange thing she called a shower. Hayden bathed separately and once again donned the robes that made her shapeless and sexless. As she fastened the robes closed, she said, "I believe that I can get you into the place in which the truths of history are sheltered. It is locked, but I am studying to be an approved guide and so I have access denied to others."

"I would expect that your access would be guarded more closely," Anders said.

"Why? Approved guides are penitents among penitents. It is they who know most deeply how we must mourn our arrogance and mistakes."

Anders scratched his beard. "And you?"

Hayden did not answer.

At the Schola, Hayden took Anders in tow and bore the brunt of the hostile stares. Once, someone said something to her in a circumlocution that Anders could barely follow. She brushed the comment aside with a directness that made the penitent's face wrench into a knot of stunned anger.

Hayden pushed past the penitent and lead Anders through the labyrinthine corridors of the Schola to a library filled with books and penitents. Anders drifted towards the shelves, but Hayden grabbed him by the elbow and led him to a locked door set in the back of the library. There she produced a flat sliver of crystal with metal patterns embedded in it from within her robes and tapped it against the door. A click sounded from within the door and Hayden pulled Anders inside.

The room was gloomy and dimly lit. "To save power," Hayden explained. "There are few people who visit this room. Most do not care about the truths of the past, or consider the extravagances of the past to be shameful."

Anders did not so much walk as he did drift down the rows of the books. There, in the gloom, he saw some names that he knew from the World Gone By and many he did not. Here, the philosophers of whom the elders spoke; there, a name of a historian to survive the World Gone By. But Aristotle and Tacitus were too old, too far removed from the cataclysm that claimed all of history.

Hayden watched silently as Anders combed through the books. He pulled one, and then another, thumbing through them and placing them back on the shelves with a reverence that the penitent had never before seen.

"Too old," Anders muttered, staring angrily at a book. "Too old. Where are the more recent history books?"

Hayden did not know and did not answer. Anders began pulling books from shelves with more abandon, skimming and flipping through the pages and placing them on top of the shelves instead of in the freshly vacated spaces. For nearly an hour, he scoured the stacks until at last he found what he was looking for and sat cross-legged in the middle of the aisle with the book in his lap.

The penitent passed the time by reshelving the books disturbed by Anders' search. Their privacy remained secure and undisturbed.

Anders' face held a frown that deepened as he turned each page. "We went to the moon. To other planets and other moons and rocks and icebergs in the sky. And then we stopped. We stopped dreaming." He did not voice the question that hung in the air, but Hayden understood what he sought.

"We were arrogant," she said. "We colonized those worlds physically and mentally. We forced our culture upon other races by broadcasting our entertainment to the stars. We were not goddesses. We were privileged, until finally a species that was strong enough to fight back against our colonial aggressions took exception and brought their war machines to Earth. It is thus that the World Gone By went by. At least," she added, "that seems to be the consensus of the truths of the past."

Anders slammed the book closed and dropped it on the ground. "You knew."

"We are penitents. We lament the crimes of those who donated biological material for our births and the privilege that they abused. The purpose of the Penitent City is to atone for the crimes of the World Gone By."

"And yet," he said bitterly, "you build towers that reach for the sky and walk upon roads that are unnaturally smooth while machines carry your burdens from tower to tower."

"They are alters of shame, meant to always remind us of the sins of our biological donors. Hence the hideous and embarrassing phallic shape of a tower, instead of something more appropriately genderless."

"No wonder they gleam in the sunlight. You must polish them incessantly. No doubt you take great pleasure in the polishing while you mourn your fathers' crimes."

If Hayden understood his own circumlocution, she gave no sign of it. Anders had to assume that she did, as her kind was given to speaking so, and that she chose to ignore the intimation. "It is the machines of the Schola that maintain our towers," she said. "We would not know how. The shame was thrust upon us by the Offended."

"The invaders?"

"The Offended," she said, but nodded as she corrected him once again.

"I would see these machines."

"You see them every time you look at our city."

"I would see where they come home to rest when they tire."

"There is a courtyard in the center of the Schola, and in the center of that, a small building that the machines enter." Hayden shrugged once, remained silent for a short time, and then shrugged again. "We will see if my keycard will take us inside the machine's home. Follow me."

Her key did not, in fact, work, but Raider's Bane did. At another secluded and locked door, this time hidden behind a thatch of overgrown bushes, Anders brought his axe to bear on the door. It cut through the metal but came to a sudden halt a fraction of an inch into the door. It jarred Anders' arms and shoulders and made his palms sting. He was sure that the noise would summon the penitents, but at last he remembered that they worshipped sheep. No one would come. Even Hayden was cowering against the wall.

There were small windows that the machines came and went through just outside of Anders' reach. Raider's Bane could make the reach easily, though, and Anders used its blade to pull stones away from a hole. The mortar that held the stones in was crumbling, and Anders had little trouble in making the hole big enough for even his broad shoulders to fit through. The machines did not seem to be interested in maintaining their own home.

"What are you going to do?" Hayden asked as Anders prepared to climb through.

"Kill the invaders' machines," Anders answered. "Every single one myself, if I must. But the ancients often used a central device to control their machines in the World Gone By. I hope that there is a.... computer? that I can terminate. Either way, I will destroy the machines that maintain a culture that keeps us repressed and ashamed."

"You'll kill the city!"

"So slowly you won't even notice it," Anders said, thinking of the way fences slowly crumbled and the way weeds tried to claim gardens. "But in the end, we'll be free to grow again."

Hayden waited an hour, maybe more. When Anders emerged, his face was drawn and his eyes full of a nameless horror. Hayden, though she was braver than most she knew, was from a culture whose natural inclination was to the safety and comfort of ignorance. She did not ask what Anders saw there, and instead followed him back to his rented room.

If she noticed that the machines of the Penitent City were sluggish and unstable, she did not say anything. She did not say anything at all, in fact, but in Anders' room, she offered him the only comfort she knew how to show.

The machines began to die. They did not so much fall out of the sky as they did drift lazily to the ground. Anders, too, seemed to be dying and refused to leave the room. Hayden brought him food that he rarely touched and paid the rent.

When her monthly shame did not come in the following week, she thought about terminating the ball of cells inside her. Experiencing menses was bad enough, a reminder of a biological identity she could not avoid, but to actively be harboring another creature inside of her—it was shameful. Hideous. Those who were born with a female gender and found themselves so infected usually spent the time of their pregnancy in hiding, lest they offend those around them. Most opted to terminate the process instead.

Penitents did not breed very fast.

Hayden, for a reason she could not name or articulate, chose not to terminate. For a reason she could still not name or articulate, she felt no shame in telling Anders—the *father*. The word should have stuck in her throat. She wanted to be angry at the word as it drifted around inside her head, but she could not. Instead, she stood naked in front of Anders and pressed his hand to her belly.

"I'm pregnant," she said, and nothing more. Anders nodded and said nothing at all to her announcement, but she thought that there might have been some spark of life in his eyes that night.

90

And she was glad for it.

"I want you to leave the city with me," Anders said to her the next morning. He was fresh out of the shower, his first in days, and she was showering as he watched the sky. The machines were all but gone now.

Hayden felt the heat bloom in her cheeks. It was only when she felt the heat elsewhere that she knew it was not shame. "Why?"

"You're carrying my child," Anders said, "honor demands that I care for both you and my child. Also, life will start to get hard here without the machines that maintained the city. I would have you living somewhere safe." The only sound for a long stretch of time was the arrhythmic melody of water falling as Hayden scrubbed herself. At last, Anders finished, "And I have grown fond of your presence."

Hayden opened her mouth, but Anders shook his head and said, "No. I am a man, not a Penitent. I will speak like a man. I have grown to love you. You cared for me as I struggled with what I saw inside the Schola. You have proven yourself a brave and courageous woman in a land of sheep, and I would have you for my wife. We will have brave and strong children who will greet the world with their heads raised in defiance."

She shut off the water but did not push aside the door. "Tell me," she said to the fuzzy shape of Anders behind the door. "Tell me what you saw inside the machine's home."

The shape of Anders turned away from her and hung its head. "I would not."

"If you truly think me that courageous…"

"It is a terrible thing."

"Many of the truths of the past are."

91

"History," he corrected.

"Much of history is," she said.

"The Secret History of the World Gone By," he said, "is secret even from you and yours."

"If I am to leave with you, they are no longer mine."

Anders' shape nodded. "We are your Offended. There was no invasion. The machines under the Schola were of human provenance, parts clearly labeled in the tongue of the World Gone By. I was confused at first, but as I stood in the wreckage of the central machine, I began to put together the True History of the World Gone By from what I had read that day. There was a second machine-brain there, and I confirmed what I suspected through the machine. It talked to me," he mused, "and answered my questions very helpfully.

"The Penitent culture was not forced on us by invaders from the stars. The penitent culture existed always inside of humanity, like a tumor.

"Like a tumor, it grew from something good. At some point we realized we'd treated other human beings very poorly. The World Gone By repented of its ways and allowed those marginalized peoples to be part of the culture. But for some, that was not enough. They insisted that we should shame the culture who did it, even hundreds of years after the offense. Every concession, every justifiable apology was met with a demand for more. When women were scorned, it was not good enough that they be given the same rights as men. They demanded to be the same as men. Even though they are not the same. Even though they deny what they are by pretending to partake in the form of man.

"So it was in all of the final days of World Gone By. For every concession, righteous or not, there was a demand for something greater. In the end, a cult that worshipped a bland and homogenous equality gained the upper hand in the politics of the World Gone By. We stopped going to the stars because it was shameful to do something that wonderful. We stopped because it made people uncomfortable that some people could do it and others could not. We stopped excelling because not everyone could excel. The educated became sheep because they did not want to hurt the feelings of the students they taught and did not make them think difficult or painful things. We—no, the elite—became penitents who had neither men nor women because it was hurtful to affirm differences between the two, and that there are ways that men and women are expected to couple and ways in which they are not.

"The penitents are all that is left of the World Gone By," Anders said, "because the World Gone By could not bear to be anything special any longer."

Hayden pushed aside the door and wrapped her arms around Anders. She was still wet from her shower, but he did not protest. "Is the city truly going to die?"

"The penitents cannot maintain it," he said. "They will be forced to abandon their city and live with the tribes. They will be forced to be men and women again."

"So that we can excel again?"

"So that we can excel again," Anders confirmed.

"Take me to your people," Hayden said. "I will be your wife if you will treat me well."

"I would not be a man," he told her, "if I did not."

Anders left the Penitent City in the spring of his manhood, with his axe, Raider's Bane, at his back and his wife at his side. Her belly and breasts were not yet swollen with child, but in due time they swelled and her hair grew long. In the course of things, a girl was born, and Anders and Hayden begat more children and raised them as proud men and women.

And when the Penitent City finally fell, the children of Anders and Hayden welcomed those refugees into their tribe and the future with their heads held high.

THE SOCIAL CONSTRUCT

By

David Hallquist

***The customizable perfect child delivered straight to your
door!***

It was time to change the sex of their child, again. William sighed.

Jess was still playing with her trucks and blocks and other toys
from before. Her dolls, forlorn, waited in the corner largely unused.
She continued to be as rambunctious as ever, thought that might
just be a condition of being two.

This was not how things should have turned out.

Initially, William and Georgia had wanted a son. Their single
child was, naturally, not directly conceived between them. The
purpose of sex was for recreation and identity, not procreation.
Their donated eggs and sperm had been tested and then combined
into hundreds of embryos in the first phase. Since they had desired
a male child, half of the embryos, with the undesirable XX
chromosome, had been discarded. In the second cull, embryos with
chromosomal errors, as well as ones with markers for possible
genetic defects had been culled as well. Additional removals had
taken place later, as the happy couple had decided upon the desired
height, weight, eye, hair and skin color. They had wanted the perfect
child, of course, and only one of the developing fetuses would be
brought to term. In the final cut, they got to see projected images of
what their son would look like as an adult. They spent hours
together over coffee selecting among scores of images and features;
it had been just like buying a new car. Eventually, they had agreed

on what the perfect son would look like, and the remaining developing fetuses were then disposed of, out of sight.

They had gone to see the little squirming infant that was their son in the clinic. Wrinkled and wet, straight from the tanks, they could not hold him yet for his skin was still too delicate. Networks of tubes, for maternal immune treatments, blood sugar balance and a whole host of other complex chemicals were flooded into and out of his tiny body by this replacement umbilical cord. He remembered the frowns of the staff: it was unseemly to view their child so early, most people waited until they had the finished product delivered.

The happy moment of delivery had been a ring of the doorbell. Their child had arrived, sealed in a small life-support unit wrapped with thermal padding. Opening the cocoon, they embraced their new son. The same cocoon would also serve as a mandated child seat while driving, and handily fit into a recess in their car. So from time to time, their son went back into the cocoon, as they traveled, while he was amused by the interior screen to keep his cortical development engaged.

His early learning and development had taken place at the Development Center, of course. Who had time to raise a child? Still, in their time with him, they had also used downloaded enrichment activities to help his development along, and bought toys for him as well. Every element of growth had to be properly tailored to properly socialize young Jeremy.

Recently, they had changed their minds, and decided they wanted a daughter instead. Daughters were trending, after all. The process had been simple: they had packed Jeremy into his now larger cocoon, and the clinic had picked him up, and then delivered their daughter a few days later. It had been exactly like returning a defective product.

There had been no need to witness the actual process, where his external genitalia were removed via surgical lasers, a vaginal urogenital slit was cut open, and artificial estrogen glands were implanted. She would then be able to develop all of the secondary sexual characteristics of womanhood as she grew. That she would never be able to bear young with the artificial organs implanted was irrelevant, since who had live children anymore? Educational and enrichment training would focus on her new feminine orientation and she would know nothing of her prior life as a boy. After all, gender was simply a social construct.

Still, both William and Georgia watched with growing concern as their child did not change as she was supposed to. She continued to love her trucks and blocks; and the racing game remained her favorite.

They discussed the matter over coffee in the kitchen, while their daughter was away at the Development Center.

"We can send her back to the clinic for a reversal." William brought up. "I understand the process is simple. They just need to switch out the glandular implants and create new artificial organs. It's all a pretty standardized procedure for a child of her age. Gender's a social construct: we can change her back now, and then later if he wants to become a girl again, he can switch back. It's not a big deal."

"You always wanted a son, I get it." Georgia scowled. "This is all about you, isn't it? You want to control the destiny of our child, and make her a copy of you. You just cannot accept that she is really who she is."

William sighed. "I don't know who she really is, yet. She's two."

"That's not what we were promised!" Georgia slammed the table. "The clinic, the Development Center, everyone said that the sexes are fully interchangeable. They said human personhood is a social construct. So, we should be able to have Jess as a girl."

"Ok, Georgia." William smiled. "We can wait. Maybe the enrichment training will take hold and she'll be happy as a girl. If not, she can always change back later, when she wants to."

"No. No more. They promised us we would have the child we wanted." Georgia looked away. "I want an abortion."

"Isn't two a little late for an abortion?" Will asked delicately.

The verbal explosion that followed was epic in scope. The argument raged on throughout the night, and reached a crescendo of breaking glass that painted the interior of the kitchen with the contents of beverages and preserves. When the police came, Georgia had graciously declined to press changes for verbal abuse.

The next day, young Jess was packed into her cocoon for return to the clinic. She was told she was going to meet new friends, and not to cry. The white truck from clinical services arrived and picked up the generic cocoon, and the men in white coats loaded her into the truck with a number of other cocoons, most smaller, a few larger. And, just like that, she was out of their lives, forever.

AT THE EDGE OF DETACHMENT

By

A.M. Freeman

What if you were not alive, but the executioner was at your door?

Thirteen years. Only one year more and he would be thirteen. Finally he'd be considered alive.

The official papers would be filled out, and he could become his own person. He had only to wait one more year, then he would be Detached. He would officially choose his name, he could celebrate his birthdays, he'd have his own papers, his own rights, and his freedoms. He had been so sure, positive, that he'd make it.

Just like so many other kids at this stage, he dreamed and hoped for that moment. He imagined what it would be like to be a *real* person. He had even planned what he wanted to do: go to schools and learn new things, go on adventures and see the world, and be certain he'd have a future. All had been going well: Mother had been happy, he was being more of a help than a burden to her, freedom and humanity had seemed within his reach. But now, this broken arm might cost him more than just climbing trees for a while.

He wished he could be in a tree now, out in the woods behind his neighborhood. He liked it out there; it was much better than this cramped house. It was out there where he and his friends would meet—out there where he could say what he liked—out there where he kept his secret. He'd never told Mother, since it was something he shouldn't be able to do, but he had learned how to read.

This had happened some time ago, while spending the day in the woods with his friends. On that day, they had found a vault half buried in the ground. There were many strange and old things in that vault, but most of all, there were books. Having not been allowed any formal education, none of them knew what the books said or meant. But over time, and with any information they could glean from home and the books themselves, together they learned to read.

Some of the books were boring, to him at least, but others were full of stories. Wonderful, incredible stories from times far past. And on these stories, he and his friends had thrived.

They were fascinating stories. But to them, almost unbelievable. He and his friends argued over whether such a time could have existed, where most children would have a mother and father at the same time. Or if it was true that back then, kids started learning in schools only four or five years after birth. Of course, there were rumors that richer families paid for private tutoring for their children—before they were fully developed. But there was never any evidence. They had enough money to keep things like that quiet.

Could there really have been a time where everyone lived like that? In a big family, going to schools, living and working where and how they wanted?

While he believed there was truth in these stories, not all of them could agree or decide what was real or not, and it troubled them. So together they'd built a dream and a promise: they'd make it to the age of Detachment, they'd learn, and they'd find the truth. He wanted to find the truth so badly; he hated being kept in the dark, pushed aside like he wasn't even there. But he had ruined any chance of that. All because he'd climbed a tree a little too high, fallen, and now was stuck with this.

The crippled arm hung heavy against his chest in the homemade cast. It was something he'd learned in one of the books, something called a splint. However, having only one hand and the materials in his room to work with, it was a lot sloppier than the picture in the book had been. But with two sticks, thick paper, and some string, he'd managed to pull it together enough to support his damaged arm. Plus, the many hours he'd been stuck in his room had numbed it some.

He looked at the cast. With all the names crudely scribbled on, it looked like a grave yard. He had put them there himself, for his own sake. If he was going to have to leave, he wanted to remember his friends who'd gone before him.

Donna, she'd stayed out too late.

Ricky, he'd kept forgetting his chores.

Little Jim, he was too much of a stress and wasn't healthy.

And then there was Emme.

Everyone said Dependents, like him and all his friends, didn't really have life until they were Detached at puberty. It was said they couldn't really feel or understand things yet. But if anyone had life it was Emme, and if there were any feeling to be felt, he knew he felt them.

Emme was the nicest, sweetest, kindest, most beautiful girl ever. Or at least, she *was*.

She had asked too many questions one night, when her mother had gotten home drunk.

But Emme was always like that, curious about everything. She'd been one of the first to figure out how to read. Then had been able to help the others, especially him.

101

Her mother owned a gun, so at least it was swift for her.

Sometimes he wondered where the kids went when they were Disposed. *Can the un-alive die?* He wondered, as his finger traced Emme's name. He hoped he wouldn't find out, but he had seen the look on Mother's face when she'd seen his broken arm. He had seen that look before, when her career demanded she eliminate stress and focus on her work.

That stress happened to be his two-year-old sister.

She was on his cast too. Lucy the Cutie, that's what he'd liked calling her.

Mother had that same look when she'd seen his arm that morning. But what scared him more was that it had stayed even as she'd left for work.

She would be back anytime now. He worried what she would say, what would happen next. Worried that his arm would never get a chance to heal.

He knew she needed rent, not to mention those shoes she'd had her eyes on, and he was already cutting in on expenses. He knew, he'd seen the bills.

If only he had been able to make it one more year. He was so close...

He heard footsteps. There was the clicking of heels, but also the stomping of serval pairs of boots. He froze, realizing Mother wasn't alone.

His heart jumped in his throat as all his worst fears flashed before him. The rush of panic made him jump towards the window. But the sudden lurch sent a stab of pain through his broken arm. He bit his lip hard to stop himself from screaming and tasted blood in his mouth.

Tears filled his eyes and blurred his vision as he cradled his arm and looked frantically for an escape.

The footsteps were closer—he could hear voices. Something was happening to his head. He was suddenly hyper focused on analyzing the closet, the window, the door—looking for the best way out. Because all he could think about was running, escaping, not dying... staying alive.

But how can I die if I'm not alive? The thought cost him a precious few seconds, and by then it was too late. The footsteps stopped, keys jingled, and the doorknob turned.

Through the partly open door, Mother's head poked in, a sweet smile on her face.

"There he is. Come on in gentleman," she pushed the door open, and five burly man in white coats walked in. One of them was holding a brief case. Mother stayed outside.

He looked at the men. He knew what they meant, and this brutal realization made his voice crack as he asked, despite already knowing and dreading the answer; "Mother, what's going on?"

He didn't take his eyes off the men. He hardly even blinked, and his feet started backing him towards his closet. He had a distant hope that maybe he could hide in there until he woke up from this bad dream. He hoped this was a dream. This couldn't really be happening.

"I've thought about it a lot," Mother said, still hovering in the door way, "and now is just not a good time. That arm will only cause you pain, and it would be better for my health and security if I didn't have to support you with that. It's for my health and wellbeing, darling, and yours."

"And the money," the words slipped out before he could stop them. Something strange was happening to him: his heart was beating faster, he could feel the blood pumping through him, and he

103

had a heightened sense of the danger he was in. She was going to have him Disposed of, he knew she was. She'd just said it herself, in a roundabout way. There was no way he was going to get out of here now; not with this arm, not against five man twice his size and strength. But something bubbled up inside him, an anger and defiance he'd never felt before, and he realized something. They were liars... they were all liars. But they weren't going to take him— not without a fight.

"I'm sure they'll give you a lot of money for my body. Just like you got that fat raise after you killed my little sister!"

"Honey, you know better than that. Lucy was never really alive, just like you aren't, it won't hurt."

"Lies!" he shouted. Mother looked startled, but he didn't care. She wasn't his mother, not like the ones in the stories. She was an imposter, a sick mockery.

The men made a semi-circle, trapping him in the corner. He ran back and forth, looking for an escape and shouted, "You didn't hear her scream! You had your daughter murdered and you were too much of a coward to stick around and hear her scream!"

Mother's face grew red with rage, "That is enough child! Don't make this harder than it has to be. This is for me, don't you love your mother?"

"You are no mother, you selfish witch!" He could no longer feel the pain in his arm, and his eyes blazed as he ran back and forth, sweat pouring from his brow and his heart drumming in his ears. "Why should I love you when you don't love me?! You are not a mother, mothers don't kill their own children!"

Mother's face was a mask of total insult and horror. "I gave birth to you! Do you know how hard that is?!"

"You mean how they doped you up on drugs and cut me out of your stomach so you could parade me around until you got bored or

I become too much stress? You mean like that? Just like you did with Lucy?!"

His hands shook as he stopped pacing and looked at her. Anger and disgust settled in his stomach like a boiling fire. He felt the pain from all those times she'd rejected and neglected him when he needed to be held. The despair he'd endured when the only times he had received her affection was in the company of others. All the unjust acts and fake love she'd given him boiled and writhed, burning away any faith he had left in her.

His voice, hardly more than a whisper, came out like sheets of ice. Every word trembled with venom as he stood still and clenched his fists, looking at her with a gaze that turned from pain, to hatred.

"You may have grown me in your stomach, you may have even let me have your food and shelter, but you were *never* a mother to me."

Mother was beyond speech. Her eyes bored into her son, but her rage had no affect him.

Her anger was inflamed by his resilience to it, and she snapped her fingers. The men started moving closer.

But he didn't stop. He started pacing again, then sprinted back and forth, his blood racing as he shouted, "A real mother loves her children! She cares about them first! She holds them when they're crying! She doesn't go out late and leave them without dinner! A real mother doesn't *Dispose* of her children! Because I am alive! And Disposing is killing! Don't kill me!"

The men had grabbed him. Each of his limbs were held by one of them, and they lifted him up in the air. Sudden panic hit as they trapped him, and he struggled and yelled,

"I'm alive! Don't kill me! Don't kill me! I'm ALIVE!" He thrashed in their arms, blood pumping in his ears. His breath came hard and short, and his mind raced.

As he struggled, he saw scenes from his short life flash before him. Little Lucy, and her death, and friends he'd lost in the same way. He remembered his friends, the books, and Emme. And he wondered: If he could think, he could feel, he could reason, if he could do everything the adults could, how could they think he wasn't alive?

For the first time, his mother looked unsure, watching the boy struggle and scream with such intensity. And she glanced at one of the specialists in their white coats.

"Don't worry ma'am, it's an underdeveloped reaction in the brain. This happens sometimes—nothing serious. You just go relax; this won't take long." The man set the brief case on the bed and opened it.

When the boy saw it, he began to thrash harder and scream louder. The man pulled a long white cloth from the case and tied the gag in the boy's mouth. He stared at his mother as she slowly turned from the door—his eyes wide and truly afraid.

He tried to scream her name, to get her to come back and see what she was doing. He had no love for that woman, but maybe if he could get her to turn back, to see what she was really doing, maybe he could break the cold bubble she lived in.

But in the end, he knew she wouldn't. He'd seen her do this before, and too many like her had done the same. Now it was his turn to be condemned by her. Condemned by this whole damned world. This world that was so different from the one in the stories he'd read. This world that so easily excused life not its own. This world that had no love.

She didn't love him—she hadn't loved either of them. It was only a status symbol to look like you cared about your children.

He heard his own voice screaming inside his head, then the man with the brief case was pulling on white gloves. He strained his neck to look at the doorway. Mother was gone. He felt a stab of pain as all hope suddenly drained from him.

The man in the white gloves picked up a long, curved needle and began walking towards him. The boy's terror was beyond measure. As he fought for his life he managed to get the gag out, and his screams were shrill and horrific, "NOOOOO!!! I DON'T WANNA DIE! I DON'T WANNA DIE!!!!"

As he jerked and screamed, the pain in his broken arm became unbearable. He looked at his cast, now twisted and falling apart. His eyes focused on Emme's name as the needle went in, and a last thought lingered in his mind. *Maybe, maybe I will see her again.* Then the pain hit, and a split second later, the numbness. He threw back his head and screamed one last time, then went completely limp.

The money was paid; his body put in the back of a cold van to be cut up, used, and distributed; and the mother put on a short dress and went out for a drink.

A HISTORY OF SAD PUPPIES

By

Larry Correia and Brad R. Torgersen

How sci fi began to fight back.

Whence Puppydom?

By

Brad R. Torgersen

Origin stories. Everybody loves 'em. The Marvel Cinematic Universe exists because of a string of successful origin stories, writ large. Everything (and everyone) has to start somewhere, right?

The phenomenon—as known in literary Science Fiction and Fantasy—of Sad Puppies, began with a piece of humor.

Larry Correia is not only a terrific New York Times bestselling storyteller, he's got a funny bone too. Essential equipment, that; if you're going to be an out-of-the-closet nonconformist in the sanctified—sanctimonious?—halls of literary SF/F.

Larry knows what history has taught us: totalitarians hate spontaneous laughter. It is unscripted, uncontrolled, and it can be directed at Those Who Must Never Be Made Fun Of. So when Larry decided to take a Delta Tau Chi approach to pointing out that SF/F's so-called Most Prestigious Award (the Hugo) was typically given out for all kinds of political and insider-clubhouse reasons unrelated to whether or not a given book or story actually has traction with a broad, fun-loving audience, he didn't nail up a manifesto. He told a joke.

We've all seen the animal shelter ads: where a big-eyed, sad-looking dog stares forlornly into the camera, guilt-tripping the hell out of you while an ever-so-serious voice drones on and on about the plight of millions of unloved pets languishing in gulag-like shelters across the nation. And you—yes, you there, in the easy chair, eating a slice of cold pizza—are the only thing standing between that trembling creature, and an untimely demise.

Televised sermons are tailor-made for lampooning. Doncha think?

Larry spun it thus: across the world, puppies dwell in eternal sadness, because SF/F awards are given to boring crap that very few people read. Thus the only way you—yes, you!—can bring happiness and joy to puppies everywhere, is to vote for books and stories which are actually fun, actually have a fan base, and might actually be said to give the readership a good time.

It was a lark. A one-off. A poke at the truth. But just a poke. It might have ended there, in 2013. But Larry had dared to speak openly, a sentiment which was already on the minds of many. The Hugo awards were skewing wonkish, and favoring message-laden, politically-progressive esotericism, at the expense of "pulp" readability. It had been more and more like that since the dawn of the new century. Even past Hugo winners were muttering about the problem—under their breath of course, and strictly off the record.

So, in 2014, Larry got organized. He was on to something. Sad Puppies had touched a nerve. Good, on the part of those who'd grown to dislike the wonkish slant of recent Hugo-winning work, and bad, on the part of those who wanted the Hugos to skew even more wonkish, become even more of a political statement, tip even more to one side of the political spectrum. One does not point out that the emperor has no clothes, without ruffling a few feathers.

Sad Puppies 2 perplexed and alarmed the SF/F literary establishment. Because for the first time in recent memory, people outside of the SF/F literary establishment—common readers and ordinary fans—were having an impact on the Hugo results. Books, stories, editors, and authors, who were not among the usual list of pre-approved—cough, always progressive, cough—established names, were actually making the final Hugo ballot. This was blasphemy, among those who make it their business to ensure that the Hugos (and "proper" SF/F by extension) are vetted and checked, according to a very specific set of social and political criteria. More alarming still, the "movement" (as political progressives are wont to label everything) only appeared to be gaining momentum. Now that the hoi polloi were actually achieving a visible impact, they were getting excited. People from outside were actually getting involved! The carefully-crafted tradition of Hugo back-room-dealing was in jeopardy. Commoners? Being allowed to decide what's good in Science Fiction and Fantasy?! Obscene.

The denizens of straight-laced Omega Theta Pi were deeply unhappy with the fact that the rambunctious lot from Delta Tau Chi were messing up Faber College.

Sad Puppies 3, launched in 2015, became the proverbial Faber homecoming parade. It was pure pandemonium. Some of which you may already be aware of, and some of which may be new to you. I am reasonably certain a metric ton of digital ink—not to mention a few pages of traditional press—were expended on the affair. Some of it pro, a lot of it con. I like to think that the folks from Omega Theta Pi showed themselves for who they really are: CHORFs (Cliquish, Holier-than-thou, Obnoxious, Reactionary Fanatics) so obsessed with keeping their totem out of the hands of unclean and dirty Delta Tau Chi members, that the CHORFs would rather obliterate the totem completely, lest their control be lost.

In the process, everything Larry Correia said, during Sad Puppies and Sad Puppies 2, was proven correct.

The CHORFs lost by winning. Sort of like how Hillary Clinton was the "popular" nominee, but Donald Trump is actually going to the White House.

Proof that you can do everything right—have the superior press game, the superior money game, the superior celebrity endorsements, and all the favorables anyone could desire—and still blow it.

Meanwhile, the rallying cry of Delta Tau Chi—Sad Puppies!—reverberates on. This book is proof of that. These stories would not exist, without authors and readers and editors who all see the problem for what it is. And while we can be certain that the Hugos will become (for the foreseeable future) an even more insular, more cliquish, more progressively-politicized award—any bets on how many allegories against the Trump administration are being written, even this very instant?—the tinfoil has at last been peeled off the rotten Science Fiction TV dinner. There is no going back, for Faber College. The veneer is gone. Poof. The ghetto is exposed. As a ghetto. Which pretends to be a country club—to include Ed White shaking his golf club at Larry Correia, while Ed is shouting, "The man's a menace!"

Consider this book our way of ripping the cover off the car stereo built into Larry's golf bag, and turning up the volume.

As for Senator Blutarsky? I think he switched parties, to the Republican side—in the wake of 9/11/2001.

A Selection of Sad Puppies Posts

By

Larry Correia

A Very Special Message (from Sad Puppies 1)

Every year thousands of pulp writers slave away in the word mines for as little as five cents a word…

(show picture of very sad looking author, sitting in bathrobe, listlessly typing, surrounded by empty cans of Coke Zero and cheesy puff wrappers)

Yet, despite providing hours of explosion-filled enjoyment to their readers, most pulp novelists will never be recognized by critics, and in fact, they will be abused by the literati elite.

(show extra sad looking pulp novelist, more than likely an overweight guy with a beard)

Literary critics stuffed this pulp novelist into a dryer, and ran it at high temperatures for nearly five minutes without even a sheet of fabric softener.

For generations, literary critics and college English departments have looked down at pulp novelists and refused to give them awards…

(show old-timey picture of HP Lovecraft, show old-timey picture of Robert E. Howard, show old-timey picture of Robert E. Howard punching out a Tyrannosaurs Rex while a woman in a chainmail bikini holds onto his leg)

Even though those guys are totally freaking awesome, and Conan the Barbarian is a thousand times more awesome than the Great Gatsby, you wouldn't know it by listening to literary snobs.

113

The hoighty-toighty literati snobs prefer heavy-handed, ham-fisted, message fiction.

(show picture of sci-fi readers giving up in frustration as they read yet another award-winning book where evil corporations, right wing religious fanatics, and a thinly veiled Dick Cheney have raped the Earth until all the polar bears have died and the plot consists entirely of academic hipster douchebags sitting around and talking about their feelings)

Much like Michael Vick, literary critics hate pulp novelists and make them fight in vicious underground novelist fighting arenas. I actually did pretty good, until Dan Wells made a shiv from a sharpened spoon and got me in the kidney. Never turn your back on the guy that writes about serial killers, I tell you what.

Only you can stop literary snobs and their abuse of pulp novelists...

Voiceover Guy (from Sad Puppies 2)

The ugly truth is that the most prestigious award in sci-fi/fantasy is basically just a popularity contest, where the people who are popular with a tiny little group of WorldCon voters get nominated and thousands of other works are ignored. Books that tickle them are declared good and anybody who publically deviates from groupthink is bad. Over time this lame-ass award process has become increasingly snooty and pretentious, and you can usually guess who all of the finalists are going to be that year before any of the books have actually come out or been read by anyone, entirely by how popular the author is with this tiny group.

This is a leading cause of puppy-related sadness.

Looking back at the Results of Sad Puppies 3:

As you all know by now, the Hugo Awards were presented Saturday, and No Award dominated most of the categories. Rather than let any outsiders win, they burned their village in order to "save it". And they did so while cheering, gloating, and generally being snide exclusive assholes about it. This year's awards have an asterisk next to them. It was all about politics rather than the quality of the work. Even the pre-award show was a totally biased joke. In addition, they changed the voting rules to make their archaic rules system even more convoluted in order to keep out future barbarian hordes. They gave as many No Awards this time as in the entire history of the awards.

So like I said yesterday... See? I told you so.

People have asked me if I'm disappointed in the results. Yes. But maybe not in the way you might expect. I'll talk about the slap in the face to specific nominees in a minute, but I can't say I'm surprised by what happened, when it was just an extreme example of what I predicted would happen three years ago when I started all this.

I said the Hugos no longer represented all of Fandom, instead they only represent tiny, insular, politically motivated cliques taking turns giving their friends awards. If you wanted to be considered, you needed to belong to, or suck up to those voting cliques. I was called a liar.

I said that most of the voters cared far more about the author's identity and politics than they did the quality of the work, and in fact, the quality of the work would be completely ignored if the creator had the wrong politics. I was called a liar.

I said that if somebody with the wrong politics got a nomination, they would be actively campaigned against, slandered, and attacked, not for the quality of their work, but because of politics. I was called a liar.

That's how the Sad Puppies campaign started. You can see the results. They freaked out and did what I said they would do. This year others took over, in the hopes of getting worthy, quality works nominated who would normally be ignored. It got worse. They freaked out so much that even I was surprised.

Each year it got a little bigger, and the resulting backlash got a little louder and nastier, culminating in this year's continual international media slander campaign. Most of the media latched onto a narrative about the campaign being sexist white males trying to keep women and minorities out of publishing. That narrative is so ridiculous that a few minutes of cursory research shows that if that was our secret goal, then we must be really bad at it, considering not just who we nominated, but who our organizers and supporters are, but hey.... Like I said, it is all about politics, and if it isn't, they're going to make it that way. You repeat a lie often enough, and people will believe it.

It isn't about truth. It is about turf.

We saw all sorts of arguments this year. They'd nitpick everything they could to make us the evil outsiders. When it was just me, they made it all about me. When it was bigger than just me, they spread the love (though I still got labeled as a sexist, racist, homophobic, woman hating, wife beater with zero evidence, which is always a treat) and went after our supporters. People who agreed with us were misogynists and our female supporters became tokens.

There was lots of virtue signaling. They represented purity and tradition, basically all goodness, and since they used up all the goodness, ergo we could only be motivated by greed, spite, and hate. Since most of us never said anything outlandish or offensive, they picked the most controversial figure they could from an allied movement, and ascribed everything they've ever said about him to all of us, and if we failed to denounce sufficiently, said we must be the same. Meanwhile, they don't have to denounce their assholes, and instead continue to shower praise and awards on literal NAMBLA supporters.

I'll skip over the boorish behavior from Saturday night, the SJW panic attacks from being triggered at the freebie table, and an editor cursing at probably the meekest, politest author I know, and talk about the actual categories. I've only had time to give the numbers a cursory glance, but it looks like you've got five to six hundred Sad Puppies, five to six hundred Rabid Puppies, and about 3,000 CHORFs and allied useful idiots, with the remainder being normal fans. This year there was about 1 of us to every 3 of them.

Right off the bat you can look through our nomination numbers from all of the categories and see that the crying about our super evil slate voting was nonsense. The actual numbers between the various Puppy nominees varied wildly, with some Puppy favorites falling just outside of the short list where we can see the same thing. Yeah, I figured that. All of those charges about voting in lockstep? Nope. The only real lockstep slate vote went to No Award.

No Award is for nominees who are not award worthy. Notice that on these nominees they railed against their identities, the philosophies of who liked them, and the politics of how they were nominated, but we seldom if ever heard anything about the quality of their work. Quality of the work had nothing to do with it. The NA crowd can cache it however they want, they're defending tradition, this is their thing, it is special to them, they're TRUEFAN, they've been attending since the '70s, we're outsiders, we upset them, how dare we! So on and so forth, but ultimately all those NA categories came down to politics over quality.

Let's look at a few of our record five No Award categories. This is where we get to the part where I'm actually disappointed. I knew there were a lot of biased assholes in fandom, but I was surprised at the depths they'd sink.

Kary English is a damned fine writer. I don't even know what her politics are. We picked her as one of our nominees because she wrote a really solid story. She got 874 votes for best short story. I believe that is one of the highest number of votes for a short story in Hugo history. No Award got 3,000.

That's asinine. Honestly compare Totaled to some of the short stories that they had no problem with before... That vote had nothing to do with quality, and everything to do with turf. You assholes are celebrating punishing her, and you justify it because you don't like people like me.

But that's not the category that is really absurd. Let's look at Best Editor, Long Form.

Now, a little background on Best Editor, and why there is a Long and Short form. It used to be just Best Editor, only it usually went to short fiction magazine editors. Until Patrick Nielsen Hayden complained one year that he'd edited most of the Best Novel nominees (well, that's a shock) and he didn't ever get to be Best Editor, so they made a category for him to win every other year (literally).

But there are no cliques or bias!

Editor Toni Weisskopf is a professional's professional. She has run one of the main sci-fi publishing houses for a decade. She has edited hundreds of books. She has discovered, taught, and nurtured a huge stable of authors, many of whom are extremely popular bestsellers. You will often hear authors complain about their editors and their publishers, but you're pretty hard pressed to find anyone who has written for her who has anything but glowing praise for Toni.

Yet before Sad Puppies came along, Toni had never received a Hugo nomination. Zero. The above-mentioned Patrick Nielsen Hayden has 8. Toni's problem was that she just didn't care and she didn't play the WorldCon politics. Her only concern was making the fans happy. She publishes any author who can do that, regardless of their politics. She's always felt that the real awards were in the royalty checks. Watching her get ignored was one of the things that spurred me into starting Sad Puppies. If anybody deserved the Hugo, it was her.

This year Toni got a whopping 1,216 first place votes for Best Editor. That isn't just a record. That is FOUR TIMES higher than the previous record. Shelia Gilbert came in next with an amazing 754. I believe that Toni is such a class act that beforehand she even said she thought Shelia Gilbert deserved to win. Fans love Toni.

Logically you would think that she would be award worthy, since the only Baen books to be nominated for a Hugo prior to Sad Puppies were edited by her (Bujold) and none of those were No Awarded. Last year she had the most first place votes, and came in second only after the weird Australian Rules voting kicked in (don't worry everybody, they just voted to make the system even more complicated), so she was apparently award worthy last year.

Toni Weisskopf has been part of organized Fandom (capital F) since she was a little kid, so all that bloviating about how Fandom is precious, and sacred, and your special home since the '70s which you need to keep as a safe space free of barbarians, blah, blah, blah, yeah, that applies to Toni just as much as it does to you CHORFs. You know how you guys paid back her lifetime of involvement in Fandom?

By giving 2,496 votes to No Award.

So what changed, WorldCon? We both know the answer. It was more important that you send a message to the outsiders than it was to honor someone who was truly deserving, and that message was *This is ours, keep out*. That's why I'm disappointed. I wanted the mask to come off and for the world to see how the sausage was really made, but even I was a little surprised by just how vile you are.

Same thing with Editor, short form. Mike Resnick has the wrong politics, but he makes up for it by being a living legend, and a major part of fandom for decades. He's super involved and has helped launch more careers than anyone can count. When they went through and broke down Hugo winners by politics over the last couple of decades, he was one of the few who was good enough and famous enough to still win. He should've won this year, big time. But nope. Brad Torgersen endorsed him. Send the message. Same category, Jennifer Brozek, I have zero idea what she believes about anything, despite working on stuff that was worthy before, No Award, because Larry Correia endorsed due to her quality work on Shattered Shields. Send the message.

Resnick and Weisskopf losing is particularly galling. CHORFs don't care about tradition. You have no honor. You only care about protecting your turf. You're inclusive and welcoming, provided the newcomers kiss your ass and don't get uppity. And old timers? Heaven forbid somebody with badthink endorses them, because then they either have to debase themselves and beg for mercy, or you'll burn them too. I talked about how this poisonous culture scares many writers into self-censoring before, and you gave them a great example too. Stay in the lines or else.

Oh, and all that bullshit you spew about fighting for diversity? Everyone knows that is a smokescreen. You talk about diversity, but simultaneously had no problem putting No Award over award-nominated females because they were nominated by fans you declared to be sexist. Wait... So let me see if I've got this straight, you denied deserving women like Toni, Cedar, Kary, Jennifer, Shelia, and Amanda, just to send a message, but we're the bad guys? I don't think so. Or as one of our female nominees said, this Puppy has been muzzled.

So who really won the Hugos this year? It was 3 to 1 in votes against the two Puppy factions, so they beat us in numbers big time. I'm not going to try to spin that (hell, after the media blitz about how you noble Fans were bravely holding off an invasion of hateful white male hatemongers of hate, I'm surprised that's all you got) they own Worldcon. At least now they finally admit that. For the Sad Puppies, I don't know what they're planning to do next. I'm not in charge. Kate Paulk is. Sarah was supposed to be in charge this year but she fell ill. I wanted to wash my hands of this thing last year and Brad asked me to come back. Over three years the Puppy numbers went from a handful, to hundreds, to over a thousand. The question now is do we want to keep throwing money at a bunch of ungrateful bastards who keep changing the rules to forbid us, or change tactics. Either way, not my call, not my problem. I'm sick of this crap.

No Award is the big winner. Only time will tell, but for FANDOM and the CHORFs I think you've got yourself a pyrrhic victory. So many of you don't seem to realize that this isn't just about the awards, and culture wars are a spectator sport. WorldCon was shrinking and greying, and now you can rejoice as it goes back to the comfy way you like it. You want to know why? Read this.

"Attending the Hugo Awards from the perspective of a 12 and 14 year old."

I took my kids to WorldCon to expose them to Fandom and I've consciously shielded them from any of the politics of the kerfuffle associated with the literary "sides" that were in play.

When we attended, we had good seats and they were excited to see if some of their choices would make it.

Let's just say that my boys ended up being exposed to some of their categories being utterly eradicated from eligibility due to this thing that I'd shielded them from.

They couldn't understand why their short story choice evaporated into something called "NO AWARD."

As I briefly explained, the audience was cheering because of that decision and the MC made a point of saying that cheering was appropriate and boos were not.

My kids were shocked.

Shocked not by not winning but by having an entire category's rug being pulled out from under it and then having all the adults (many of which were old enough to be their grandparents) cheering for something my kids looked at as an unfair tragedy.

I'll admit to having feared this outcome – yet this was my children's introduction to Fandom.

We are driving home and they are of the opinion that they aren't particularly interested in this "Fandom" thing.

I find that a great shame – and I blame not the people who established the ballots to vote for (for my kids enjoyed a great deal of what they read on the ballots), but as my kids noted – they blame the ones who made them feel "like the rug was pulled out from under me."

I'd offered Fandom my boys – my boys now reject them.

And yes, the picture below is just before us walking to the Hugo ceremonies. They're excited about it all. I just find it a pity that they didn't feel anything other than bewilderment and bitterness toward the people in the auditorium after the ceremonies.[1]

That's the future you elitist exclusive snobs want. Sasquan talked about their record numbers, and record attendance, record supporting memberships, record votes (not to mention record

---

[1]Originally published at http://www.michaelarothman.com/2015/08/27/worldcon-and-the-aftermath/

money), but then to commemorate it, you gave them an asterisk for violating your secret gentlemen's agreements, and told them their kind isn't welcome in Trufandom. Thinking about the asterisk though, didn't any of you special snowflakes watch Community? None of my people got any awards, so it isn't our flag that's an anus. But fly your anus high, WorldCon, because those two kids will probably be published authors themselves, having fun with other Wrongfans at other cons by the time Gerrold finishes the next Chtorr book.

The real winner this year was Vox Day and the Rabid Puppies. Yep. You CHORFing idiots don't seem to realize that Brad, Sarah, and I were the reasonable ones who spent most of the summer talking Vox out of having his people No Award the whole thing to burn it down, but then you did it for him. He got the best of both worlds. Oh, but now you're going to say that Three Body Problem won, and that's a victory for diversity! You poor deluded fools.... That was Vox's pick for best novel. That's the one most of the Rabid Puppies voted for too.

Here's something for you crowing imbeciles to think through— the only reason Vox didn't have Three Body Problem on his nomination slate was that he read it a month too late. If he'd read it sooner, it would have been an RP nomination... AND THEN YOU WOULD HAVE NO AWARDED IT.

And if that doesn't prove my original point about this fucked up system being more about politics than the quality of the work, I don't know what will. One of the only two fiction works that actually received an award this year would have been a Rabid Puppy nominee except for timing, and you would've No Awarded the winner just to send your little message.

The outrage this summer is all about politics and protecting turf. Look at the nomination numbers. There is a significant correlation between the amount of butt hurt and who was supposed to have made it.

http://www.thehugoawards.org/content/pdf/2015HugoStatistics.pdf

Other than the Puppy noms, look through all the supporting categories and look how tiny their numbers are. Yeah, the Puppies crushed them and locked them out, but not through malicious slate voting. It doesn't take a lockstep slate to beat a system that is so pathetic a couple dozen friends can swing it.

The cliques are small and inbred. Don't believe me, think about who our biggest haters are, and then scroll through the list and see who didn't get Hugo nominations because my side showed up for once. Check out Fan Writer. Look at the list of who would've made it if it hadn't been for us. Funny. Most of those names look familiar, usually because they're ranting about sexist/racist hate boogeymen.

Same thing with Best Related Work and the other little categories. No wonder Hines has been on the warpath. We interrupted his destiny. As GRRM said, he's served his time, damn it! Hell, if we'd not shown up culture warrior Anita Sarkeesian would have been a nominee, and you say that we're the ones who involved GamerGate? And for all of Empress Theresa's bloviating about us keeping off the 2nd volume of the Heinlein dialogs, that's a smoke screen because it wouldn't have made it anyway. Oh, and there's Glyer 45 Hugos. No wonder he's pissed. If it hadn't been for Puppies his title would be Glyer 46 Hugos. Sheesh. Scroll down that list. Lots of familiar names with pathetically small vote counts that would've otherwise made it, but there are no entrenched cliques. Uh huh.

Anyways, I'm glad it's over. I can't wait to see what new exciting ways they come up with to slander anyone who disagrees with them next year.

IF YOU WERE A HAMBURGER, MY LOVE

By

Ray Blank

A parody of the Hugo-Nominated, Nebula-winning "If You Were a Dinosaur, My Love"

If you were a hamburger, my love, then you would be lightly grilled. You were sanguine during the great E. coli pandemic of 2046, and your dread of Martian flu meant you never lingered at barbecues, back when people still ate outdoors. You'd be a meaty burger, a real whopper, an eight-hundred-pounder, reflecting the ample human girth made possible by living in our low-gravity environment. Thick rich ketchup would ooze across your skin, not evaporating into a toxic mist, like it did when we crosslinked the matter transporter to the microwave oven and tried to feed people mid-beam. Most of all, if you were a hamburger, you would be rare.

If you were a lightly grilled beef patty, then I would become a waitress, so I could serve you. I'd butter your buns, like in the old days before runaway nanites made milk products sentient. I'd lay you on a bed of lettuce and tomato, and cover you in processed cheese. They say the thought waves emanating from modern dairy and vegetables can scramble the psychic senses of police clairvoyants, thus preserving us from incarceration if we violate sexcrime statute S84.

If we violated sexcrime statute S84, and got away with it, then I would sing to you afterward, especially show tunes from *Hello, Dolly!* and other decadent bourgeois relics of the postmodernist

125

precivilization. You wouldn't sing back, because it's absurd to suggest a hamburger might sing, though they can sizzle from time to time. However, a neural link to my smartphone would allow you to play those ringtones that most closely correspond to whatever music floats through your burger mind.

If you were playing a ringtone on my smartphone, it would probably sound like the song you're playing me now. Beep. Beep. Beep. The tone of your life support machine is bittersweet. You're more machine than human, but that's not much of a change; we're both 178 years old, and joining the Cyborg Union was cheaper than health insurance. My heart beats with yours. They should—they're both running the same software, and it's synched to Greenwich time via a satellite uplink. But when they removed your chrome and plastic outer casing, I gazed upon your organic vestiges and thought fondly of traditional foodstuffs rarely seen outside of a holographic library.

If we visited a holographic library together, then I would use my cyborg shapeshifting skills to assume the form of a giant onion ring, so you wouldn't appear quite so weird to all the kids who run around and mash the buttons on the interactive displays instead of learning anything. People would weep at the memory of slicing onions, and impressed by the spectacle of seeing us together, the librarians in the genetic department would clone a real pig just so they could top you with genuine bacon.

If you were joined in secular matrimony with a slice of bacon, I'd try not to be jealous of you preferring a bit of piggy-in-the-middle to playing with my ring. I'd be sad, and crying, and wailing loudly, and wearing the white dress I bought for our wedding, but I wouldn't do any of that to make you feel uncomfortable. On the contrary, I'd really really want you to marry a sliver of processed pork if you're sure that's what you wanted. It just happens to be the case that white shows off my complexion, and the color would help to hide any stains if you drip mayonnaise on me. So marry the bacon, if you must, but don't come crying to me if the resurrected heads of 17th century statesmen currently serving on the Supreme Court decide to interpret *Clutterbuck v. Homogenate Margarine Substitute* as justification for rescinding the universal human right to divorce.

If I was wearing white at your wedding, I'd also want to wear something old, new, borrowed and blue, even though I wouldn't be the bride and that's what brides wore until our Artificially Intelligent overlords banned all forms of neopagan ritual, especially those which assigned different roles according to gender. To keep things simple, I'd borrow some stinky old blue cheese and incorporate it into a new hamburger recipe, and then wear that as a hat. The smell of my daring fashion statement would make it obvious you're no longer the only hamburger in the world, which should make you smile, instead of complaining that I'm embarrassing you in public like usual.

If you weren't the only hamburger in the world, or a cyborg which is almost fifty percent organic, then maybe you would have successfully fought off those ex-military androids who returned from the failed mission to conquer Io. Being homeless and intelligent synthetic lifeforms, they were entitled to fight you for your living quarters, even though you bought that apartment with money you borrowed from your parents. I had some sympathy for your plight, but democratic decentralization inevitably means rioting should be protected as an exercise of free speech. I watched helplessly whilst they kicked you in the taco, and pounded your brain into sweet and sour sauce. Sadly, the androids were careful not to mix their regrettable but perfectly legal ultraviolence with a prohibited activity like badwordscrime. They gave me no excuse to call the thought police. Though you were very angry at the time, you must admit the androids were pretty ingenious, using comically outdated phrases to deprecate you whilst they viciously pounded your skull. They called you a malcontent, and a vagabond, and a rogue, and a rotter, and a cad, and a bounder, and a ne'er-do-well.

When one of them called you a eunuch jelly, I lifted my phone, thinking that might be badwordscrime, but the smartphone AI corrected me, saying "eunuch" was a legitimate reference to a recognized gender reassignment.

If you were a hamburger, my love, you'd be a great big fatty burger covered in cheese and bacon and pickles and relish, and then your enemies would eat you, and then they'd suffer heart disease, and possibly flatulence too. It's fair to assume the androids would eat you. They don't really need food but they like to appear like ordinary people, and I know I'd want to eat you, but only if I didn't know you already. Or maybe eating you would rust the androids' innards, though it's possible the grease might actually be good for them. Anyhow, let's suppose the androids started dying from heart disease because they couldn't afford health insurance either. How I'd laugh at that! Whilst they were lying in their hospital/autoshop beds, I'd slink up to them using my shapeshifting skills, and show them a live update of their credit rating, which would demonstrate their medical bills had doomed their robotic offspring to a lifetime of indentured servitude.

If I laughed at ruining the credit rating of the androids' children, then eventually I'd feel a little bit guilty, because you shouldn't punish the daughterboard for the sins of the motherboard. But I'd only feel guilty to make it clear how superior I am to an android, because they lack a full range of emotions as appropriate for every situation. And then I'd laugh a bit more, because I really am superior. Ha!

If you were a hamburger, my love, then I'd be happy because that would mean cows aren't extinct, and the closest analogue to beef would no longer be cockroach pâté. But cows are extinct, thanks to the cull which saved us all from methane overload. So it's with a heavy heart that I give permission to recycle you into Soylent Green, because you'll never be a hamburger, though you're dead meat now.

IMAGINE

By

Pierce Oka

Who is willing to help the victims of an all-powerful state?

"You'll be accompanying me today on your first field response." Two men walked down a white paneled hallway tiled with shiny black squares. One man, the elder and the taller of the two, walked with an air of boredom, his legs precisely measuring two-tile steps. The younger man walked with a nervous but excited gait, checking the pockets of his long white coat repeatedly to make sure he hadn't forgotten anything. They stopped at an elevator at the end of the hall and the tall man lazily extended a white sleeved arm to push the down button. The door hissed open and soft music began wafting out of the elevator shaft.

"Surprisingly fast, these elevators," said the young man as they stepped in.

"Efficiency is the hallmark of our Society," replied the other as he cleaned his glasses on his coat. "It's why we have to be so strict with our citizens; too many freedoms and they forget the main goal."

"Is that what we're heading out for today?" asked the young man, raking his fingers through his fair hair.

"Today we are headed to apprehend a disturber of the peace. Our target is charged with racism, sexism, homophobia, and aiding a criminal. Order must be restored swiftly." The young agent fell silent for a moment in thought. The elder agent listened with amusement as his partner began to reverently join in the Societal Anthem floating out of the elevator's speakers.

"Imagine no possessions/ I wonder if you can/ No need for greed or hunger/ A brotherhood of man..." He had trained many like him before. Give him a few months and his naive fervor would dissipate as he realized all the lofty ideals for which the Society stood were merely a useful tool for controlling the masses. The elevator came to a gentle stop and the two men exited into another white and black hallway, the younger now trying to match the measured steps of his elder. They passed into a side room near the large entrance to a garage.

"You have your choice of peacekeeping tools, though I'd recommend something small and unobtrusive; our target shouldn't give us too much trouble." The senior agent selected a small pistol and snapped the holster onto his belt. His partner examined several weapons in succession. A triple-barreled rifle. Impressive, but rather heavy. A stun baton. Too utilitarian. A crowbar. What the hell? He chose an intimidating-looking pistol and strapped it to his belt. The two men then exited the armory and headed into the garage.

"Hey, Amber, hurry up!" Dawn called down the sidewalk to her friend. A young woman came pelting down the concrete, her red hair flapping in the breeze a stark contrast against the standard issue grey scarf looped around her neck. She caught up to her friend, taking deep gulps of air and resting her hands on her knees.

"Why again is it so important that we get there so fast?" she asked between breaths.

"If we get there too late, all the good jobs will be taken. Do you want to be stuck with pipeworks for a year?" Dawn pushed a few light strands of hair away from her face, and made a pointed gesture towards a small crowd around a large building. "C'mon, you can already see the line forming down the street."

"Can't we just walk for a little bit? I'm totally out of breath. If anyone passes us we can start running again, okay?"

"Have it your way then, lazybones," said Dawn, ruffling her friend's hair, "just don't blame me if you get 'sustainable power worker'." The two walked on in silence for a bit until Amber let out a squeak of surprise she quickly stifled.

"W-what is *that*?" She gestured across the street.

"The stocks? It's an old time punishment I think, didn't know if they would still bring it out or not. See the sign?" Dawn pointed to a block of black text on the base of the stocks: HOARDING FOOD— FAILED TO LIVE FOR TODAY. "That guy probably hasn't eaten in a few days, to make up for the food he tried to keep."

"Shouldn't we go help him? He looks like he could drop dead any minute now."

"Didn't you see the sign? It's people like him that are trying to drag our Society back into the Dark Times, who don't want people to share and talk about this being greater than Humankind." Cameras on the nearby street lamps detected Dawn's rising voice and swiveled towards her in case any altercation should occur. They soon turned again, however, when a man in a grey habit interrupted the beam plate in front of the stocks and began feeding something out of a bowl to the food hoarder. "See?" said Dawn, "Another one of these nuts, and he's in some funny getup, definitely non-issued. I have half a mind to slam one of the red buttons right now, but we've got to get to the Ministry of Occupations fast!" She strode determinedly down the street.

"This isn't the Dawn I remember from high school," ventured Amber after a minute or so of uncomfortable silence, "What's happened to you? It hasn't been that long since we've seen each other."

"Are you criticizing how I think?!" said Dawn, whirling about on Amber. "Do you know what Professor Hage has to say about criticism?!" But whatever it was Professor Hage had to say about criticism Amber never found out, because at that moment a small gravtruck swung around the corner and two men in white coats came out, weapons raised.

A small door opened out onto a side street and a dark beard jutted out of the doorway. The beard was followed by a nose and face as Brother Edmund peered cautiously into the alleyway. This was a mad risk, he thought to himself, aiding a condemned man while going out openly in his habit, but he hadn't become religious in this day and age to live a life of ease. That man locked up in the streets needed to eat, and there were few that would help him do that. Cradling a pot of stew in his arms, Brother Edmund stepped into the street and began walking briskly. Turning right at the first intersection, he swung about to face the third door on his left. This door, like most doors in the Society, was a dull color, which, like most dull colors in the Society, had a pretentious name like Rodeo Beige or Italian Same. Closer investigation however, would reveal a small fish symbol carved into the door by the doorknob. Brother Edmund knocked thrice upon the door, which swung inward just enough for him to squeeze through.

"Heading to Fourth Street, Brother?" asked the plump, kindly looking woman that had opened the door.

"Yes, to help that poor fellow locked up for 'hoarding food', the nonsense." Brother Edmund stepped over the threshold and the woman quickly closed the door behind him.

"I know, they expect us to believe that the bread will keep on coming and the trains will keep running and the perfect Society will go on forever. No need to worry about the next day! Just live for the moment and it'll all work out fine!"

"Be careful, Martha," he said, cracking a wry smile, "they might have bugs in the houses now. More and more of the side streets are getting crime spotters installed." The two walked farther into the house, which Martha had managed to make look cozy despite the utilitarian design of Society furnishings. They entered the kitchen, and Martha shifted aside a large floor tile.

"Ha! My husband's been an electrician for the past decade; he'd wire them into the neighbor's house. They're always spouting off Society claptrap and praises." Brother Edmund set down the stew pot and began to climb down the ladder into the tunnel under the floor. "You be careful now," she added as she lowered the pot down to him.

"As always. God bless you Martha."

"Careful, they might have bugged the tunnels," she said, smiling. Then all was dark as she pushed the floor tile back into place. Brother Edmund fumbled about in the hood of his habit for a moment before pulling out a small flashlight. With his path illumined he began to walk down the tunnel. Water dripped from the ceiling as he passed under potholed Fifth Street, and the small ring of light in the distance marked Fourth Street. The brother emerged from the old electricians' tunnel behind a large dumpster, and glanced around the corner for any officers of the law. All he saw were two young women, preoccupied with some discussion, so he left his hiding place and approached the man in the stocks. As he did so, he felt as though he had passed through a current of some kind, and noticed the crime spotters swiveling to fix their glassy eyes on him. If he ran now, he could escape. Brother Edmund looked up at the man, saw his gaunt face and pleading eyes. No, he had not come to run away at the first sign of danger.

"Whatever you do for the least of my brethren, you do for me." The thought echoed in Brother Edmund's mind. How could he leave this poor man here? Uncovering the pot, Brother Edmund offered the man a ladle full of stew. He eagerly gulped it down, and croaked out through cracked lips:

"Thank you."

"Thank God," said Brother Edmund, "I am only His lowly servant." He gave more of the stew to the man.

"Odd-looking clothes you're wearing. Won't you get in trouble for that?"

"They are a sign of obedience to God; no threat would make me wear otherwise."

"That remains to be seen," broke in a clipped, authoritative voice.

The young agent's arms shook as he kept his pistol trained on the disturber of the peace. "Just drop the bowl and come with us," he said, trying to force the nervousness out of his voice and sound authoritative. The target paid no attention to his command, and continued to feed something out of a ladle to the criminal. "If you don't stop now, your sentence will be worse!" The man in the strange and offensive garb set down his pot, which made a hollow, ringing sound as it hit the sidewalk. It seemed as though he were going to listen to the agent now, but instead he made some odd gesture with his arms and began to head down the street. "Halt or I'll shoot!"

"Leave him be!" came a woman's voice from behind, followed by another's:

"No you idiot, they're the law!"

"Shoot him." The third voice came surprisingly close to the young agent's ear. The elder agent had stepped up behind him. The young man readjusted his aim and thumbed off the safety of his gun. His irregular breathing made it difficult to keep his pistol trained on the escaping man, who was approaching an alleyway. But he couldn't do it. He couldn't shoot. The older agent sighed, raised his gun, and fired. As the echoes of the gunshot died, the noontime chimes sounded over a public speaker and the Societal Anthem began to play:

"Imagine there's no Heaven/ It's easy if you try... "

GRADUATION DAY

By

Chrome Oxide

A glimpse of state-run education to come...

I was so proud of my daughter that even though I'd never met her, I wanted to spy on her one last time. As the anonymous sperm donor I had no parental rights, but she was the only child I'd ever have.

Today was her Graduation, I mean her Exit Day. After eight years at the Karl Marx Safe Space Educational Gulag she had been exposed to everything the government information czars decided was appropriate for her to see. Even though it seems like yesterday, it was eight years ago that she graduated, I mean exited from high school. She was about to leave academia behind and become a productive adult member of our society.

I pulled my keyboard and monitor from my pocket and expanded them to full size. A quick touch brought up the Gulag map. The screen was full of glowing dots indicating the location of the privacy tracking chips implanted in all citizens at their birth. The signature of my daughter's chip showed her near the center of the campus quad. Because privacy was important to her she disabled public access to her selfie drone when she started at the Gulag. That delayed my search because I needed to drone hop the data streams among the government, university, public access, private, pirate and selfie drones hovering over the campus.

The first drone I jumped to hovered at the east edge of the quad and focused on a white woman lying motionless on the ground. The tears in her clothes and stab wounds on her torso and throat were visible from this angle. A group of heavily tattooed non-white men were pulling up their pants. It wasn't rape because there hadn't been any rapes on campus since the government had banned white men and their rape culture from attending the Gulag. The courts had ruled that after centuries of oppression by the white male patriarchy any actions by minorities were a legitimate form of political protest.

I gasped with horror when I realized the races and genders were mixing in public when they normally stayed in their single-color and gender safe spaces. Only the excitement of Exit Day would cause them to abandon the safe spaces they'd struggled to acquire.

Because of my White Privilege, my education ended in high school where I was trained as a programmer. Five minutes into my first job I became a criminal when I hacked the national database and inserted a datahound to record any queries into my record. My shameful white male heritage was linked to my record because all white males that survived to puberty and didn't have gender reassignment surgery were required to donate sperm to the government sperm bank.

Two years after my hack a data query that I thought was a criminal investigation turned out to be a DNA search for red hair and green eyes. I was surprised any female would consider me a suitable donor because scientists were still unable to remove the CRuSH Gene (Cisgender, Racist, Sexist and Homophobic) from white male DNA. A red-haired, green-eyed white woman selected my sperm because she wanted a red-haired, green-eyed daughter.

Thirty years ago was the only time I viewed my daughter's mother. It was during the delivery and the following week because the Afterbirth Abortion Activists live-streamed the event. They also streamed their attempts to convince the mother to terminate the parasitical growth that for nine months stole nourishment from her body before it escaped from her womb. Nine months of reproductive slavery is mild compared to the twenty-one years of

136

child-rearing slavery that follows a birth. The mother of my daughter resisted their demands for an abortion. She hired bodyguards to protect herself and my child.

Any male that impregnates a female without asking her for permission is guilty of rape. Since I hadn't asked her for permission to violate the sanctity of her ovum when she selected my sperm sample without my permission, the government ruled me guilty of rape and had sent enforcers to execute me. In addition, the Afterbirth Abortion Activists placed a reward for my death to prevent me from ever raping another woman again.

I was running out of time, so I found a government drone hovering above the center of the campus quad. Piles of rocks were placed around the quad for when women, gays or infidels needed to be stoned to death. Non-white men with scimitars wandered around the campus. The camera was focused on the inspirational school motto carved into the sidewalk, "Free Speech Is Too Valuable To Waste On People Who Disagree With Us." On the sidewalk nearby someone had chalked messages for the students. "Kill Jews." "Kill White People." "Kill Pigs." I was glad to see that even though diversity of thought was encouraged no one had written anything hateful.

As I hopped among the drones looking for my daughter, I noticed a man of color, wearing robes of many colors, stalking across the quad wielding a bloody scimitar. He screamed, "Allahu Akbar" and then beheaded a woman who was not of color. I switched to another drone because I didn't want to invade his privacy. Once I started running I'd never have a chance to check the government news sources to find out what the sword wielder's motives were.

Before I hopped to another drone I spotted my daughter, her red hair bright in the morning light. She was talking with another white woman. Both of them turned to face away from the beheading. The other woman pulled out a hand gun and held it in her open palm

137

like it was a snake about to strike. I jumped to a closer drone and zoomed in to read the engraving on the side. "Use this gun to force the greedy 1% to share their wealth."

I boosted the volume and filtered out the other sounds to hear their conversation.

My daughter said, "How can you hold that thing? Guns are scary and evil."

"I know. I don't want it, but I have no choice. Since I received my participation trophy in community activism and wealth distribution, it is my duty to use this thing to fight the greedy oppressive patriarchal society. It is unfortunate that the wealthy don't understand that this is for their own good and the good of society."

Like all good citizens I supported sharing the wealth. It was unfair for any person who wasn't a contributor to political campaigns or a hereditary member of the government to own more than anyone else.

"My drone hasn't arrived yet. I wonder what my career will be."

"I'm sure whatever career the government selects for you will be the right one. The government never makes mistakes."

"That makes me feel better."

The other female looked around, whispered, "Today I'm self-identifying as a lesbian Hispanic female. What race and gender are you today?"

If I didn't know better, I would think she was scared. But with police, guns and white males banned from campus, I knew there was nothing for her to be afraid of. I slapped my head and mentally apologized for providing them with CRuSH motives when they were only being sensitive to the privacy needs of the other individuals on campus.

My daughter looked around and whispered, "Today I'm self-identifying as a gay black male."

White males are prohibited from self-identifying as anything other than themselves because of their White Privilege and defective DNA.

"Do be careful about cultural appropriation."

"I will."

They hugged each other without asking for permission. I shivered. If a white man hugged any female without written consent he would be rightfully arrested and charged with rape.

After they separated and wiped the tears from their eyes, an official Gulag delivery drone paused in front of my daughter. It dropped a note and a participation trophy into her hands along with a gun. I zoomed in on the gun. "Use this gun to eliminate White Privilege by eliminating all whites."

The trophy was inscribed with the following words. "Congratulations. This trophy honors your occasional presence on campus while enrolled in the eight-year course of study on the evils of the CRuSH white oppressors."

She opened the note. "You are assigned to the Afterbirth Abortion Activists to provide post-birth abortions to evil oppressive white men. Your first assignment is the sperm donor rapist of your mother."

While I accepted the rightness of her career and assignment, I was unhappy that it applied to me. My monitor caught the reflection of a tear rolling down my white face into my red beard. With my go bag on my shoulder, I rolled up my monitor and keyboard and stuffed them in my pocket. My daughter had grown up to be just like I imagined her mother was. I was so proud of her.

HYMNS OF THE MOTHERS

By

Brad R. Torgersen

Do the mothers always know best?

The trog's body was both pale and stiff, as he lay at the base of the southwestern wall. He'd fallen a long way, onto the boulders and debris heaped in either direction. Dinah had never seen a dead person before. The mothers talked of death as if it were a disease, long since vanquished by medicine. The oldest of the mothers was said to have lived for hundreds of years. Dinah herself was just a lyte—in the latter half of her second decade. She and her classmates were on a rare field trip skirting the wall's perimeter. It was only her second time seeing the outside. In the distance was the vast, green bulwark of endless forest, extending up to the foothills of the far mountains. Also in the distance—in the opposite direction—was the shattered hulk of one of the dead cities. The mothers knew about those too. The dead cities had been made by people, long ago. Before the war that ruined the world—so that the Earth could be made whole again.

Dinah turned her eyes from the poor trog, and gazed up the hundred-meter face of the wall proper. There were several balconies two-thirds of the way to the top. Only the mothers were allowed to visit those perches. The trog must have been called to perform some chore for a mother in need of manual work. How or why he'd gone over the edge... well, it didn't matter. According to Mother Eilan, a trog's life wasn't worth much. Dogs and cats possessed more value. They at least provided pleasant company. Trogs were boorish, and kept apart from lytes and mothers alike. When they were seen, it was only for short periods. Either lugging

141

furniture and hardware, or trooping in a tidy column to their next task—with a watchful beta standing over them, its punishment flail at the ready.

"Do you think he jumped?" asked a voice to Dinah's left.

"Why would any creature do that!?" Dinah exclaimed.

Shervet—also a lyte, and Dinah's best friend—was still looking at the trog's body.

"It's unlikely he tripped," Shervet said. "The railing on each balcony is at least a meter or more high. The trog would have had to climb up on top, and push off. Look how far the body is from the wall. He was moving forward as he dropped."

"So many broken bones," Dinah said, shuddering—her eyes still averted. "I hope his end was quick."

"Sympathy for a trog?" Shervet chided.

"Even a trog deserves at least a modicum of compassion," Dinah replied.

"Don't let the mothers hear that," Shervet said, turning and walking to Dinah's side. "You know what they say about trogs."

"Short-tempered, short-sighted, short-lived," Dinah said, in a somewhat mocking tone—repeating the line from the hymn which had been taught to them since Dinah had been old enough to grasp the meaning of words. Until this unpleasant discovery, it had never occurred to her what that particular hymn really meant. The trogs were almost always out of sight, and out of mind. But now? Now, one of them lay smashed and lifeless at her feet. Even he had been a child once, albeit following in the footsteps of his elders—from the moment he was deemed capable of using tools.

"We should tell the others," Dinah said.

"What for?" Shervet asked. "Not like it'll do him any good at this point. Besides, a trog ground crew will be around eventually. They

142

can collect the body, and put it through the crematorium. Come on, let's keep walking. We've only got two hours left in the morning. Mother Eilan will be upset with us if we're late returning to the rendezvous point."

Dinah took a final look over her shoulder, her mouth turned down in a slight frown, then nodded her head in acquiescence. She and Shervet slowly resumed picking their way through the rocks.

It was a relief, stepping back inside the wall. Everything was clean, and in its designated place. Trees, green lawns, walking boulevards, the various sculpture-like buildings that the mothers had created over the centuries. All of it intimately familiar. Dinah and twenty other lytes all moved in a relaxed, orderly formation, with Mother Eilan gliding at their side. It was said that Eilan was over two hundred years old. She possessed the stately grace of one who had long ago become accustomed to authority. Her movements were fluid, yet strong. On her shoulders were the straps of her day pack—a somewhat more robust version of the smaller packs each of the lytes had carried outside. Presently, Eilan steered the formation into one of the circular vestibules that accessed their school house. While Shervet and the others went to store their packs in the cubbyholes that lined the vestibule's walls, Mother Eilan approached Dinah and bade the young woman to have a seat at Eilan's side.

The polished, symmetrical stone bench was cold to the touch. A huge, transparent skylight allowed the sun's rays to flood down into the vestibule, where the white marble floor reflected that light to every part of the space.

"Your brow is creased," Mother Eilan said quietly. "I would know your thoughts, Lyte Dinah."

Dinah shifted uncomfortably. "It's just good to be back in," she said.

143

"Does the outer world disturb you?"

"Yes," Dinah admitted. "More than I thought it would—even having been outside before."

"You saw something unusual this time?"

Dinah hesitated. Neither she nor Shervet had told anyone about the dead trog.

"I saw... I saw enough, to know that the outer world is dangerous."

"Indeed," Mother Eilan said, patting a hand on Dinah's thigh. "That's why the wall exists. It was the first thing the original mothers created, when the great rebuilding commenced—after fighting had stopped, and many decades of silence passed. You also saw the dead city?"

"Yes."

"It's nowhere visible from inside the wall—for a reason. We don't need a corpse from the past reminding us of the terribleness from before true civilization was born. Occasionally, I voice the opinion that we should make the effort to go and tear down the dead city. Completely. But then I am reminded by my seniors that time will do the work, as surely as anything else. Besides, we don't have enough trogs for the job. And that's a good thing."

"Trogs... " Dinah said, and swallowed hard, remembering the body. One thing suddenly occurred to her. Why had the trog been naked? All trogs wore the customary, dull coveralls of their kind. The one outside the wall hadn't had so much as a napkin to cover himself with, nor boots on his feet. Only the silvery collar of obedience around his neck.

"You're not giving me the full truth," Mother Eilan suddenly said, in a sharp tone. "Out with it, girl. Now."

"Yes ma'am," Dinah said dutifully, and swallowed hard a second time; before continuing. "When we paired off to explore outside, Shervet and myself wound up finding... well, we found... I'm so sorry, Mother Eilan. It was a trog!"

"A trog? Beyond the wall? Did the trog molest you in any way!?"

"He was dead," Dinah quickly blurted. "And no, this wasn't one of the wild trogs rumored to still be living outside. I know, because all he had on, was the collar. Nothing else."

Mother Eilan suddenly stiffened, her gaze turning from Dinah's eyes—to stare into space just in front of their feet.

"You're sure it was dead?"

"Lifeless as a stick in winter," Dinah replied. "And so broken from the fall, I doubt even a strong beta could have survived a similar accident. We came across the body under one of the balconies."

"Yes," Eilan said, "I imagine you did."

"What does it mean?" Dinah asked, suddenly sensing that it was Mother Eilan who wasn't divulging the full truth.

"It means nothing," Mother Eilan snapped. Then, seeming to remember herself, her posture softened, and she placed a comforting hand on Dinah's shoulder. "Or at least, it means nothing of concern to you. Trogs are, as you know, a necessary component of our society. But their uses are limited. My seniors would be alarmed to learn of a feral trog from the subterranean stables, wandering around outside. But a deceased trog? That seems to be the kind of problem which has neatly solved itself."

Dinah looked into Mother Eilan's eyes—bright with purpose and intelligence—but dared not probe with further questions. Dinah had learned, as all lytes must learn, that knowledge was not the same thing as wisdom. Wisdom would come with time, and patience. All would be revealed, so that by the year Dinah herself

145

was of age to ascend to motherhood, much that now seemed opaque, would be clear.

If any of the other lytes had been paying attention to Mother Eilan's sidebar, the lytes didn't show it. Eavesdropping was a punishable offense. When a mother pulled a lyte aside for one-on-one counseling, this was for that specific lyte, and her alone.

"Now, we have more classwork for today," Mother Eilan said, quickly standing. "Was there anything else you needed to tell me, before you walk to your desk?"

"No, ma'am," Dinah said.

"Good. Put the poor trog out of your mind. Its time on this Earth was going to be quick, regardless. Like fallen snow melting in a spring afternoon."

Dinah nodded, and trailed the rest of the lytes flowing out of the vestibule. The comforting blanket of routine would do much to soothe her nerves. But the image of the dead trog—face down, on the stones, his body twisted—could not be easily banished from Dinah's mind.

The opening hymn of class now concluded, Mother Qez was at the lightboard, using her fingertips to call up imagery from the school computer. All of the lytes in Dinah's age bracket were now receiving weekly inservices on motherhood—the life soon to be— since they were just a few years shy of achieving true maturity. At twenty, every person would take up the mantle of adulthood. To include participating in the procreation lottery.

"As you can see," Mother Qez said in an academic tone, "the total number of lottery selections is, annually, very small. This is one of the most important aspects of our society, and I cannot stress it enough. We will not grow our nation beyond the confines of the wall. It is an artifact erected to protect us, yes—to ensure that our

146

country is now, and always will be, a safe space. But it's also a reminder, that procreation without limits was one of the reasons the old war occurred. We now limit ourselves, so that our footprint on the surface of the Earth remains modest. People will never again spread over the land, consuming everything in sight—like a plague of crickets."

Out of the corner of her eye, Dinah could see Mother Eilan nodding her head—an affirmation of Mother Qez's statement. Doubtless Mother Eilan knew the rote texts of history as well as any school instructor, but this particular aspect of a lyte's education was always reserved for Mother Qez. Who was rumored to be over three centuries in age; though her body had achieved that timeless quality all senior mothers seemed to have. Not young, but also not old. She was seasoned. Polished. Like the use-worn wooden handle on an artist's paint brush.

The question light over Shervet's desk flicked on.

"Yes, Lyte Shervet?" Mother Qez asked.

"Knowing what the lottery is, and why we need it, is one thing, ma'am. What I'd like to know is, just how are babies made?"

A hushed bubbling of giggles quickly went through the lytes—Shervet had put words to what they'd all been thinking, but had been too sheepish to ask. A pregnant mother was a rare thing indeed, and pregnancy brought with it a tremendous amount of deference, as well as veneration. But the pregnant mothers never talked about how they became pregnant. And once a child was born, she was immediately placed into the communal nursery, where all mothers would function as one—to rear the next generation of lytes.

Mother Qez's ordinarily small mouth, cinched itself up into a tight knot. She absently rapped a knuckle on the lightboard, considering Shervet's pertinent question.

147

"You know that menstruation is the body's monthly way of cycling," Mother Qez said. "You've also been taught that pregnancy is impossible, through much of that cycle. And that, for a short time every thirty days—give or take—there is a window during which a mother can conceive. What's not shared with you until you actually achieve maturity, is the precise process whereby the eggs each of you carry, are fertilized. It is not secret, so much as it is sacrosanct. A lesson you will each have to wait to learn, in the fullness of time. Suffice to say that, once you have given birth—as a selectee of the lottery—you will then receive your companion; to keep with you for the rest of your life."

Mother Qez tapped the small, metallic disc resting on the skin below and behind her left ear. All of the mothers had them—at least the ones old enough to have won the procreation lottery. Once your birth was completed, at whatever age you happened to be when your number came up, the companion was surgically implanted. And seeming immortality attained.

Or, at least, as close to immortality as could be achieved through science.

How the companion worked, was also something the senior mothers kept to themselves. Additional knowledge to be gained— by the lytes—when enough years had elapsed. An aspect of society Dinah found endlessly frustrating. But it was the way of things.

Dinah's glance at Shervet told her that Shervet wasn't satisfied, but also wasn't going to argue with Mother Qez, either. There were many rumors forever circulating among the lytes—about the how and the why of the universe. Surely the mothers knew, for they themselves had once been lytes. But the mothers kept quiet, and knowledge was dispensed to the younger generation over an achingly gradual schedule.

"It is a mistake to know too much, too soon!" Mother Eilan had once shouted, banging her palm on the very same lightboard that

Mother Qez now used. The lessons of the dead world from before the war, seemed to inhabit many conclusions of many lyte-inspired conversations. "Capability, without responsibility!"

Hesitantly, Dinah pushed the desk button to illuminate her own question light.

"Yes, Lyte Dinah?"

"Ummm," Dinah said, working up the nerve to complete her thought; if Shervet could do it, Dinah could.

Now it was Mother Eilan who was also looking at Dinah, in addition to Mother Qez.

Dinah's face suddenly felt very hot, so she released the button.

"Never mind," Dinah said.

"Oh no," Mother Qez said, her eyebrow arched. "You're not getting off the hook that easily. I know your file, Lyte Dinah. I know the kinds of thoughts that knock around inside your head. Ask your question—I'll let you know if it can be answered."

"Shervet wants to know how babies happen," Dinah said haltingly, "but what I want to know is, how do trogs happen?"

Mother Eilan practically leapt from her chair at the back of the class, while Mother Qez stepped to the rear several paces, and bumped her elbows against the lightboard.

The entire class had fallen silent. Now here was a matter few truly dared broach.

"Also a question that must wait, until you are selected—and made ready," Mother Qez said.

"Do we give birth to trogs, as well as lytes?" Dinah asked, pushing through her embarrassment. The picture of the dead trog was foremost in her mind now. He'd been as fragile as any lyte. What were his feelings, up to and directly before the end? What had been his hates? His fears? His loves? Had he even known love at all? Dinah opened her mouth to speak again, but was suddenly cut off.

"Of course not!" Mother Eilan practically shouted from the back of the room. "The trogs are inhuman!"

Mother Qez held up her hand, looking to her junior mother—as if to request calmness.

"Your mind seems to be following a dangerous path," Mother Qez said, turning her head and eyes to look at Dinah. "I admire the boldness of your curiosity. That is the mark of a lyte who will do much good for our country. But only if your mind is disciplined. On the origins of the trogs, I can speak no further. Not because the truth is not known, but because the truth—at this time, and in this class—would be harmful to you. Suffice to say that you will know eventually. You will all know. Now, let's continue. I want to discuss the mechanics of the lottery proper, before going into more detail about the communal nursery."

Mother Qez's fingers began to manipulate the lightboard, but Dinah's mind was very far away from the lecture. It stayed far away until Mother Qez called for a break. The various lytes stood up from their desks—to stretch, and use the lavatory. Dinah herself absently got out of her seat, and joined several other lytes as they sauntered out of the room and down a hallway to where the toilets and wash basins would be.

A yellow sign blocked their path, guarded by a towering beta.

"No entry," the beta's voice stated firmly. Despite the beta's size, its voice was high-pitched. Like every other inch of the beta's pink skin, the beta's scalp was smooth. It didn't blink as it stared down at the lytes, who fidgeted with physical discomfort.

"Is there a problem?" asked Mother Eilan's voice from behind. She was walking toward the growing collection of lytes, all trying to look past or around the beta guarding the lavatory entrance.

The beta's manner turned from stern, to gentle—almost obsequious. "Yes, Mother, there is a problem—for which I deeply and profoundly apologize. One of your kindred instructors alerted the maintenance center to the fact that this particular lavatory is experiencing mechanical problems. I immediately brought a work crew over to deal with it. I do want to apologize again for this extreme inconvenience."

Mother Eilan seemed to accept this at face value, then clapped her hands three times.

"You heard what it said, now, quickly—over to the east lavatory. Before someone makes a mess!"

The lytes collectively moaned a complaint, then hurriedly shuffled off to the far lavatory in a different part of the building. Dinah was last in, and had to wait for a clear toilet stall. She felt like bursting, before she got a chance to sit down, and relieve herself. Then she allowed herself the luxury of remaining, and waiting. She was on the far side of the lavatory, away from the wash basin. When the other lytes had vacated, Dinah was alone—and in her solitude, able to think. The matter of the dead trog continued to bother her. The fact that Mother Qez was tight-lipped about the origin of the trogs, bothered Dinah more. Surely they weren't pulled—alive and whole—out of the ground. Somebody had to give birth to them. Even if they weren't people. Cats made kittens and dogs made puppies. The trogs—

Suddenly, footsteps proceeded into the lavatory. Two pairs of feet. Adult, by the quality of the sound. The two mothers were in mid-conversation, their tone hushed. Dinah thought it sounded like Mother Eilan and Mother Qez, but could not be sure.

Dinah held her breath, as the two mothers conducted their personal business just a few stalls away. Had they seen Dinah's feet? She deftly pulled them up off the floor, clutching her knees to her chin.

"... she's too inquisitive to hold back with the others."

"... it's the damned field trip outside the wall, she saw one of them."

"... a trog? Let me guess, that was Ouphon's toy who jumped last night."

"... Ouphon shouldn't be violating the law!"

"... Ouphon isn't the first, and won't be the last."

"... How can you just say it like that? As if it doesn't mean anything?"

"... Of course it means something. It means Lyte Dinah may have to be placed on an accelerated learning track, and taken out of the ordinary school environment. Her dormitory partner, too. Shervet? They both saw the body. Unfortunate, that Ouphon didn't think to tell anyone before it was too late."

"... Ouphon clearly didn't want to get caught, nor admit what she'd been doing with that trog!"

"... Nor should she. I'd have probably kept my mouth shut too. Anyway, if confronted, she'll deny it, regardless. And so what? It's not like a dead trog is a crime. Ouphon will just have to get over not getting any more 'service' in her auxiliary suite—inside the wall. You have to admit, that's a clever place to do it. Isolated. Far from the busy buildings. Trogs are not an uncommon sight, performing wall maintenance."

"... You almost sound like you want to try it yourself."

"... Any woman who hasn't thought about trying it with the trogs—"

"... Disgusting!"

"... Yes, well, maybe."

Eventually the voices were drowned out by the sound of running water, and then the adult footsteps receded.

Dinah breathlessly lowered her feet back to the floor. After a bit of cleaning up, she was out the lavatory door, and heading back to class. Doubtless Mother Qez had resumed instructing, but Dinah couldn't be dinged for lateness—the lavatory closest to the classroom had been out of order. What really terrified Dinah, was the conversation she'd overheard. Too many unanswered and unanswerable questions, pushing at the front of her consciousness.

Ten meters before making the classroom door, Dinah stopped short. The beta she'd seen earlier, was leading three trogs out the way they'd originally come in. One of the trogs was pushing a cart on wheels. Another was carrying a large box with a handle on the top. Both of them were stooped, and had long hair that sprouted from both their heads and their faces—silver in color, and dirty by the smell of it. The third trog was different, though. Young. Black haired. Perhaps as young as Dinah herself? Unlike the older trogs—who simply stared ahead, and shuffled, without speaking—the young trog noticed Dinah, and made eye contact with her.

There was an instant of connection of one mind, acknowledging another. The young trog, whose eyes—as bright as Mother Eilan's—were both warm, and suggesting of intellect. He hesitated for a moment, the mop handle in his hands temporarily forgotten. Dinah suddenly thought him beautiful.

That was all it took, and the beta was coming down on the young trog like a lightning storm.

"Eyes front, you waste of skin! Eyes front!"

The pain flail lashed, and a current-charged cascade of agony caused the young trog to scream.

"No! No!" Dinah found herself yelling, trying to step between the beta, and the trog who convulsed on the floor.

Almost instantly, the door to the classroom popped open, and Mother Eilan was standing at the doorway, her voice bellowing commands.

"Stop that, this instant! Get out of here with your crew! Lyte Dinah, you will report to my learning chamber at once! MOVE!"

The beta lowered its flail, and smiled a smile filled with yellow, crooked teeth.

"Oh, most assuredly, Mother, and I do profoundly and deeply apologize for the interruption! I will ensure that this young one is properly disciplined and dealt with, away from the campus. Do please pass my apology to the rest of the staff. I am so very sorry for this. Terribly, terribly inappropriate."

The beta's eyes promised murder at the young trog—who was shakily climbing to his feet.

Dinah tried to look into the young trog's face—to see again, what she had so briefly seen—but the trog's eyes remained fully forward, and his head was bent low, as he hurriedly kept after the other trogs; even going so far as to mimic their age-worn shuffling.

Shervet joined Dinah at their dormitory window. It was dark. Dinah should have been asleep. Or at least in her bunk. The faint light from a half moon, filtered in through the window's transparent material. Outside, the tops of trees and buildings could be seen, all shadowy and silvered at the edges.

Dinah quietly hummed a bit of music, to try to calm herself. It was from one of the nursery hymns they all learned, as small girls. About how there was harmony in all things, when all things knew their places. A sensible enough hymn, for the communal nursery— where mothers worked around the clock to keep toddlers and youngsters in line. The hymn had always brought Dinah comfort. It

154

spoke of finding refuge and support in structure. But now? Now, the words seemed empty.

"Today was just bad luck," Shervet said, placing a hand on Dinah's shoulder.

"Bad luck for us both," Dinah replied. "I'm not the only one being pulled out of class."

"Punished for being nosy," Shervet said. "Figures."

"I wonder if they'll move us out of the dormitory too?" Dinah asked. "I think we're being taken out of class, more to protect the other lytes from our 'nosiness' than anything else."

"Probably," Shervet replied.

A short silence elapsed, as the two lytes stared out into the night.

Then, Shervet's hand slowly slid across Dinah's triceps, to the opposite shoulder, where Shervet's fingers began to trace little circles.

Dinah stiffened.

"Is now not a good time for the touch?" Shervet said, freezing her movement.

"I'm sorry," Dinah said. "I don't mean to be rude. It's just that... I can't... Maybe some other night."

Shervet's arm dropped, and she turned to go crawl into her bunk. It was a two-person room. With narrow beds to either side of the window, and shelving above the bunks. A mere two meters separated them. But suddenly Shervet felt very far away.

"Wait," Dinah said. "Don't be cross. It's not you. It's me."

"You never didn't like the touch before," Shervet said, a hint of petulance in her voice. "Maybe it would take your mind off the trogs? That's all you've been thinking about, ever since this morning."

"I can't stop," Dinah said, making fists in her short hair—as if to pull it out at the roots.

"I can't either," Shervet admitted. "I was hoping the touch would take both our minds off of it."

"But it's not just what we saw," Dinah said. "It's what I heard. You weren't there when I listened to the mothers talking in the lavatory. You were right, about how he died. He jumped. But that's not the most shocking part. The mothers talked as if a different mother were... well... you can infer a lot from the way people talk about a thing, without really talking about it."

"What are you getting at?" Dinah Shervet said, her feet dangling over the side of her bed.

"Did you notice, how the dead trog was naked?"

"Now that you mention it, sure."

"It didn't make sense, until I heard the mothers talking about Mother Ouphon. They referred to the naked trog as Ouphon's 'toy' and how Mother Ouphon would just have to 'get by' without him."

"Okay... " Shervet said hesitantly, still not getting what Dinah was driving at.

"Ouphon and the trog... Shervet, Ouphon and the trog were doing the touch!"

"That's gross. But why would the trog jump?"

"I don't know. If it had been Mother Eilan doing the touch with a trog, she would have jumped—to spare herself the shame."

"Maybe the trog was ashamed too?"

"Maybe. Shervet, we've discovered something. Something we've not yet been told about, but also something that's not supposed to happen. Not among the mothers, anyway. But I think it's happened before. Maybe it's still happening now? Something the mothers don't want to admit, or at least don't want to talk about openly with each other."

"Doing the touch with a trog, sounds disgusting," Shervet said. "They're stupid, smelly, and filthy."

"Yes they are," Dinah said. "But the dead one outside the wall, he wasn't smelly or filthy. He was as clean as you or me—ignoring the blood."

Dinah watched her friend's features, in the dim light from the window. Shervet's mouth frowned, as she seemed to be trying to puzzle something out.

"What if... what if the question I asked in class today, and the question you asked... have the same answer?" Shervet finally said.

Dinah felt a prickle run up her spine.

The next morning, Dinah and Shervet were ordered to pack their belongings. Two large, plastic chests were brought by two young trogs, and their requisite beta master. It wasn't the same beta as Dinah had encountered the day before, but she was certain that one of the two trogs was the same one who'd been hit with the punishment flail, for daring to meet her gaze. The trogs stood outside the dorm room door, speechless, heads hung low and eyes on the floor, while Dinah and Shervet gathered their clothing and belongings, and carefully deposited it all into the chests. The trogs were ordered in, to pick up and carry the chests—each one far heavier than most lytes would care to handle—and then the trogs trailed along behind Dinah and Shervet as one of the dorm mothers led them through a service corridor ordinarily not accessible to lytes. Halfway down a connecting hallway, Shervet began muttering to herself. When the dorm mother called for a halt, Shervet confessed to having forgotten something back in their old room.

The dorm mother sighed in annoyance, then bade the beta to have the trogs rest their burdens on the floor.

"What could you have possibly left behind?" the dorm mother asked.

"It's a smaller chest. Mother Wyo gave it to me a long time ago, and said not to open it until my ascension to motherhood. I keep it under my bunk, so that it's out of the way."

"Is it heavy enough to require a trog's muscles?" the dorm mother asked.

"Probably," Shervet said, her face now bright red.

The dorm mother looked around for a moment, then threw up her hands in exasperation, and snapped her fingers at the beta.

"Come. Bring one of the two. The other stays here, with Lyte Dinah."

"Mother," the beta said—its voice high-pitched, like that of its kindred, "I do not believe it would not be wise to leave a trog unsupervised. They can be troublesome if left out of the watchful eye of a responsible master."

"Are you saying you were foolish enough to bring a known problem trog into a dorm?" the dorm mother said sharply.

The beta almost choked. Then rushed to explain himself.

"Oh, no, ma'am, no, no, it's not that. It's just... well, if something were to happen—"

"I am sure it will be fine," Shervet interrupted, her face still red. "It was my fault for leaving the second chest. The sooner we retrieve it, the sooner we can be on our way. I apologize for the inconvenience and interruption."

The beta seemed to want to argue its point further, but decided against the idea, bowing its head once, then clapping one of the two young trogs on the butt. The young trog began to hurry off, with

Shervet and the dorm mother in the lead, and the beta following watchfully behind.

Suddenly, Dinah found herself alone with the trog who seemed very much like the one from the day before. He kept his eyes on the ground, his posture stiff. Afraid.

"I'm sorry the beta hurt you yesterday," Dinah said.

The trog in front of her, kept silent. He didn't so much as alter his breathing.

"It is you, isn't it?" Dinah asked, aware of the fact that this was very much against protocol—to directly interrogate a trog, without first going through a beta—but she was intensely curious, and there might not ever be another opportunity to talk to a trog without any adult supervision present.

"Please," Dinah said. "Just let me know that it's you, or not. If you can't look me in the eye, at least show me somehow. I know, let's try this—if you remember me from the school, and were unfortunately punished for looking at me, stamp your right foot on the ground two times."

At first, there was nothing. Then, hesitantly, the trog lifted his right foot, and gently tapped the sole of his boot on the cement floor twice in succession.

"It is you!" Dinah exclaimed, suddenly delighted.

Then she remembered herself.

"Please," she said. "It's important to me that you understand what I am saying, and that you believe me when I tell you that I did not want you to get into trouble. Certainly I didn't want that beast of a beta taking out its anger on you. I know lytes aren't supposed to care. We're not even supposed to spend much time in contact with trogs. But I'm not like that. I think there's a case to be made for courtesy, as well as kindness. Especially when—"

The young trog raised his face, and Dinah stopped short. Yes, this was the one. His eyes—the same intelligence, the same warmth—could not be mistaken for another's. Her heart skipped a beat, when he said just a single word.

"Gebbel."

Dinah was shocked at the deepness of the trog's voice. In truth, it was the first time she'd ever heard a trog form a word at all.

"What?" Dinah blurted, surprised.

"Do not forget. My name, is Gebbel."

Then the trog's face aimed back down to the floor, and footsteps in the distance told Dinah that the dorm mother was coming. Very quickly, the beta, Shervet, and the trog carrying Shervet's second chest, returned. Gebbel stooped and hefted Dinah's chest, then he and the other trog—who now carried Shervet's two chests, one atop the other; with obvious strain and discomfort—began to walk behind Dinah and Shervet, as the dorm mother led them through two more connecting hallways, and finally out into a large plaza.

Dinah wasn't familiar with this place. It was one of the areas reserved strictly for the mothers. Paving bricks formed pathways in between or around variously-shaped fountains. Trees grew tall, providing shade from the sun as it approached midday. On the other side of the plaza, a large, multi-storied building awaited. The dorm mother pointed to it and said, "Go there. Mother Uroz is waiting for you. You do not know her, but she will know the both of you. She will show you to your new place of residence, and give you further direction."

"Will we be able to see any of our friends, or old teachers?" Shervet asked nervously.

"In time, yes. But Mother Uroz will be able to tell you more. I bid you goodbye, and wish you well."

The outer door—somewhere on the flank of the dorm—snapped shut, and Dinah walked woodenly next to Shervet, as they crossed the plaza to their new home.

Things weren't much different from before. The hours and schedule were almost exactly the same. Dinah and Shervet even shared a room, built for two. But this room was much larger, and actually had a lavatory of its own. Incredibly small, compared to the communal dorm lavatories Dinah was used to. But the exclusivity of the tiny two-person lavatory seemed almost obscenely luxurious. Neither Dinah nor Shervet could get over it. For a full week, they took turns simply relishing the quiet privacy of the thing.

Class was more exclusive too. Dinah and Shervet took lessons with only four other lytes, all of varying age. Mother Uroz seemed to have the same timeless quality that Mother Qez possessed, and a dignified manner of speech and movement that suggested great age. Their school subjects were the same, the opening hymns the same, but the material concerning motherhood was greatly enhanced and expanded. Including details on the companion, about which almost nothing had been said by any of the mothers before.

"Your companion is the key," said Mother Uroz. "It will be with you from the first day, after your one and only birth. Once implanted, the companion monitors all of your body's life functions. It also runs the army of microbe-sized machines which will be introduced into your bodies—to ward you against diseases, cancers, sclerotic arteries, and other problems. Without the companion, each of you would die in a matter of decades. With your companion intact and fully functioning, life can be extended dramatically."

"How dramatically?" Dinah asked, after turning on her question light.

"Nobody really knows," Mother Uroz admitted. "We've had the companions for as long as I've been alive. To my knowledge, no woman ever given the companion implant has ever died of old age. They have died of other things—usually accidents and injuries—but old age? No. Not yet. Perhaps, not ever."

"What's it like," Shervet said, leaning forward into the illuminating halo of her own question light.

"What's what like?" Mother Uroz asked.

"To live so long," Shervet said. "Years upon decades upon... centuries. Do you ever get bored?"

Mother Uroz's brow creased, and she seemed about to dismiss the question, then she closed her mouth and considered further. Before responding, she drew up a stool in front of the lectern from which she ordinarily orated, and sat down; her hands folded.

"In the regular schools, we'd not be obliged to answer such an audacious question. But as you're all aware, this is not a regular school. Each of you has been, in different ways, deemed precocious. This is a blessing, and a curse. Your minds may be ready to accept knowledge at an uneven or accelerated pace, but your hearts may not be. When a lyte is brought to me, it's because her imagination is adventuring into territory well beyond her ken. My job is to try to guide you all down the correct paths, without stunting or discouraging your intellect. Our nation needs powerful minds. It's how we managed to re-forge a better world for ourselves. Here, inside the wall. When all else surrounding us was ash."

"Are you old enough to remember the war?" one of the other lytes asked.

"No," Mother Uroz responded. "That was long before my time. But I was like you, once. And when my questions threatened to explode out of my skull, I was brought here. The senior mothers helped me to understand. Eventually, I attained motherhood, experienced my one birth, gained a companion, and when I'd lived many, many decades beyond the years of a lyte, I returned here. To help ones such as I had been find their places in our society."

Shervet still leaned forward at her desk, the question light not yet darkened.

"Which," Mother Uroz said, chuckling at herself, "does not address the original point, Lyte Shervet. Let me put it this way. I have lived three hundred and forty six years. During that time I have seen our nation inside the wall create many wonderful things. We have grown. But not without balance. There are many more of us now, and we're capable of doing many things. But our progress is restrained. Sensible. To include long journeys beyond the wall—into the wilderness."

Now, all the question lights on all the desks illuminated.

Mother Uroz chuckled again.

"Yes, I know. You've not been told—until now—of the expeditions. Doubtless when some of you are ascended to motherhood, you will have an opportunity to venture out on some future quest for knowledge. Depending on your professions. Going outside for days, weeks, even months, is not for the delicate. There are things you will see out there—places you will visit and experience—which will change you forever. And it's the change which keeps life interesting. I am not now, who I was one hundred years in the past. And I was not then, who I was one hundred years prior. And so on, and so forth. If there was no opportunity for change, then long life would seem like a prison."

"Like with the trogs," Dinah said under her breath.

Mother Uroz's back straightened.

"What about them?" she said, and suddenly Dinah's face was turning bright red—Mother Uroz had keen ears.

"Short life would seem to be as much of a potential prison, as long life," Dinah said quickly. Then shrank into her seat, hoping she could stop being the sudden center of attention.

"We're pretending that a trog has the capacity to grasp what it would mean—to live a short life, versus a long life," Mother Uroz said confidently. "I've had more than my fair share of experience with their kind. In a sense, the trogs are one of nature's truly unfortunate cases. Almost smart enough, to be civilized. Almost long-lived enough, to attain the kind of wisdom one needs to be a productive member of society. But not quite. Always... not quite. Like a stunted child just intelligent enough to be aware of how she doesn't measure up to everyone else. We do the trogs a favor, by employing their strength for practical projects that require muscle."

"And what about the betas?" Shervet asked.

"A beta is merely a trog we—the mothers—have chosen to elevate to a higher grade of awareness."

"How?"

"The same medical science that gives us the companion, gives us the ability to make a trog into something more than what it is."

"Then why not all the way?" Dinah asked—her question light staying off. She'd forgotten all about pushing the button. And Mother Uroz didn't seem to care.

"All the way to what?" Mother Uroz responded.

"If we can take a trog and make him into a beta, why not take a beta and make the beta into something more like us?"

Mother Uroz smiled, and shook her head.

"Do not mistake the limits of our medicine, for lack of compassion. We have tried. Oh yes, our country has tried. The first mothers worked endlessly to uplift the trogs. It's in the records, which some of you will see eventually, if you yourselves decide to

164

practice medicine. We tried so hard to improve the trogs' existence—to make them like we are. But it never worked. The closest we could come, was the betas. So, we did what we could with both species. We gave them roles in our world. Roles for which they are most aptly suited. Which is a far, far better thing, than banishing them to the outside. There is no hope beyond the wall. I've been out there to see it for myself. No creature would ever want to be condemned to a life outside. Here, on the inside, the betas and the trogs at least have some form of civilization. Clothing. Food. Sanitation. None of you understand precisely how valuable things like clothing, food, and sanitation can be; until you're forced to do without them."

"Can trogs make baby trogs, the way a mother makes a baby lyte?"

Dinah's last question—asked of Mother Quez, earlier—stopped Mother Uroz short.

"What?" she blurted.

"It makes sense," Dinah pressed. "Lytes come from mothers, and eventually turn into mothers. The trogs must also come from other trogs. But we've never seen a trog be pregnant. What little we see of them at all. Can trogs even get pregnant?"

"No," Mother Uroz snapped, and then wiped a hand along the side of her face with exasperation. "I mean, it's more complicated than you suspect, Lyte Dinah. I was briefed on your specific precociousness, before your arrival here. I know what you saw, that morning, during the field trip. Doubtless the dead trog was a horrible thing to discover, and when you've seen something horrible—believe me, I have, more than once—the image sticks in your brain. It fascinates you. So now the trog takes up space within your soul. You cannot get rid of him. You need to understand him. To know what happened, and why."

165

"Yes!" Dinah practically shouted, realizing Mother Uroz understood her predicament.

"But," Mother Uroz said—with the mothers, there was always a caveat, "the specifics of procreation—trogs, betas, lytes, mothers—is something not even I can discuss freely, until all of you have had more time with me. To properly prepare you. Some of you might be ready now. Others might not be ready ever. We're striking a happy medium, and hoping that even with an accelerated learning curve, we're not exposing you all to too much, too soon. If we did that, we'd be destroying exactly what we're desiring to build in you. A proper education."

A little sigh of disappointment passed through all the lytes. Except for Dinah. Dinah felt a kernel of anger burning in her stomach. Once again, the mothers were being deliberately opaque. It wasn't fair to Dinah, or Shervet, or any of their new classmates. More than that, Dinah was beginning to suspect that it wasn't fair to the trogs either.

Occasionally, Dinah caught sight of her trog—Gebbel—while she was walking the plaza. Funny, she thought, that she'd come to regard him as hers. Almost always, Gebbel was part of a work crew, engaged in some aspect of plaza maintenance. Trimming the verge, or re-laying the pavers into a new configuration. He never looked up at her, whether Dinah was near or far. But she sensed that he was aware of her presence, and deliberately trying to not let it be known. The betas would notice, and make their displeasure felt with their pain flails.

There were other trogs with whom Dinah began to acquaint herself, too. Some of them were regulars inside the school, performing some aspect of building maintenance, or carrying equipment at the behest of an instructor. Most of the trogs were obviously old. But a few of them were young, and it was one of the young ones—who seemed to always be helping Mother Evlun—who showed up mysteriously in the school hallways one night.

Dinah only saw him, because she was out of her bed, trying to pace off her insomnia. She'd not slept well since departing the old school. Many nights, she lay in her bunk and stared up into the dark, unable to quiet her mind. Until literal exhaustion swept her off to oblivion. On this particular night, she'd decided to actively attack the problem, and slipped out of her bed with a mouse's care, so as not to disturb Shervet, who softly snored.

If trying to lay still wasn't doing her any good, Dinah was going to burn off her anxious energy. A stroll ought to do the trick. But lytes were forbidden in the plaza after dark. So the interior of the school—that section portioned off for quarters—was all she had to work with.

Dinah didn't get a close look at the young trog. She spied yellow light coming from the end of one of the many corridors—usually, at this hour, lit simply by the moon's pale energy; passing through windows in the walls—and peered around the corner just in time to see the trog being beckoned through an adult's apartment door.

Mother Evlun's to be precise. No beta in sight.

When the door closed, Dinah could not contain her curiosity. So she soft-footed her way toward the door, and waited at the archway for over a minute—looking as shadows moved around in the thin band of yellow light that projected beneath the edge of the door itself.

Then, the light went out. And as Dinah stood there, motionless and listening, the most unusual sounds began to come from inside. Muffled, of course—the doors here were as thick as they'd been at the old school. But the intensity of the sounds escalated, until a rhythmic thumping against furniture could be heard, along with skin slapping skin.

For a moment, Dinah almost screamed in alarm—because it sounded like Mother Evlun was being hurt.

Dinah kept quiet, though, when Evlun's voice distinctly cried out the words "More!" and "Yes!" in repetitive, breathless, interpolated succession.

These were not the sounds of harm being done. In fact, as Dinah listened intently—her head practically pressed to the door proper—she realized that what she was hearing was something similar to the touch. But much more energetic and feral than anything Dinah had ever done with Shervet. It seemed as if Mother Evlun and the young trog might shake the apartment apart. Then both Mother Evlun and the Trog engaged in a drawn out, mutual groan—that seemed to last for many seconds—and silence returned.

Eventually, light returned beneath the door. Dinah's heart leapt into her throat, and she scurried back down the corridor the way she'd come, until she was hidden again behind the corner. She watched from a safe distance as the door opened, and the young trog reappeared—adjusting and buttoning his dirty coveralls. Mother Evlun's head appeared, as did her shoulders, which were bare. She and the trog both looked to the left, and then to the right, waiting and listening. Then came the most astonishing thing of all. Mother Evlun pushed her head forward and pressed her mouth to the trog's mouth. He pushed back. And for several seconds, the two of them seemed to be rubbing faces. Then contact was broken quickly, Mother Evlun shut the door, and the young trog disappeared in the opposite direction—seemingly navigating in the dark with the swiftness of a cat.

Dinah slipped back into her room, and laid down on her bed. Her heart was beating heavily in her chest. What had she just witnessed? Everything about it seemed obscene. No, worse than obscene. It was an abomination. And yet, the remembered sounds of

Mother Evlun exclaiming "Yes!" and "More!" could not be wiped from Dinah's mind. Those had been the sounds of joy, uttered with uncaring abandon. Is that what it would be like, to do the touch with Gebbel?

Dinah spent the rest of the night wondering.

Weeks passed into months. The shock of discovering the dead trog, had faded. But Dinah's curiosity about live trogs, was greater than ever before. Twice more, Dinah observed the same young trog visiting Mother Evlun's apartment in the middle of the night. Each time, Dinah told Shervet all about it—the following morning—but Shervet didn't seem to care.

"Bad dream," Shervet said, in annoyance. "Why let it bother you?"

At the behest of Shervet, Dinah did not persist in taking late night walks. If Dinah got into serious trouble, it was said that a second relocation would be in order—this time, not to a school for lytes who were precocious, but to a penal farm for lytes who were truly mischievous. Those lytes would be denied motherhood, as well as a companion. They would become short-lived workers like the trogs themselves. Kept away from the rest of the country, in a kind of exile for women who did not or would not behave. Something Shervet feared greatly, because she knew that she and Dinah were treated as an informal unit. If Dinah were to be punished, it was likely Shervet would pay the price too—as an accessory.

Occasionally, Dinah and Shervet would indulge in the touch. Or rather, Shervet would visit Dinah's bed, and initiate—with Dinah going along to get along.

But there was an unsatisfying quality to the act, now. Something was most definitely missing, though Dinah couldn't put her finger on what it was. Which simply frustrated Shervet, who seemed to have no such problem enjoying the moment. Until it became clear that Dinah could not reciprocate.

A distance grew between them, which words alone could not close. No matter how much Dinah apologized.

Then one day, after Shervet had demurred to attend class—on account of not feeling well—Dinah returned to their room, to discover that Shervet and all of her things were gone. Even the small chest kept under Shervet's bunk.

When Dinah rushed to tell Mother Uroz, the older woman simply wrapped an arm around Dinah and guided Dinah into Uroz's learning chamber, at the back of the now-empty classroom. Uroz slowly shut the learning chamber's door, and then sat down at her large instructor's desk. An aquarium filled with brightly-colored fish, sat at one corner of the surface, while ancient-looking bound-paper books were arranged between bookends on the opposite corner.

Dinah's chair—across from Mother Uroz—felt uncomfortable, despite padding.

"I don't understand," Dinah said, sniffling at a piece of tissue which Mother Uroz had offered.

"I could see it coming," Mother Uroz said. "Even before your arrival here. We don't often get paired lytes, but when we do, it almost never lasts. Sooner or later, one of the two tires of the relationship, and requests to be separated. The pain will be something you have to deal with in your own time, and in your own way. I would tell you not to take it personally, but that's impossible. I know for a fact."

"How?" Dinah asked.

"Within a year of coming here, when I myself was a lyte, Mother Cedra—then Lyte Cedra—moved out of our room. And she didn't even tell me why. I just... came back to the room, and she was gone.

Moved to a new class with a new instructor, too. We seldom talked after that. I seldom talk to her, even now. It's just something I've learned to live with. You will too."

Dinah drew her knees up to her chin, and hugged them tight.

"It hurts," she said. "Everything hurts."

"And it will keep hurting," Mother Uroz said. "Even many, many years from now. You just... learn to live and be happy, despite the hurt."

"But it's not just about Shervet," Dinah said hotly, staring across the desk with watery eyes.

"I know," Mother Uroz said.

"How?!" Dinah barked, surprised at her temerity in addressing a mother without using the expected manners and deference. But given the rawness of her heart, Dinah did not, in that moment, particularly care about being well-behaved. She wanted answers.

Mother Uroz steepled her fingers. "So much like I was," she said softly, as if to no one in particular.

The older woman reached a hand under her desk, and there was a slight snapping sound—as if a switch had been thrown. The bubbles in the aquarium suddenly grew in number, until their noise was practically an irritant. There was something else, too. A kind of low, electronic pitch. Just loud enough to be detectable, but underlying the frenetic burbling of the aquarium.

"A necessary distraction," Mother Uroz said. "To mask our conversation. Because what I am about to tell you, cannot leave this room. There are more ears here, than ours. Will you swear to me now, on your own life, that what is divulged between us, stays between us?"

"I swear it," Dinah said.

"Do you promise it by your very blood?"

"By my blood, I swear it!" Dinah said, leaping out of her chair and extending her hands across the table.

Mother Uroz took them—the older woman's grip reassuringly strong—and then she released Dinah's fingers, and told the lyte to sit back down. And listen carefully.

"We travel the same path, you and I," Mother Uroz said. "Many of the questions that now crowd inside your skull, once crowded inside mine as well. I was not an easy student for the senior mothers to deal with. It seemed like I was always half a step from exile. But I managed to stay just this side of their expectations. Eventually they sent me here, and here is where I learned the truth."

Dinah had forgotten all about the tissue in her hand. She barely breathed, as Mother Uroz continued to speak.

"There was a time, long ago, when trogs and lytes lived amongst each other. Before the war which ended all wars. Before the companion, and our longevity as mothers. The trogs were in charge of the world, then. Yes, I see the shock in your eyes. It's historical fact, nonetheless. Hundreds of countries across the Earth, were all run by trogs—with very few exceptions. They could never stop fighting with each other. They still can't keep from fighting. That's why we created the betas. To keep order and discipline. But there were no betas then, nor mothers. We lived with the trogs, and they lived with us. We did the touch—trogs and lytes with each other—and made billions of babies."

"Shervet was right," Dinah said, almost gasping.

"Oh, you both more or less figured it out. All you needed was confirmation. Yes, to this day, we still need the trogs—to make lytes. And they need us to make trogs. When a mother gives birth—her one and only child—the female babies are put into the communal nurseries, to become lytes. The male babies are turned over to the betas, who make them into trogs. Which are kept separate, so that

172

they can be properly harnessed and controlled—and their violence can never again rule the world."

Dinah's face expressed her horror at what she'd been told.

Mother Uroz quickly continued.

"Or at least, that's the logic our society has relied upon since the wall was erected many long years ago. It's the fable we tell ourselves, to justify maintaining the status quo."

"But how can we call ourselves superior?" Dinah demanded. "We treat them as animals, but trogs are... they are people too!"

"Not all of us agree with the law," Mother Uroz said. "Which is why I do the work that I do. So as to identify and shepherd lytes who will bring sorrow to themselves, by knowing and asking too much—then expecting things to change."

"But they should change!" Dinah said emphatically. "I mean, Mother Evlun has been doing the touch with a trog, right under your noses! A law isn't a law, if it's conveniently broken by people who should know better!"

"Mother Evlun? Really? I didn't know that."

"I've heard them several times."

"You've been busy paying attention to other womens' personal business. If I were one of the other instructors, I'd have you punished for it. But I won't. What got you curious about Mother Evlun, anyway?"

"Because nobody tells lytes anything. You give us half-truths, and expect us to wait for the rest of the story—and you act like we're just supposed to accept this."

"That's because most lytes do. Most. Which again, brings us to this conversation in this room. You're right. A law isn't a law, if it's broken without consequence. I can't expect you to understand yet, because you're not a mother. When you're of age, one of the secrets that is finally shared with you, is that doing the touch with trogs is not only allowed, it's expected."

Dinah's mouth hung half-open.

"How else do you think the egg is fertilized," Mother Uroz said. "By magic? With another egg from another mother? No. The trogs complete the procreation puzzle. We provide the eggs, but the trogs provide the sperm. You are offered a choice: artificial insemination, or direct mating with a trog. Some women try the latter, don't like it, and resort to the former, until pregnant. Other women try the latter, like it, and become pregnant in the ancient way. And out of those women, a few cannot let it go. They enjoy it too much. So that, long after the birth is over, and long after gaining a companion, these women yearn again for the experience. Enough to risk violating the law. So they make arrangements. Yes, it's against the code of our country, but are we going to throw every mother—who secretly has a trog on the side—into exile? No. It's a tolerated violation. We don't openly talk about it."

"Even when something goes wrong?" Dinah said.

"Like what?"

"Like when a mother becomes pregnant for the second time."

Mother Uroz tapped the metal disc below and behind her ear.

"The companion sees to it that no mother, so quipped, need ever worry about becoming pregnant again."

"But what about when a life is in peril?"

Mother Uroz opened her mouth to say something, then seemed to catch Dinah's drift, and frowned for several seconds—before continuing.

"I don't know the specific reason why you found a dead trog outside the wall. But I can guess. Liaisons with trogs are supposed to be short-lived, like the trogs themselves. I am wagering whichever mother was partaking of the trog who jumped to his death, she'd let it go on too long. Allowed herself to become attached. Or, worse yet, allowed the trog to become attached. When she tried to break it off, the trog despaired. So he ended his life."

"I can't imagine anyone—trog or no—choosing suicide, simply because he's losing the touch with some mother," Dinah said. "But I can imagine choosing suicide, if the trog has fallen in love; and gets hurt."

"A trog can feel in such a sophisticated way?" Mother Uroz said, raising an eyebrow.

"You tell me!" Dinah said loudly. "You have all the answers!"

Suddenly, Dinah began to weep again. But this time, it wasn't just sniffling. It was a hard, unrelenting ache in her stomach, that caused her to lean forward and wail openly. For Shervet. And, in a sense, for Gebbel too. Because it was Gebbel—the picture in her mind, of his lovely face, of imagining his hands on her skin, his lips on her lips— which had distracted Dinah enough to ultimately drive Shervet away. One relationship, carelessly shattered. Another relationship, unfortunately impossible.

In the space of a single year, the whole world had stopped making sense.

Mother Uroz waited patiently. When Dinah collected herself— more tissue being offered from Uroz's hand—the older woman reached for one of the books on the corner of her desk. She opened it, and removed a piece of paper. She slid it across her desk, and Dinah took it.

There were words arranged on the single page. Lyrics.

"You know all the hymns officially sung in school," Mother Uroz said. "But this is one of the forbidden hymns."

"Forbidden? Why?"

"This hymn tells of the time before the wall. Before trogs, and lytes, and betas. When there were simply boys and girls, and women and men. The hymn hints at a legend—about another nation, which survived the war, very far away from our own. Where men and women live and work together still. As equals. I've been on expeditions which were sent to find this country. We were never successful. But some of us still believe it exists. Maybe you will be the one to find it?"

Dinah stared into the fish tank, watching the colorful creatures dart to and fro—disturbed by the increased turbulence from the bubbles.

"Finding such a place," Dinah said, after a long pause, "would not change anything inside the wall."

"Maybe, maybe not. But we have to hope. Meanwhile, you must learn to have two lives. There is the life that you live, for the outer world. Where you show the other mothers that you are a good, proper member of our society. Then there is the life you live for you. That you share only with similar minds. There are not many of us, but we do exist. And we work together to prepare for a time when there may be a real opportunity for change. Without it needing to be a war."

"You expect me to be happy living and speaking a lie?"

"No," Mother Uroz said, matter-of-fact. "But none of this is about your happiness, Lyte Dinah. It's about your survival—preparing you for the reality of the universe in which you live. I could just let you go, and see you eaten alive in exile. Or I can offer you the outstretched hand of camaraderie. It's not an easy way, this thing I am offering you. But it is a way. And in time, you will help others to also find the way. Perhaps, beyond anything either one of us can now expect. Are you willing to walk that road?"

Dinah held the piece of paper in her hand, and silently read the words to herself. As Mother Uroz had promised, the hymn spoke of

176

a far-away land, where males and females built a new nation—together. A place where some of the learning and artifacts of the time before the war, had been preserved. Of a life utterly unlike the one Dinah knew inside the wall.

Her hand began to tremble. Could it be? Was there such a country? She imagined walking down a boulevard, with Gebbel at her side—no need for ducking and fearing any armed betas. Dinah pictured Gebbel with a smile on his face. Perhaps, even a child at his feet? No, more than one. Several children. Theirs. Made with the touch.

"Show me," Dinah said finally, and reverently placed the paper back onto the desk. "Show me everything, Mother Uroz. I am ready to learn."

The older woman smiled broadly—the first time Dinah had ever seen such an expression on her instructor's face—and clapped her hands together with satisfaction.

By His Cockle Hat and Staff

By

John C. Wright

***What if the life we really want does not come from the
changes we think we want?***

> *"And how should I know your true-love*
> *From many another one?"*
> *O, by his cockle hat, and staff,*
> *And by his sandal shoon."*
>
> *"O lady, he is dead and gone!*
> *Lady, he's dead and gone!*
> *And at his head a green grass turf,*
> *And at his heels a stone."*

The Friar of Orders Gray—Thomas Percy (1729–1811)

-1-

There are much easier ways than killing yourself.

We have all heard the endless argument about the best method
of insertion, and I know the advantages of taking over your self's
life in the new world. You have his clothing and his money, for one
thing, not to mention opposable thumbs, and you can start to bend
history back into the right direction, the way things should have
gone had Hell never broken the world, nor Mesmer.

But consider the disadvantages.

-2-

I am ashamed to admit that, at first, the idea that I was a
sleepwalker amused me. It was the kind of thing one reads in

romances by Wells or Wiene, but never sees in life. In our peaceful and unexciting world, the idea of being a somnambulist seemed so... exotic.

The first time was when I woke up at midnight, roused by the barking of a dog right outside my dressing room window, to find myself on my feet, facing the full-length looking glass. I was barefoot, but otherwise completely dressed in trousers, waistcoat, jacket and tie. But the tie had been tied improperly. A polite knock came at the door.

"Come!"

"Just me, sir. Was there anything you needed, sir?"

It was my valet, Roberts, blinking and yawning.

"Why are you awake at this ghastly hour?" for the church steeple of Saint Anne's was ringing midnight, coming across the waters of Lake Quinsigamond. "Good God! Why am I?"

"That, I cannot say, sir. I heard you moving about."

"Moving?"

"In the wine cellar, up the back stair, down the servant's hall, front hall, kitchen, pantry. You do know that the boards creak more loudly when you tiptoe? If you don't mind my saying, sir."

"Why was I tiptoeing? It's my house!" This house had stood here in Regatta Point Park since my grandfather fled to America with all his wealth, changing his name from *von Wardszawaschwig-Glücksburg* to *Ward* and left all the dynastic insanity and warfare of Europe far behind. There have been three wars in Europe since then, in 1912, in 1939, and again in 1985 when the last Czar fell and the Kaiser of Greater Germany claimed all the Russian lands as his; but American was involved in none of them.

"You woke Mrs. Ferris, too, but she, kind soul, will say naught. She heard the drawers opening and shutting in the library. Your desk drawers. And then the sound of rattling the roll top, as if you'd forgotten where you'd put the key. I thought I would ask?"

"Well, if you find an answer, Roberts, by damn, tell me. I was asleep in bed. I was dreaming about a world where I lived in a grey box that shouted at me all the time—" It had sounded a lot more sensible when I was asleep.

That was not the last episode of sleepwalking, nor the worst.

The worst was when I was absent for two days in March. The servants reported that I rose as normal, spoke as normal, but instead of going to the Tool and Die, told Roberts that I was visiting relatives, summoned a hansom, and vanished. I woke up, remembering none of this and thinking it was March 27th on the 30th.

The hansom was an automatic, and, since this is not Germany, the company keeps no trip record in the autodriver.

The last episode—that I recall—was when I woke, this time properly dressed, at the Grafton train station, with a ticket to Rhode Island in my hand. The station was an echoing and empty cathedral around me, and I felt like a ghost. Evidently I was waiting to catch the midnight train.

So, it was no longer exotic or quaint to be afflicted, but frightening.

The shop foreman had everything well in hand, and practically ran the place anyway, so I awarded myself a permanent vacation until I found a cure.

The family doctor directed me to a specialist, who recommended a program of dieting and healthy exercise. And, when nothing changed, I went to other specialists.

One recommended I avoid eating meals in the evenings, or anything that might cause stress. The next had me lie on a couch and reminiscence about any hidden feelings of hate or guilt about

181

my father. The next suggested that my sleep should be interrupted one hour before and again one hour after midnight, which was a strain on Roberts and on me, since neither of us got an uninterrupted night's rest.

The next and last was a doctor named Fish. He had me put a bell on my bedroom door, and proscribed trazodone hydrochloride. He said, "I have a patient down in Coventry, lovely girl, with the same problem. Sleepwalking. Seems she was in a coma for six months, after half-drowning in a boating accident, and woke up of a sudden for no reason I could find. Now she is normal, except for these fugue states."

One day in April, I found myself suddenly awake wandering the streets of Coventry, over an hour away by train or motor, with a black bag in my hand.

My wristwatch, which I was wearing on the wrong wrist, said it was two in the morning. I opened the bag. There was a little stoppered bottle of brown glass, a rag, a screwdriver, pliers, a crowbar, several yards of rope, a roll of duct tape. There was also, oddly enough, a number of magnets, including an electromagnet shaped like a flashlight whose current could be adjusted.

Obviously the doctor's mention of a similar case provoked something odd in my subconscious mind. I thought he was more dangerous than the disease.

I lost my specialist and hired a detective. I found a man named Braun to watch my movements and follow me. He was a big, buff fellow in a loud checkered green coat and a yellow hat with a frightening mass of red side-whiskers, but he said I would not see him shadowing me. He had a chubby and cheerful face, and the cold, dead eyes of a killer.

Braun also talked to shopkeepers and confirmed that I had bought the contents of the bag with my own money. The brown bottle came from a shop that catered to butterfly collectors. It was chloroform.

I only had two more episodes after that: the first was when Roberts stopped me from calling a hansom at one in the morning. By then, I was really curious as to where I was going, so I asked him, if it happened again, to let me on my way, trusting Braun to follow. The second episode was when I awoke on the night-train to Coventry.

He said I would not spot him, but I did. Braun was seated in the next car, dressed very nondescriptly. Braun was holding up a newspaper to hide his face, just like something out of the motion pictures, but now shorn of his noticeable red whiskers, which apparently had been fake to begin with. There was no sign of his green suit or yellow hat.

I sat down in the seat opposite, and he folded the newspaper. Without a word, he took a photograph from his breast pocket and handed it to me.

For a moment, I could not breathe. It was a picture of the most beautiful girl I'd ever seen. In the photograph, she was wearing a simple white dress, standing by a tall, half-open door, and smiling. There was a bow in her hair, large enough that the fabric could be seen on either side of her ears. She had an oval face, large eyes, and a mass of dark hair worn simply. The doorposts were marble carved to look like tree trunks twined with ivy leaves: a somewhat eccentric style.

"Who is she?" I spoke loudly enough for Braun to hear me over the sound of the train wheels clattering, but not enough to wake any passengers napping in a nearby seat.

"I was going to ask you the same thing," he said. "Seems you hired a dick named Dooley to find her. This was on March 27th. I know old Dooley. Sure, there aren't that many Pinkertons in the

Yellow Pages. When I found out we had the same client, I met him after hours to swap drinks and swap gab."

"Can this Dooley give me her name and address? I have to see her!" I blurted this out before looking from the photo to his face, which had a look of scorn and skepticism on it.

"Her name is Mary Ward, same last name as yours, but Jane's *Families of New England*, or Black's *Who's Who* does not show any connection with you, nor do any courthouse records. She lives with her father, Lester, and younger sister, Vivian, at Ivy House, Coventry. It was built by Artemas Ward. That is, General Ward, later, Senator Ward."

"Not our branch of the family," I said. "And this Dooley says that I—"

"That you hired him. You paid him by barter, using your mother's diamond earrings, as if you had forgotten how to write a check on the checkbook that he saw in your pocket. He also says that, two weeks ago, in a stolen tuxedo, you tried a little bit of gatecrashing to break into Vivian Ward's debutante ball in Boston, being held in the Ritz-Carlton, no less. That's when Dooley washed his hands of you. He thinks you are up to something, some elaborate scam or scheme—"

"I am a sleepwalker," I said. "I have been in what the doctor calls a fugue state, and afterward I don't remember—"

"Su-ure. If that is the story you are going to tell the coppers when you get caught, good luck to you! As an alibi, on the other hand, it stinks. You put me on the witness stand, and I tell the jury I think you are faking the whole time."

"You have to believe me!"

The look of skepticism darkened and settled on his face, as if moving in for permanent residence. "It took me less than two hours at the public library to bone up on sleepwalking: it lasts a few

184

minutes, and people do not get dressed, look up names in the phone book, take a cab across town, and have a forty-five minute meeting with a private detective. You can pay me what you owe, including the price of this train ticket, and then we are quits."

Yes, I did go see Dooley the next day. He did not want to see me at first, but I offered him one hundred dollars per hour just to talk to me. Dooley was an older man, bald and wrinkled, quiet and sedate in his motions. I mean he made no more noise than a cat walking over the floorboards of his clean but tiny little office. I could well believe him expert at his job: his face was one I have already forgotten.

Dooley added some details to Braun's account. He showed me my signature on his work memorandum, except....

"That is not my signature."

"Whose might it be, now, that being the case, sir?" Said he with a mild lift of one eyebrow, and a mild half-smile.

"Leonardo's," I muttered.

When I was young, the schoolteacher forced me to do all my writing with my right hand. But I heard that Leonardo Da Vinci kept a diary with his left hand, written in mirror writing, backward, so for a long time I kept a left-hand diary, like him, and learned to sign my name that way. The left-handed signature matched.

Dooley also said that my voice had been strange. I spoke in a higher pitched tone, as if I were trying to sound like a child, or a girl, and had odd ticks or twitches when it came to my words.

"Well," said Dooley, "F'rinstance, when you did not shake hands, and you did not stand up when Miss Floret, my secretary, came in, and you said *'I think every person is entitled to his or her own opinion, to suit him- or her-self'*—sounds a bit odd on the ear, don't it? But I don't think it is enough to make out an insanity plea, or whatever business you are trying to pull off."

185

And no other private detective after that would take the case: as Braun had said, they swapped drinks and gossip, and had been told to steer clear of me.

So I lost my detective and hired a guru. That is surely a sign of some sort of mental degradation. I began to wonder what sort of horrible crime I was no doubt about to commit.

His name was Ashwathama. He was thin as a rail and brown as a nut, but he had the kindest eyes I have ever looked into.

I would sit on the porch on a straw mat, going through the routine of breathing, of meditation, of auto-hypnosis. The guru made me wear a magnet on my forehead. Said it would balance my internal energy flows or something. I mounted it on my mother's tiara, since that was the only way I could get it to sit right above my eyes in the spot where he wanted.

Ashwathama said to me in his calm, singsong voice, "You might think this is some ancient Eastern art of my people. Put that thought away from your head! The power of magnets to influence the mind and body is well attested by modern physicians, that is, those who are willing to look beyond what they know for a deeper truth. Maximillian Hell was a Jesuit from Vienna who investigated the properties of energy disturbances that can be magnetically corrected. Anton Mesmer perfected the art. He called it animal magnetism. It can be used to plant suggestions in the mind, but that is not its true purpose. It opens the mind, silences the noisiness of conscious thought, allows you to hear the whispers."

"Whispers from where?"

Ashwathama said, "There are worlds beyond this world, and souls who move through them. You will find your answers within. The one who is haunting you—is you!"

And he touched me lightly on the chest, just above my heart.

I became diligent in my practice of meditation and auto-hypnosis. I was searching for a buried memory or a hidden split personality or a dream—I don't know what damned thing I was searching for.

I did it day and night, six days a week. By day, I would stare at the lake water. It was a long and narrow lake, and I could see the houses and trees on the far side. I would watch sailboats or canoes float by. There was a big red Irish Setter that would sit beneath the trees, hidden by the bushes, to one side of the broad back lawn leading to the lakeside. He came every day just at the same time I did: I thought of him as a friend and wondered who owned him. I suppose I would not have noticed him in this distance were it not for the meditation, and the clarity of mind it brought.

At night I did my exercises and stared at the sky or its reflection. My eyes were getting more sensitive. The stars seemed so bright to my eyesight it was astonishing. I could see their colors and pick out individual stars in the band of the Milky Way.

On the first day of May, without moving or closing my eyes, I had a dream.

-3-

They are going to kill the girl I love, the girl I have lived with, and with whom I have shared my life for three years. I still remember the day when we exchanged dormitory keys. I knelt and handed her my key in a little square velvet box, just like some romantic cis-male from the bad old days, the time of darkness, proffering a ring to his or her mate-for-life, back when life-partnership was still allowed.

You know, at times I wonder how dark those times of darkness were.

It was Rob who told me, the clerk from the Sharing, Caring and Giving Department. His name had originally been Roberts, but now was Property-is-Robbery. He had been my downie during Gender

187

Clarification in education camp, just enough to fulfill our non-hetero requirement, but he liked girls as much as I did, and we were the only two boys in camp not proscribed to take Ritalin or soma, so he was the only guy I could have an intelligent conversation with. I know that sounds totally smart-ist, but there it is.

He slid into the seat opposite mine in the cafeteria, holding his gray plastic tray of gray health gruel. "Like a cabbage juice?" he said, passing the gray canister to me. I said no, but he shoved it into my hand anyway, and reached over and popped top open, so that the loud, grinning, blaring music of the health-and-nonviolent-nutrition announcement came ringing from the little can, and enthused and cheery voices of young people reciting various government warnings and advice in gushingly jolly words, carefully pitched so that it was not clear if the speaker were male, female, cismale, shemale, transmale, ubermale, undermale, othermale, antimale, nomale, everymale, or one of the other approved gender selections.

I noticed that the song was the same as the recording on the carrot juice cans, and no one bothered to change the word from *carrot* to *cabbage*.

Beneath the blanket of the noise, he whispered, "Dice, they're going to mum your *Ho*."

Mum was slang for mummify, that is, deprive her of fluids until she was dry as a mummy and died of thirst. *Ho* was slang for any female or he-male of the feminine gender role, a downie rather than topper.

"*Mary!* It cannot be!" Unthinkingly, I used our little private love-name we shared. That was the name on her birth certificate, before the Naming Inequality and Community Equality Act. Names that came from particular ethnic or self-identification groups were thought to be exclusionary and discriminatory, and so Mary was assigned the name Crusading-for-Womens-Equality, or Lity for short. Mine was Workmans-Paradise, or just Dice.

I lowered my voice and lowered my head toward him, "How do you know?"

"Share, Care and Give tracks all the supplies. The Death Panel kills someone, you can see it on the invoice lists, what equipment gets checked out. Name on the tag was her doctor's name, Nonagression-something-or-other."

I felt as if my skull were a balloon ready to burst under a terrible internal pressure. The sensation that everything was unreal, a nightmare, was choking. Lity is an Agent of Otherwhere, like me, a Great Dreamer. We were in the Revision corps. She and I were immune from the population cull, and the organlegger lottery.

Someone walked by carrying a tray. Since having private conversations is exclusionary, I had to shove my face into Rob's face and kiss him, so it looked like we were engaging in a public display of affection, as we have a right to do.

He pulled away, a look of impatience on his face. I suspect he is not thrilled by non-bio-binary stuff, but I do not judge. That would be biologist.

I said, "There must be some mistake. I would have been informed! I am her husb—I mean, I am her partner. The US Constitution says we have rights! That amendment that they passed last year, it says we have rights! All of them!"

The UN permitted the United States to pass an amendment just last year, despite the opposition of the wreckers and saboteurs, which provided that everyone, male and female, etc., man and animal, had each and all and every right both legally and morally to everything and anything. It was called the Perfect Amendment, because there was no more need to pass any more Amendments, or even laws.

Everyone had all the rights they could imagine. Special agents, called Notification of Amnesty and Noncompliance officers, but

189

which everyone called Nannies, just made an on-the-spot decision based on the circumstances without being tied down by precedent, or written law. It was amazing to me that such a simple solution to the complex problem of how to govern people had never been tried before.

Oddly enough, the cheerful tones of the singing can of cabbage juice is what gave me the heart I needed to fight this thing. The people all cared for each other: that was our law! Everyone voted, everyone made all the laws, everyone had all the rights! Lity was immune from the normal rationing of medical care. Ours was a wonderful and progressive country, and any society that cared enough to tell me the calorie count and the salt content and the allergy sensitivity number of a can of juice, to force every can to tell everyone who opened it exactly how much and how fast he should drink it—that society would not allow such cruelty to occur.

I was able to bribe a guy on the waiting list with my recreational pharmacy chit, because I didn't use the stuff (not that I judge anyone who does! That would be druggist!), so it was only three weeks later that I got the chance to see my supervisor, Do-Your-Best. He is an older man, (not that I am ageist or mannist) who walks without making noise. He is gray and balding (but I am not hirsuteist or colorist).

He sat at his gray desk in his cubicular gray room, which was much larger than mine. He even had a window view, looking out onto the gray concrete wall across the alleyway.

He said, "There is no evidence she is still alive. If there is no parallel version of her in the target line, she could never have made the insertion in the first place. And the host always rejects the influence of the possessor after a month or two: the brain cannot hold two active minds. Logically, it is not possible that her host both exists and has no brain!"

190

I said, "But there are cases where the possessor was inserted into a host who was not a pure parallel! It happened when there are twins in the target line! There was that case of Rudolf Rassendyll, where our agent landed not in his own body, but the body of his cousin. And I have heard that the Tibetans can insert into the bodies of people unrelated to them! That fellow we sent to Alcatraz, Ashwathama, he said he could possess the body of an ape, or—"

"Cases of twin possession are very rare, and that guru—well, it would be an act of cultural exploitation to discuss the results of Tibetan research. As for agent Crusading-for-Womens-Equality, her glands and nervous system may enable some other candidate to achieve the insertion across the paracontinuum. We cannot be selfish when others are in need!"

I said, "Her contract with the recruiting office says she is safe from organ donation if she goes comatose in the line of duty."

Do-Your-Best fitted his fingertips together. "Ah, that is as that may be. Certainly that is what the *words* on the contract say." He gave me a quirky half-grin, tilting his head forward and gazing at me archly as if peering over the upper rims of imaginary eyeglasses. It was the expression of a man who shares an unspoken joke.

I said, "I—of course that is what the words say—she and I are in the corps. We go to other parallel worlds for you. Our bodies are empty while we are gone, and need life support. You cannot just kill her."

Do-Your-Best's face kind of closed up. He looked disappointed, as if I were supposed to catch on to the unspoken idea without imposing on him the task of speaking it. "The attorneys have gone over her contract. It appears that there are certain emanations from a penumbra of rights to which she is entitled, including the right to die with dignity. And the panel, of course, has the right to help her make that hard decision in the fashion that is best for everyone. The contract is a fluid and living document, subject to change as circumstances require. She cannot hide behind that flimsy bit of paper!"

"But—but—she has a right to life!"

He gave me look of withering contempt. "That is the way antiabortionist fanatics talk! They hate the health of women! Do you hate the health of women? Euthanasia is a health issue!"

I said, "We project our mind into parallel worlds for you! For the cause!"

He said, "And if the cause requires her self-sacrifice, the corps will accept it with gratitude."

If I could not appeal to his loyalty, perhaps I could appeal to his self-interest. I made my voice calm and even. "You know how rare the Hell and Mesmer trait is, and how many candidates, even if they do test positive, wash out of basic training! Rarer still is to find a stickler, someone who can maintain permanent possession, overcome the thoughts of their host mind without any cross cultural contamination!"

He shook his head wearily. "There are only a finite number of beds in the hospital ward set aside for the Revision Corps. You know we are gearing up for a major effort, and pulling our agents out of other timelines for this one."

Of course I knew. The Central Committee had been discussing it for over a year: We were preparing a thousand volunteers for an engagement in a world where women never got the vote.

The problem was that the timeline faded into and out of availability unexpectedly. And if we cannot find the deviation point, the crux event where their line split off from the homeline of true history, we could not proceed.

"I know about the Big Push."

"It will be our most popular intervention yet! It will silence all talk of cutting our budget! No one, not even the bitterest enemies of goodthink, will dare defend a world without female suffrage! We will be using every agent, just as soon as the crux point is identified, and we can all make a safe mass insertion. So we will be needing all the beds, and there is no room for someone we cannot make room for."

I could not believe what I was hearing. "But then you also need her! She is a trained agent! She was on a mission when she went missing."

I did not tell him that I knew which world it was: Earth Fourteen. It was the one where American built a city on the moon, and was using it to build rockets for manned interplanetary exploration. Her mission had been to introduce into their press and popular entertainment the Social Justice Narrative, using the methods of Critical Theory as developed by the Frankfurt School. She was to preach and teach that the space program was immoral, on the grounds that its funds ought to be spent on earth, on the poor and downtrodden. The hope and pioneer spirit something like a successful space program inspired spelled the death to all our social justice narratives. Once men were proud and confident, able to accomplish something, they developed a false consciousness, and no longer realized how oppressed they were, and no longer were willing to hate and retaliate against the persons identified to them as oppressors.

I mean persons, of course, not men. Animals, too. I do not believe humans are special. I am not specialist.

He said, "Whether she was on a mission is not information you are cleared to know! But if she were on a mission, then why did she fail to return, and wake? If she had no doppelganger in the parallel continuum, she could not have inserted in the first place. If she had a doppelganger, even sticklers cannot remain in continuous possession, even with the willing cooperation of the host, for over a month, because the mutual brain activity creates the very same magnetic disturbances in the nervous system Hell and Mesmer so carefully examined, and which forms the basis of Mesmeromagnetic Paracontinuum Ectoprojection. But the other possibility is that the host died while she was in possession. So she is truly dead, and there is no need to keep the body alive. It would be a violation of her right to die."

So much for my supervisor. I got a different story out of Rob when I saw him next.

Rob told me in a whisper that technicians examined her brainscans very carefully before they flatlined. The signature was not consistent with the magnetic contour needed to insert herself into the line where she was assigned, Earth Fourteen. There was no sign of her. Her double on that world had been contacted by another agent, and she never returned the recognition countersign. It was apparently the native born host, not a sleepwalker.

Equality must have substituted another magnetic signature during her launch meditation, or remembered an old one.

He said, "You are not going to get anywhere going through the channels. Who has the resources to look for someone who abandons her or his post?"

My last recourse was a trump card that overrode all normal red tape: I would go to the Amnesty Officer. The one for my district had an even longer waiting list than my supervisor had, but I was able to threaten someone very high up in the queue by hinting I had overheard a sexually aggressive joke. He, of course, had probably never made a joke in his life, but he did not need the grief, and so we swapped places, and I got his interview slot.

The interview went badly. The Nanny was an old gray-haired lady whose face was a wrinkled sagging sack of bitterness and despair, and whose eyes were dead. If I had touched those eyes with my finger, they would have been hard and dry, like touching two pallid pebbles.

We met at her dormitory cube, which was larger than mine. All four gray walls were tuned to the national public channel, and so were speaking in soft, soothing, cultured tones about the need to reduce the Caucasian population to zero, so as to prevent strain and overcrowding on public resources, as more undocumented pre-citizens from the Middle East and China were arriving. The volume was very loud, and the speaking voices were interrupted periodically by rousing rock opera music, blaring with trumpets, screaming guitars, and a pre-teen girl shrieking four-letter-words at the top of her little lungs. I think it was the new, all-inclusive non-nationalistic National anthem that the government was focus-group testing in this broadcast area, but I am not sure. Microphones and speakers are mixed in with every batch of concrete from which everything is made, dorms and workhouses and walls and roads, but officers of her rank should have been able to turn the volume down. More likely she was half-deaf and had turned it up.

It made the conversation so difficult, I am not sure the Nanny heard me at all.

She said sternly, her wrinkled jowls wobbling, "You should be ashamed! There is no place in civilized society for someone who is named Crusading-for-Womens-Equality. That excludes and insults transsexuals and quasisexuals. One does not need to have a vagina to be to a woman! Not to mention her name is Islamophobic. What kind of horrible, sick person is named *Crusading*? Are you insane?"

I protested. "But—we were assigned those names! We go to jail if we don't use them!"

Maybe my voice was loud, but then again, the six-year-old girl screaming cusswords from the gray walls was also very loud.

"You can petition to have your name changed! It only takes a few years and the legal fees are quite reasonable if you take out a guaranteed loan. But anyone named Workmans-Paradise could not understand anything. I am amazed you dare to show your face in public, with a sexist and faithist name like that! *Paradise!* Pah! Now get out of here!"

I stood up, slowly. "But—there is something else."

"Spit it out, you snot-brained limp-mugged retard!"

"I want to have the body. If they kill her. So I can bury her. May I—if I might be allowed—"

She pushed a button in his desk, and told her sergeant to come escort me out. She did not look at me, but spoke to the thug who appeared in the doorway. He was rough and red-whiskered gorilla of a man, round-faced, but with deadly coldness in his eyes. "Kick this snotlicking filth out, and don't be gentle about it. We are going to grind his cis-female bitch up for dogfood, and he, knowing how hard it is to get everyone to recycle, and knowing how important animal rights are, wanted to bury the body in some sick, faithist ritual in the ground, contaminating the groundwater!"

The sergeant drew his truncheon. And, no, he was not gentle about it.

I was clever. Instead of submitting to the beating as we are taught in education camp, I fought back. Once, one of my slaps actually caught him on the cheek. I bet that stung! But my plan was that if he did sufficient damage to me, I might be able to get into the hospital through the shorter list for the military officer emergency room, rather than the longer civilian list.

Well, it sort of worked and sort of did not. I sat in my gray little cube of a room, with the walls all lecturing me on how to be a better person, eat right, be a good citizen, and avoid wrongheaded thoughts, for several days. And the beating had done no permanent harm, broken no bones.

196

In fact, I was perfectly fine by the time I was invited to the hospital. I walked there, past all the motionless and empty cars on the road, motorcars left over from the pre-rationing days. It was late in March, and the last snow of winter was mingled with the first hail and freezing rain of spring, so that the mush of frost was covered with a layer of slick ice. The line in front of the hospital stretched a block or two. I saw two old folk who had frozen to death while waiting in queue, but the soldiers just laughed when someone asked them to move the bodies. They were there to open fire on the crowd in case another rationing riot started. There was a woman weeping because her baby had died in her arms from the cold. People were laughing at her and scolding her, asking why she was so stupid as to bring a sick baby out into cold like this. There is not much to laugh about these days, so I am happy that the people found a source of amusement, as for the woman, I shoved her out of the way so that I could get into the emergency room doors.

The nurse was sitting and smoking, staring at the blank screen of her broken computer, and the fume of cigarette smoke had filled the room, and I was able to bribe her with a bottle of vodka, and so get my chit stamped. There was a man missing an arm and a leg in the bed I was assigned, still hallucinating from the pain of recent surgery, but since his chart said he was a heteromale with one lifelong partner, this put him on the low-priority list, I was able to get the hospital sergeants to turn him out of the bed for me. I heard him screaming and raving in the snow outside, while the patients who had been waiting all night amused themselves pelting him with snowballs.

I waited patiently until there was no one on duty. It did not take long. Hospitals are always short staffed, and when prisoners are assigned to act as nurses and doctors, most of them simply make a break for it, as if there were some place to run to. I got up, unclipped the clipboard from the foot of the bed, found the wing set aside for Revision Corps, and opened the magnet cabinet with a crowbar.

Inside, neatly labeled, were the electromagnets, each one programmed with a different induction rhythm designed to stimulate the Sylvian fissure area of the brain, which Hell and Mesmer long ago discovered was the source not only of so-called psychic intuitions and flashes of Deja-Vu, but the way to tune one's brainwaves into the brain of the near-identical twin brain of your doppelganger in the parallel world.

There was only one place I knew her doppelganger would not be under observation by other agents-in-place. That was the invasion ground, Earth Seventeen, the one where women never got the vote. It was said to be a tricky place to enter, since the insertionist is supposed to meditate on the deviation point before calling up the hypnotically coded names and words to make the transition, and neither I nor anyone knew the point for his world. But I knew that if I entered it, I would be the only Otherwhere agent there.

Also, nearly all the magnets had been programmed for Earth Seventeen.

I returned to my bed, made a note on my chart that the patient was comatose and needed intravenous feeding and so on, slipped on the head band with the magnets held in place above the correct three areas of the skull, and I lay me down.

And the rest you know. I have been looking for this world's version of Equality Ward, my life-partner. Her name here is Mary Ward.

I have been trying, off and on, for three months now to locate her and talk to her. I tried to break into her sister's party just to see her; I even went to her house with chloroform and a rope to kidnap her if need be—I am that desperate! I will not be stopped! It is a matter of life and death, the life and death of an innocent girl that I love with all my heart.

Now, I might as well tell you, since you can probably see it in my thoughts anyway, that I did finally manage to find your key and open the roll top desk where you keep your mother's jewelry. Making an electromagnet is absurdly simple: all one needs is an iron bar and a coil of electric wire, and the needle-sized electrical batteries you people here make are wonders of miniaturization. I placed other slivers of iron into the coronet you place on your head for your meditation, but these were attuned to my personal frequency, to enable me to gain a more complete control of your body.

Nonetheless, I mean you no harm, and I ask you, no, I *beg* you, for your help. Help me talk to her! I don't know your world and don't know your ways. Even getting one of those automatic taxicabs or whatever you call them to carry me where I wanted to go was nearly impossible for me.

I must see her. But she has these people living with her that will not let me in the door. What do you call them?

If I had not been out of ideas, I would not have allowed the other version of me to become aware of me.

-**2**-

As I sat on my balcony, dreaming, the alien thoughts welling up in me, memories of another world, another life, I found my limbs had fallen asleep. I could not move them. I assumed that even if the alien half of me could force me to move, I could not force myself to think. Indeed, the meditation allowed me to hold my thoughts quite blank, so that there was nothing for my rather desperate other half to do.

I understood, believe me. These thoughts seemed to me like my thoughts, my memories, and the underlying personality was the same: while I would never even dream of shoving a mother with a dead child aside, or throwing a cripple out into the snow, on the other hand, I had been raised by a loving mother married to one man her whole life. I had not been sexually abused as a child by one after another of a series of my mother's violent live-in lovers. I had been punished as a child for hitting a little girl once, not punished for refusing to box a little girl in gym class. And I cannot say I do not know how I would have turned out had I been raised under those circumstances: for I remembered exactly how I had turned out.

I could not even blame myself for attempting first to act by stealth and trickery rather than openly.

Had I been him, raised as he was, without a father, running with a gang from a young age, trusting no one, being fed on nothing but lies his whole life—lies about the nature of man, lies about the nature of truth, the nature of the world, the nature of marriage, lies about economy, lies about politics, lies about the races, lies about wealth and how it is made, lies about history, lies about science, and topped off with the hugest lies about the most trivial things imaginable, such as weather reports—I would not have trusted me either.

I would have done the same thing had I been him. I know, because, after all, I was him.

I felt my lips move: "You have to help me!"

Did I?

"You saw her photo."

I did. It had been love at first sight.

"So you want to see her, too."

That I certainly did. I would do anything to see that face again.

"I met her in school. We were assigned to the same room at Wesley. You were supposed to meet her, but something kept you apart, some accident in this world."

In this world, Wesley is an all-girls college.

"Who are those people who prevent me from seeing her?"

Her parents.

"Marriage was abolished in my world. The government has no part in how to define love! Marriage is just a way to transfer ownership of a woman from her father to her husband. Women in our world are free."

Well, in this world, no father in his right mind would allow a gentleman caller to visit his daughter unannounced, alone, with no reason or explanation given. Small wonder he threw you out the front door. What did you expect?

"I told him I was a sexual compliance inspector, pulling a surprise inspection on his daughter's vagina, to make sure she had performed penis-in-vagina sex with blacks and hispaniards, penis-in-anus with nethermales and vibro-in-vagina with the right number and racial classification of other nonhetfemales or otherhets and the other approved minorities."

You are lucky he did not kick your teeth in. Damn! The only reason why I do not kick your teeth in is that they are my teeth, too.

"Then you will think of a way to see her? You know me, you've seen my thoughts. You know I would never harm her."

Give control of my body back to me, and I will ponder the question. Otherwise I sit here with my mind blank, and your version of Mary Ward dies.

And when I raised my hand to snap my fingers, it worked.

-3-

I watched myself without understanding what I saw. I made a phone call or two, first to her college alumni office, then to some family friends, and then to an opera house. That evening, during the intermission, I saw the girl, Mary, in the crowd. She had an odd look on her face, a poker face, calm and watchful, wary, while the other young ladies around her were laughing and chattering gaily. I walked up to the tall older man who was hovering near her, and introduced myself. This was her father. He and I spoke briefly about a series of inconsequential issues; he introduced me to his wife, and I bowed over her hand, mentioning how envious any unmarried man must be of someone who has found domestic bliss.

And that was all. Mary, the daughter, I was not introduced to, even though it was obvious I could not keep my eyes from her.

It seemed that I was a wealthy and eligible bachelor in this strange world where people owned their own property, and for some reason, that made me desirable in the eyes of parents looking to find a match for their daughter—but why it would be their concern was opaque to me. I assumed that the father and mother would join us in a foursome.

Each moment that crawled by was another moment in which Equality might be killed back in my home line, but there was apparently no way to hurry the matter. The next week I was invited to the theater with Mr. Ward, who came with both his daughters. This time was I allowed to touch the hand of Mary Ward and bow over it, and pay some flattering, meaningless compliment to her.

Sitting in the theater seat, watching some meaningless play whose point I could not understand—why could the Italian fellow not simply ask the girl on the balcony to pencil him in on her sexual congress schedule? And once she was done servicing him, he could then try to get to know her? What was all that business about the name? Why were the men always fighting?—I found that I had a few questions for myself.

I could put myself in a very light meditative trance, and I found I could ask and answer questions without having to move my lips or talk aloud:

The great discovery of Hell and Mesmer was at first misunderstood, and thought to be some sort of psychic or magical effect, hypnosis or astral projection, or visions of paradise, purgatory or inferno. But later researchers discovered that the other worlds visionaries discovered in their dream journeys were all this world, the material world, the only world that exists; merely worlds occupying a might-have-been.

Simple magnets can stimulate this area of the brain, at least of some people, and tune them into a different brain as one might tune a radio. Training in autohyponosis and meditation is needed as well. The target brain must, of course, be identical or nearly so: it has to be your brain, your own, merely the 'you' as you would have been had the past taken a wrong turn.

We, of course, dwell in the best of all possible worlds, and so the mission fate imposes on us is to bring these unrealized and aborted versions of history back into line with true history, and impose on them the ideas and ideals they should have enjoyed had their horrible mistakes and thoughtcrimes never been made.

The key is the rhythm or sequence, almost like a melody, of the magnetic stimulant. Each world has its own rhythm, its own code, that unlocks the brain. This is partly based on the length of the deviation, how long ago the two histories divided, and partly based on a subjective knowledge of what went wrong and when. Hence, when a new world is discovered, the first priority of the advanced scout is to find a library or a wise man or newspaper archive, and see when and where the deviation event took place.

I saw an opportunity as the theater was being let out. I happened to be standing directly behind Miss Ward, and very near a hansom that her father had called, when he and the mother were greeted by someone shouting cheerfully over the murmur of the crowd. They both turned and stepped away for a moment, while other impatient members of the crowd, men in black and ladies as gorgeous as tropical birds in their plumage, stepped between us, blocking the view.

Before I could stop myself, I took Mary roughly by the arm and forced her up the step into the interior of the hansom, stepping after her, and slamming the door. Then I paused, looking in panic at the unfamiliar line of keys and switches and buttons that formed the automatic cabman.

I said, "You fool, what are you doing?"

She said, "Being abducted, apparently." The girl was maybe four years younger than I was, a vision of perfection with her wide eyes and stormcloud masses of dark hair. Her evening gown displayed her naked, perfumed shoulders and a daring amount of cleavage, her delicate and sinuous arms were hidden in long gloves as black as the tails of two unlucky cats.

I said, "Your methods take too long! Equality could be dead already!"

She said, "Abducted by the least competent kidnapper on the continent." She took a small silver key out of her purse, put in into one of the slots on the dash board, and said, "Home!"

And the hansom rolled into motion. The engines on this world are completely silent, but the hansoms have little silver bells on their fore and aft lanterns that jingle, and the tall, spidery and gaily painted wheels make a pleasant sound as they clatter over the cobblestones.

I took the variable-output electromagnet I had cobbled together in the Tool and Die shop and showed it to her. "This device will allow your soul to project itself from your body into another world, like this one, but with a different history. A better history."

"Re-eally?" She drawled. This version of her had the same way of arching an eyebrow and tilting her head that was impossibly lovely, a Greek statue of the nymph or goddess brought to life by alchemy. It was an elfin look, playful, half-scornful.

My right hand leaped up and slapped the instrument out of my left hand, and I grabbed the wrist as it tried to grab my throat. When I bit painfully into the thumb, I was not sure which I was trying to do the biting. It was a somewhat self-defeating sort of brawl, no matter how you look at it.

There is no way it should have happened, because my meditative and autohypnotic skills have been honed by years of practice, whereas my skills—the native me—were those of an amateur. I found myself wondering who this Ashwathama was?

During the struggle, I stood up and banged my head against the roof. This world does not have seatbelts, but, then again, their vehicles move sedately.

The instrument spun through the air and landed in her lap. She spread her knees and caught it neatly in a triangle of velvet.

I managed to spit out my hand and gasp. "You must believe me! This is tuned to my home line. You have a—a twin—a twin sister you never knew, who needs your help. If you wake up in her body, for just a moment, and let the doctors see you with your eyes open, moving your fingers and toes, then they cannot kill her!"

She said, "That depends, doesn't it? There is no rule against euthanizing a perfectly healthy person, is there? If she knows something the Nannies think people have a right not to know. The right not to be offended outweighs the right to free speech, or the right to life."

I looked at her, a slow realization breaking on me. Her eyes were not those of a stranger.

I stopped fighting myself. Both of me stopped. Me and the other me were more interested in that odd remark than we were in prolonging the pointless one-man wrestling bout.

The other me was slightly swifter on the uptake, "You are Equality Ward, aren't you? Lity? You are also Dr. Fish's patient, the girl with sleepwalking problems?"

She said, "You are the native Ward. Your voice is pitched lower." She tossed the instrument at me, and I caught it. She said, "You are also right-handed. My Ward is left-handed."

I heard myself say, "The nuns beat left-handedness out of me with a ruler."

She said, "Such a thing would never be permitted on our world. Nuns are not permitted either. And, no, I was not actually sleepwalking, that was an act, to explain why I forget things I should have known about your world and about my doppelganger's life in it. It is—" she could not suppress a smile. Dimples appeared in her cheek. Her eyes glittered and danced. If I had not already been in love with her, I would have fallen, then and there, just seeing that impish look. "—it is an interesting life here."

I said, "Interesting how?"

She said, "High pitched again. That must be my Ward. You mean to ask what do I find more interesting than you?"

I said, "Something like that..."

"I have four suitors here, plus my father's manservant who dotes on me. They kneel to me as if I were a queen, and offer me gifts and tokens as if I were a goddess. None of them have struck me. Not one. Two of them met by accident on the way to my father's house: they smote each other in the face. For me. And I have a father here, a father who cares for me as if I were a precious jewel. And my mother talks to me."

"Your mother back home talks to you!"

"No, she talks *at* me. It is not the same thing. She gets mad when I remind her that I was raised by the daycare nurses, not by her, and that she has no right to tell me what to do. Sometime she forgets my name."

I said, "Where is the Mary Ward from this world?"

She said, "Still in the coma, as far as I know. Her brain activity is not interfering with mine in any way. There is no pressure, nothing trying to shove me back, nothing. It is the only case like this I ever heard of. Usually we kill the host to make the possession permanent."

I said, "You should not have told me that!"

"High-pitched Ward. Why? Are you lying to yourself?"

I said, "No. I just don't like killing myself. I never have, and I believe me when I say that, because I can see it in my mind."

"Low-pitched again. You know, that voice makes little shivers go up a girl's spine! Why don't you talk like that at home?" she laughed, and it was the silver bells of elfland. "It sounds like Invader Ward does not have Native Ward under control. But I would not trust you if I were you, Native Ward. We can kill our host memories just by concentrating, by mesmerism. We can also hide thoughts from our host. You did not know that our thoughts have been trained to kill? Through autohypnosis, we can trigger the amnesia mechanism already present in every brain. This mechanism is natural to humans: they are the reason why we forget so many of our dreams in the morning. "

I said, "There are much better ways than killing yourself."

She raised her pretty little nose in the air, and snorted. "Is that scruples? Or weakness?"

Suddenly the girl looked remarkably less attractive to me. I said harshly, "It's strength. The same strength that allowed me to cross to this world no one seems to be able to enter, and track you down. They are going to kill your body back home!"

She shook her head. "Now I cannot tell which one of you is talking. You know as well as I that losing that body will not kill this mind here, not as long as I have a safe and empty body to inhabit here. I could probably wake her from the coma—I can almost feel her thoughts, like a word on the tip of my tongue—she's been this way since a boating accident some months ago. But I won't. Her mind is like an empty house, all swept and garnished. "

I did not like her tone, so I pulled back my hand to slap her, but I stopped myself.

She looked on as I grimaced and hissed. She said, "It looks like the native has an advantage. That is unusual. We are trained at this."

I said, "I don't know what I was like in your world, but I made about as big a wreck I could make of my life as a rich, young, empty-headed and empty-hearted young man can make. My Dad cut me off without a penny until I had earned ten thousand dollars in some honest work. The church charity would not feed me, since I was able-bodied, so I had to find work or starve. I worked as a dogsbody in a factory that made gauges and jigs until I earned the respect of a master who took me on as a prentice. Do you know how many vices I had to give up to do that, no to mention how much sleep I lost and meals I skipped? I don't think your paramour can force his way into my head any more forcefully than all those lovely, seductive vices I so adored. And your man does not have the heart to fight me if you are not on his side. So what gives? Why are you not on his side? Why didn't you go back?"

She shook her head, "I don't know what Invader Ward told you, but your world is safe, for now, because of me. You see, I am the agent that they sent to find the deviation point. Once they know that, they can tune their instruments and concentrate their thoughts all the better."

"And you don't want that? Why not?"

"My people can take over anyone whose doppelganger is alive in this world. We have thousands of agents. No matter what they had been doing here, they will all have an epiphany, leave their old lives, go into politics, into journalism, into entertainment, and start spreading the message by hints and whispers, never obvious, never naming ourselves, never saying what we are. We never need to be seen coordinating our message, we just let it seep in. If it takes a hundred years, we let it. History is on our side. There is nothing you can possibly do to stop us. So you want me to stay here."

I said, "You did not answer my question. Why are you no longer loyal to your world? What do you want?"

She said, "I like this life! What business is it of yours? What do you want?"

I said, "I want you to wake up the version of Mary Ward who comes from this world."

She said, "That will force me out!"

I shrugged. "You are a trespasser. Why didn't they tell me—invader me—what your mission was?"

She said, "You are so naïve! The Revision Corps can only show an unmitigated string of successes. If I fail, the mission never took place, and I was sent to the moon-city world, Earth Fourteen. Only if I succeed was I ever sent here, Earth Seventeen."

I said, "But you did succeed. You discovered the deviation point. You will be a heroine when you return."

She shook her head. "I can tell you are still mostly the native. My Ward would never say 'heroine'. I think my Ward has probably figured out what is going on, even if you have not."

All of me was agreed on the action. I snatched the device out her lap, and pressed it again her head. Sending her home would save her body, and perhaps her life. And it might allow the Mary from this world to wake up.

She said, "If I go back, I will be a *dead* heroine. They will kill me to keep the secret silent."

That made my hand waver. "What is so terrible?"

She spoke rapidly, her eyes on that instrument like the eyes of a bird watching a snake. "The suffragette Mrs Pankhurst succeeded in my world because the English were unwilling to force feed her when she went on hunger strike. It was a tactic she learned from the Russians. In my world, their revolution succeeded, and was widely admired. Her success was also admired, and the public believed that the anti-suffragette women lacked the courage of any convictions. No one in my world believed that women should bear and raise children as their lot in life, and no one was allowed to say that one wife cannot do both at once."

I said, "I know the rest. The income tax shifted the soul of America from Wall Street to Washington. Ambitious men entered politics instead of business. The abolition of alcohol trampled the state's rights still more, and encouraged nationwide crime rings, and this led to a nationwide police force called the FBI, who were permitted to carry guns. The popular election of Senators eviscerated the Senate of its prime function, which was to protect the states from the Federal government. And the women's vote went for ever bigger government, and the government started ruling in a feminine way, with nagging on labels, and public services messages, and reprimands meant to force the races to get along as if we were all unruly children instead of grown men. The male approach to law making, which was to have a few, simple, and clear rules that every man of honor respects, all that eroded into nothing. Honor eroded into nothing. Government by law was replaced by government by compassion. But government by compassion is not very compassionate. And the mothers did not raise their children, and so the whole generation of brats came to maturity, still children—nagging, whining, spoilt children. Children who would not work at tough and honest jobs. Children who could demand a handout from the government as a matter of right. And these children voted a straight ticket of filthy self-indulgence: to allow no-fault divorce, to allow contraception and abortion and to make all women into men in thought and deed. And at the end of that road is your mindless world of lies and gray walls that scream at you."

She said, "Don't send me back to that world! They have the right not to be offended there. No right is more terrible than that. It means I have no rights at all, because anything I do, even being alive at all, might offend someone."

"Sorry, my darling, but you are not meant to be here..." But when I brought up my other hand to twist the knob and turn it on, I grabbed my own wrist instead and forced the instrument back toward my own head.

But then I realized that sending the Invader back to his home—now that we both knew the deviation point—would be tantamount to inviting an invasion here. That thought unnerved me. I was weakening. The little flashlight magnet came ever nearer my head. I pressed victorious, pushing the little flashlight magnet ever nearer my head.

Not until it was too late did I realize what I was trying to do: the magnetic pulse could also be tuned to trigger the amnesia reflex, which would allow the possessor to kill the host, even a strong host who was doing a good job of resisting. As soon as the magnet touched me, I would die. As soon as it touched me, I would be triumphant, and Lity would be safe.

Inch by inch, I began forcing the magnet away from myself.

I gasped, "Help me!"

Lity said, "If you kill the native, you can take up permanent residence with me, here, and we can live in this lovely and romantic world! No one lies here—well, not compared to our world. When they talk about honor and chivalry and romance—they believe it! When husbands walk out on their wives, they are punished! Punished at law! This whole world is like a paradise for women, a huge romance novel!"

That encouraged me. It actually did help. I did not have the training after all; I had done this before, for years; whereas I had never fought a mental battle like this.

The magnet touched my head. I screamed in rage and triumph and panic as I saw my own fingers groping for the switch. Closer and farther, closer and farther my fingers twitched and writhed like worms.

I was thrown out of my seat and against the dashboard when a big red dog ran up alongside the hansom, passed it, and fell down on the road right in front of the vehicle. An automatic circuit in the driver brought the hansom to a dangerously abrupt halt. I took advantage of the confusion by throwing the device out of the window.

But I could not stop myself from stepping outside of the motionless cab and merely picking it up again. But then the dog leaped to his feet, wrestled the device out of my surprised hand, and ran off a few feet. He put the device down, and stared at me, his tongue lolling.

The hansom was on a small and winding back road, with trees to both sides, and the moon behind a cloud with a silver lining. The night wind was blowing strongly, and sounded as if an insubstantial giant were wading through the trees, but there was a scent of pollen in the air, a hint of springtime.

Lity had climbed out of the hansom behind me, hugging herself and shivering. "Don't all the men of this world carry guns? Shoot the thing, and get the inducer. Use it on yourself, and we can live here happily ever after."

I took a step forward, but now my force of will was returning, and I was going through some of Ashwathama's exercises in my mind, making my soul like an ocean, a substance that yields but never surrenders, that always returns whenever it is shoved back. Unwillingly, I took a step back.

"That happy ending may not work out, partner mine," I said. "I am having, damn it, second thoughts."

She snorted in disgust, and strode forward, hips swaying in her silken gown, her heels clattering on the roadstones, as she marched toward the dog. "I have always been an animal rights activist! Come here, doggy, doggy! There's a good boy and/or girl!" This was all in the least soothing tone of voice imaginable.

"Your girl does not seem to get the hang of dogs," I said to myself, aloud. And I answered in a slighter higher pitched voice, "Yeah, well, she's always been sort of a city girl."

The dog put the device down, barked at her outstretched hand, growled, flattened his ears, and said, "Back off, lady."

She stepped backward pretty quickly. In fact, it was a nimble jump, and skipped back behind me and hid behind my shoulder. It was something she never would have done back home, turn to me for protection. I felt an odd tension in my spine, a tension I had not realized was there, suddenly vanish like a slip knot pulled free, and my spine straightened. I raised one arm and reached behind me, as if to shield her. With my other hand, I reached through the open door, and under the seat cushion of the cab, and took out a tire iron.

I said to the dog, "Who the hell are you?"

The dog said, "Someone with cleaner language than yours, brother. Not every beast has the divine gift of speech: it is best not to demean it."

She pointed a trembling finger at the dog. "It's impossible! Impossible! Dogs don't talk! Not on any world!" I had never seen her shake before. Perhaps it was just the cold. She was not dressed very warmly.

I said over my shoulder, "So says a woman from another dimension who can cross between alternate timelines by autohypnosis, and take over empty bodies."

213

She said, "It's impossible. That's you. Don't you recognize the tone, the rhythm of the words? Don't you recognize your own voice?"

I stared at the creature. He sat down on his hind legs, and raised his nose, peering at us. At that moment, the moon came out from the behind the clouds. The moon was bright enough and low enough to cast the beast's shadow across the road toward us. The full moon was not that far above the dog's upright ears. The device was invisible in the moonshadow, but no doubt was between the dogs paws.

I hefted the tire iron in my fist. "Speak up, pooch."

"That is Father Francis to you, Frank."

"How can you talk?"

"It is one of the disciplines I learned from Ashwathama. I am not actually talking, I am merely making you understand what my mewls and growls mean."

"Who—What are you? Where do you come from?"

"She is right," said the dog, nodding at Lity. "I am you. One of you. As to where I am from, that requires an explanation. Rudolf Maximilian Höll in my world was cherished as a wise and brilliant discoverer. The evil of allowing some men to take over the bodies of other selves in parallel worlds was so obviously horrible, that the art was placed under strict and draconian laws. What could it be used for? One cannot carry any physical goods from world to world. Only ideas, literature, inventions, philosophy. Höll shared his discovery with his other selves in the other worlds. In so doing, he broke the world. Before about 1750 AD, all the history lines were parallel, and all events are the same. After that point, thanks to the different uses the different Höll versions made of the discovery, the worlds diverged, becoming less and less alike. Like you, Francis, I am a member of an order that seeks to persuade the shattered worlds to rejoin the main trunk of history again."

214

I said, "What makes the different lines differ? I assume there is one where the South won the Civil War? Another where the American Revolution failed?"

The dog said, "She knows."

Lity said, "It is nothing like that. Philosophy is the only thing that makes a difference in history. All the wars turn out exactly the same. All the people are the same. Hegel was a philosopher in my world who inspired a man named Marx, who inspired the Progressive movement. There are others named Nietzsche, Comte, Schopenhauer, J.S. Mill. But especially a man named John Dewey! If it were not for him, my home timeline would not exist at all. And Rawls, of course."

The dog said, "In mine there were men named Søren Kierkegaard, Friedrich Hayek, G.K. Chesterton, C.S. Lewis."

I said, "There are all these writers in my world, too. Why are the different worlds different?"

The dog said, "In her world, they listened to Hegel, Marx, Nietzsche. In mine, they did not."

"That is the only difference? Whom you listen to?"

"Whom you follow. The Ashwathama of my world is ageless, born with a magic jewel in his brow that protected him against any attacks of ghosts, demons, stinging insects, venomous serpents, vicious beasts. He is immortal, was cursed by heaven to roam the age of this world for the slaying of the five innocent sons of Draupadi, wife of Pandavas, those heroic brothers, sons of fallen angels and mortal women. In your world, he hid himself for shame, and so he is unknown, thought to be a myth like the Wandering Jew or the Flying Dutchman. In my world, he repented utterly; he came to be the most famous and holiest sage of India. He met with Höll after seeing from afar the world-shattering discovery to be made, and traveled across land and sea, no easy journey in those days. He taught the Jesuit and learned from him. Together, they unlocked the deeper secrets of so-called animal magnetism, and discovered a variation on the art which involves no abduction of another man's body, using only a willing animal as a vessel. So you see me here. Back home I have a body like yours. Exactly like yours, in fact. Well, my haircut is different."

It was too weird to take in. "No, wait. To cross between worlds, you have to have an exact match of brain to brain, close as twins, or closer! Maybe a cousin can sometimes, ah—" But I remembered the rumors about Ashwathama from my world being able to possess an ape.

The dog snorted, which is an odd noise for a dog to make. And he bared his teeth, but only because he could not smile. "And you think the silly little magnets are what do the work? It is your faith in them, my son. It is a placebo effect. The real mechanism is purely spiritual, purely a matter of the mind. It is a matter of love. All you need to do is find a dog willing to be your dog, and you must be willing to be his master. He is glad for the company. Dogs get lonely too."

"But—you are living as a dog! Sleeping in ditches, eating raw rats! What is worth life as a dog?"

"To spread the gospel. Everyone from the Hegelian world, they spend their lives spreading their sick gospel, a gospel of envy and license and despair, and yet neither Dice nor Lity counts the cost, or regrets being thrown into one strange world after another."

"But why not just come into my head, like I did? Like he did?" I said, pointing at myself.

"To be sure, there are advantages of taking over your self's life in the new world. You can steal his clothing and his money, for one thing, not to mention opposable thumbs. But consider the disadvantages."

Now the dog stooped his head, and, taking up the device once more in his jaws, he bit. The metal cracked and shattered under his powerful teeth. With a toss of his head, he spat out the fragments.

I said, "What the—why did you do that! Now she is trapped here!"

The dog said, "But you are safe."

I said, "Until I build another one. It only takes an hour, and materials one can get at any hardware store."

"You will not have an hour." The Irish Setter turned his nose toward the girl. "You now have a choice to make, and it will save you or damn you. Fear not! I could never hurt you, my child. You are the image and likeness of my own beloved Marianna, whom I wed on her deathbed and lost to consumption. Nor will I harm you, Francis Ward or Workmans Paradise. Both of you, like me, fell into a very dark place in your life. Francis, you pulled yourself out by hard work. I, by prayer. Dice, you will pull yourself out of your dark pit by the virtue of love, of which there is no greater power in the universe."

I said, "What do you want of me? Either of me?"

He said, "From world to world I have hunted you down, doggedly—if I may be permitted that expression—chasing you, seeking you, and only now finding you. If I told you for how long I sought, you would not believe me."

I stepped back, half-urging and half-pushing Lity back too, and hefted the tire iron. "Hunted us for what?"

He said, "I am a Dominican, one of the Hounds of God. I have hunted you across the world to find you and forgive you. To offer you the opportunity to be forgiven for your black crimes, your murders, your lies, the abduction which occurs each time you possess one of your twins on another world."

217

She looked at the scattered bits of the device, the only thing that could have forced her brainwaves out of synchrony with the body she now inhabited. "Forgiven, eh? For living my life the way I chose? So what happens if I tell you to go to Hell, instead?"

The big Irish Setter raised his mouth to the night sky and let out a long, high, mournful howl.

Immediately, the wind picked up, and the hansom cab behind us rocked on its shock absorbers, swaying. The clouds rushed like a dark armada under full sail. The trees lashed their branches like harts rearing and shaking their antlers. The moon vanished behind a cloud, and darkness spread as if a giant hand had extinguished a candle flame.

I exorcise thee, every unclean spirit, in the name of God the Father Almighty, and in the name of Jesus Christ, His Son, our Lord and Judge, and in the power of the Holy Spirit, that thou depart from this creature of God, Mary Ward which our Lord hath designed to call unto His holy temple, that it may be made the temple of the living God, and that the Holy Spirit may dwell therein. Through the same Christ our Lord, who shall come to judge the living and the dead, and the world by fire.

I could not tell if the words were coming from the howling mouth of the dog or the howling voices of the wind. Lity threw herself on her face, regardless of the dirt and cold of the road, the hardness of the roadstones, the fineness of her dress. She was crying out something, babbling hysterically, begging.

I was too, before I even knew what I was saying.

The wind died down immediately, as if a window in heaven had snapped shut. Leaves and dust fell directly to the ground in the sudden, eerie silence.

The dog said, "I will hear both your confessions. As for penance, you both already have guessed what would be proper to ask of you, without my saying."

I said, "Our penance is to return to our world, and die."

"No. To return to your world, and fight. Sell your coat and buy a sword."

"If you banish us back to our world, the powers that rule there will kill us."

He said, "You will not go back unarmed. You have been trained by your masters to suborn and undermine whole nations, races, and civilizations through slow and patient lies. You therefore know, with no further need for instruction, how to uplift and heal whole nations, races, and civilizations with the truth, which you will be impatient to tell, because you will burn with love of truth. I will tell you a name you can call upon to banish the spirits possessing your leaders who have made your world into an imitation of Hell."

I said, "The struggle is hopeless!"

He said, "And if this lady discovers that she truly and deeply loves you, now that she has seen that, like the men of this brighter and saner world, you are willing to chase her beyond the end of the world, defy all authority, cast aside all caution, and protect her with your life and soul and indeed to die for her, what then? Is she worth challenging a world to single combat?"

I lifted my face out of the dirt of the road. I saw Lity also kneeling. Her face was toward me, but, in the gloom, I could not see what her expression meant.

I said, "Her love will arm me with such a sword as could crack the sky from its crown to the horizon, and topple the wreckage into hell, to crush the screaming demons. For her, I would fight a thousand worlds."

The dog cocked his head and raised one ear, looking at her.

She said to me, "I have been waiting my whole life for him to say that to me. Not those exact words, but—damn you! What took you so long! So many wasted years while I waited and wondered!" There were tears in her eyes. Who understands women?

She said to the red dog, "Thank you. Die or live does not matter now. I found him. I have been living with him for five years. Only now, just now, have I found him. You helped me find him."

He said, "That is what the office of a dog is for."

I said to the dog, "You are a priest. You can marry us."

The dog said to her, "And you, my daughter, your penance shall be to restore the Mary Ward of this world to wholeness before you depart. I will not charge you to tell no one of the deviation point of this world: no one of the Hegelian world would be allowed to believe it. And, now, my son, step away. Her words need privacy while I hear what her contrite heart must say."

I stood up and said, "But you can marry us, right? The old fashioned unbreakable marriage vows that last until death?"

The dog said, "Perhaps you should ask the girl, first."

-1-

As it turned out, I ended up performing two weddings on that world, one that night, and one exactly a year later, in the woods, with no humans save for Mary and Francis, her parents, and her wide-eyed sister, Vivian. The birds and beasts, the roebuck and stags, rabbits and foxes and lambs, dogs and cats and leopards who had gathered around to witness were men and women from my world, who had taken time away from the summits and audiences with kings and presidents to be here. And a great lion came to bless us all.

So, you see, there are advantages to avoiding doing any harm to yourself, but only good.

Lord, forgive me for how jealous I was, for Mary looked so much like my beloved bride, whose embrace I never knew, wedded for an hour! There are happier worlds than mine.

> *"Yet stay, fair lady, turn again,*
> *And dry those pearly tears;*
> *For see, beneath this gown of gray*
> *Thy own true-love appears.*
>
> *"Here forced by grief and hopeless love,*
> *These holy weeds I sought;*
> *And here, amid these lonely walls,*
> *To end my days I thought.*
>
> *"But haply, for my year of grace*
> *Is not yet passed away,*
> *Might I still hope to win thy love,*
> *No longer would I stay."*
>
> *"Now farewell grief, and welcome joy*
> *Once more unto my heart;*
> *For since I have found thee, lovely youth,*
> *We nevermore will part."*

The Friar of Orders Gray—Thomas Percy (1729–1811)

THE RULES OF RACISM

By

Tom Kratman

How charges of racism work for the Left and the Right

The Left's 20 Rules of Racism:

1. If you believe that general intelligence exists, is heritable and at all testable for, you're a racist.

2. If you point out that liberal philosophies and programs intended to have a good impact have had a disproportionately bad impact on the ethnicities targeted by liberals, you're a racist.

3. If you notice that other cultures have some problems, you're a racist.

4. If you notice your own culture has had some successes, you're a racist.

5. If you try to identify subcultural problems, you're a racist. If the problems existed or got worse under liberalism, see item 2, above.

6. If you're mainstream American culture, and don't hate that culture, you're a racist.

7. If you're capable of noting unpleasant facts about subcultures and discussing them without your brain fogging, you're a racist.

8. If you won't kowtow and grovel as soon as someone accuses you of racism for one of the reasons above or below, you're a hopeless racist.

9. If you do not believe that mankind is a tabula rasa for liberals to make whatever they think would be good to make of man, this week, you're a racist.

10. If you don't take personal responsibility for all the evils of slavery, you're a racist. This is true even if you only arrived from Poland last week.

11. If you're white, you're a racist.

12. If you're white and just arrived from Poland last week and don't accept that you're a racist, you're a racist.

13. If you try to interject logical thought into a discussion of culture, you're a racist.

14. If you refuse to admit culture is a racial matter, and a liberal wants to conflate the two, you're a racist.

15. If you believe that race and culture are indistinguishable and a liberal decides that you shouldn't conflate the two, you're a racist.

16. If you believe that black or Hispanic girls who are paid by liberal-inspired programs from the age of 13 to have babies will have babies, you're a racist.

17. If you believe that girls of whatever color who are paid to have babies will then have babies but then, insensitively, observe that a smaller percentage of white girls do, certainly because they haven't been targeted for as much "help" from liberals, you're a racist.

18. If it doesn't bother you that the truth offends liberals, you're a racist.

19. If your name is Tom Kratman and you write and in your writing your heroes and heroines tend to be from minorities while your villains are white liberals, you're still a racist.

20. If you read The Bell Curve, you're a racist. On the other hand, if you didn't read it but wrote a scathing review on Amazon anyway you might not be a racist provided you take personal responsibility for 300 years of slavery even if you just arrived from Poland last week.

The Right's 20 Rules of Racism:

1. Anyone responsible for three hundred years of slavery would have to be a lot older than you and me.

2. There has to be some genetics in "racism's" DNA, some DNA in its gene pool, or it just isn't racism.

3. Racism could be eliminated in the United States if we could just eliminate the white liberals who so plainly depend on it so much and do so much to keep it going.

4. Reality isn't racist: The reality is that there are pond-scummy gallows bait in every group. Some of those will be more of a problem to their own group than to you (see Rule 14, below). Some will be more of a problem to you precisely because you're not a member of their group. It is wise, not racist, to avoid the latter. In Boston, this may be referred to as the "Evelyn Wagler-George Pratt Rule," and that's not code. Odd exception to half of Rule 4: Jesse Jackson would much rather be followed by a white on the streets of DC, at night, than a black.

5. There have been two instances in recent history where the concept of "honorary white" held sway. One was in apartheid South Africa where, for example, Japanese were considered "honorary white." The other was when, in relation to the Trayvon Martin shooting, the American mainstream media made Hispanic George Zimmerman an "honorary white." This is not entirely a coincidence, since (see Rule 18) the very liberal American media is as racist in their way as ever the Afrikaner Broederbond was in its.

6. Nobody really thinks whites are as evil as portrayed by white liberals and black demagogues. If they really thought so, they'd be too afraid to ever leave the house, since a) there are a lot more whites, b) those whites are much better armed, c) they're more likely to be veterans of the Army's and Marine Corps' ground-

gaining combat arms, and d) they have an historically demonstrated cultural aptitude for mass, organized violence.

7. People who insist you're speaking in code insist on it because they believe it's true. They believe it's true because they really do speak in code and can't imagine anyone who does not speak in code. It's not racist to think those people are idiots, nor to note that they're mostly white. (Exception to rule: When conservatives talk about guns and zombies? Especially in terms of using the former to kill the latter? Yeah; "zombie" is code for "liberals of any color." See Rule 6, above.)

8. It's not racist to note that white liberalism managed to do in about thirty years something that three hundred years of slavery could not, seriously damage the black family, generally though not universally, and ruin it completely over wide swaths.

9. Speaking of slavery, the bulk of slave raiding and trading in Africa was black, usually Islamic black (see Rule 16, below), on black. The Arabic word for black and slave is the same, "Abd." And the first registered slave owner in Virginia was black. Pointing this out to liberals, white and black, is always fun.

10. It's not racist to wish that our first black president had been Thomas Sowell.

11. The "Some of my best friends" defense against a charge of racism is no defense... unless it happens to be true. Sometimes it's best expressed to a white liberal as, "You don't have so much as a day in uniform, do you, dipshit?"

12. The system of education that white liberals have inflicted on inner city blacks is a crime against humanity. No amount of money that they toss at it helps to overcome the elimination of discipline liberalism has caused. It's neither racist to note this... nor wrong.

13. The various college and university minority "studies" programs, because they give a useless pseudo-education, and at very high cost in both money and time, are racist in their effects.

14. Most black crime is black on black crime. It is racist in its effects to deprive the black community of the social good that comes from executing black criminals that prey on other blacks.

15. It takes a white liberal idiot (Lord, forgive us our redundancies) not to understand the difference between casual sex with a member of another race and marrying and investing one's entire reproductive effort in a member of another race. See, e.g., http://www.tomkratman.com/yoli.html. Dipshits.

16. Islam is not a race. Detesting Islam is not racist. There is nothing in Islam which genetically compels either slightly tanned Palestinians or totally white English reverts to pray toward Mecca five times daily, to self-detonate in crowded squares and movie theaters, to find offense in just about everything, nor even to clitorectomize their women. Flash alert: Lysenko was wrong. Dipshits.

17. When a liberal accuses you of racism, rejoice; it means the dipshit knows he or she is losing.

18. The worst racists are liberals, mostly white ones, who assume that blacks and hispanics are so inferior that only affirmative action in perpetuity would give them a remotely fair chance. (That this also keeps a lot of liberal white social workers and bureaucrats employed is, of course, merely incidental. Ahem. Dipshits.)

19. There was a conservative argument for a kind of affirmative action. Unfortunately, all the money's already been spent on employing white liberal social workers and bureaucrats, and we're broke now, so that ship has sailed. Again, blame dipshit white liberals.

20. Screaming "Racism! Raaaacissssm!" on the part of a white liberal, when the matter in question has no DNA in its gene pool, no genetics in its DNA (see Rule 2, above), is the surest proof that said white liberal is genetically defective. And a dipshit. And it's not racist to point this out.

WORLD ABLAZE

By

Jane Lebak

In a totalitarian regime, can you trust the beggar at your door?

On the second trip to my door to retrieve the rest of my grocery rations, I find a man on my steps staring at the bags full of good things he no doubt has been denied for days, if not weeks. He looks up, rain-soaked hair dripping onto the threadbare shoulders of his coat. I say, "Do you need something to eat?"

He stares uneasily as I lift the remaining bags. "Well, come in," I say. "Let's get you a meal."

Still in silence he follows me into the kitchen. I turn on the kettle. Using the fresh bread, I make him a sandwich thick with ham and cheese, then lay it before him along with mustard and pickles. Before I finish saying, "I have no lettuce," he's already set into the sandwich. At the counter I make three more, sealing each in plastic, then open a package of apples and another of carrots. When I look up the man is staring at me, a woman who is at least twenty years older and two skin-shades darker than himself.

He rasps, "I can't get work because I'm a Christian." I nod. His gaze hardens. "Have you already called the authorities?"

"I've called no one." I pour some tea to steep, then I bring a worn backpack from the closet and load it with the sandwiches, the fruit and carrots. "I can't give you more than a few days' food, but this should keep you for a while." I find the cast-off backpacks at thrift stores, and each stands ready with a toothbrush, toothpaste, soap, socks, and a towel. The man trembles as I hand him the bundle, a hole carefully patched at the top, but at least it won't draw attention like new gear.

He looks into the bag. "Are you a Christian?"

I return to the counter. "I'm actually a Dominican nun in hiding."

His eyes widen.

"And I can recognize an informant, so you'll meet your quota if you want to. But take that anyhow, because you'll need food until the deposit clears in the bank, assuming the authorities pay you what they claim they will."

He goes pale. I put three bottles of water into the backpack and hand him a fourth. He cracks the cap and bolts down the whole thing in four swallows.

His raspiness wasn't an act—he sounds ill. "How did you know?"

"You're not the first." I set his tea before him along with honey and the skim milk issued by the ration cards. It's been years since we've had cream or butter.

He drinks the tea as quickly as he drank the water. "You could die if I turn you in." He sounds stunned. "You could have refused me at the door. Why didn't you?"

"Because you just told me you're a Christian, and you're not." I take a seat at the table. "But someday, when you eat your dinner, you'll be saying grace."

In the hospital where I work as a nurse, I count off a rosary on my fingers as I move through the day. Back in the Philippines, my mother's generation used strings of beads, but if anyone found them on me today in Baton Rouge, I'd forfeit my life. It comforts me to consider that our Blessed Mother would rather I remain alive to pray again than insist on doing things the traditional way. Even my name had to go. I took permanent vows as Therese, named for the saint on whom I was Patterned, but my name tag (and my official ID) says only *Reese*.

The informant hasn't turned me in. I don't know if he or any of the other informants ever became Christians, but I do know there have been five, and despite the government's rewards, none have made that call.

It's a morning of bedpans and medications, worried patients and belligerent ones as well, sometimes in exactly the same body. Christ breaks the government's prohibitions to dwell all around me in the antiseptic halls: in the man clasping his dying wife's hand, in the first-time mother learning to diaper her newborn, and in the clerk navigating the system to obtain approval for a patient's elective procedure.

In room 2856, I come to my favorite patient. A radiologist waits at the foot of the bed, her head bowed. Although it's a private room and the door remains closed, I draw the curtains around a middle-aged black man's bed and bow my head as well. "Good morning, Your Excellency." And then I present him a fist-sized box with a test-tube full of wine and a wafer I baked in my own kitchen.

John Shaller underwent a back-alley consecration as Bishop five years ago with me and two other covert nuns in attendance. The Church moves around nowadays without any kind of permanency except for the people it inhabits—no buildings, no property. We've got a cottage industry changing IDs and moving the newly-created people from city to city. A homeless man showed up one evening and it turned out to be the Archbishop from New Orleans, come to ordain a replacement for Bishop Ruiz after his execution. Bishop Shaller spends days unloading cargo ships, but nights are for a clandestine Mass and as many other sacraments as he can.

In non-theological terms, we refer to this as burning the candle at both ends; he's been hospitalized with pneumonia. The radiologist in the room is Sister Miriam, aka Miri. Every day I can, I

231

bring bread and wine. Sister Miriam is able to smuggle in a page with the day's readings. While I check his vital signs and fill out his chart, he says Mass in thirteen minutes. Once finished, the paper folds into squares tiny enough to slip beneath my wristwatch.

Before I go, he says, "Do we have access tonight?"

"Yes, your Excellency." Then I open the curtains and push his bedside table nearer.

In the evening, I wheel Bishop Shaller to the ultrasound room. The radiologist signs off that he's here, then escorts in a Chinese woman wearing a nurse's uniform even though she's not yet a nurse. Catholic nuns used to run hospitals; nowadays we infest them.

Bishop Shaller sits in his wheelchair, out of breath, while I boot the computer. It takes three successive pass codes, each one telling us, "Password incorrect. Try again" before the ultrasound machine becomes a Pattern machine. I say, "Do we have the Pattern piece?"

Bishop Shaller removes a jewelry box from his bathrobe pocket, and within it I find a single wooden bead.

"Nice." Wood works so much better than clothing, although anything organic will do. A wooden rosary is as strong a Pattern piece as anyone could ask for. I load the machine, and it begins analyzing.

Sister Miriam sets a cap on our postulant's head and attaches electrodes to her wrists and ankles.

The postulant looks nervous, so I say, "Whose Pattern did you choose?"

She twists her shirt in her hands. "Saint Faustina of the Divine Mercy."

"Oh, I like her, even though she was a little snippy with Saint Therese of Lisieux."

The postulant pauses. "Was St. Therese your Pattern?"

I nod.

Bishop Shaller rises from the chair long enough to give her Communion, bless her, and renew her preliminary vows.

The computer indicates it's loaded the Pattern, so Sister Miriam begins the process.

Patterning takes half an hour, but it's a half hour of intensity. When I took my Pattern, I found myself remembering long passages of *The Story Of A Soul* word for word as they settled into my heart and changed the way I thought. I felt an intense love of the ordinary world surrounding me, the individual moments all given me by God my Father. Later as I came back to the real world as if breaking the surface of the ocean and taking that first breath, I realized just what a treasure God had given us by creating our very lives. Yes, even a Church living in persecution. Yes, even in Masses whispered beside bed pans and Final Vows taken in muddy alleys.

The postulant whimpers, "Talk to me." She's pale. "Talk to me."

It works best if the subject stays quiet, so while Sister Miriam moves the wand over her temples, I say, "You know we discovered Patterning completely by accident? God gave us this gift when someone learned something about violins. A scientist named Selah Merced learned that when you play the same melody repeatedly, the sound physically changes the wood to make the violin more attuned to that particular series of sounds."

The postulant nods, still frightened, and Miriam asks her to keep still. Saint Faustina spent a lot of time feeling out of her depth too, so that's probably a good sign. I continue, "Well, someone applied the Selah principle to all wooden items and discovered they picked up patterning from the alpha waves a person's brain produces during prayer or meditation. And we can reproduce those vibrations and project them onto other organic material."

Wood is the best for preserving patterns, but wool works too. Fragments of bone are the least effective because they picked up everything the person did, not just prayers. I've always wished we could take a Pattern off a fragment of the True Cross.

The postulant whispers, "I'm going away."

I squeeze her hand. "No, you're being enhanced. You're having Saint Faustina's pattern worked into your standard brainwave pattern so it will be easier for you to achieve her style of spirituality, but you were already a bit like her. You wouldn't be able to take a pattern very different than yourself." I watch the screen over Miriam's shoulder while Miriam runs the wand over all the places of her brain that God might make His home, dialing the intensity in and out to train the most spiritually sensitive areas.

"There are so many different kinds of saints, so many different lights before God. You've found one like yourself, and you're letting her lead your path. Relax. Try to pray."

At the end of the Pattern, our postulant wipes the gel off her head and neck with a white towel. We lock out the ultrasound machine so it's ready for performing ultrasounds again. Bishop Shaller hears our postulant's final vows, and at last her soul matches the name on her ID card: Tina. Miriam brings her upstairs, and Bishop Shaller climbs into his wheelchair, exhausted, so I can return him to his room.

I hand him the bead in the box. "It feels like I'm touching mercy."

He tucks the box into his robe without a word.

When I return from my shift, the rain-dampened informant skulks on my walkway, a dangerous habit because the peace officers are just as likely to arrest him for begging as they are to arrest me for Christianity. With each six-hundred square foot house identical to all the rest, it's a wonder he was able to find mine at all.

He whispers, "I need to know more."

I hand him Sister Miriam's slip of paper with today's readings and the collect prayer. He pockets it as I say, "Are you hungry?"

He nods. I say, "Leave, and forget your backpack on my front steps. In half an hour, remember it and come back."

Five minutes later, as I make him more sandwiches, I think about the slip of paper I've just handed to an informant. It could be my death. It could be his life. The reading for today: *I've come to set the world on fire. How I wish it were already burning.* It's burning now. Father against son, brother against sister, neighbor against neighbor. We're well and truly on fire, and Jesus, you can come back. Except you're still waiting, waiting to collect one more soul, and then one more, and one more after that, each one a little different from all the ones before, never to be seen again and therefore too precious to leave unfinished. Little treats for you as each of us finds you and reaches for you and our hands grasp yours. You call one more soul, and then it's so good that you reach for the next.

There's a rapid banging at the door, followed by the bell ringing twice. My death, indeed. It's easy to think about arrest and martyrdom while slicing cheese, but my heart pounds, and then again someone beats on my door.

At the entrance I find a grey-uniformed peace officer, and at her side, the informant.

So this is how I surrender my life to You. Please God, forgive the informant.

The drizzle doesn't bother the peace officer. She gestures to the informant. "He's been hanging around. Is he bothering you?"

Is he bothering me? Is that all? Not a surrender of my life, but a chance to protect his?

"I work at the hospital, and I have his backpack. I wanted him to come get it." I hand him the bag. "Thank you."

The officer looks unconvinced. She says, "If he's harassing you, tell your husband to get rid of him."

I say, "My husband died."

The informant exclaims, "What?"

I nod. "On a Friday afternoon, in an unnecessary police action."

The peace officer shifts her weight.

"He did it to save me," I tell the informant.

The informant hesitates before speaking, but then understanding dawns on him. "He sounds like a great guy."

I'm in dangerous territory, a peace officer at my elbow, but I have to grasp the opportunity God's given me. Perhaps this is how I surrender my life after all. "He'd have done it to save you, too."

The informant stares at the ground. "I doubt it. It sounds like he'd be too good to ever talk to me."

"I knew he was too good for me too. But he called one day, and I answered." My voice softens. "He had this way of making you good enough."

The peace officer snatches the bag from the informant and yanks open the zipper, then dumps out everything I've packed: the food, the fresh socks, the book. Yes, a book, its worn jacket proclaiming *Perfect Uniformity Of Our Minds*. Every citizen has at least one edition, courtesy of the government. Half the patients I care for clutch their copy as they die. She shoves everything back in, then barks at the informant, "Get out of here."

He hefts his bag and leaves. The peace officer stares him down until he reaches the main road.

When she turns back to me, I say, "Thank you for looking out for me. I know it's not an easy job, especially when people fear you, but it's important work."

She could have arrested us both if she'd opened the book and found the jacket wrapped around a copy of *An Introduction To The Devout Life*. Instead of condemning me, she says, "Well, be careful. Feed that type and you never get rid of them."

No, and neither does God.

Sister Faustina is having difficulty adjusting after her final vows. I know it happens sometimes, but when we cross paths, she's unsettled. "Maybe I made a mistake," she tells me in a supply room. She's restless. She doesn't want to hide. She clutches my hand and says, "Reese, I'm not being careful. It's not like me. I've stayed underground for years, so why now?"

I say, "Stay with me," and I bring her to hear Bishop Shaller say Mass. His Excellency is going to be released this afternoon, so I won't receive Communion for a while. Although there's a network of priests living underground, they're difficult to reach, so receiving the Eucharist daily has been like venturing into the sunlight after weeks of rain.

Faustina slips out of the hospital room while I finish the Bishop's discharge paperwork. "I'm worried about her. There shouldn't be this difficult an adjustment to final vows." As I hand him the clipboard, I remember her gripping my hand during Patterning. *I'm going away.* "I wonder if her Pattern didn't take."

Bishop Shaller says, "Just keep praying for her," and he signs his paperwork.

I push his wheelchair to the entrance, per regulations, and then he gets out of the chair and walks out the front door. Again per regulations. The hospital has designed so many routines to protect itself from accusations, but then again, those routines have helped us hide for years. Whenever I appear to be doing something strange, no one concludes I'm hiding my illegal beliefs but rather that I'm following regulations in their best interests not to know, and they already have too many of their own. By the grace of God I can juggle them all; can perfectly fulfill the hospital's requirements so they will leave me alone to follow God's.

In the cafeteria, I take a seat near an Urgent Care orderly whose nametag reads Kell but who is actually a seminarian named Michael who, for obvious reasons, had not been Patterned on his namesake. "Long shift?"

He looks exhausted. "This is the first time I've sat down in twenty-three hours."

I bow my head as if sad for him, but I'm saying grace over the bowl of oatmeal and protein powder. I've been fasting for my informant for two reasons, the less obvious reason being that I can't feed him with food I've already eaten, and therefore the cafeteria lunch seems more than appetizing. Thank you, Jesus, for protein.

When I look up, I say, "I need you to think about something." Code for prayer. He nods. "There's a new nurse who just joined us. She went to the Faustina school, and she's very unsettled."

He pauses. "Faustina school?"

I nod. His confusion remains, and he continues, "I didn't think anyone from this part of the world could go to Faustina."

I frown. "Why not?"

"No source material." He leans closer so he can speak lower. "From Faustina, it's all stone or metal. "

The trade in relics is its own system of caves and tunnels, one I've never delved because the contacts are so very in the crosshairs. I can drop a slip of paper into an incinerator or count off a rosary on my fingers, but dealers carry their condemnation on their persons. My informant could accuse anyone of Christian beliefs, but imagine if I carried a theca with the gloves of Saint Padre Pio. Anyone who knows a dealer doesn't even whisper that she knows.

It's possible someone has a wooden rosary of Saint Faustina and Kell hasn't heard about it. It's also possible that someone unscrupulous only said he had it. The devil tempts us all, and who knows what currency he'd use against someone in that line of work? I just rejoice God never called me to it.

On the other hand, Bishop Shaller needs to know there's a question as to his pattern-piece's authenticity. So I peck my way through the computer system and obtain authorization for a follow-up nurse visit in seven days. An electronic summons goes out, and Bishop Shaller's employer confirms an appointment. He'll come to me.

Every day I tuck a sandwich and a snack in a plastic bag beneath the flowers at my fence. I wrap the fruit in a piece of paper. A clever person might notice the papers have writing on them, and a reading person might notice the writings tell the story of a special man with a special mission. Every day, the food disappears from the plastic bag, but the previous day's page has returned, flattened where it was creased.

I continue praying with Sister Faustina, but the Divine Mercy chaplet holds no more joy for her. She's restless. She's been reprimanded for speaking back to a doctor. The longer we work together, the more I find myself convinced she didn't take her sponsor's pattern, whether through failure of the method or failure of the medium. She and I are folding bandages in a stock room when I say to her, "Do you regret your vows?"

She says, "I've never wanted anything else, and I still don't. But this hiding, it's wearing on me."

I say, "What do you want to do?"

She crumples a bandage in her fist. "I want to fight."

"That's not what your role model would do."

Her eyes gleam. "No, and I chose her for that. As a child, I got into so many fights, but everyone told me to be like her, gentle even when people acted so nasty. I thought her pattern would help me be more accepting. But now, it feels just like when I was a kid."

I lower my voice. "What if the pattern was faulty?"

She shakes her head. "Then God let the Church destroy me, and I have to accept that."

Cold inside, I clutch her hand. "Tina, no. That's not right."

She says, "It's surrender."

I say, "That's not surrender. God made you the way you are, not to be destroyed."

She walks away. I spend the next half-hour changing the dressing on a patient's infected wound while the sick woman screams at me that I'm killing her and the one in the next bed complains endlessly of the stench. She is Christ, wounded and filled with the pus of humanity's collective infection. I am Christ to her, maybe the only Christ who will ever touch her without flinching.

And at my fence, I imagine Christ again, starving in both body and soul, stealing an apple from the shelter of the corner post and devouring snippets of the Gospel on shreds of paper that smudge in the endless drizzle.

Seven days. My informant keeps taking his apples. My Sister settles down to her routine and abides by her improvement plan. My Bishop arrives for his appointment, and I escort him to a treatment room, fill in his chart, listen to his lungs. I murmur, "The pattern piece of Faustina may not be legit," and I fill him in.

He makes no reply. I say, "We need to stop using it."

"On the contrary." He hands me the box with the bead. "You have another candidate tonight. He's to take the same Pattern."

I say, "It's illegitimate. It's done harm to Tina."

He shakes his head. "It's real." And when I wait, he says, "You are under obedience not to sabotage the Patterning. You must go through with it."

I look at the box, wondering whose spirit I hold in my gloved hands.

He says, "We don't need another Faustina or another Gemma Galgani. Look around you. It's time for boldness and authority. We could have fire and uprising, so why waste our saints on hidden lives? "

Hidden lives. Tears spring to my eyes. "The Holy Spirit knows what we need. The Holy Spirit will send us the right saints for our time."

He says, "The Holy Spirit sent us Patterns, and it's up to us to use His gifts. We don't need more victim souls right now, more counselors and recluses."

"How do you know what we *do* need? Won't the Church just stagnate?" I clutch the box until it hurts my hand. "Who could have predicted a Saint Francis? Who could have designed a Teresa of Avila? We never knew we needed them until they appeared, and then God sent them, and it was right. But to design them—to override our own souls—"

"It's not an override. You told Tina that yourself. It's a boost." Then he pats me on the shoulder. "Don't let this injure your pride. We can pray the Holy Spirit sends us the souls we need, or we can use His gifts to ensure we have them. You're under obedience, and right now, we need more of Oscar Romero."

That's who I'm holding in my hand. A martyr Archbishop and a galvanizer of the people, and now Tina's guiding light.

I am under obedience. I am not allowed to sabotage the Pattern, but when Sister Faustina brings down our new candidate, I make sure she sees and recognizes the bead. Our new candidate is a middle-aged man with bags under his eyes and a permanent limp. I say, "Our Bishop has left instructions to change your Pattern."

Faustina says, "Whose is that?"

As Miri starts up the ultrasound machine, I tell her. Her eyes darken, but she says nothing, and I don't disturb her during the process because I know she's praying. She's not praying for mercy. Now that she's stopped fighting herself, she's praying against injustice.

The rain begins to let up. I may never see the sun again, though, because at home, four police cars and a riot van idle before my house. They must think they're coming for a dangerous criminal rather than a Christian. May God have mercy on my informant. Myself I surrender, but not him, not until he finds You.

Four peace officers meet me on the sidewalk, and a fifth shoves my informant before me. "Do you recognize this man?"

He's just as threadbare as before, his jacket soaked and a pocket half torn off. "I do."

The peace officer who previously came to my door says, "We know you've been giving him things."

I gesture to his threadbare appearance. "I've been leaving him food. He was starving."

She holds out a slip of paper. "We found this on him. Was this yours?"

I see on the page a handful of words from Luke. *You know how to interpret the appearance of the earth and the sky; why can't you*

242

interpret the present time Why don't you judge for yourselves what is right?

The informant snarls, "I told you, I was going to plant it on her and turn her in for the money!"

The peace officers pull him back with a jerk.

I look at him. "So you're an informant who can't turn in any real Christians?"

"Pathetic, huh?" It's the first time I've ever seen him smile.

I smile in return. "That's why I was leaving food for you."

He glares at the officer's hand gripping his arm. "And no matter what happens, I'm glad you did."

The rain drips off the state-issued tree shading my front steps. One of the officers says, "I say we arrest them both and let the magistrate sort it out."

They conference by their vehicles, leaving me and my informant with the rain dripping on us both. Using my thumb and the rain, I trace a cross on his forehead. I murmur, "I baptize you in the name of the Father, and of the Son, and of the Holy Spirit."

His eyes widen. Relief.

The peace officer returns. "We're going to search your house," she says, but then my informant bolts between the houses and across the next street, and the officers shout even as one of them wrenches me by the arm.

The pain brings tears to my eyes, but I'm not running. I'm praying. I'm praying for a hungry man who's been fed, praying that God gives him the dexterity to outrun a radio signal. They can search my house, and I know they will. They've searched before and have found nothing. More important right now is that they never find him.

They don't find him. They don't find anything in my house, but they spend the next week tailing me everywhere. Tina keeps advocating for her patients. I keep cleaning wounds and folding bandages. The Bishop does his work at the dock by day and at night with the people. And one morning, as I take the bus to work, I find an abandoned building spray-painted in red: *I have come to set the Earth on fire.*

I have no doubt the Holy Spirit sent my informant to do just that, a fire we never predicted and never would have made for ourselves. How I wish it were already ablaze.

AMAZON GAMBIT

By

Vox Day

What happens when a military unit formed for PR reasons is given an actual combat mission?

Lieutenant Colonel Max Kruger stood at attention and saluted as General Markham, SUBCONCOM, debarked from the flyer with the ease of a man four decades younger and strode across the landing pad towards him.

"At ease, Colonel," the general ordered. "Good to see you. Now, come with me, we've got a lot to discuss before the press conference."

The general had four centims on him and was walking quickly, so Kruger had to lengthen his stride in order to keep up with the taller man.

"The Grkese signed the contract?"

"They did indeed," the general confirmed. "And the Duke himself selected you as the contract CO, Max."

"Honored," Kruger murmured, as expected. And it was true, he did feel honored, although he wasn't exactly surprised. Of the various officers in the Rhysalani Armed Forces qualified to command low-tech forces, he not only possessed the best record with regards to successfully completed contracts, but he had beaten Col. Thompson, his closest rival, rather soundly at the Duke's Command Challenge last year. "I presume it will be 3rd Battalion?"

The 3rd Battalion of the Ducal Marines specialized in low-tech combat, particularly combat below TL10. Kruger had served with them on two previous deployments, both of which had taken place on Dom Sevru. The men of 3rd Battalion were trained to be able to fight with everything from swords and shields to plasma cannon and sub-atomic armor.

"No," the general replied, to his surprise, as they entered the elevator that would bring them down to the heart of the airbase command center. "The Lord General suggested that this would be the ideal opportunity to show the subsector what the 11th Special Battalion can do. And the Duke concurred."

Kruger couldn't hide his astonishment. Or his dismay. He looked at his superior in disbelief, and while he saw everything from amusement to sympathy in the older man's eyes, he detected no sign at all that his leg was being pulled.

"Dear God, you're not joking!"

"Afraid not, Max. The Duke has spent a fortune training and equipping those women for the last five years, and he's decided that it's about time to see a return on that investment."

Kruger didn't trust himself to speak. The first five or six responses that sprang to mind would have earned him at least a reprimand, if not a court-martial. The next three, if uttered openly by an officer of the Armed Forces, technically amounted to lèse-nobilité and would theoretically merit a firing squad. So he said nothing.

The general grinned nonchalantly and raised an eyebrow. He knew damn well what Kruger was thinking. "He's not wrong, Max. Their negotiators were so impressed that they paid triple our usual rate. Half up front."

"They did? Why the Hell would they do that?"

"Well, as I understand the sales pitch, our highly trained female soldiers have proven to be much better communicators than their male counterparts, and as a result they are considerably less

246

inclined to needlessly break things and kill people. In this particular case, the estimated savings in infrastructure damage when taking and occupying the primary objective alone is expected to more than make up for the increased cost of the contract."

"Assuming we can complete it. What's the tech level again?"

"Seven."

This time, Kruger couldn't restrain an oath. The general raised an eyebrow, then slapped Kruger on his oak-leafed shoulders as they approached a door with a pair of Duke's Marines on either side.

"Try to keep it clean for the cameras, Max. If you don't know what to say, just smile and declare that you've got every confidence in the troops. Do your best to sell it. God knows we've all had to tell a few humdingers in our day. Your record speaks for itself, so let it do the talking. Now, you've got an hour to review the contract and meet with the battalion's officers before the press conference, so I suggest you hop to it."

"Yessir," Kruger said morosely. "Any chance I can get out of this, General?"

"None at all, Max. None at all."

Four hundred and ninety-seven women stood at parade rest, their ranks stretching out nearly to the horizon, awaiting his review. Accompanying him was Captain Tango, a cold grey-eyed woman who was half-a-head taller than he was, the commander of Easy Company. The two other company commanders followed them, Captains Kreuz and Mills, both of whom were slender, attractive women who carried themselves with the easy confidence of professional athletes. All three women were impressive, all three had done the battalion credit at yesterday's press conference, and in other circumstances, Kruger would have been proud to have them serve under him.

As it stood, however, he wondered if the most straightforward solution would be to simply fry his brain with the Ikoni-17 service laser he was wearing on his right hip.

He walked past the ranks of uniformed women, who straightened and saluted as he passed them by. His eyes narrowed as he walked, taking in long legs in knee-high boots, ill-concealed swellings of firm, high-set breasts, and straight, attractive noses on one pretty face after another. Where were the squatty, foul-mouthed bull dykes, the hard women with faces like roadkill and chips on their broad, oxen-like shoulders? Then the unwelcome reality struck him. They hadn't just given him an all-female battalion, the whole damn unit was made up of poster girls. Like a long-dead Russian Czar, who selected his elite regiments based on height, the Duke's 11th Special Battalion was, to put it in marketing terms, an extremely media-friendly outfit.

Silently, he cursed the Duchess as he walked past one tall, attractive, fit young woman after another. A good one-third of them were taller than he was. What he was reviewing wasn't a combat unit, it was a bloody Praetorian Guard!

After the review, he dismissed the battalion with a few meaningless words about their upcoming deployment, then retired to a conference room to meet with the three company commanders, as well as the lieutenant in charge of the battalion staff platoon and the battalion's senior sergeant.

"Ladies, we have a problem," he informed them. "I need to find out whether you're in this to win, or if you're here to go through the motions."

"In it to win it, sir!" Mills, Kreuz, and the lieutenant, who was a pretty young blonde, chorused. Tango and the sergeant were more circumspect.

"What motions, Colonel?" Tango said.

He took a deep breath. "None of this goes beyond this room. Understood?"

"Sir!"

"I've gone over the briefings as well as everything I could find about the situation on Ulixis between South Grkas and the Foundation. And I've reached an inescapable conclusion. You're being set up to fail. Correction: we're being set up to fail."

There was a long moment of silence. The women looked at each other. Tango sniffed contemptuously, as if his assertion was nothing new to her.

"Are you sure that's not just the opinion of an insecure man who's afraid an all-female unit might show up the rest of the Duke's soldiers?"

It wasn't, technically, insubordination. Kruger did his best to keep a straight face as he answered her.

"While that is certainly possible in theory, Captain, it is also the considered opinion of an officer who has participated in 37 combat deployments and commanded twelve of them. Every single one of those twelve contracts paid in full, Captain, eight of them with a performance-related bonus. I've read your record, Tango. Two off-planet deployments, neither of which involved so much as scratching your nail polish. So, what exactly do you know about the situation that I don't? Precisely what am I missing?"

The other women were staring at the grey-eyed woman, who, much to Kruger's surprise, laughed. It was a higher-pitched, more feminine laugh than he would have expected. "Not a damn thing, sir. Sorry, sir."

Well. That was a surprise. He dismissed her apology with a gesture. "Never mind that. Here's my read. You know the brass billed us at three times the usual rate, and they arranged to get paid half up-front. That means that even if we fail, they walk away with more than they would have gotten if they'd pitched 3rd Battalion. I did some asking around yesterday, and the scuttlebutt is that Lord Grey has been looking to disband this battalion for the last three years. Whether you realize it or not, you're the Duchess's darlings, so the Lord General can't simply shut it down without coming up with a good excuse. A debacle on Ulixis will give him the ammo he needs, which explains why he pitched you instead of 3rd."

"Why did they give the command to you, sir?" asked Kreuz. "We heard you were the best."

"That's exactly why. Because if the Duke's best and most handsome lieutenant colonel can't beat a few stone-throwing savages with you, what use can you possibly be to anyone? I'm their show pony, and they're throwing me to the wolves just to make the fall look good. To cover up the fact that they're running a scam."

The women looked at each other again. Mills, who might have been pretty if she had a less prominent nose, appeared as though she was about to cry. "What are we going to do, Colonel?"

"We have two choices. One, we do what we're supposed to do, we go through the motions, and we fail. Presumably with an eye to minimizing casualties, of course. Two, we figure out a way to beat the bastards and we come back here with their peckers in our hands."

"Do you really think we can do that, sir?" Tango asked. "I mean, I thought you said we were being set up to fail."

"We are!" The women jumped as Kruger slammed his hand on the table and roared at them. "But who said we have to? I'll be damned if I'll let them trash my perfect record just so some damned accountant can hand the Duke an excuse to keep his bloody wife from going mental!"

He glared at them. "You ladies may not be able to fight your way out of a paper bag, but that doesn't mean we can't find a way to get the job done. I just need to know that you're willing to do what it takes. Whatever it takes."

"We'll do whatever it takes, Colonel," Tango assured him frostily. "And don't think the 11th can't fight. We'll show you we can."

Kruger snorted bitterly. "No, you won't. We'll start with you, Captain. Have Easy Company on Field Bravo at zero eight hundred in their running gear tomorrow morning. It's time for you parade ladies to start learning what combat is."

Sergeant Hollis was, according to both Captain Tango and Lieutenant Cahill, the meanest, baddest brawler in Easy. She, and five other women that the captain had hand-selected, were standing in front of the rest of the company, stretching, throwing kicks, and shadow boxing, as Kruger approached them. He was followed by eight Marines from 3rd Battalion and a pair of Navy squids who looked though he'd just extricated them from the brig. Several of the men had broken noses and facial scars, five of them were over-muscled hulks with the swollen muscles indicative of genetic modification, and all of them looked like hardened killers.

"Hollis!" Kruger pointed to the sergeant. "The captain tells me you're tough."

"I can hold my own, Colonel."

"We'll see about that. Do you see Corporal Enz there?" Her ponytail bobbed as she nodded. "Well, I want you to do your damndest to take him out with your bare hands. Fight dirty. Do whatever it takes to win. Understand?"

She looked uncertain, but she nodded.

He glanced at Enz. "As for you, Corporal, don't hold back. Just try not to kill her if you can avoid it."

"Colonel!" Tango tried to interrupt but Kruger cut her off.

"We're about to be deployed on a tech-seven planet, Captain. The enemy isn't going to invite you to a tea party." He nodded to the two assigned combatants. "Get to it!"

Hollis was game. Her face was a mask of pure determination, and she kept a good guard up to protect it as she warily circled the larger Marine. The sergeant was stocky and muscular, but even so, she was at least eighty kilos lighter than the corporal. For his part, Enz rotated to keep Hollis in front of him while holding his hands carelessly just above his waist.

"Hai!" Hollis shouted as she suddenly rushed forward and threw a left jab. Her form was textbook-perfect, but Enz simply leaned back and slapped it aside with his own left. Hollis stumbled with the force of the deflection, briefly exposing her right side, but she quickly caught her balance and whirled around, her guard back in place. Unnecessarily, as it happened, since Enz hadn't followed up on the momentary opening. He had merely rotated in place, a faint smile on his face, with his eyes still locked on her. Hollis resumed circling, and when she rushed in again, this time her jab was a feint, followed by a powerful right rear hand.

Again, her form was crisp. She kept her guard up and her hip snapped smartly. But the blow never landed. Hollis had barely begun to extend her arm when Enz's right fist caught her chin in a half-cross, half-uppercut. There was an audible crack. The blow snapped her head back and sent her crumpling to the ground like a rag doll. The watching women, Captain Tango included, gasped.

"She's out cold. Get her to sick bay," Kruger ordered. "Make sure her jaw isn't broken. Well done, corporal. James, you're up next. Who you got for the private, Captain?"

Private James's opponent was a Private Saipano, a tall young woman, lean like a panther, who had apparently been trained in some form of kickboxing. She threw a pair of beautiful high kicks with flawlessly crisp technique at James, who ducked the first one,

252

then caught her foot on the second and jerked it forward as he twisted. Saipano screamed in fear as she was pulled off her feet, then thrown nearly four meters through the air as James spun around 180 degrees before letting her go. The woman landed hard on her side, but managed to roll over and rise to her feet, just in time to be kicked in the stomach by the much bigger man. James stepped back as Saipano curled up in a ball, and Kruger waved him off as the medic rushed to Saipano's side and kneeled down beside her.

"She's spitting up blood, Colonel. She may have broken ribs or other internal injuries."

"Get her to sick bay," he told her. Then he turned to Tango. "Who's next?"

The captain grimly indicated the next woman, whose honed form showed the unmistakable sign of considerable time spent in the gym, but no sooner did she find herself squaring off against a big, scar-faced Marine who loomed over her than she lost control of her bladder. The Marine laughed, sparking cries of anger and outrage from the women of Easy Company.

Kruger waved the smirking Marine off and turned towards Tango. "Seen enough?"

"This is sadistic!" she hissed. "Sir!"

"No, Captain, this is combat, and it's the gentle kind at that. What would be sadistic is putting these soldiers up against primitive warriors who are carrying swords and axes and spears, who are trained from childhood to use such weapons, and who outmass your troops on average three-to-one. They aren't going to stop coming at you just because one of your frightened little girls pissed her pants, Captain."

"That's not fair!"

"War isn't fair."

"You are demoralizing these women before the deployment, sir!"

"Better demoralized than dead. What I'm trying to do is to knock some sense into you, Captain. Into all of you." He raised his voice. "Hands up, Easy Company! How many of you thought you were ready to go into combat against men yesterday?"

A few dozen hands went up, some of them slowly and uncertainly.

"How many of you still think you're ready?"

Only five or six remained up.

"Good. Now who wants to go next?"

Not a single hand remained aloft. Kruger turned back to Tango. She glared at him, but finally, she nodded.

"You've made your point, sir. We can't fight them. Not hand-to-hand, at any rate. Are you going to report that the battalion isn't combat-ready?"

"Hell no!" Kruger grinned at the company commander, whose pretty face was flushed with chagrin. "There's more than one way to kill a man. And there are more ways to take a city than a frontal assault."

The Ulixian sky had a faint purple tinge to it, particularly in the morning. No doubt there was some perfectly good scientific explanation for that, Kruger assumed, but he didn't care why there was a purple sky, he just liked the way it looked. It was rather refreshing being on a low-tech planet; outside the spaceport anything that didn't operate on pure muscle power, animal or human, was banned under both world and Ascendancy law. Life was considerably slower, and the population was more spread-out, lending a bucolic holiday air to the deployment.

But there were men living on Ulixis, and wherever there were men there were differences of opinion. And wherever there were differences of opinion, sooner or later, there was always war. Kruger didn't know why South Grkas was warring against the Eighth-Day Foundation, nor did he care; what concerned him was that the contract required the 11th Special Battalion of the Rhysalani Marines to take the Foundation city of Noötrine within four months of landing. Nearly one month had already passed without the battalion doing much more than patrol some of the border villages and occasionally engage in minor skirmishes, skirmishes in which they usually came off considerably worse than either the Foundationers or the Grkese.

The Grkese were rapidly losing confidence in both Kruger and the Rhysalani Marines, which was entirely understandable in light of the minor engagements, and, more importantly, how the battalion had not yet made any sort of move towards Noötrine. But unbeknownst to their employers, the 11th Special Battalion was making substantial progress.

"Colonel, we have word that the first three girls have been spotted in the city," Tango told him as she climbed the hill behind him. "Route Alpha is confirmed."

"Do we have any word from them?"

"No, but there were no signs of visible mistreatment. Corporal McCall was wearing a blue ribbon in her hair."

"That's good." The blue ribbon was the sign that everything was going according to plan. Prior to arranging for the infiltration, a series of codes had been arranged, but the simplest one was based on ribbons. The Foundation women favored long hairstyles that involved ribbons, so communicating in this manner was unlikely to raise any suspicions on the part of the Noötrinese.

"Do you want to increase the volume?"

"No, let's play it safe. The reports have been consistent. We need at least 200 soldiers inside before we can act. Three hundred would be better."

"That would make maintaining the visibility profile more difficult."

"I know."

Kruger wondered if he dared take the risk. Given how well-known the presence of the battalion was, the women couldn't simply disappear. If they did, someone might make the connection between the shrinking battalion and the sudden appearance of a number of suspiciously fit young women in the city of Noötrine. No, the greatest risk to his plan was that it would be prematurely uncovered, not that their initial strike would be too weak. There was no reason not to stick to the plan.

Resisting the urge to meddle was sometimes the hardest part, he reflected.

"Thirty-seven more days, Captain."

"I know sir. It's going to be hard to keep the Grkese from complaining."

Kruger shrugged. "I don't know that we want to. The louder they complain, the more convinced the Foundation is that we're not doing anything dangerous. Let them whine."

Three more weeks went by. Kruger and the company commanders continued to go through the motions, hoping that their doubled-up duty schedules would conceal the fact that more than one-fifth of the battalion was now mysteriously absent. Kruger put up with twice-daily visits from the Grkese generals with an indifference bordering on arrogance, which only infuriated them all the more.

"You have done nothing, Colonel Kruger! Nothing at all! The city is not invested, you have not engaged the Foundation's forces, and as far as I can see your poor excuses for soldiers have not left the barracks in more than one month!"

"That's a fair summary, General," Kruger admitted. He was leaning back in his chair with his boots on his desk, a pose he'd learned seemed to particularly annoy the Grkese officers. "Sometimes the most efficient way to fight is to do nothing at all."

"Nonsense!" shouted the general. "Do you think you will placate us with cheap aphorisms? I will have you know the king is seriously contemplating writing a complaint about your performance to your superior officers!"

"Is he? Well, tell him to give my best to the brass."

"Do you think you're going to get away with this, Colonel? Do you think we are so stupid that we don't know you think you can just accept our money, then sit on your fat asses and do nothing! You are thieves, Colonel! Nothing but thieves!"

"You're going to regret those words in a few months when you're all falling all over each other to tell me what a strategic genius I am," Kruger said.

"I find it very difficult to believe you are engaging in strategic anything," the general said. "Unless you are strategically working your way through your soldiery one-by-one."

"Eppure si muove."

"What's that?"

"One more thing you won't understand." Kruger spread his hands. "Look, General, you've admitted you don't know what is going on. And you don't. You're government has already sunk a considerable amount of resources into me and my battalion. You did it because you couldn't beat the Foundation on your own. So, why don't you let the very expensive forces you hired, and their very brilliant commander, do our job the best way we know how to do it?"

The general stared at him. He was a tall, slender man like most of the Ulixians; the planetary gravity was two percent lighter than that of Rhysalan and four point two percent lighter than Ascendancy Standard. He tugged at his orange-striped mustache in a thoughtful manner, then nodded curtly. "Perhaps you are correct. There will be time enough for recriminations later. But so help me, Colonel, if your Duke has played us for fools, your mercenaries will never find employment anywhere on this planet again!"

"We prefer the term 'contractors'," Kruger drawled. "But I take your point, general. Now, I have a question for you. How many men do you have ready for when we crack the gates?"

"The gates?"

"Of Noötrine," he said patiently. "The city you are paying us this princely sum to assist you in taking."

"I don't understand."

"I am aware of that. You don't need to understand, you merely need to have your men established at a forward base sufficiently close to the city to permit them to approach the walls under cover of darkness. I'll provide you with a staff officer so long as you swear to guard her virtue like your own virgin daughter's; she'll let you know when to advance from the base."

The general stared at him, his eyes narrow with suspicion. But he nodded, slowly, as if he understood, which Kruger very much doubted. He pointed a stubby finger at Kruger, and for the first time since he'd entered Kruger's makeshift office, he smiled. It was a crafty smile of man who believes he has just drawn a winning hand.

"Ah, you play the cards close to your chest, Colonel. I like that!"

Yeah, I'll bet you do. "Five thousand of your best men, General. We'll get the gates open, never you fear about that, but as good as my girls are, all they can do is give you the city. You want to keep it, you're going to have to take it firmly in hand."

The general extended his hand, and Kruger removed his boots from the desk, swiveled his chair, and stood up to take it. The man's hand was pudgy, but his grip was firm. "You have no siege engines, no miners, no ladders, and you make no moves of any kind that I can see. Perhaps you are a magician, Colonel?"

Kruger smiled blandly as the general suggestively brushed his nose in a gesture that indicated cunning. Let him think we managed to smuggle some banned tech in. An anti-gravity generator, or a tractor beam to pull the gates open, explosives to blow them, or chemicals to melt the walls. Anything that would keep him and everyone else looking in the wrong direction.

It was three days before H-hour. They'd been lucky so far, but Kruger couldn't help thinking that their luck was bound to run out at some point. He now regretted not doing anything to give the rumors some teeth, maybe arranging for a set of fake generators to be set up around the perimeter, or even sending out a trumpeter once a day to circle the walls and sound a magic horn. The infiltrations had proceeded apace, and he held sufficient hostages to bolster the weakest link in the chain, the traffickers, but every soldier inside the enemy city was one more risk piled on top of all the rest. If his experience was any guide, the spark that set the fireworks off would probably be struck at the most inopportune moment.

The problem was that putting his girls into position early could be that very spark. There were Foundation spies all over the city, and while he was confident none of them were privy to the fact of the Battalion's declining numbers, even a nighttime departure wouldn't be enough to prevent either their actions or their numbers from being marked. What they needed, he decided, was a distraction, and one that would justify the Battalion exiting both the barracks and the city in as cloaked and confusing a manner as possible.

Then he smiled. The answer was inherent in the question posed. He lifted the silver bell on his desk and shook it, sending a pair of metallic notes echoing off the stone walls. A staff sergeant opened the door and poked her head in.

"Colonel?"

"Get me Captain Tango."

"Right away, sir!"

It wasn't long before Tango entered. She was wearing a sleepsuit that looked a size too small and was breathing hard as if she'd just run through the corridors to get there. Her eyes were initially bright and anticipatory, although after he outlined his modified plan for her, she looked downright unsettled.

"Moving up the departure isn't a problem, Colonel. We can be on the move within five kilosecs. I'm a little more concerned about the idea of setting fire to the city. Won't that violate our bond?"

"It's not a violation per se. Although we certainly want to avoid paying any reparations. It only matters if we get caught." He shrugged. "So don't get caught. Besides, there have been rumors about Foundation saboteurs floating around since we got here. Might as well put some meat on those bones."

"Yessir," she said dubiously. "I'll give Lieutenant Whitworth the detail. She's clever enough. What about the hostages?"

"Find a lodging, dose them, lock them in, and tell the proprietor to release them tomorrow morning. This will be over one way or another before they can get any word to Noötrine."

"Sir!" She saluted and left. Kruger looked around his office. For all the crudities and the candles, it had served him well enough. Still, he was looking forward to getting back to a planet where there were showers and the women weren't off-limits. Too many of the girls, including several of the officers, had made it clear that they wouldn't mind a little fraternizing with a superior officer and he wasn't sure how much longer he could hold out.

Unless he missed a beat, that Tango had been wearing freshly applied lipstick tonight. She didn't look bad, not bad at all. He laughed bitterly. Bloody close quarters and nothing to do could send even an ice princess over the edge.

Dawn was breaking and the weary 11th Special Battalion was within sight of the ridge that overlooked the city beyond when Kruger spotted a rider rushing towards them. It was Corporal Reynolds, one of the battalion's shorter soldiers, who had been assigned to the overwatch team more than a month ago.

"Colonel, it's a good thing you're here. Two of the girls were spotted wearing red ribbons yesterday evening!"

"And you're just coming to tell me now?"

"The lieutenant said it was too dangerous to ride at night, sir!"

Kruger closed his eyes and counted to ten. Then he counted to ten again. The propensity of his soldiers to prioritize their own safety over the mission never ceased to astonish and enrage him, but he had learned that voicing his opinion on the matter did nothing but provoke waterworks. After counting to ten one more time, he felt calm enough to address her without resorting to expletives.

"Are there any signs of the guard being called out? Are they on alert? Do we know how many were taken?"

"No, no, and no. Sir. As far as we know."

Kruger nodded. There was nothing for it now but to hope that whoever had been taken would have the sense to keep her mouth shut. The mere act of speech would be sufficient to give any of the women away as off-worlders, and it wasn't exactly a secret that the Grkese had hired female contractors. Then again, if the Foundation only ID'd one or two of them, they'd assume they were spies or

261

perhaps assassins. As long as the girls had the steel to not spill the only secret that mattered, their capture wouldn't make a difference as far as the mission was concerned.

He turned to Tango. "Launch the signal at midnight. Tell the girls to get some shut-eye now, we're going in tonight. And send a rider to the Grkese commander, tell him he's got to be in within 200 meters of the gates at zero dark fifty."

Kruger looked back at the column of two hundred fifty exhausted women behind him. They had taken thirty-six kilosecs to cover what would have taken one of the other battalions closer to twenty. Their sisters had been taking all the risks and putting in the hard work laying the foundation for tonight's action, but would they be up to finishing the mission? He'd done all he could over the last month to prepare them, but now there was only one way to find out.

The transport had come out of hyperwave, and planetfall on Rhysalan was scheduled in just over one ship's day, when the captain summoned Kruger to his cabin. The Navy man was uncharacteristically respectful when he arrived, which made him suspect that someone important had already taken advantage of the restoration of communications to hail the ship. His suspicions were confirmed when the captain promptly announced that His Grace the Duke of Rhysalan was on the screen and waiting for Kruger before making himself scarce.

"Lieutenant Colonel Kruger, 11th Special Battalion, your Grace," he announced himself. He didn't remember if he still needed to bow when he was only in the virtual presence, rather than the actual presence, of the Duke, so he awkwardly ducked his head in the hopes that the gesture would pass for the deed if he did.

"Well done, Colonel! I wanted to be the first to congratulate you for your spectacular success in completing the contract!" The Duke was a man in his middle forties, handsome in the way that only aristocrats who have married for beauty for several generations can achieve. His voice was so rich and mellifluent that it sounded like a voice-over.

"Thank you, your Grace. It is my honor to serve your noble House." The bank transfer from the Grkese must have cleared, Kruger thought. The Duke was so cheerful he was almost giddy.

"The Lord General tells me the casualty figures were unusually low. Remarkable, Colonel, simply remarkable!"

"I could not have done it without the 11th Battalion," Kruger told him honestly. "Their commitment to the mission was... total."

The Duke beamed. "I'm so very pleased. So is my wife, for as you know, the 11th Special Battalion was her particular brainchild. She wished to congratulate you herself, Colonel, so allow me to convey my sincere appreciation to you and your officers again before I transfer you to her now."

"Honored, Your Grace," Kruger said dutifully. A moment later, he found himself facing the flashing eyes of an angry woman in her thirties. The Duchess of Rhysalan was said to have once been the most beautiful woman on the planet, and although her pale cheeks were now bright crimson with rage, she was still breathtakingly lovely.

"Are you the bastard who ruined my battalion?"

Kruger stifled the laughter that threatened to erupt from deep within him and blithely assumed the blank face of the professional soldier who admits to knowing absolutely nothing more than his name, his rank, and his identification number.

"Lieutenant Colonel Alfrix Kruger, Commander, 11th Special Battalion, Your Grace."

"I heard what you did, Commander! You turned those brave, brave women into whores! How dare you? You're neither an officer nor a gentleman, you're nothing but a pimp!"

"Your Grace, with all due respect, would you be happier if we were coming home with 68 women in body bags instead of pregnant? Those brave women risked their lives and put their bodies on the line for the mission, and they got the job done without losing one-tenth as many soldiers as any other battalion would have lost." He didn't think it was necessary to mention the 53 troops who had contracted venereal diseases; the medics told him they expected to be able to clear all of the infected women before the battalion made planetfall. "Hell, they're bringing home future reinforcements!"

He realized he'd gone too far with his last line when the Duchess began to blister his ears with an obscenity-laced rant that would have made his old drill sergeant blush. He took it as impassively as he could manage, allowing himself no more than a faint smile when she finally shrieked incoherently and closed the connection.

The old Greek strategist had it right, he mused to himself. Pleasures capture the passions and corrupt even the most courageous. Hell, correctly harnessed, pleasures could even capture walled cities!

And yet, one thought haunted Kruger. What had they thought, those poor Foundation soldiers, all those officers and guards, at that moment their sweet, compliant lovers had given them le coup de grâce in the place of le petit mort.

He thought of Captain Tango's eager, lipsticked smile, and he shivered.

ELEGY FOR THE LOCUST

By

Brian Niemeier

When you have the chance to redress the injustice of your birth...

It wasn't an epiphany; more like the dawning awareness of something that had long subsisted beneath or above notice—an insect on a page that one only sees when it scuttles across a letter. By the time I'd recognized the idea, it had burrowed too deeply under my skin to dislodge.

Since time out of mind I had languished in the grip of a merciless yearning that I resisted with all my strength. When the longing overwhelmed me I would seek potable respite at the Red Crow teahouse. But not even the local burned wine—the sole consolation of living in Iye—could drown my envy of Marthen Lumac.

No. Envy was too mild a word for my loathing of the cosmic farce that I was Janeth and not Marthen.

Shame poured from the hollow of my heart and filled my chest with scarlet fire. Every burst of rowdy laughter was a judgment of the drunken dockhands against my lowliness in light of Lumac's glory. Every sour glance from a sloe-eyed serving girl scorned my dull brown mop and pale skin in favor of Lumac's golden hair and bronze complexion. Certainty of my temporal, spiritual, and moral poverty robbed my wine of sweetness.

My very being had become unbearable torture. Yet I never entertained self-murder; not due to any proscription of my lukewarm faith, but because death would forever deny me the answer that waited just beyond reach.

There in the raucous gloom, over a half-empty glass gone cold, the idea revealed itself to my tormented mind. I resisted at the urging of my conscience, but undermined by lethargy it soon succumbed.

In that hour I knew that my pain had but one remedy. I must become Marthen Lumac.

I staggered out into the damp night, leaving a pair of brass coins on the rough, stained table. Little remained of the pittance I earned by translating certain volumes in Lumac's private library from the native Shianese, but the prospect of reliving my destitution was the least enticement down the irrevocable path I'd chosen.

The air was heavy but clear, and as I passed along the seaside lane I saw the monument looming over the wharf ahead on my right. The pillar of black stone taller than a ship's mast had been raised when Shianmar had overthrown the last Tral emperor and allegedly marked the site of Almeth Elocine's landing on the Thysian continent.

More recently the column had been sanded square to honor the first Guild fleet, which had flown over the same shore on its way to conquer Elocine's home isle of Annon.

The black pillar aroused in me the bitterness of broken hope. The Charter War had coincided with my preparation to enter the College of Augurs in Mizraim—an oversight that proved my blindness to omens. By the time I gained appointment to the priesthood, the Steersmen's Guild was fully established.

I looked away from the monument and the shadowy sea beyond. But a salt-scented wind recalled the death of my vocation to sail the stars and bring civilized religion to the heathens of Keth. Even before my consecration to Bifron, taking the auspices upon the birth of a child or the eve of a new venture had fallen out of favor among the old nobility. The new merchants who succeeded them despised all priestcraft and placed their faith in Workings.

Wrath and sorrow racked my soul as I remembered how, almost overnight, the cult that had bound an empire which once ruled one quarter of the world had dwindled to a forgotten remnant. A last glimmer of the faith remained in Shianmar, and I was assigned to serve the spiritual needs of a small trading company in Iye. A salt breeze brought me there. And there I languished, merely half a world away, instead of treading the soil of a distant sphere.

Resigned to fate's decree that I remain on Mithgar, I served as best I could until the company folded; its generations-long line of owners impoverished by the princely fees that Guild Steersmen command. I had thought myself condemned to penury when a friend's pity obtained for me an introduction to Marthen Lumac and employment in his house.

The cobblestone lane turned away from the shore and curved upward between tight rows of buildings with gabled tile roofs. The sea breeze gave way to a stagnant miasma of old cooking fat, rotting garbage, and urine. Seedy figures crouched on doorsteps, huddled in twos or threes, and cast furtive looks as I passed.

I never stopped to ask directions. It seemed that my feet knew where to go.

On the next street corner I saw a red wooden post capped with a golden pyramid—a symbol of the native Atavist faith—which called to mind a familiar artifact.

The sculpture, composed of four gold triangles the size of my palm, resided in Lumac's third floor gallery. His home was built in the Western style with four stories clad in fine white limestone, as befit the city's chief liaison to the Guild. Comparing his palace to my rented hovel elicited a sensation like a slap to the face.

A face, I vowed, that would soon disgrace me no more!

I emerged from my grim reverie in front of a building rife with peculiarities but also possessing a strange familiarity. Its design was of the old fashion, with a prominent central structure flanked by two symmetrical wings stretching back beyond sight into the dark. The whole rambling edifice was surmounted by two-tiered fired clay roofs with stone statues of grotesque beasts standing watch at the peaks and corners.

The place was—or had been—the manor house of a distinguished family. I pictured it as the home of a port official built on what had been Iye's outskirts before the city had overrun his estate. The house had changed hands more than once over the years if the corroded temple bells, the faded signage advertising room rates in four languages, and the crude mural of a slender woman massaging a smiling man were trustworthy auspices.

I could not discern what manner of trade the current householder engaged in. The wind chime depicting Zadok and Thera suggested an outlet for cheap curios. Whether the establishment was open or closed likewise eluded me, since the ornate lanterns bracketing the door were unlit; but light flickered behind the small squares of colored glass that made up the front windows.

How long I stood debating on the threshold, I cannot say. Some reflexive aversion, as if I were facing a trap that had caught me before, prevented me from ringing the doorbell. Yet the certainty that leaving would doom me forever to existence as myself kept me from returning to the street.

The wind chime played a single desolate note despite the lack of a breeze. As if some curse had been broken, I bolted toward the door, threw it open, and barged into a candlelit vestibule.

"Welcome, Janeth," an affable, airy voice greeted me from the shifting darkness beyond.

I recognized my name, pronounced almost as a sigh, as having been spoken by the one man who had cause not to shun it—my only friend in Iye, in all of Shianmar; perhaps on the whole sphere of Mithgar.

268

"Where are you, friend?" I asked, for I knew him only by that term of affection.

"Here." My friend's lank, somewhat stooped form materialized from the shadows to my right. The dry floorboards creaked under his sandal-shod feet, elsewise I would have thought him a figment of my troubled mind.

I looked about from the candles set on the wax-encrusted windowsill to the carved willow trim on the yellowed plaster walls, to the scuffed floor. My nose detected the ghosts of spices and incense.

"What business brings you here?" I pondered aloud.

My friend's mouth formed a thin smile. "The same that brings you." He withdrew a key on an iron chain fine as thread from his faded blue coat and turned back toward the darkness. "Come. The Prior is waiting."

Moved by fear of abandonment to my fate, I plucked a beeswax candle from the sill and followed. My friend passed through a circular arch and turned left into a darkened hallway. Though my candle shed no light on his path as I walked behind him, my friend sauntered down the corridor as one would stroll through a garden at noon. My quivering light revealed walls defaced with graffiti that defied interpretation.

Dust motes dancing in a shaft of pale light betrayed the presence of a window in the left wall ahead. My friend continued past the unglazed opening without pause, but I ventured a glance through the window, if only to assure myself that a wide world existed beyond these dark dusty confines.

In the half-light of a moon partially veiled by scraps of cloud, a broad courtyard stretched between the building's two wings. Sunk into the bare soil was a cluster of stone-ringed holes too shallow for wells. The grit heaped against their walls bespoke long disuse.

Before I could study them further, dark clouds hid the moon and left my poor candle as the sole source of light.

At length my friend came to a halt. The rattling of metal on metal said that we'd reached a door, which he was unlocking with his small iron key. Rusted hinges soon creaked, and we advanced only a few paces before my friend stopped again and faced left.

"Shut the door, won't you?" he said. "We mustn't be disturbed."

Acting on deeply ingrained manners, I turned back to the door we'd entered through and pulled it closed. The latch clicked. Trying the knob, I was somewhat disturbed to find that the door had locked itself behind us.

Hinges squealed again, and I turned to see that my friend had opened the door in the left wall. We proceeded through and began a descent down a narrow flight of dirty steps. Each stair bowed discouragingly beneath my underfed frame, and I released a breath I hadn't known I'd held when we set foot on a solid floor of packed soil. My next indrawn breath tasted of vinegar and old bread.

"This way." Though he spoke at conversational volume, my friend's voice retained the quality of a whisper. He led me into a cool chamber so large that the candlelight touched neither walls nor ceiling. The shadows did relinquish the skeletal remains of a winepress—its great overarching timbers riddled with rot.

We passed between parallel rows of barrels big enough for a man to sit upright in and came to a door of iron-bound planks in a mortarless stone wall. Unlike every other feature I'd seen within the house, this door looked newly made.

My friend stood at the door and knocked. The cavernous chamber returned no echo. My stomach tied itself in knots as I waited in the silent gloom.

The door opened inward with hardly a sound. My expectation of a stout, broken-nosed guard was dashed when I instead saw no one standing inside the doorway. Unless my senses deceived me—and the mounting dread vying with my forbidden desperation may well have clouded my eyes—the door had opened on its own.

Yet the oddity I'd witnessed brought at least one comfort—the room beyond was filled with warm steady light.

My friend passed through the door and stepped to one side, affording me an unobstructed view of the chamber. A continuous wall of rough stone encircled the room, and a vaulted stone ceiling hung overhead. The orange-yellow light shone from glass orbs the size of a man's head ensconced atop twisted wrought iron lampstands upon intricately woven rugs. I counted a dozen such lamps—no doubt the products of some Working—positioned along the curve of the wall.

"Come, Janeth. A gentleman does not lurk in doorways."

The invitation, delivered in a mellifluous voice normally reserved for malakhim, was issued by a man seated at an oak table elegantly carved in the Stranosi style yet lacquered after the Shianese fashion. Even from across a room that could have served as a lecture hall or a minor temple, I clearly saw that his fair face retained the glow of youth while projecting the confidence of one in the prime of life. A perfect mane of silver hair fell to the midpoint of his neck.

My first steps upon the soft carpets were halting, but my stride quickened as I approached the table. The singular man seated behind it closed the cloth-bound codex he'd been reading in the light of a miniature Worked lamp. His robes rustled as he rose to greet me, and I saw that they were cream-colored silk embellished with gold. A short cape colored and shaped like butterfly wings encircled the upper third of his lean body.

How did you know my name? I nearly asked aloud before my sense of courtesy intervened. Surely my friend, who maintained his vigil beside the door, had made me known to this gentleman who'd rounded the table to stand before me.

"I am Prior Sed," the silver-haired man introduced himself, eschewing a solemn bow and extending his open hand like a freeman of the West.

As I shook the Prior's smooth, firm hand, my eyes wandered past the table and the folding Midraist scribe's chair to another door set directly across from the entrance. It, too, was of recent construction and boasted stouter timbers and more iron bands than the door I'd come through.

"Your presence gladdens us," said the Prior.

I hastily returned my full attention to my host, whose hair, I was astonished to see, wasn't hair at all but thin strands of silver wire growing from his scalp.

The Prior's face fell. "Have I given offense in some way?"

"No—no!" I stammered, scrubbing a hand through my frazzled hair. "It's just that... I am not entirely certain why I am here. I left the Red Crow down by the wharf perhaps an hour ago. My steps seemed aimless, yet now I feel that each step inexorably led me here."

The Prior nodded with the patience of one used to instructing the ignorant. "Take heart. You would not have come to us were you not in great need of our aid."

For the first time since I'd come to Iye, a spark of hope kindled in my heart. Perhaps that was why, though I did not know this man from Nessh, I suddenly poured out the contents of my heart to him. I confessed the unbearable wretchedness of my lot and my unquenchable envy of Marthen Lumac.

"You wish that your station and Lumac's were reversed?" the Prior asked when I'd finished.

Hearing another give voice to the deepest longing of my heart emboldened me to abandon decorum.

"Yes!" I cried, clutching the Prior's hand in both of my own. "I wish it in every respect. Lumac's appearance, his wealth, his prestige; his very selfhood—all must be mine, or failing that, death!"

The Prior smiled, and said what I did not expect. "An unconventional request, but not unreasonable."

Momentarily dumbstruck, I stared into the Prior's hazel eyes and realized for the first time that their irises were oblong, not unlike a goat's.

"Can such a thing be done?" I wondered aloud.

The Prior slid his hand from my grasp, returned to the table, and retrieved the bound volume lying upon it. He turned back to me and said, "Our order acknowledges and extols but one absolute— freedom. We take what we will from other cults and philosophies for the ultimate liberation of all."

A memory of my own lapsed tradition sounded a warning. "Are you necromancers?"

The Prior gave a deep, resounding laugh, and my friend by the door joined him. "We are young compared to the disciples of Teth," said the Prior. "Yet they will never exhaust the object of their inquiry, while we hasten ever closer to realizing our goal."

"How?" I asked, not bothering to hide my desperation. "How can I be freed from this torment?"

"Perhaps you have heard of transessence," the Prior said. "The Guild claims a monopoly over it, but the Mystery of exchanging the properties of substances has been known to the Gen since time immemorial."

My limbs shook. I licked my lips. "Can transessence exchange the qualities of two men? Will you use it to make me all that Lumac is?"

The Prior drew back slightly as if offended, but compassion filled his face. "Do you think us so cruel as to leave you a prisoner to

273

yourself while we stand by with the key? All are equal here, and none may pass judgment on another. If none can condemn you, then you are free. And if that freedom does not sanction the sovereign choice to define your own being, then it is no freedom at all."

Having heard all I needed, I fell to my knees. "Your words are music sweeter than any hymn. Free me, I beg you!"

"Take care that passion does not become rashness," said the Prior. "We have not yet discussed the price."

My heart sank like a lead ball cast into the sea. "I am but a poor librarian. My meagre stipend is all but spent, and what little remains must feed me for the rest of the month."

The Prior raised his hand, signaling silence and reassurance. "When you are Marthen Lumac, then you will have Marthen Lumac's wealth. But we have no lust for coin. There are other, far rarer goods which entice us."

I thought I heard a dolorous groan from beyond the far door. A memory surfaced unbidden of a sow on my uncle's farm that had died while giving birth, and my hackles rose. But resurgent longing burned away my fear.

"What must I do?" I asked.

The Prior bade me rise and presented the book to me. I took its rough hemp cover in my hand and studied the title written in fluid brushstrokes—Elegy for the Locust.

"Go forth," the Prior said, "and return, bringing Marthen Lumac with you. Nothing more is yet required."

Wiser men would have carefully laid their plans. But my desire was my master, and I hastened at once to Lumac's house. Insisting that I had obtained a rare tome that our master would wish to see at once got me past the night watchman. I was told to wait in the library while the watchman woke Lumac's valet, who would in turn wake the master of the house. I agreed but first made a detour to admit my friend through the kitchen door.

When Lumac, clothed in a red and gold silk dressing gown, strode into the library, my friend immediately subdued him with a cloth drenched in sweet-smelling liquid. I helped to lay Lumac's statuesque, unconscious body upon the reading table, and my friend made strange signs before laying his hand on the victim's throat.

After a moment my friend went to the door, opened it a crack, and spoke to Lumac's valet in the rich voice of his master. He said that he would be deeply absorbed in reading for an indefinite length of time and gave a stern warning that he was not to be disturbed. Then he dismissed the servant back to bed.

When I asked, my friend explained—once again in his own airy whisper—that he had borrowed Lumac's voice via a temporary application of the same transessence that would soon invest all of Lumac's qualities in me. The Prior also had another Working that would make the transfer permanent.

After making certain that the valet had gone, we hauled Lumac out of the library and locked the door behind us. Transporting Lumac's tall, limp form back to the winery was a harrowing adventure in itself. But with the aid of a threadbare cloak snatched from the garden shed, we disguised him as a drinking companion passed out from a night's revelry.

The candles at the old manor house had all been extinguished. Still, I retraced my steps along the dark halls, down the narrow stairs, and through the vast cellar with remarkable ease for one who had only made the journey once before. The door to the Prior's chamber opened of its own accord as my friend and I approached, and we laid Lumac on the table.

The Prior offered me his own chair, and as I sat catching my breath I noticed a new personage in the room. This unknown figure stood against the wall to my right, dressed in a black wool doublet and breeches with a matching cloak over all. The deep hood concealed his face.

Before I could ask about the stranger's identity, the Prior announced his intention to begin. Eager to obtain the object of my longing at last, I readily agreed.

The process proved amazingly simple. I sat beside the table where Lumac lay as the Prior performed esoteric motions of his hands and arms synchronized with his breathing. He would consummate each cycle by laying one hand on Lumac and the other on me.

At first I felt nothing, and I admit to having harbored growing doubts. But after one touch of the Prior's hand, I felt aches in my muscles and bones, and my clothing became suddenly tight. A while later I risked a look at my hands and saw their former pallor replaced with a warm bronze tan.

Partway through the process Lumac began to stir, but my friend had already bound him in thick manacles and leg irons. The man on the table kept issuing grunts and groans like one waking from fitful sleep until the Prior finally lowered his hands and stepped around to face me.

"Look," he said, pointing to where Lumac lay.

I did look, and I saw to my horror and delight that it was I who lay in chains upon the table.

No, I thought, not I. There lies the wretch Janeth Wainlass. That ill-omened name is no longer bound to me!

To banish all doubt, the Prior drew an octagonal hand mirror from his robe and turned its bright surface toward me. The firm jaw, flinty eyes, and golden hair reflected back at me gave a name to the transcendent joy fountaining up in my soul.

"I am Marthen Lumac," I said in a voice like a deep, expertly played woodwind.

"You possess all of his physical qualities," the Prior said. "Only one thing is still lacking."

The prior turned to the cloaked figure standing against the wall. "Flez, we are ready."

Flez advanced from his place at the wall to stand before the Prior, who guided him to the end of the table where Lumac's—no, Janeth's, head tossed restlessly. Looking over my shoulder, I saw why Flez had needed a guiding hand when he drew back his hood to reveal cauterized indentations in place of eyes. Wispy hair the color of dirty snow framed a marred face that I recognized as inhuman.

"You are a Gen!" I exclaimed in my new pleasing baritone. "How do you walk free in a town controlled by the Guild?"

The Gen ignored me and pressed his gloved hands to Janeth's temples. My old self's beady eyes popped open, and his groans became shrieks that my friend muzzled with his cloth.

My umbrage must have shown, because the Prior said, "Flez cannot answer you. He is a veteran of Annon, and the Guild were not gentle with their prisoners. His eyes were not all they took from him."

Revulsion coursed through me. "That is monstrous! Can you not make him whole?"

"The Guild laid Workings on him to prevent it," said the Prior. "We work tirelessly for the day when our transessence surpasses the Brotherhood's. Until then, Flez is pleased to lend us his unique abilities."

At these words, the Gen released Janeth's head and stepped behind my chair. His spidery fingers sought my temples, sending a chill down my spine.

"What is he about?" I demanded.

"You have Marthen Lumac's body," the Prior explained, "but you lack his mind. A man's thoughts and memories are integral to making him who he is."

My outrage abated. "This Gen can bestow such intangible gifts?"

"Indeed," the Prior said. "Flez wields a power—rare among even his exalted kind—arising not from prana, but from the will and the soul. With it he shall impart to you the contents of Lumac's mind, and your transformation will be total."

I sat back in the chair and tried to relax, but anticipation and anxiety churned the waters of my mind. Into those choppy depths the Gen soon poured a torrent of memories, notions, and impressions. In a moment, the lived experience of another lifetime mingled with that of my life as Janeth. My potent new voice rose in a scream.

The greatest surprise was learning that Lumac—that I—had not been invulnerable. The new memories brought new fears, insecurities, and vices. Lumac's confusion about and sporadic resentment toward women took me aback. There were a hundred trivialities that he thought to be of monumental importance, and a few secret lusts that repulsed me.

Less surprising was Lumac's disposition toward Janeth. As was the case with his other servants, he'd hardly thought of his librarian at all. But the high regard in which he'd held Janeth's scholarly expertise on the rare occasions when he had thought of him confounded me.

No matter. All of that was in the past. I swelled with pride to think that I would be a better Marthen Lumac than the name's former holder had ever aspired to be.

I stood and voiced my gratitude as my friend dragged the feebly struggling Janeth toward the far door. A mournful whine emanated through the sturdy wood, but I had already gone before the door was opened.

The splendor of the next several days exceeded my grandest dreams and passed just as quickly. Invigorated by my second chance at life, I grasped Lumac's with both hands. I dared what he had not, took the risks he'd avoided; met every challenge.

As days became weeks and then months, I slowly became aware of a nagging discontent that grew by the hour. The delicacies of Lumac's table lost their savor. Political jousts with the guildsmen became dull routine. I woke in cold sweats on more nights than not.

Gradually I withdrew to the solace of the library, where I sought the cause of my malaise. After countless hours of study, meditation, and even several attempts at augury, I found the answer.

Arriving outside the old manner house, I nearly despaired to find it under new management. Gaudy signs named the former winery as a museum of dubious oddities. But I steeled myself and shouldered my way past the outraged proprietors and into the long hallway.

Leaving the staff's protests behind me, I came to the familiar door and cursed when I found it locked. My pounding on the ancient wood finally caused the door to be opened from the inside, and I heaved a shuddering sigh of relief to see my friend greeting me with his thin smile.

"Master Lumac," he all but whispered. "It is a pleasure to receive you again."

He turned and started down the stairs. I needed no invitation to follow. The large casks were still in place, as was the door to the Prior's room, which opened when my friend knocked.

An odor both fleshly and artificial hung about the room. It called to mind the specimens preserved in jars that an itinerant natural philosopher had displayed in the town square during my boyhood. I knew the memory as Lumac's, and therein lay the problem.

The Prior—still dressed like a colorful insect emerging from its cocoon—sat at the table with Flez stationed behind him like a solid shadow.

"Master Lumac," the Prior greeted me as he rose. "You honor us with your presence. We of course appreciate the generous donations from your library and your purse. May we be of further assistance?"

I marched up to the table and slammed my hands down upon its lacquered surface. "It's the memories."

The Prior's face remained placid. "There are those who find infused knowledge difficult to assimilate. Are you having difficulty digesting Lumac's?"

"No!" I said. "The trouble isn't digesting Lumac's memories; it's that I am Lumac, but I still don't regard his memories as my own."

The Prior steepled his fingers and pressed them to his mouth. "I see."

"The problem isn't having Lumac's memories," I said, "it's having Janeth's. As long as I remember being someone else, I'll never fully be Lumac!"

"Take heart." The Prior smiled as he guided Flez around the table to stand behind my chair. "Soon you will have no memory of being anyone other than Marthen Lumac."

It wasn't sudden inspiration; more like the dawning awareness of something that had long lain beneath notice—an insect on a ledger that one only sees when it crawls across a number. By the time I'd recognized the idea, it had burrowed too deep under my skin to remove.

280

For as long as I could remember, I had struggled in the grip of a fierce yearning that I resisted with all my strength. When the battle turned against me I would retreat to my private study. But not even Kethan liquor—worth the outrageous expense of importing to Iye—could drown my envy of Eadoard Scrof.

No. Envy was too weak for my hatred of the fact that I was Marthen; not Eadoard.

I knew that my pain had only one cure.

TEST OF THE PROPHET

By

L. Jagi Lamplighter

How do you save someone who's fallen in with radicals?

Shazia adjusted her wet *hijab* for the fifth time and lay the thick wool rug over the barbed wire covering the low fence. She glanced left and right through the rainy gloom, but there was no one around—neither men nor ghosts. Placing both hands on the top of the rug, she confidently swung both legs over the fence. Vaulting had been one of her specialties, back on her high school gymnastics team.

The skirts on the tunic part of her gold and teal *salwar-kameez* encumbered her, catching on the rug. Her left foot struck the fence instead of clearing it, plunging her face first toward the cement.

Catching herself with her hands, she curled into a roll. Lying on the abandoned street, her palms smarting, rain falling onto her face, Shazia wondered, not for the first time, if coming to Peshawar to save her cousin Kabir had been a tremendous mistake.

"I remember when our city was known as an open city," Kabir's older sister Chana had told her four days earlier, as they rounded a corner at breakneck speed, barely avoiding a rickshaw and a brightly-painted bus that looked like a work of tribal art. The two young women were driving to the market to buy fresh fruit, chicken, and perhaps a syrupy *Jalebi* or two. "Peshawar was a jewel in the crown of Pakistan. The City of Flowers! Travelers came from all over the world to see the Khyber Pass and learn about our place in the Silk Road. And now?" She gestured out the window at the tall, dangerous-looking fence they were passing. "Checkpoints everywhere. Barbed wire. Sand bags. Blast walls. Cousin, it is terrible!"

Shazia did not answer immediately. Another near miss—this time with an entire family of four all perched on one bicycle—had caused the car to lurch so violently that it felt as if her stomach were stuck somewhere in her throat. It did not help that the Pakistani drove on the left side of the road, like the British who had once colonized the land. To Shazia, it looked as if all the oncoming cars were in the wrong lane heading right for them.

"Zahilda Kasmi came from Peshawar, you know?" Chana said, noticing Shazia's discomfort. She turned her head and grinned out from under her red headscarf. "Maybe I will emulate her when my children become old enough for school, hmm?"

It was clear that Chana's intent was to tease, but Shazia had no idea what the comment meant. All she knew was that there was a horse-drawn vegetable cart coming around the corner, and her cousin was not looking at the road.

"Who?" she yelped, pointing ahead.

"You do not know Zahilda Kasmi?" Chana deftly avoided slaughtering the horse with her automobile. "She is famous! She is Pakistan's only female taxi driver. No other woman drives a taxi. At the age of thirty-three, her husband died. Taxis were not very expensive, so she bought one and began carrying passengers to support her four daughters and two sons. Her family hated this. They threatened her with death, but she did not yield."

"No other women drive taxis?"

"None." Chana shook her head hard for emphasis. "At first, Zahilda wore a burka, to protect herself from unwanted attention, but when she realized her customers were all good people, she stopped wearing it. Eventually, she became president of the

Pakistan Yellow Cab Drivers Association—and remained president for twelve years."

Ahead was a checkpoint. Chana merely looked annoyed, but Shazia's heart beat rapidly. She was carrying her Pakistani passport, from before she became an American citizen, but it was old, and technically, it was illegal.

She was supposed to have turned it in when she obtained her first return visa. But she had forgotten it that day. So rather than make the long trek to the embassy another day, she had pretended that she had always been American and just handed the clerk her American passport. Now, traveling in Pakistan, she found that she was harassed less if people did not know she was American. She lived in a constant fear, however, that someone would discern something wrong with her old passport and detect her deception.

Despite her trepidations, the guards merely glanced at her name and nodded. Shazia breathed a sigh of relief as they drove on. She wiped her sweaty hands on the silk of the bright peach and gold tunic of her *salwar kameez*, which she wore for the same reason that she carried her old passport.

It was easier to blend in when she looked like a local.

She sighed.

How cowardly she was being. No one seeing her sweating in a car would have believed that she was the same Marine Lance Corporal Hayak who had distinguished herself so ably in Afghanistan.

She even had a medal—just like the Cowardly Lion.

It was strange how much tiny things like outward garments mattered. It had been easy to feel brave and competent in fatigues and combat boots. Somehow, it was much harder when dressed in pretty silk trousers and a long gold-embroidered, dress-like tunic. She needed to pull herself together, *salwar kameez* or no *salwar*

285

kameez. If she did not, she would not be able to accomplish what she had come to do.

Shazia glanced over at her pretty, vivacious cousin, one of her favorite childhood playmates from before her family moved to America. Chana was now the mother of two little ones, with a third one on the way. She looked so calm and self-possessed in her cream and fuchsia crepe silk *salwar-kameez* and her bright red *hijab.*

"Chana, why do you wear this thing?" Shazia leaned over and tugged on her cousin's *hijab.* "You did not do that when we were young. You had such thick, luxurious, black hair! There is no law saying women have to wear head coverings in Pakistan. Why do you wear one?"

Chana's animated face grew even prettier as she lowered her lashes. "It pleases my husband."

"But... why?" cried Shazia. "Because it shows he is a bully who can push his wife around? Because it makes him look good in front of his buddies?"

"No! Nothing like that!" Chana looked appalled. "It honors him. He loves knowing that no man but him sees my hair. I tell you, Shazia. Is it annoying? Yes. Sometimes. But not as annoying as high-heeled shoes."

Shazia gave a grudging grunt of acknowledgement. She, too, hated high-heels. Of course, she still wore them when the occasion required.

"It may be annoying at times," Chana continued, "but it is worth it."

"Worth it for... what?"

Chana smiled mysteriously. It was a feminine expression, a mixture of secret joy and demureness. With a start, Shazia realized that, while she had read about such expressions in books and seen them in movies, she had never seen it on a real living person before.

"For that moment, behind closed doors, when I take off the scarf," Chana's dark eyes shone, "when my hair comes down, all shining, like a black waterfall, and I glance at him over my shoulder.

"Oh, Shazia! You should see his face! It is erotic. It is romantic. You have nothing like that in the West. All the romance has been sucked out of your lives because everything is naked. The hair. The bosoms. The thighs. You have no mystery left."

"There is more to life than mystery," retorted Shazia. "I don't want mystery. I want forthrightness."

"And that is why you are not yet married," her cousin replied firmly. "Without mystery, there is nothing between a man and woman but rutting bodies. That I do not want."

Shazia stared out the window at a man selling green parrots, which he kept under a large wire cage attached to a stick, so the whole device looked like a giant stiff butterfly net. She wanted to object, but she thought of her past relationships with men she had known in high school, at college, while she was serving in the military. There had been no mystery, and, for the most part, there had been no romance.

Her freedom-loving soul cried out against the *hijab* and all that it represented; however, some tiny part deep inside of her argued that maybe Chana had a point.

They spent the next hour walking among the brightly-colored booths of the market and eating sweet, sticky, vaguely pretzel-shaped *jalebi*, one of Shazia's favorite childhood treats. Vegetables of all kinds, including some she had not seen since she was a child, filled the street-side market, the top of which was covered over with ripped burlap that blocked out the sky—so that it almost felt as if they were shopping inside. Other booths held cascades of fish, sizzling round *naan* cooked over flames in a fire pit built into the floor, ripe mangos and huge yellow melons, and woven baskets overflowing with fluffy, peeping goslings. The sights, the smells, the jabbering in many languages, it was all familiar and yet overwhelming.

As they returned to the car, their arms laden, Shazia found the courage to ask the question she had flown halfway around the world to have answered.

"And Kabir? How is he?" She wanted to sound casual, but her voice shook.

"Oh, Shazia," Chana's whole face crumpled. She put down her packages on the back seat of the car and grabbed her cousin's arm. "I am so worried for my little brother! He has joined the Taliban! Here! In Peshawar! Where those monsters, those butchers, killed over a hundred and thirty of our children—while they were studying in school! The burned the teachers alive and made the children watch! One class was even in the auditorium, studying first aid. And one of the butchers cried out, 'The children are under the benches. Kill them all.'"

"Oh, Chana!" Shazia put her own bags into the car, before they slipped from her arms.

"They killed our cousin Umar! You never met him, Shazia. He was just a baby when you were last here. But, he was such a good boy! Reliable and strong. He had made house captain!"

Chana shook with rage. Shazia hugged her cousin. The two young women held each other and rocked back and forth, both crying.

"Shazia!" wailed Chana. "I don't know what to do about Kabir!"

"I will talk to him," Shazia assured her. "That is why I came."

In the end, speaking to Kabir turned out to be harder than she had expected. Chana sent a message. Shazia was certain that the moment he heard that she was here, her favorite cousin and dearest childhood playmate would drop everything and rush to her side.

Kabir did not come.

After four days, she could not wait any longer. Her visit would soon be over. Like Mohammad and the mountain, if Kabir would not come to her, Shazia must go to Kabir.

Using Google Earth from her tablet, she mapped out the way to the lot where Chana said Kabir and his cronies gathered. She scoped it out twice, once on foot and once by taxi—Chana's story of the female taxi driver had given her the idea. She noted all the checkpoints, guard posts, and barbed wire fences. Then, she sat down and made a list of what she would need, relying on her experience serving in Afghanistan.

She had limited her walking and taxi rides to places she could see without having to pass through a checkpoint. The main reason for her convoluted approach was that she did not want to meet any guards when she was alone. Without Chana, she might be called upon to talk, and she was not certain she could remember her old accent. If they caught an American woman traveling alone, she would be retained for questioning for sure.

This had not been the case when she was a girl. When she had first planned this trip, she had not been afraid to use her American passport. Two weeks ago, however, she had run into her neighbor, Sumaira Elahi, who had just returned from visiting Pakistan with her husband. They came from a village not too far from Peshawar. Taliban fighters who had been pushed out of Afghanistan now resided in their village. Her husband had been forced to spend his entire visit hiding in his family home. They would have hanged him in the town square had they caught him, merely for the crime of living in America.

Things were not as bad in Peshawar; at least she did not think so.

289

Still, she would rather not put the matter to the test.

When the next day dawned chilly and gray, Shazia greeted it with a grin. A cold, rainy day was just what she needed. In times of relative peace, she knew, guards had a tendency to get sloppy. They did not like to venture out of their posts when the weather was nasty.

This meant that of the three routes she had considered, the one that ran close to the old tenth-century Khyber Gate would be the best. The nearest guard posts were farthest from the places she wanted to go. It was her best chance of crossing over undetected.

Eager to draw as little attention as possible, Shazia had chosen a dull teal and gold *salwar kameez*. Then, taking up a matching dull teal scarf, she had asked Chana to show her how to wear a *hijab*. Her cousin had been delighted to do so, demonstrating how to put up one's hair and chatting on about the joys of catching a good husband.

When Chana had withdrawn to put her children down for a nap, Shazia had grabbed her bag and slipped away.

Now she laid on her back on the wet street, in the shadow of the Bab-e-Khyber—an immense, castle-like gate that marked the beginning of the Khyber Pass, beyond which was the no man's land between Pakistan and Afghanistan. This ancient pass through the Spin Ghar Mountains had been part of the trade route known as the Silk Road. The pass was so old that it had been traveled by the forces of Alexander the Great.

Beyond the towering stone gate, with its round, crenellated pillars and top bridge, stretched the barren wastes of the Spin Ghar. From her vantage point, as she rolled to her knees and rose, she could see the muzzle of machine guns nestled between the crenellations on the top of the round towers.

Shazia stuck her rug back in her large cloth bag and hurried onward. Crossing the road that ran east of the great, stone Khyber Gate, Shazia headed toward the old fort. She walked head down with a brisk sense of purpose. She had learned as a young girl that if you acted as if you were in your rightful place, giving no sign of furtiveness or uncertainly, you could go many places that might otherwise be off limits.

It was Kabir who had taught her this.

Her thoughts wandered backward, recalling a time, two decades before, when she had been a little girl, and Peshawar had still been a happy place to live. This was before her family had moved to America. Having but one sibling of her own, a much older brother, Shazia had spent all her time with her cousins, Chana, her older sister Fabiha, and their younger brother, Kabir.

Of all of them, of everyone alive, Kabir had been her favorite.

They had been inseparable.

Memories flooded her: Kabir laughing as they rode a bicycle together, nearly crashing into their uncle's longsuffering donkey; Kabir squatting in the dust, teaching her to shoot marbles like a boy; Kabir seated beside her at the feet of their great grandmother, listening with huge eyes to tales of Arabian Nights of Saladin and Solomon and Aladdin and dangerous djinn.

Great-grandmother Anahita was of Persian blood. Her family claimed descent from the Magi of old. This, she explained to her spellbound great-grandchildren, was why they could see ghosts. She charged them never to speak to anyone, who was not of Magi blood, of what they saw—not even their fathers—or they would find themselves the recipients of a very unhappy fate. She emphasized this point with six grisly stories of the tragic fates that befell those who revealed that they could commune with spirits, stories that had caused Kabir and Shazia to shiver with horrified delight.

291

Hunching beneath the cold rain, Shazia moved swiftly across an open area behind a line of houses, passing a muddy garden and brightly-colored laundry someone had forgotten to take in before the rains started. She passed an old lady tending an old cart with faded blue wheels, overflowing with grapes, and a cart selling brightly-colored magazines. At the corner, dark stains on the pavement marked the place where a woman had recently been stoned to death for adultery.

Shazia thought of all her girlfriends back home who dated married men, of her co-workers and fellow Marines who had cheated on their wives. She shuddered. Sometimes, even she had trouble believing America and Pakistan could exist in the same century.

To the side of the blood-stained rock had been the spot where Shazia had vomited two days ago, when the nausea that came with seeing ghosts had struck her. It was because she had seen the poor woman's ghost that she knew what had caused the dark stain on the street. Chana had gotten them past the guard's checkpoint that time, so she had not needed to climb over the barbed-wire fence. Seeing her cousin's distress, Chana had inquired whether Shazia had eaten something that did not agree with her, or, with a sweet but wicket smile, if she might be pregnant? Apparently, Chana had forgotten about such incidents from their youth.

If only Shazia had thought to ask Great-Grandmother Anahika, while she was still alive, why it was that seeing spirits always made her feel so ill.

Until recently, Shazia and Kabir had kept in touch by Skype. It was when he stopped calling that she began to suspect something was wrong. It had been over a decade since she had seen Kabir face to face. The flight to Pakistan was so long that the family had decided on a reunion in London, with Shazia's family traveling from the US to England, and Kabir's coming from Pakistan.

They had met up at Trafalgar Square. Shazia had been an awkward, budding girl of thirteen. Kabir had been tall and lanky, with a veneer of teenage cool. A few minutes together, however, had revealed the same vibrant boy she had loved. She remembered the two of them running through the pigeons with their arms stretched, watching the startled birds fly up into the air. She remembered seeking out a birdseed vender and laughing as they watched their avian companions mob the seed. And then, laughing again when their antics caused Kabir to slide on the stones covered with pigeon droppings, his arms windmilling as he fell. How funny he had looked when he stood up again, his garments streaked with white.

During her recent flight, she had scheduled a day's layover in London. When she returned to Trafalgar Square, the pigeons were gone. The city had outlawed the selling of birdseed and chased the birds away. A man with a fierce-looking hawk was on patrol to make certain that no pigeons returned.

The surface underfoot was less treacherous, true. Yet, the memory of the empty square without its mob of feathered friends made Shaza's eyes prick with tears.

Shazia shook her head. Rain in her eyes was bad enough. She needed to stay alert, focused. And yet, as she rounded the corner and started across an abandoned parking lot toward where she believed Kabir and his associates to be, she could not help recalling her favorite memories of her favorite cousin.

Her clearest memories of Kabir were of walking to and from school. Shazia's family had been progressive enough to send their daughter to school. That was one reason they had eventually moved to America. While they lived in Peshawar, however, Shazia and Kabir had attended the same form, so they walked to and from school together.

She could remember Kabir striding beside her so proudly, in his role as her male protector. Most of all, however, she remembered the day they came upon the cockfight.

They had been coming home from school on a lovely spring day. Blossoms were everywhere in the City of Flowers, and the air was heady with perfume. They had been walking together along the packed dirt road that led down the hill to their neighborhood, swinging their book bags and singing a song that they had learned in class.

Ahead of them was a gathering of grown men, all shouting and cheering. Eager to investigate what was causing such excitement, the two children had run forward, darting through the crowd.

"Remember," Kabir had whispered to her as they slipped between the grown men, "look like you're supposed to be here. No one ever bothers you if you do that."

The mass of men had turned out to be a hollow ring. At the center, two black roosters strutted and pecked at each other. All around, men hollered encouragement and called out bets. Kabir had stood for a moment, watching one bird try to peck out the eyes of the other, then he had turned away, dragging Shazia by the hand.

"Come away," he had said in disgust. "This is no place for a girl."

But he did not say it the way boys said such things in movies, as if girls were not worthy to be present. Rather, he said it with respect, as if she were made of finer stuff than the brutes who shouted and howled around them—as if the good things in life were worth cherishing, worth protecting.

It had made her feel very good.

"When I grow up, I am not going to do stupid things like that, making poor animals fight," Kabir had said confidently. Shazia knew he loved their chickens. "Only a swine would behave so. A barbarian. Someone with no civility. When I grow up, I am going to put a stop to such cruelty. I will make the world a better place."

At that moment, as they walked along the dusty, flower-hemmed road, Shazia had sworn a solemn vow, the most solemn vow of her life. She had vowed to Allah above that, when she grew up, she would help her cousin accomplish his goal.

That was why she had become a Marine—because when the time came for Kabir to make the world better, she wanted to be capable of helping.

Under the shadow of the sandy walls of the old Jamrud Fort, Shazia lifted her bowed head and looked around at the broken concrete, the sand bags, the weary faces of the lone old man heading in the other direction with his cart and his patient donkey. She thought of the City of Flowers as it had been in her youth.

It did not look like a better place.

She heard their voices before she saw them. Using her military training, she crept forward slowly, staying behind cover. Of course, back in Afghanistan, she had worn city camo, not a teal and gold flowing dress with pants that looked like something out of *I Dream of Jeannie*.

A cold black hatred of all things Taliban gripped her heart.

This may have been a good thing, because when she peered around the corner from behind a low cement wall, in the midst of her hatred, she was thinking like a Marine—so she did not cry out.

Lance Corporal Hayak never cried out.

She was not so sure about Shazia, the young woman in the *hijab*. She might have called out. It was hard to remember who she was when dressed in these clothes.

Ten young men stood around a kneeling figure, arguing with each other. They were not dressed in the turbans and dirty robes of the Taliban, but in the tight black paramilitary garb of Islamic State extremists, with black headgear and black scarves across their faces. One young man held a naked scimitar. The kneeling figure wore the uniform of a Pakistani soldier. A burlap bag covered his head.

No!

Shazia slipped out of sight and pressed her back against the concrete wall, her heart hammering. They were going to behead the soldier. And Kabir was among them. Even at this distance, she had recognized his eyes.

He was the young man with the scimitar.

Kabir was going to behead a man!

How different those eyes were. Where was his compassion? His clever wit? Where was the joy that had set him apart from all others she knew? His eyes, the eyes of all those young men, had been filled with a rabid, feverous hate.

Think, she told herself, *breathe, stay calm.*

She moved back until she could see them again, peering from behind her cover. She had planned to wait until the meeting broke up and then approach Kabir. But she could not let this murder go forward.

She wanted to save the soldier, but, even more than that, she wanted to save Kabir—save him from becoming the very kind of man he had vowed, the day of the cockfight, that he would never be.

But save him... how? Here he stood, part of a crowd that surrounded a hapless victim, even as those men had ringed the fighting birds.

Shazia moved behind the wall again and sat there, struggling not to weep. Marines did not weep.

What had become of her hero? Why had she suffered so, forcing herself to face things no young woman should ever have to face—death, mutilated children, the smell of burnt flesh, and worse horrors she did not like to recall—just to be worthy to aid him? Had all her hopes and dreams come to this?

Were they to die today on the edge of a scimitar?

The very thought made her ill. She doubled over with nausea.

As she squatted behind the cement wall, her head between her knees, a searing pain shot through her head. Her vision became double. The broken glass and pebbles on the ground before her seemed to reproduce themselves, producing their twin.

No! No! Not now!

The waves of nausea grew stronger. Leaning against the cement wall, her fingers pressed against her temples, she made herself breathe deep, slow breaths. She had managed to control herself during her entire tour of duty, even though the war-torn countryside of Afghanistan had been full of ghosts. If she could keep herself together then, she could do it now.

The nausea retreated, but her head still throbbed. Slowly, she turned and leaned around the corner of the wall, looking back at the young men to see what the "gift" passed down to her from her Magi ancestors would show her.

The air above Kabir and his fellows swarmed with monstrosities. Some were horrible, ugly creatures with horns and forked tails. Others looked like snakes or scorpions. Still others were black clouds with fiery eyes. The *marid* towered over the others, tall as giants—cruel horns jutting from their forehead or huge tusks thrusting from their upper lips.

She recognized each kind of evil djinn from her great-grandmother's tales. There were five types of djinn in all. Four of them were here: bad *djann*, wicked *shaitans*, evil *ifrite*, and, worst of all, five terrible, huge *marid*. They swarmed over Kabir and his friends hooting and cackling. From time to time, they swooped down and whispered into the ears of the young men. Each time they did so, the young men's eyes became more fevered, more fanatical. Their argument grew louder. One of the young men in black shoved another.

Shazia had seen dark djinn before on Muslim battlefields. She had seen evil *qareen*—the companion djinn that urged each mortal to give into base desires—whispering to their masters, inciting wrath, lust, hatred. Her Irish bunkmate could see them, too. She called them by another name: *demons*.

"Allah, Lord of Jibreel, Mikail and Israfil protect me!" she prayed fervently, mouthing the words she did not dare to speak aloud, lest she be overheard. "Save my cousin from this terrible sin. Send your angels to drive away these wicked djinn."

The young man who had been shoved lunged at his attacker. Only he never reached him. Instead, he stopped mid-step, his hand outstretched, motionless. His attacker, too, stopped moving, as if caught in the frozen frame of a movie. The other young men, too, were motionless.

As was the rain.

Amazed, Shazia reached up and touched one of silvery drops that hung suspended in mid-air. It gave slightly under her finger. Everything was quiet, hushed, everything but the wicked djinn, who still squawked and cackled. That was the only sound.

What was happening?

Footsteps sounded in the utter quiet of the frozen world. A figure walked into the grass and broken glass of the clearing in front of the frozen young men. He was seven feet tall with hair of gold that shone like a second sun. His coat was a white so brilliant that it hurt her eyes. When he came forward, the smallest of the djinn, the bad djann, fled away, shrieking. The larger ones hissed and cawed, but they continued to swarm around the heads and shoulders of the young men.

The newcomer stopped and smiled at Shazia. His face was very handsome, but his expression was kindly, like a loving father.

"Who… " she faltered.

"I am the Angel Gabriel."

Shazia's jaw dropped. "You… came?"

"Angels always come when they are called. It is just that mortals do not usually see us."

"Why can I see you?"

"That is your family's gift."

"But I have never seen an angel before!"

"Have you ever called for one?"

Shazia opened her mouth and closed it again. She could not recall that she had.

"Can you drive away the Evil Ones?" she asked hopefully.

The angel shook his head. "I can protect you. But those are the *qareen* of these young men, and other dark entities whom they have invited. The young men would have to ask for my protection themselves. I may not act otherwise."

"Not even to save them?" pleaded Shazia.

"My Father has granted free will to the Race of Adam."

"Your… father?" Shazia took a step back in confusion. "But Allah has no children!"

She suddenly became aware of how heavy and cold her wet garments were. She began to shiver. The angel regarded her wordlessly.

Shazia played with the hem of her *hijab*. "Is that not why the good djinn converted to Islam? Because they overheard the Prophet explaining that Allah had no wife and no son?"

Great-Grandmother Anahika had seen to it that she and Kabir were familiar with all the *Quran* had to say about djinn.

"Does it not say in *Sura Al-Jin*," she continued. *"Say: It has been revealed to me that a group of Jinn listened and said, 'Verily we have heard a marvelous Quran. It guides unto righteousness so we have believed in it. And, we will never make partners with our Lord. He— exalted by the glory of our Lord— has not taken a wife nor a son. What the foolish ones among us used to say about God is a horrible lie."*

A terrible horrible cacophony came from the gathering of dark djinn. It took a moment for Shazia to realize that this terrible din was an expression of mirth.

"No son!" They laughed outrageously, striking each other violently. "Oh yes. We like that part! Tell more pathetic worms of human beings. The Unaccursed One has no Son!"

She looked from the chortling fiends to the glorious, calm angel. "Are you... You are the Muslim Angel Jibrail, right?"

The angel gave her such an odd look. "Without me, there would be no Islam. I am he who spoke to Mohammad, thus making him a prophet." He frowned at the gathered crowd of evil djinn. "What Mohammad wrote down is another matter."

"What do you mean?" Shazia drew herself up, eyes flashing. "Is not the *Quran* 'Allah's perfect and complete word'?"

Laughter exploded from the dark djinn. They pushed each other and clawed and spat fire. One gigantic *marid* bent down and

300

swallowed two of the ifrites, though they eventually burst out of its body in a method Shazia wished she had not seen.

Another larger *marid*, with curling ram horns and cloven hooves stepped over the crowd and strode forward, bending down until its brutish, snub-nosed head was close to her. Too close. She could smell his putrid, fetid breath. She drew her *hijab* across her mouth.

"Mankind, those Sons of Whores!" declared the *marid*. "How puny. How gullible. They cling to their sacred texts like a dung beetle to his ball. Little do they realize that we demons have, over the generations, snuck errors into every single holy scripture upon the earth."

"Is... is this true?" Shazia took a step back, shaken.

The angel nodded.

"But... why is this allowed?" she cried.

"Mankind has been granted free will," Gabriel said sadly. "My brethren and I may but advise."

Another *marid* came and squatted down. This one looked like a sunburnt pig with huge tusks. "Sooo many errors. Big rutting errors. Little buggering errors. And do you know the prize of the dung heap? "Two turdy little words: '*Fear God.*' Everywhere those offal words appear—that was done by us."

The *marid* with the ram horns said, "Oh, mortals, those Get of Dogs, might claim these two words mean wisdom, or a hundred other explanations, but every time one of those sons of asses reads those two words, some part of him shrieks with terror, believing that the Unaccursed means him harm. Each time this happens, we win that little bit more."

Shazia understood that there were mistakes in the religions of the infidel, but...

"Even in the *Quran*, there are mistakes?" She looked helplessly at Gabriel.

301

He nodded gravely.

"The faults in the teachings, which stink like the droppings of a sick dog, let us in," said the pig-nosed one. "It allows us to sway men in our sheep-buggering direction. To fill the parts of them that should be filled with light with offal and filth."

"Whenever a prophet sins, there a door stands open for us."

"We can reach through it." The pig-nose grinned a snorty, piggish grin, "and grab his followers by their moldering tender parts."

"Thanks to our diligence," said the ram-horn, "we are winning."

"Shoo! Go away!" Shazia shouted angrily. "Leave these good young men alone! I have seen you before. In Afghanistan! Breathing on the necks of the rebels. Breeding hate! Let Islam go back to being the Religion of Peace!"

Another burst of raucous laughter, both from the two towering *marids* who crouched beside her and from the raucous djinn gang around the young men.

The ram-horn cackled, "The very first thing your Dog-rutting Prophet did—after receiving instruction from Oh-So-High-and-Mighty-Gabriel, here, telling him to be kind to the followers of the Slaughtered Lamb and the People of the Book—was move to Medina and to put those very People of the Book to the sword."

"And your bull-buggering prophet and his poxy offspring have been conquering and murdering since," snorted the pig-nose. "With the help of Mohammad's fanatics, we nearly won. We nearly conquered Europe and eradicated the... things we don't like."

"We conquered North Africa and the Middle East," said the ram-horn, "all of which had been, at that time, bathed in the blood of the Slaughtered Lamb. We owned Spain, much of Austria. We even made it as far north as Tours in France.

"The lamb. How soft!" The pig-nose giggled, a high, unpleasant sound. "How curly!"

"How weak," the ram-horn sneered in scorn. "How unable to protect his followers."

"How bloody your ancestors were," jeered the pig-nose.

"And yet, now," he continued, bragging, "we have convinced you modern sons of mares to blame the Crusaders for slaughtering the innocent Muslims." He laughed long and hard, a harsh, grating sound.

"Ooo," the pig-face joined in gleefully, adding, "and the names of men like Charles Martel have been forgotten."

"Who?" asked Shazia.

"See!" The whole gang of djinn chortled and guffawed.

"What a time that was!" the ram-horn grinned, showing ragged uneven teeth. "Back then, where the followers of the Lamb went, they stopped slavery, stopped the killing of women and children, and introduced liberties for the commoners, those gets of bulls. While your people—everywhere they conquered, they put men, women, and children to the sword. When they were generous, anyone who would not convert was demoted to second class *dhimmi*. When they were not generous, the conquered were instructed to convert or die. Or, even better for us, they just slaughtered them all. Like Boka Haram in Africa."

"That is the true face of your 'Religion of Peace.'" Chortled the pig-face.

"Why?" Shazia turned toward the angel. "Why did this all happen?"

The pig-nose snickered. "Your precious Mohammad did not pass the Test of the Prophet."

"He did not fail entirely," said the Angel Gabriel. "In the beginning, he heard me."

"Wha... What is the Test of the Prophet?" asked Shazia.

The stench of the *marid* was beginning to make her feel light-headed. She feared she might faint. She felt it necessary to remind herself in the sternest of terms: Marines *never* fainted.

The angel spoke, "All who hear the good news that I, or one of my brethren, bring must undergo a test. A test of their worthiness for the task before them. If they pass, then they are true prophets of God. If they fail, they cease to hear us properly and become, instead, false prophets."

"How do they pass or fail?" Shazia asked. "What are the criteria?"

"Faith and humility," replied the Angel Gabriel. "They must both have faith, that Our Divine Father has picked the right ones for the task, and humility, to understand that they are one servant among many."

"What happens when they fail?" she asked.

"Some judge themselves unworthy," leered the pig-face, "even though the Unaccursed has told them otherwise. They bow to fear and kiss its dung-coated behind."

"We whisper to the sons of vixen," said the ram-horn, "feeding their fears, convincing them to refuse to speak the message given to them. Or, even better, to invent a lie, to shift some of the burden—such as to say that the words came from an old man met on a mountain road or were found on some, now lost, ancient manuscript."

"And this is bad?"

"They think 'a noble lie' will harm no one," said Gabriel solemnly, "but lies are the children of the Enemy. When mortals worship a religion founded on lies, they open themselves to—in addition to their personal sins—the mechanizations of Sut, Son of Iblis."

Shazia knew from her great-grandmother's stories that Iblis, the Lord of all Evil Djinn, had five sons: Tir, Al-A'war, Sut, Dasimn, and Zalambur. Each had an unholy duty it performed. Sut's task was to suggest lies.

"Others," cackled the pig-nose, "fail to recognize their own filth. They judge themselves grander than other men. They start believing that they shit rubies and piss sweet wine. They congratulate themselves and listen to our whispers. Their preaching becomes all about themselves, and they preach to the satisfaction of their lusts—violence, sex, drink, whatever offal they desire."

"Look at your son of a dog prophet," chuckled the ram-horn. "He preached more than one wife. Even though it is written: *A man who marries two wives is a thief, for he steals the love intended for his first wife and gives it to another.*"

"Ah! But it is not written!" snorted the pig-face, waving his hoofed hand back and forth, as if admonishing. "We arranged for that to be left out."

The djinn all laughed heartily together, a terrible and maddening sound.

"At first he listened to me," the Angel Gabriel said gravely. "In the early books of the *Quran*, he listened to me and called upon his people to show kindness to the followers of Isa Iln Maryam and the People of the Book. But he soon became much more concerned with naming himself the final prophet and calling for vengeance against those who did not agree. He stopped listing to me.

"As to the Test of the Prophet," continued the angel, "when the time comes for a prophet to come into his own, the rules are told to him. Then he is tempted. For it is my eldest brother's prerogative to have a chance to lead mankind astray. The potential prophet is told

305

that it is allowed to do something that is not allowed. If he knows better, he is a true prophet. If he does not, he retroactively becomes a false one."

"You mean... like Eve being told not to eat the apple, and then the serpent told her she could?" asked Shazia.

"Exactly." The angel nodded. "Or Paris, who turned down a kingdom and earthly wisdom but fell prey to the promises of beauty and thus destroyed his civilization. Or Isa Iln Maryam, who turned down a kingdom and refused to use his heavenly powers for his own aggrandizement when the devil came to tempt him."

"Wait! You mean... Paris Alexander? The Prince of Troy?" Shazia blinked. "I had not realized that he was a prophet."

"Nor was he. But he could have been, had he not yielded to temptation."

"Weird," Shazia muttered. For a moment, her whole current experience took on a surreal quality. "I have heard of false prophets, but I have never thought before about people who were supposed to be prophets and failed."

"There have been thousands. Tens of thousands," said the angel.

"Oh."

"Most disqualified themselves immediately by doubting the message," said the angel. "The rest failed the Test of the Prophet."

"And the Prophet failed?" Shazia's voice quailed.

She thought of her devout parents and all the other good Muslims she knew, and how their faith had sustained them through times of trial. Surely, it had not all been lies. There was truth what they believed!

She *knew* it in her heart.

"As I said, at first, he wrote truly what I had spoken," said Gabriel. "He wrote of peace and of the virtue of God. He wrote many wise and true things that uplift his followers, even today. But his temptation came in the form of the same temptation Isa and Paris rejected—the promise of an earthly kingdom. My eldest brother whispered to him, enflaming his pride. When he came to Medina, he presented himself as a Jewish prophet to the Jews living there. They asked for evidence of his claim, and when he was not able to give any, they doubted him. Instead of praying humbly for a sign, he grew angry and belligerent and attacked them. Instead of using his greatness to bring peace and healing, he chose war. This choice colored his judgment. After a time, he stopped being able to hear me. He did not realize that my eldest brother, the King of the Djinn, had taken my place."

"You mean... Iblis Al-Shaitan?"

"I do."

"So the *Quran*?"

The pig-faced chortled. "One of our greatest works! We convinced the manure-eating early Imams to scramble the books of the *Quran*. To put them longest to shortest, instead of eldest to newest. So no one could tell which came first. Or which came after."

"Had this not happened," Gabriel lowered his head in sorrow, "the imams who followed would have figured out that the idea of jihad was a distortion of my message. There would have been a general movement away from the later books, and Islam might have become, truly, the Religion of Peace."

Shazia thought of the violence that currently rocked the Muslim world. She thought of her great-grandfather and how he had boasted of the great Muslim warriors of the past and of the carnage they committed upon the infidel. She thought of Raif Badawi, such a promising young man with three sweet little children, who had been sent to jail for ten years and flogged with a horse whip for the crime of blogging: "Muslims, Christians, Jews, and atheists are all equal."

Her heart cried out for her people and for their terrible wounds.

"How did this come to be?" Shazia moaned. She hugged her shoulders and rocked back and forth.

Gabriel replied solemnly, "When I came to speak to Mohammad he could have received my word in humility. Instead he chose to 'put himself above his peers in glory.'"

Shazia leaned against the cement wall. She felt a terrible pain in her stomach, as if everything firm and certain had been cut away.

"So... all Islam? We are all the servants of the dark ones?" she cried.

"Only those who lean toward the dark teachings," replied Gabriel.

"Don't feel so bad," mocked the ram-horn. "You sons of pigs are not the only ones who bend and lick the feet of the children of Iblis. Tir, who brings about calamities, rules Islam, true. But to the West is the domain of Al-A'war who spreads debauchery. The East is rulled by Sut, Lord of Lies, who rules the Communists, those filth-eating fools gobble up whatever nonsense their masters feed them."

"I do not care if the infidels are corrupt," cried Shazia, "I care about the Prophet!"

"Do not judge him too harshly," the angel said gently, "it is a very difficult task. Few succeed."

"But if the Prophet could not do it, has anyone succeeded?"

"Certainly." Gabriel smiled. "All that is needed is faith and humility. Do you not remember what Maryam said, when I brought her the Good News?"

Maryam, mother of Isa?" asked Shazia, startled. "The *Quran* does not say."

Of course! This was the angel who had brought the word of virgin birth to the mother of the prophet Isa Iln Maryam.

The angel's eyebrow actually twitched. "I told him to put that in."

The *marid* and their cohorts chortled mightily.

"What did she say?" Shazia ignored the taunts of the raucous crows of djinn.

The Angel Gabriel replied, "She said: '*Behold the handmaid of the Lord; be it unto me according to thy word.*'"

The *marid* shrieked and yowled, the noise of it hurt Shazia's head.

"Can you not rid me of these?" Shazia cried, her hands over her ears. "You said you could protect those who ask!"

Gabriel smiled, as if he had been waiting for this. "It would be my pleasure!"

The angel's brilliant white coat billowed. Only Shazia saw now that it was not a coat but wings with pure white feathers. A circle of gold appeared above his head. The halo shed hope the way a lamp shed light. In its illumination, the giant *marid* seemed puny, weak, mewling things. Crying in dismay, they scuttled backwards to hide behind the frozen young men.

Beneath the halo of the Angel Gabriel, Shazia did not feel as cold. Such buoyancy lifted her spirits that even seeing her beloved cousin in such a terrible circumstance ceased to crush her spirits.

Only once before had she ever felt such a thing. When she was six, Great-Grandmother Anahika fell ill. For days, she had lain and moaned in bed. The doctor had come and left again, shaking his head. Family had gathered from distant villages, anticipating her death. A great aunt Shazia had not previously met was an artist. She had set up her easel to draw one last picture of Anahika, though mainly she had reminisced with the other women about the old days of their youth. Most of the children were unaffected by this commotion. Adults might be downcast, but the children's lives went on.

Shazia and Kabir, however, were full of trepidation and sadness, for they loved Great-Grandma most of all.

Shazia had gone to her mother and asked to be taught a Du'a from the Quran for the healing of the sick. Her mother gave her: Truly distress has seized me, but You are Most Merciful of those that are merciful. *Shazia had murmured it under her breath wherever she went.*

But healing did not come, and Great-Grandmother would soon be taken from them. It was agreed by all.

Then, one day, the door had opened and her father had stood there. Shazia could still remember how he looked, the light framing his tall form.

"Shazia!" he had cried, scooping her up, "The doctor! He has found a new medicine! He says Anahika will get well!"

And so it had come to pass. Great-Grandmother had not died. The relatives from distant villages had to go home without a funeral. All had continued as it should.

But what Shazia remembered best was the hope that had come to her at that moment, when all was lost, and then there was Papa, surrounded by light. Hope had flooded through her, lifting everything inside of her. In later years, when times were grim, she had remember that moment, and she had told herself that if hope had come even then, when death was certain, fixed, it might come again.

How beautiful great-grandmother had looked when she was well and could again sit with the children at her feet to tell her stories. At the end of that next story session, Great-Grandmother Anihika had taken Kabir's hand in one of hers and Shazia's in the other, and she had held their two hands together, saying, "Thank you, my dear ones, for your dear love of me, and I charge you to always be true to each other. No matter what happens, put each other first and never let anything come between you."

"Stop!" cried the *marid*, cowering behind the young men. "We will not pester the daughter of a whore. Stop!"

Gabriel folded his wings. The halo vanished, leaving a cold, gloomy, gray day filled with motionless raindrops. Shazia tried to hold onto the flame of hope that had kindled inside her, but it was nothing but a memory. The feeling it had kindled slipped from her grasp, leaving her feeling empty and cold.

The angel turned to Shazia. His eyes were a deep, bottomless blue. "The real question, Lance Corporal Shazia Hayak is not: *Did Mohammad pass the Test of the Prophet.* The real question is: *Will you?*"

"Wait, what? *Me?*" she squawked.

"You are talking to *me.*" The angel waved a hand at his shining self. "If there is another qualification for becoming a prophet, I know it not."

"But that's... just because I can see ghosts."

"And why do you think you were granted such a gift?"

"But... "

The angel took a step forward. "Did you not swear a solemn vow to make the world a better place? Can you think of anything it needs more?"

Shazia wanted to object, but she could not.

"Why me?" She sputtered, "T-they will not listen to me! They will discount what I say."

"Is that so?" A flicker of amusement passed through Gabriel's eyes. "Are you also slow of tongue?"

"Pardon me?"

The angel shrugged, his eyes twinkling. "Moses joke there."

Shazia gaped at him. *Angels could make jokes?*

"Is not laughter the weapon of the angels?" asked Gabriel, smiling.

"Sorry, Old Gabe," called one of the *marid* from where they cowered, "Under our influence, the sons of monkeys removed that line, too."

"But," Shazia sputtered, still appalled by the angel's suggestion that she could be a prophet, "according to the *Quran*, a woman cannot become a Muslim preacher—women are only allowed to preach to other women."

"True," replied the angel, smiling, "but then a woman cannot be a Marine either. In Pakistan, they cannot even drive a taxi."

Shazia blinked. "Um... but to change the *Quran*, the Law, would require a prophet. And the *Quran* says the Prophet—M-mohammad, I mean—was the last prophet. There are to be no more. To change this would require a whole new religion! A woman cannot just start a religion!"

"Mary Baker Eddy did."

"Who?"

"And there have been many female prophets. What of St. Teresa, St. Juliana of Norwich, or the ancient Jewish prophetess, Judith?"

Unsure of who these people were, Shazia merely nodded.

"Mohammed wrote down what I said. That is what made him a prophet. Now I have come to you," intoned the angel. "Will you tell others what I tell you? Or shall you, too, fail the Test of the Prophet?"

"You want me to... "

"Write down my words on those occasions in the future when I will come to speak with you. Tell the world, the Muslim world in particular, the truth. Be the light that leads mankind to the real Religion of Peace."

Shazia remembered the words Maryam had spoken when Gabriel gave her the news that she was to bear the prophet Isa. Could she say such a thing? Merely accept such a dread fate without complaint? New admiration for Maryam filled her.

But was not this what she had wanted?

Had not she trained her whole life to change the world, to make it a better place? Did not she have a better chance of doing that with an angel on her side than without?

And yet, the idea sounded crazy!

"Me? Change the world?" she cried, her heart beating rapidly. "All by myself?"

"You were meant to have a helper." The angel regarded the frozen young men.

"Kabir?" Hope flooded into her heart.

The angel's eyes filled with kindness and sorrow. "Together, the two of you were meant to be called to end the doctrine of jihad."

"Is that our task?" Shazia gasped with joy, looking from the angel to Kabir. "To end jihad?"

The angel nodded. "Was that not what he prayed for, the day he wished to stop the fighting of both men and roosters?"

She pressed her hands against her mouth and then brought them together, pleading. "O, Great One, can my cousin be saved?"

The Angel just looked at her.

Shazia's jaw trembled. "If he kills this soldier... will he be no longer fit for such a destiny?"

"It will make your job much harder." The angel bowed his head. "If you can find a way to stop him from committing murder—if you can stop him and yet retain his life and yours—he will in time aid you. I can see it. Once he regains himself, he will write letters from prison that will help clarify and inspire. If he dies, your mission may be lost, and mankind will pass into yet another age of darkness."

"But... what can I do?" she cried. "If I run over and speak to him, they will kill me. Will they not?"

"Yes. They will."

"What then?" cried Shazia.

"You could fetch the soldiers—the city guard," suggested Gabriel. "I will hold the young men here a while longer, to give you time. Your cousin will be arrested, but he will live."

"And... that is the only way?"

"It is." The angel's face seemed strangely cool and distant. "I have seen it."

Turn on Kabir? Betray him to the police?

That was the only way to save the world?

Shazia gazed at her cousin, so handsome if he would only stop sneering. She glanced at those around him, the nine standing and the one kneeling and frowned.

"That man there with the bag over his head," she pointed. "He is a soldier. If I bring more, won't they grow angry at the humiliation of one of their own and shoot."

"They might," the angel said sadly. "My Father has granted humans free will."

"But," Shazia cried in great agitation, "can you tell me for certain that if I turn my cousin in, he will live. Do you know for sure?"

The angel bowed his head. "Only my Father knows all."

Shazia continued to gaze at her beloved cousin. Was this to be her fate, then? To turn on the one person she most wished to protect and betray him to the officials, so that years from now, he might write her helpful letters from prison? Allah was cruel, indeed.

What of the life he was going to have led? What of the family he wished someday to have? Was that all to be lost?

Was there no hope?

Shazia's eyes filled with tears that even a Marine would not be ashamed of.

Pulling her hijab around her more closely, she turned her back on the angel and began to walk slowly toward the Khyber Gate with its machine guns and its guards. As she walked her cheeks began to grow hot as she envisioned all the *I-told-you-sos* she would soon face from her friends at home. All of them had told her she was crazy for coming, for wasting her time, her money on such a fool's errand—all of them except her Irish bunkmate from the Marines.

Camlyn had written her a long email telling about how the O'Malley family had lost her uncle Sean after he joined the IRA. He had been shot by a cop while trying to blow up a building for the Irish terrorists group. "To this day," her friend had written, "my mother mourns her brother and regrets that she did not make the trip to Ireland to try and change his mind. You go, Lance Corporal Hayak! You save Kabir!"

Disappointing her fellow Marine was going to be even more painful than facing the naysayers. Maybe, she would just send a text: *Mission failed.*

Then she paused, for she had just recalled the words of the Angel Gabriel: *"When the time comes for a prophet to come into his own, the rules are told to him. Then he is tempted. For it is my eldest brother's prerogative to have a chance to lead mankind astray. The potential prophet is told that it is allowed to do something that is not allowed. If he knows better, he is a true prophet. If he does not, he retroactively becomes a false one."*

Had not she just been told the rules?

In the light of the angel's halo, had not she been reminded by her memory of Great-Grandmother Anahika of the two most important things in life? *Never lose hope,* and *never let anything come between her and Kabir.*

This was the Test of the Prophet. The Evil One could not appeal to her vanity. Shazia was not a vain woman. The Evil One was tempting her to despair.

Shazia turned slowly and gazed back at her cousin and his comrades through the frozen raindrops. The young men in their tight black clothing stood surrounded by jeering shaitans, ifrites, and *marids.* The angel was still in the clearing, standing motionless, shining in the gloom like a star.

"Gabriel," she cried, "what if I could drive off the djinn? They are making these young men crazy. I saw it in their eyes. If I could drive off the djinn, might Kabir and his friends let the soldier go."

"Very likely," replied the Angel Gabriel.

"How? How can I do that?"

"I cannot help you."

The djinn hooted and guffawed. They shouted out crass mocking words.

Shazia hung her head, struggling not to cry. She was a Marine. Marines refused to give up. Marines found solutions.

"Solomon!" Her head snapped up. "The *Quran* says that Allah granted him '*a kingdom over the djinn not allowed to any human after him.*' Even the Prophet could not command djinn, but King Solomon could. Could you... bring Solomon here?"

The angel shook his head. "That is not within my power."

Shazia cried in desperation, "Is there truly no other way? Something, someone, somewhere must be able to banish the dark spirits!"

The angel gazed at her with his unendurably deep eyes. "There is Another in whose name these dark ones can be banished. For it has been said: '*Even the evil spirits are subject to us in thy name.*'"

That sounded familiar, but she could not place it. From a movie, perhaps?

"There is someone else? Who?" Shazia fell to her knees on the hard ground, taking no care to avoid the broken glass scattered there. She pressed her hands together, pleading. "Please, if there is anyone—anyone at all—who has authority over these dark spirits... Anyone in all of wide Heaven... Can he not help me? Please?" She looked up at the rain-drenched sky, through the motionless drops. "If there is any power in Heaven that can drive back these dark djinn, I beg of you, please come!"

There came a sound that shook the earth beneath her. The beast-like shaitans and the black, flame-eyed ifrite fled away, leaving only the five great *marids* with their horns and fiery breath hovering over the young men. Shazia, too, quaked, her limbs trembling. Even as she shook, however, it came to her that she had heard such a sound before, on a documentary.

It was the roar of Lion.

A great golden beast came padding around the corner. It was greater than any lion Shazia had ever seen in a zoo. Its body shone like the sun, and its mane was so dark a gold as to appear black. Its eyes gazed out upon the world like two terrible lamps.

Terror seized Shazia. Her thoughts scattered like frightened butterflies. Never before had she been so scared. Not the first time she had deployed, not in her entire stint in the Corps, not even the time she crossed a field where a landmine had just blown off a man's leg to save his little girl.

Shazia screamed and leapt to her feet, hiding behind the angel, clutching the soft feathers of his folded wings.

This was clearly not a tame lion.

Yet, the beast did not attack.

The angel bowed his head respectfully, "Milord."

Shazia gasped. She had been betrayed. This glorious angel was not Jibrail, but some pretender. This beast was the horrible Iblis himself, coming to claim her.

Only the Lion's eyes were not terrible. They were mighty to behold, but it was a wonderful kind of mighty.

Looking into them made her feel as if she were so much more than a young woman who had lost her way. Looking into them, she felt like the very daughter of God.

The Lion turned and regarded the *marid*. The great wicked creatures backed up, hissing and spitting. Yet still they clung to their charges.

"You are not welcome here," their leader hissed. "No one has called You. We are within our rights."

The Lion eyed them gravely. "Tell your fellows down in the fiery pit: *Our Father is beautiful in his mercy and terrible in his justice.* Tell them that I said: *Last time, I came as a lamb and thus went meekly to the slaughter. That time has past. Soon, I shall come again. This time, I come as a Lion.*"

Ooooohhh!

Shazia's jaw dropped. "You... you are Isa Ibn Maryam!"

"That is one name for me." The Lion's tone was wry. "But it is not the name that these ones fear. It will not aid you now."

"You mean..." Her mouth was as dry as dust from the desert. "Do I have to convert? Turn my back on my people? What is it that I must do? Drink blood?"

Lion ignored her. It sat and began washing like a cat.

318

"What do I do? Must I convert to the infidel religion? Worship you? Bow down? Kiss your feet? Foreswear everything held dear to me? I have heard about you my whole life. The imams preach against the followers of the Son of God ever Friday. You will not help me unless I do some horrible thing?"

Lion drew itself up, until it looked very fearsome indeed. In a deep, deep voice, it roared: *"Do you think me so small as that?"*

Shazia shrieked and grabbed Gabriel's back, her fingers again sinking into the soft feathers of his wings.

Gabriel spoke, his voice like music, "Call upon His Name."

"Just that?" asked Shazia.

"That is all."

"B-but *why?*" Shazia cried, turning to the Lion. "Why would you help me, a Muslim? I am no one important. Not an angel. Not a king. Not a son of God. I am just a lowly creation in submission to Allah. Why would you help me just because of my asking?"

The Lion regarded her steadily.

Shazia took a very deep breath and cried out in as steady a voice as she was able: "I-I banish thee... in the name of Jesus Christ!"

The Lion *roared*.

The sound of it shook the foundations of the earth. There was a rush of darkness as the djinn screeched and fled.

Then it was raining.

Shazia stood on the grass amidst the broken glass. Rain pelted her *hijab*. Ten young men, standing around a kneeling soldier with a bag over his head, all looked at her, where she stood, dripping wet, having just shouted out a name that would mark her for an infidel.

One of the young men jabbered at her in Urdu, quicker than she could follow.

"Shazia?" Kabir cried out. "My sweet cousin Shazia? What are you doing here?"

"I... am lost," she cried in Urdu, for it was all she could think to say.

The young men stared at her. Shazia drew the edge of her hajib across her face. But she noticed a difference. The crazed anger was draining from their eyes. They looked like ordinary young men, the kind that might play basketball at the park while listening to music.

"Shazia, what are you doing here? You will catch your death in this rain. Come home. Come home."

Kabir dropped the scimitar. Striding forward, he grabbed her arm and pulled her away from the others. Under his breath, he whispered, "Don't look back. Just walk, as if that is what we are supposed to be doing."

Shazia lifted her head and walked.

"What are you doing here?" asked Kabir.

"Saving you."

"Saving me?"

"You know what you are doing here. It is wrong."

Kabir must have forgotten his own recent words of wisdom, for he stopped cold. "But it is for the glory of Allah!"

"Yes!" Shazia replied scathingly. "This is what Allah wants from you! You! Do you remember how we vowed to make a change for good? Does this look to you like good? This barbed wire? This atmosphere of fear? What kind of god would want a good boy to turn into such a bad one?"

Kabir's face grew dark with outrage, but then his face went slack. He glanced over his shoulder, almost as if he were looking for the wicked *qareen* who no longer dwelt there. He blinked twice. "Yes. You are right. I do not know what came over me."

"Come, Kabir. Let's go home," said Shazia. "We have work to do. You and I."

He took her hand and began walking again, whispering. "Don't look back."

But she did.

Behind them, the tallest of the young men kicked the kneeling soldier, pushing the man over with his foot. The soldier fell to the muddy ground, his hands still tied behind his back.

"This is no good." The tall one pulled off his face scarf. "Let's go."

The young men turned and left. The soldier lay panting on the ground, alive.

A huge golden Lion stepped forward and stood over the fallen soldier, who was writhing, trying to get free of his bonds. The Lion breathed on him. The ropes loosened. The soldier wriggled free. He ripped the bag off his head and untied the ropes securing his legs, stumbled to his feet, and ran.

He did not seem to see the Lion.

The Lion turned its head toward her. Shazia noted that it had not cost her another headache to see Him. Staring into the great golden eyes, she understood that her ghost-induced sickness was a thing of the past. From now on, she would be able to see the invisible world without pain.

In her mind, Shazia heard His words, answering her earlier unanswered question.

"You are all my Father's children."

FLIGHT TO EGYPT

By

Sarah A. Hoyt

The new segregation is just the tip of the iceberg...

Ingrid looked around the room where she'd lived for three months.

Three months.

It seemed impossible, as she stared at the pink walls, the pink-painted furniture, the statue of Our Lady Del Dolores languishing on the bedside table in a flash of purple and inartistic silver plaster swords.

The baby moved within Ingrid, his movement so violent that her too-tight blue dress seemed to writhe upon her distended stomach with a life of its own.

"You got everything now, dear, didn't you?" Dotty asked. Dotty owned this house and the pink room. She was a plump, middle-aged woman who always wore black in memory of a husband dead so many years ago that anyone else would have sickened of the monochrome outfits. She wore her hair back in a tight, salt-and-pepper bun that left her face round and unencumbered, looking like bread pudding from amid which her eyes shone like two glossy, black plums. Standing at the door to the small room, watching Ingrid pack her things into the small, canvas suitcase, she sniffed and twitched her nose, and touched a tissue to it in a way that reminded Ingrid of a white rabbit.

Of course, Ingrid repented the thought immediately, and reproached herself on her uncharitableness, as she snapped the suitcase shut and said, "I've got everything."

Her back hurt as she straightened.

Dotty didn't offer to carry the case. She just turned and walked down the narrow hallway outside the room, towards the living room. "Your husband will be here soon," she said and sniffled, and took the tissue to her eyes.

Dotty was in a great hurry to get rid of Ingrid, yet Ingrid refused to resent it. If it weren't for Dotty and her small, modest house in a working class area on the outskirts of Goldport, Colorado; if it weren't for the whole network of the Rachels, then Ingrid wouldn't have a baby moving within her; she wouldn't have to worry about the weight on her back, nor counterbalancing it by standing very straight.

She wouldn't have to worry about anything like that and she wouldn't have to stay hidden. She could go out and work. She could even visit her family in Marstown. Or move there, if she didn't mind leaving Joe behind.

Which she did, of course, she told herself, erasing the whole tempting thought of Marstown streets, of the freedom to move around, of not having to live in cramped quarters, defying authority by her very lack of action.

She felt the weight of her heavy plait of blond hair. She hadn't been able to get a decent haircut in three months. Her back hurt. The baby pushed on her bladder. Her feet hurt.

She'd lived for three months in one cramped room, unable to see strangers, unable to talk to anyone but Dotty. And now she was being evicted.

Ingrid felt her eyes fill with tears and wished she could sniffle genteelly, like Dotty. But she couldn't. And once she let the tears come, they would flood her eyes and she would bawl her eyes out like a child.

She'd never been one to defy authority.

Never before. But when authority threatens all that's important to you, even the meekest of women will rebel.

Ingrid found herself smiling, looking at the man in the art exhibit. She'd just arrived from Marstown, via the tunnel to downtown Goldport—a freshly landed art student in search of the glories of the past.

Instead, she'd got sidetracked by this small exhibition, and now by a man—a living man, a living earthling, neither art nor ancient. Although the art part could be begged.

He wore dark pants and a tight shirt that molded well-defined muscles, sculpted his broad shoulders, showed his tiny waist in sharp relief.

Standing in front of a white marble sculpture of a nymph in flight, he looked less like a real man and more like a part of the art exhibit—a polished, shining dark sculpture, throwing the lines and color of the other into relief. Only, of course, he wasn't a sculpture and he wasn't the color of dark stone.

More the color of dark chocolate, freshly melted.

He raised his eyebrows at her. "May I help you?"

"Huh?" Ingrid said, and reproached herself for her foolish lack of words.

"May I help you?" he asked, again. He spoke with a baritone that throbbed and moved something within her, something to which her heart seemed to reply in faster beats, in quicker breaths, something that was familiar and at once strange. "You looked... lost," he said.

"No, I didn't," she said, and cursed herself for her stupid frankness, but it was either that or not saying anything at all and leaving the place, shamefaced and slow, regretting it forever. "I looked like I was ogling you. Because I was." She grinned at his shocked face. Sometime between puberty and her twentieth birthday, Ingrid had realized that the most straightforward of men could be discomfited by frankness in a woman. "Did you know you're the exact color of dark chocolate?"

For a moment it hung in the balance.

His large brown eyes widened in shock, then it looked like he would be offended. But his lips twitched upwards, the corners struggling to pull upward, and finally, finally, drawing up into a broad smile. "Thanks," he said. "And you look like you're a spacer."

"Just arrived through the tunnel. Does it show that much?"

He grinned and waved his hand, mid-air, from side to side, in a so-so gesture. "There are very few pure blondes left on Earth. Only small, closed colonies manage that. So, which one produced you?"

"Marstown."

"Ah," he said. "Swede."

She laughed, charmed, having forgotten all the stories she'd heard before leaving Marstown, all the stories about how Earth was a backward pot of seething violence, where no man—there and no woman either—would be safe.

Her walk from the tunnel arrival terminal to the art gallery had been pleasant, unencumbered, a walk along a normal street of small shops and automated eating establishments that could have taken place in Marstown itself. The mix of small restaurants and smaller shops could have existed anywhere at all.

And this man seemed safe enough, sane enough, intelligent enough.

Ingrid, whom all friends swore was the original ice virgin, looked up at the soft brown eyes and melted. "My name is Ingrid Illesen."

He put his hand forward, a large hand that engulfed her small, thin one. "I'm Joseph Michaels. Welcome to Earth."

Joseph Michaels was the author of the nymphs and satyrs, the amazing, light sculptures all around, sculptures that seemed on the verge of flight. The style and some of the sculptures themselves were known to Ingrid. She'd seen them in Marstown.

"You're Joseph Michaels?" she asked, all out of breath. "You're—"

"Call me Joe," he said.

Joe smiled at her again, bathing her in the unavoidable light of his approval, as he looked her slowly from head to toe. "So, want to go out for something to eat? Maybe I can show you the town," he said.

She felt underdressed in her dark green travel suit of shorts and loose tunic. She thought he was attracted to her, but it was hard to see why.

She smiled and nodded, inanely. "Yes, yes, I'd love to."

"Any minute now, dear," Dotty said, and sniffled, and looked at Ingrid, sort of sideways, with a quick glance at Ingrid's stomach and then away. "I wish.... It doesn't seem right to send you out like this, again, but...."

But Dotty had got news, over the computer, that the government had been raiding the safe houses of the Daughters of Rachel, the Catholic organization that protected women whose babies were slated—for whatever reason—for abortion. And on that rumor, the white rabbit that Dotty was at heart had fled to its safe hole—calling Joe, making him come and remove his very pregnant wife.

Ingrid shifted from foot to foot and sighed, hoping Joe would get here quickly.

Dotty's living room was no more tastefully decorated than her guest room.

Lump-like sofas and armchairs in some molded pink material halfway between rubber and sponge took up most of the space, on the baby-blue carpet.

Statues of saints—Saint Theresa holding the baby Jesus, St. Anthony with the same baby incongruously perched atop a book, St. Joseph gazing in wonder at his flowering staff—stared out from many little, oddly shaped glass tables.

The walls continued the theme, with pictures of the Virgin being surprised by the archangel Gabriel, a painting of St. Rita in her nun's habit staring at a palm leaf as if it held the answers to the questions of the universe.

Though not a Catholic herself, Ingrid had been introduced to the pantheon by Joe's personal devotion.

Of course, Joe's devotion didn't translate itself to plaster and poorly applied paint. Or at least not in such a facile way. Joe had never been one for facile forms or simple anything.

That first day they met, he took her to dinner at a small downtown restaurant in Goldport.

At the edge of the area that Joe described as *prettied up* for the tourists from out world, it was pretty enough an establishment—with its tiny tables with checkered cloth coverings, and lit candles—for Ingrid to exclaim over it.

"I thought Earth was all grime and despair," she said, halfway through the first course Joe had ordered: a broiled fresh-stream fish, something she couldn't get on Mars.

And Joe, who'd been prattling facilely about art and the balance of masses and light, looked up from his dinner, with a sudden, wounded stare as though she'd slapped him.

"I'm sorry," she said. "I'm sorry. It's what one sees in the news holos, though. I mean...."

He shook his head. His face looked all serious, the big, velvet eyes appeared to have shaded themselves, as though darkness had descended upon Joe's thoughts. "Nothing to be sorry for," he said. "Nothing to be sorry for. It's true. What you read, what you see in the holos, is pretty much true. This," he waved his hand to include the small tables with their individual candles and the couples sitting at them, leaning over to each other in intimate conversation. "This is for tourists. For the spacers. We want them to feel happy and welcome. The rest.... The rest is where the real people live. It took me years of working in the rest of Earth to make it to the near-tunnel galleries. Years."

His veiled eyes shaded further and a soft seriousness covered his face, making him look suddenly much younger and lost, like a child with a secret sadness that no mother can kiss away.

The doorbell rang and Dotty rushed to open it, with the same half-eager rush that a rabbit might display in escaping from a bird of prey.

Joe stood there—Joe, looking gaunter than he'd been three months ago, and somehow worn down, polished down, like a pebble beaten long and hard by the tide.

His soft-velvet eyes lit up when he looked at Ingrid and he smiled. "Hi, babe."

She didn't know she would do it, until she found herself wrapped around him, her belly between them, with the baby turning and turning and kicking.

Joe kissed her hair, her eyes, her mouth. "I missed you too, babe," he said. "I missed you, too."

Still, Ingrid couldn't help noticing that Dotty turned her head away from their kissing.

Dotty had made it clear early on that though she disapproved of abortion, she disapproved of miscegenation also.

329

Earth was like that—a diminished pool of resources upon which various groups pulled and picked like vultures over one meager meal, each in hatred and seclusion of all others.

On that first day they'd met, they'd driven around after dinner in Joe's dilapidated little fly car, looking at neighborhoods, flying over empty space.

Earth had a lot of empty, ruined areas.

"Population has been falling since the migrations started," Joe said. "A lot of areas are just closed off, fenced off. Some of them are polluted beyond recovery and some...." He shrugged. "There's not enough people left to care for. The people who cared have long since gone to space."

Used to the tiny, bustling cities of terraformed Mars, and to tourism in the tunnels of the moon, the warrens of the asteroid belt, Ingrid felt lost in these huge empty spaces, so lost it was hard to conceive, hard to believe that a world as large, as strong as Earth could be dying. Dying at last, irretrievably.

She looked at Joe.

He had the car on automatic as they flew over the deserted and ruined areas of Earth. He looked out the window and something that might be tears sparkled in his velvet-soft eyes.

"Why don't you emigrate?" she asked. "Do you love Earth that much? Why don't you go to Mars? Your work is loved there."

He looked at her, surprised, as if the idea had never occurred to him, and stared at her as if he doubted her sanity. Then his eyes softened, and his laughter rippled through, like a curtain being opened. A laughter of half-relief, half-loss. "Oh, babe. The spacer colonies wouldn't have me. I'm a black man."

Joe took her by the hand and led her to the door, mumbling stiff little correct thanks to Dotty.

Only the pressure of his hand on hers, only the slight trembling at the edges of his voice told Ingrid that he felt some deep emotion. What the emotion was—happiness to see her, fear for her, relief that she was well, as was the baby—Ingrid couldn't tell.

Joe took her suitcase, and led her to his fly—the same small, dilapidated purple fly in which they'd gone on their first date.

It wasn't until she was inside, strapped into the seat—Joe having checked over the seatbelt, ensuring it didn't unduly constrict the baby—that Joe broke down and knelt on the floor beside her, and put his head in her lap and whispered, "Oh, babe, babe, what are we going to do?"

"That's not true," Ingrid had said, in that flycar, all those years ago, while Joe took her on her first flying tour of the non-tourist areas near the tunnel from the space. "That's not true." She remembered priming her lips, and hearing her own voice all edgy, civics-class prissy. "Mars doesn't discriminate on the basis of race or religion, or origin."

Joe had looked at her with his soft-sad look, the one that she was starting to recognize as his look of despair, when he couldn't explain things to her. Then he'd smiled, ruefully, and said, "You're right. But, at any rate, they don't want me."

He'd taken her to her touristy hotel and refused to come in for a nightcap, and she thought that was the last she'd see of Joe Michaels, sculptor extraordinaire and, obviously, a confused Earthling.

But the next morning he had called her and they'd spent most of her three months on Earth together. Together every minute.

331

Ingrid put her hand on the back of Joe's head, and patted him distractedly.

He wore his hair very short and, though she'd have sworn it had been pitch black just three months ago, it was now entwined with silver hairs. Had he worried that much?

"What's wrong?" she asked. "What's wrong, love?"

"The visa," he said. He sniffled and it was a strong, unmistakable sniffle, nothing like Dotty's lady-like whiffs. "They denied me a visa again. And you. Because you're pregnant. Pregnant by an Earther."

"I see," Ingrid said. She felt very tired and the baby kicked within her, but she tried to make her voice strong. Joe had always been the strong one, but now she must support him.

She saw many things she'd never been able to see, never been able to understand when they'd first got together.

And suddenly, suddenly, like a fire burning within her, she felt very happy that she had hidden with Dotty for those three long months, that the baby was still alive and strong within her. "Then we'll have to find a place to hide until the baby is born," she said.

Six months after returning to Marstown, six months of daily calls to Joe to hear his soft, low voice, his laughter, his comments full of that cutting wit that reached something deep within her, something no other man, no other human being had ever reached, Ingrid had decided to go back to Earth.

This time, she'd had to ask for a visa from Earth—a resident visa.

It had come together in no time at all—unlike Joe's visa to Mars, which had been blocked again and again and again, with the vague excuse that Joe had undesirable characteristics.

They'd never told Ingrid what the characteristics were.

She suspected it was his lack of respect for authority.

As they sat in the fly, in the driveway of Dotty's little rounded workmen's cottage in the outskirts of Goldport, a voice sounded, out of nowhere, surrounding them: *Warning*, the voice blared. *You are the subject of suspicion by the peace keepers of Earth. Do not attempt to take off or make any sudden moves. We will be searching your fly for the presence of a woman with an unauthorized condition.*

Ingrid didn't know what to make of it.

But the voice galvanized Joe into action. Jumping up, muttering who knew what under his breath, he programmed a take-off route, his fingers fast and assured on the keyboard of the flycar.

As they took off almost vertically and Ingrid, pushed into her seat, tasting bile risen to her throat, she managed to ask, "What?"

"Peacekeepers," Joe said. His fingers danced on the keyboard. "They've been following me around. They've been raiding safehouses."

And while they took off, the viewport showing them narrowly missing the steel-blue side of a hovering police fly, Ingrid thought that at least Dotty's feelings had been justified.

They'd been married for three years, and living together in their studio apartment at the edge of the tourist section of Goldport.

Just a vast room with broad windows. The bed took up a little corner of it, as did the miniscule, outdated cooker, and the rope on which they hung their changes of clothes.

Most of the space was taken up by rock and chisels, clay, paint, unfinished canvas.

Ingrid's own work was becoming known, but nothing like Joe's, which was bought in every corner of the human worlds.

And though Ingrid realized this was not the best place to bring up a child, she couldn't understand why Joe's face closed so when she told him she was pregnant.

"I thought you liked children," she said, defensively, feeling a little offended that he didn't want this, the product of their love—as much a joint work as their art.

"I love children," he said. "And I would love your child." But his eyes had gone that veiled, shaded softness she'd come to recognize, and he whispered, "I just hope it's a girl."

"Where are we going?" Ingrid asked, out of breath, pressed into the seat, the baby kicking frantically within her as though looking around for a way to escape the added pressure of acceleration. "Where are we going?"

"To the tunnel," he said.

Twisting her head by an effort of will, Ingrid looked out the rear viewport of the fly and saw the steel blue police cruiser still in pursuit.

"I thought we didn't have a visa," she said.

"We don't," Joe said.

Ingrid stood in the medical center, three months pregnant and cursing Earth's slowness to do this. The medical center itself seemed designed to drive an ill person to the grave: a large, cavernous space with no chairs to sit on, and a long, long counter separating the ill from the medtechs, as nurses and medical assistants were uniformly known on Earth.

Sick people sat on the floor, in whichever pattern and waited, waited, waited.

Every once in a while a name was called and either a medtech cautiously opened the door at the end of the counter to admit a patient to the sancto sanctorum of the inner rooms where tests were run by de-facto med machines, or test results were announced to a patient, in a hushed voice, by a medtech leaning earnestly over the counter.

Ingrid had already been in and been scanned by the med machines. So, now, she stood at the counter and waited for her test results.

On Mars, she would have been tested months ago—she and the baby. She would have known by now if anything at all was likely to go wrong with the pregnancy.

But Earth's health care was slow and slapdash, working—if it could be said to work—on the principle that the more serious the illness the longer the line, the more painful the waiting period.

The young man who finally came up to the counter and said, "Mrs Michaels, we have your results," was a grave young man—light brown color, with slick black hair, and a serious, intent expression on his oval face. He spoke very quickly, as if he didn't want to hear what he said. "This is the result." He handed her over an electro paper imprinted with tiny black characters. "As you can see, your baby would display antisocial characteristics, and we advise you to have it aborted. The list of abortion centers is at the bottom and your insurance will cover it fully."

"What?" Ingrid's head swam. She felt sick, and smelled the sweat of the other patients suddenly, too sharply, too strongly. "What?"

"Your baby displays antisocial characteristics and we...."

335

"How can it be antisocial?. It's a three-month-old fetus." Her voice rang out loud, like a scream in her own ears. No one, she noticed, turned to look.

The young man sighed. He looked all around, his eyes darting, darting, then looked at the paper. He opened his hands. "Look, Mrs. Michaels. You're pregnant with a boy."

"And...?" Was this everyone's obsession, that she should only have girls?

"Well," the young man licked his lips and stepped back, as if afraid she would slug him across the counter. "Well... your husband is of African ancestry, see, and if you look at statistics, there is a genetic tendency for black men to commit more crimes."

"What?" Her head felt as if it swam on the end of her neck, like a ball ill-balanced on a straw. "But—"

"Look, it's a fact of life, that's all. And with such statistics, we can't really expect the government of Earth to support your baby. So, so as not to impose on the commonwealth, not to make us support the costs of violence later in life, we're asking you to abort this fetus. If you do not comply, a court order can be pursued."

Ingrid didn't hear the rest of it. Her dizziness, the revulsion at such naked, unimpeded racism, colluded with the queasiness she'd felt ever since she'd first got pregnant, and Ingrid threw up on the floor, next to the counter, before the horrified eyes of the med tech. How could strangers decide the life and death of her baby before he was even fully formed?

"We can't go to the tunnel," she said. The tunnel was the popular name to the wormhole that connected to the outer planets. "Not without a visa. The guards—"

"Watch me," Joe said, his teeth clenched, making his voice sound funny. "Just watch me."

"Genocide is what it's called, babe," Joe said. He sat on their bed, and looked at her with his softest, saddest gaze. "It's been going on for the last twenty years."

"Every black male?" she asked, puzzled, wondering how the world hadn't risen in revolution.

Joe twirled the little electronic paper in his hands. "No. Of course not. Just those that are genetically predisposed. They tell you that here. The race is just an aggravating factor."

"But...." She sat beside Joe. She'd ridden home in a haze, hoping that it would all turn out to be a nightmare, that Joe would tell her a way to get around it. She could feel the baby alive within her, not a weight yet, but a presence, a living presence. Joe's baby, her baby. She loved Joe. She wanted this baby. Though she had nothing in the abstract against abortion—unlike Joe with his Catholic faith—she had never thought of applying it to herself. Damn it, other creatures in this stage of development might be fetuses, but this was a baby and she wanted him.

"But I thought the genetic determinants of violence were not so well defined. I mean, we've never managed to define them that well in Marstown." She forbore to say that their health services were better and their screening more sophisticated. Which, at any rate, Joe already knew. "I mean, the same genes that, according to this print out code for violence, I learned in school as potential coders for risk taking and creativity."

Joe shrugged. "They can't code them any better than that, no. They use genetic clues, but then the rest is statistics. So, any potential black babies with these genes that might or might not indicate violent tendencies but that are often found in violent criminals get aborted."

"They can't do that, can they?"

Joe had stared at her, held her hands. "I'm afraid they can, babe. But there's this organization. It's called Daughters of Rachel and they shelter women who.... Well.... See, after the baby is born, he's a citizen and they can throw us in jail—or they can throw me in jail and deport you. But they can't kill him."

She didn't want to be at the mercy of any Catholic organization. "Why didn't you tell me to use contraceptives?" she asked.

He looked at her, looked away, and she felt very stupid. Of course. Of course. Joe couldn't have. His Catholicism wouldn't allow it. But, damn it.... It was better than this.

She felt very mad at him for a moment. For just a moment.

"It could have been a girl," he whispered. "A little girl. Our little girl."

That whisper broke Ingrid's rage. That soft sound of longing in his voice spoke of how much he wanted her to have his baby, how much he wanted their child.

She took in breath sharply and wondered how anyone could possibly think this man was violent.

And they'd made love on the narrow bed in their studio.

The fly sped through the air, with the police cruiser giving chase.

"They won't shoot," Joe said. "Don't worry. They'd never shoot. If they kill us it's murder. They wouldn't do that. They will kill us before birth, but not after."

Ingrid hadn't even thought they could be in danger of being shot at. All she could think was that Joe looked angry.

His clenched teeth made his face look harsh, hard, every plane, every angle too clearly defined.

He turned the fly car on manual, moving very fast amid the tall buildings in the tourist area of Goldport.

"It makes it harder for them to shoot," Joe said, with a quick look at Ingrid. He looked as though afraid of what the acceleration would do to her. "If they should forget themselves. Cheer up, babe. You're going home."

She didn't have time to think about it. At the end of the street loomed the tunnel.

It stood out in the open air, with ticket takers—and visa checkers—on either side of it.

People walked through it, of course. After getting their papers checked, of course.

They didn't have papers.

Ingrid realized they weren't stopping the fly either. The tunnel was big enough, oh, big enough—a ragged opening like a burn in the scenery, ten feet high, twenty feet wide—and at the bottom the figures of little people walking across.

The tunnels had to be that big for some physics reason. Ingrid recalled her lesson on this in elementary school. But she couldn't remember the reason.

"We can't fly into it," Ingrid screamed.

Joe grinned.

"Watch me."

Antisocial, she thought.

Antisocial. Maybe Earth authorities were right. Maybe Mars authorities were right. Undesirable characteristics.

It was all his fault the baby wasn't right. All his fault.

Ingrid opened her mouth to tell him that, but the wave of something, like a strong gust of wind, hit her as they entered the tunnel.

Below her, she could see the astonished, up-turned faces of people looking up, guards and commuters and everyone, everyone.

The wave, a vague tingly feeling while walking, crushed and rattled the fly as it dashed through at top speed, to career, nose first, into the sands of a wide Martian plain.

Ingrid whipped forward and lost consciousness.

The news holo showed Joe, in his best clothes, the same black pants and shirt that Ingrid had first seen him in.

The woman interviewing him was all but visibly licking her lips, and Ingrid smiled, in amusement, as she held her son up at her shoulder. She'd just finished nursing, and patted the baby, trying to make it burp.

"So, you say that the antisocial characteristics that Earth identifies are actually based on statistics?" the newswoman asked.

"Well," Joe shrugged. "This has been going on for two hundred years, this type of thought. Only the form changes. Why should it surprise you now? Ever since profiling started influencing police work, it's been a double-feed system: more people of certain ethnic backgrounds get investigated, therefore more get arrested, therefore statistically they appear to commit more crimes. Genetics is just a new dressing for an old wound. If you give government enough power, they end up dividing people in groups. Statistical groups. Setting group against group, so none will challenge their power." He spoke glibly, but his eyes looked soft and sad, in the way Ingrid knew so well. "Holding the power of life and death over the individuals they refuse to see. The more power any state has, the more indiscriminate its use, and the more they'll enshrine the prejudices of its people into law. Or even create prejudices, for the sake of power."

"And it took yours and your wife's escape here to make our government realize this and stop denying visas to Earth citizens because of such profiling?"

"Right," Joe said. In public he wouldn't speculate on whether Marstown officials knew too well what they were doing. He'd done it often enough in private to Ingrid. But he wouldn't alienate Marstown public opinion. The public opinion that had kept him from being deported, and rallied around this well-known artist and his very pregnant wife who had so romantically flown through the tunnel and into Mars.

That Joe had spent three days in the hospital with a concussion hadn't hurt either. Or that Ingrid's family had spread the story as far and wide as they could.

The newswoman, a polished piece with an expensive haircut, shook her head over the idea of certain people being persecuted solely for their race. "And you? Are you going to make your life here on Mars now that you've been granted a visa?"

Joe hesitated.

Ingrid, watching the cast, knew how much he missed Earth and saw his desire to return in that little flinch of his, that tiny hesitation.

"We'll stay here. My wife and myself. At least for a while. But my son might want to go back eventually."

The newswoman smiled and licked her heart-shaped lips. "Your son. What did you call him again?"

Joe looked straight at the camera and smiled, as though his smile were aimed at Ingrid, in their small suburban Marstown home, and at the baby she held.

Which it was.

"Moses," he said. "We called him Moses."

CONTRIBUTORS

Milo Yiannopoulous
(https://www.amazon.com/Milo-Yiannopoulos/e/B01MZ5RC5Q/)

Ben Zwycky
(https://www.amazon.com/Ben-Zwycky/e/B00GN7W3LS/)

Nick Cole
(https://www.amazon.com/Nick-Cole/e/B004W47QXE/)

E.J. Shumak
(https://www.amazon.com/E.-J.-Shumak/e/B00V6H1T4W/)

Ray Blank

Matthew Ward

Joshua M. Young
(https://www.amazon.com/Joshua-M.-Young/e/B00OM8RLJE/)

David Hallquist

A. M. Freeman

Larry Correia
(https://www.amazon.com/Larry-Correia/e/B002D68HL8/)

Brad R. Torgersen
(https://www.amazon.com/Brad-R-Torgersen/e/B004FVMF1M/)

Pierce Oka

Chrome Oxide

John C. Wright
(https://www.amazon.com/John-C.-Wright/e/B001IR1FZS/)

Tom Kratman
(https://www.amazon.com/Tom-Kratman/e/B001IXNZFA/)

Jane Lebak
(https://www.amazon.com/Jane-Lebak/e/B004FRUOLY/)

Vox Day
(https://www.amazon.com/Vox-Day/e/B001JP3CVO/)

Brian Niemeier
(https://www.amazon.com/Brian-Niemeier/e/B00ZG6V7SW/)

L. Jagi Lamplighter
(https://www.amazon.com/L.-Jagi-Lamplighter/e/B0028OGMLM/)

Sarah A. Hoyt
(https://www.amazon.com/Sarah-A.-Hoyt/e/B001HCVAX6/)

Made in the USA
San Bernardino, CA
27 January 2017